HERE I AM

ALSO BY JONATHAN SAFRAN FOER

FICTION

Extremely Loud and Incredibly Close
Everything Is Illuminated

NONFICTION

Eating Animals

HERE

I AM

JONATHAN
SAFRAN
FOER

HAMISH HAMILTON

an imprint of Penguin Canada, a division of Penguin Random House Canada Limited

Canada • USA • UK • Ireland • Australia • New Zealand • India • South Africa • China

Published in Hamish Hamilton hardcover by Penguin Canada, 2016
Simultaneously published in the United States by Farrar, Straus and Giroux,
18 West 18th Street, New York 10011

The president's speech, in the chapter "Nothing Is Not Political," was adapted from a speech President Obama gave, in 2010, after the earthquake in Haiti. The poems quoted from in Part VII are Franz Wright's "Year One" and "Progress." Radiolab, Invisibilia, 99% Invisible, and Dan Carlin's Hardcore History offered the inspiration for the podcasts Jacob listens to.

www.penguinrandomhouse.ca

Publisher's note: This book is a work of fiction. Names, characters, places and incidents either are the product of the author's imagination or are used fictitiously, and any resemblance to actual persons living or dead, events, or locales is entirely coincidental.

LIBRARY AND ARCHIVES CANADA CATALOGUING IN PUBLICATION

Foer, Jonathan Safran, 1977-, author
Here I am / Jonathan Safran Foer.

ISBN 978-0-7352-3293-8 (hardback)
ISBN 978-0-7352-3294-5 (electronic)

I. Title.

PS3606.O38H47 2016   813'.6   C2016-902468-7

Book design by Jonathan D. Lippincott
Jacket design by gray318

Printed and bound in the United States of America

10 9 8 7 6 5 4 3 2 1

Penguin Random House

For Eric Chinski,
who sees through me,
and for Nicole Aragi,
who sees me through

CONTENTS

HERE I AM

I

BEFORE THE WAR

GET BACK TO HAPPINESS

When the destruction of Israel commenced, Isaac Bloch was weighing whether to kill himself or move to the Jewish Home. He had lived in an apartment with books touching the ceilings, and rugs thick enough to hide dice; then in a room and a half with dirt floors; on forest floors, under unconcerned stars; under the floorboards of a Christian who, half a world and three-quarters of a century away, would have a tree planted to commemorate his righteousness; in a hole for so many days his knees would never wholly unbend; among Gypsies and partisans and half-decent Poles; in transit, refugee, and displaced persons camps; on a boat with a bottle with a boat that an insomniac agnostic had miraculously constructed inside it; on the other side of an ocean he would never wholly cross; above half a dozen grocery stores he killed himself fixing up and selling for small profits; beside a woman who rechecked the locks until she broke them, and died of old age at forty-two without a syllable of praise in her throat but the cells of her murdered mother still dividing in her brain; and finally, for the last quarter century, in a snow-globe-quiet Silver Spring split-level: ten pounds of Roman Vishniac bleaching on the coffee table; *Enemies, A Love Story* demagnetizing in the world's last functional VCR; egg salad becoming bird flu in a refrigerator mummified with photographs of gorgeous, genius, tumorless great-grandchildren.

German horticulturalists had pruned Isaac's family tree all the way back to the Galician soil. But with luck and intuition and no help from above, he had transplanted its roots into the sidewalks of Washington, D.C., and lived to see it regrow limbs. And unless America turned on the

Jews—*until*, his son, Irv, would correct—the tree would continue to branch and sprout. Of course, Isaac would be back in a hole by then. He would never unbend his knees, but at his unknown age, with unknown indignities however near, it was time to unball his Jewish fists and concede the beginning of the end. The difference between conceding and accepting is depression.

Even putting aside the destruction of Israel, the timing was unfortunate: it was only weeks before his eldest great-grandson's bar mitzvah, which Isaac had been marking as his life's finish line ever since he crossed the previous finish line of his youngest great-grandson's birth. But one can't control when an old Jew's soul will vacate his body and his body will vacate the coveted one-bedroom for the next body on the waiting list. One can't rush or defer manhood, either. Then again, the purchase of a dozen nonrefundable airplane tickets, the booking of a block of the Washington Hilton, and the payment of twenty-three thousand dollars in deposits for a bar mitzvah that has been on the calendar since the last Winter Olympics are no guarantee that it's going to happen.

A group of boys lumbered down the halls of Adas Israel, laughing, punching, blood rushing from developing brains to developing genitals and back again in the zero-sum game of puberty.

"Seriously, though," one said, the second s getting caught on his palate expander, "the only good thing about blowjobs are the wet handjobs you get with them."

"Amen to that."

"Otherwise you're just boning a glass of water with teeth."

"Which is pointless," said a redheaded boy who still got chills from so much as thinking about the epilogue of *Harry Potter and the Deathly Hallows.*

"Nihilistic."

If God existed and judged, He would have forgiven these boys everything, knowing that they were compelled by forces outside of themselves inside of themselves, and that they, too, were made in His image.

Silence as they slowed to watch Margot Wasserman lapping water. It was said that her parents parked two cars outside their three-car garage because they had five cars. It was said that her Pomeranian still had its balls, and they were honeydews.

"God*damn it*, I want to be that drinking fountain," a boy with the Hebrew name Peretz-Yizchak said.

"I want to be the missing part of those crotchless undies."

"I want to fill my dick with mercury."

A pause.

"What the hell does that mean?"

"You know," Marty Cohen-Rosenbaum, né Chaim ben Kalman, said, "like . . . make my dick a thermometer."

"By feeding it sushi?"

"Or just injecting it. Or whatever. Dude, you know what I mean."

Four shakes, and their heads achieved an unintended synchronicity, like Ping-Pong spectators.

In a whisper: *"To put it in her butt."*

The others were lucky to have twenty-first-century moms who knew that temperatures were taken digitally in the ear. And Chaim was lucky that the boys' attention was diverted before they had time to slap him with a nickname he would never shed.

Sam was sitting on the bench outside Rabbi Singer's office, head lowered, eyes on the upturned hands in his lap like a monk waiting to burn. The boys stopped, turning their self-hatred toward him.

"We heard what you wrote," one said, thrusting a finger into Sam's chest. "You crossed a line."

"Some fucked-up shit, bro."

It was odd, because Sam's profligate sweat production usually didn't kick in until the threat had subsided.

"I didn't write it, and I'm not your"—air quotes—"*bro.*"

He could have said that, but he didn't. He also could have explained why nothing was as it seemed. But he didn't. Instead, he just took it, as he always did in life on the crap side of the screen.

On the other side of the rabbi's door, on the other side of the rabbi's desk, sat Sam's parents, Jacob and Julia. They didn't want to be there. No one wanted to be there. The rabbi needed to embroider some thoughtful-sounding words about someone named Ralph Kremberg before they put him in the ground at two o'clock. Jacob would have preferred to be working on the bible for *Ever-Dying People*, or ransacking the house for his missing phone, or at least tapping the Internet's lever for some dopamine hits. And today was supposed to be Julia's day off—this was the opposite of off.

"Shouldn't Sam be in here?" Jacob asked.

"I think it's best if we have an adult conversation," Rabbi Singer said.

"Sam's an adult."

"Sam is *not* an adult," Julia said.

"Because he's three verses shy of mastering the blessings after the blessings after his haftorah?"

Ignoring Jacob, Julia put her hand on the rabbi's desk and said, "It's clearly unacceptable to talk back to a teacher, and we want to find a way to make this right."

"But at the same time," Jacob said, "isn't suspension a bit draconian for what, in the scheme of things, is not really *that* big a deal?"

"Jacob . . ."

"What?"

In an effort to communicate with her husband but not the rabbi, Julia pressed two fingers to her brow and gently shook her head while flaring her nostrils. She looked more like a third-base coach than a wife, mother, and member of the community attempting to keep the ocean from her son's sand castle.

"Adas Israel is a progressive shul," the rabbi said, eliciting an eye-roll from Jacob as reflexive as gagging. "We have a long and proud history of seeing beyond the cultural norms of any given moment, and finding the divine light, the Ohr Ein Sof, in every person. Using racial epithets here is a very big deal, indeed."

"*What?*" Julia asked, finding her posture.

"That can't be right," Jacob said.

The rabbi sighed a rabbi's sigh and slid a piece of paper across his desk to Julia.

"He *said* these?" Julia asked.

"He wrote them."

"Wrote *what?*" Jacob asked.

Shaking her head in disbelief, Julia quietly read the list: "Filthy Arab, chink, cunt, jap, faggot, spic, kike, n-word—"

"He wrote 'n-word'?" Jacob asked. "Or the *actual* n-word?"

"The word itself," the rabbi said.

Though his son's plight should have taken mental precedence, Jacob became distracted by the fact that this was the only word that could not bear vocalization.

"There must be a misunderstanding," Julia said, finally handing the paper to Jacob. "Sam nurses animals back to—"

"*Cincinnati Bow Tie?* That's not a racial epithet. It's a sex act. I think. Maybe."

"They're not all epithets," the rabbi said.

"You know, I'm pretty sure 'Filthy Arab' is a sex act, too."

"I would have to take your word for it."

"My point is, maybe we're completely misinterpreting this list."

Ignoring her husband again, Julia said, "What has Sam said about this?"

The rabbi picked at his beard, searching for words as a macaque searches for lice.

"He denied it. Vociferously. But the words weren't there before class, and he is the only person who sits at that desk."

"He didn't do it," Jacob said.

"It's his handwriting," Julia said.

"All thirteen-year-old boys write the same."

The rabbi said, "He wasn't able to offer another explanation for how it got there."

"It's not his job to," Jacob said. "And by the way, if Sam *were* to have written those words, why on earth would he have left them on the desk? The brazenness proves his innocence. Like in *Basic Instinct.*"

"But she did it in *Basic Instinct,*" Julia said.

"She did?"

"The ice pick."

"I guess that's right. But that's a movie. Obviously some genuinely racist kid, with a grudge against Sam, planted it."

Julia spoke directly to the rabbi: "We'll make sure Sam understands why what he wrote is so hurtful."

"Julia," Jacob said.

"Would an apology to the teacher be sufficient to get the bar mitzvah back on its tracks?"

"It's what I was going to suggest. But I'm afraid word of his words has spread around our community. So—"

Jacob expelled a puff of frustration—a gesture he'd either taught to Sam or learned from him. "And hurtful to *whom*, by the way? There's a world of difference between breaking someone's nose and shadow boxing."

The rabbi studied Jacob. He asked, "Has Sam been having any difficulties at home?"

"He's been overwhelmed by homework," Julia began.

"He *did not* do this."

"And he's been training for his bar mitzvah, which is, at least in theory, another hour every night. And cello, and soccer. And his younger brother Max is going through some existential stuff, which has been challenging for everyone. And the youngest, Benjy—"

"It sounds like he's got a lot on his plate," the rabbi said. "And I certainly sympathize with that. We ask a lot of our children. More than was ever asked of us. But I'm afraid racism has no place here."

"Of course it doesn't," Julia said.

"Hold on. Now you're calling Sam a *racist*?"

"I did not say that, Mr. Bloch."

"You *did*. You *just did*. Julia—"

"I don't remember his exact words."

"I said, 'Racism has no place here.'"

"Racism is what racists express."

"Have you ever lied, Mr. Bloch?" Jacob reflexively searched his jacket pocket yet again for his phone. "I assume that, like everyone who has ever lived, you have told a lie. But that doesn't make you a liar."

"You're calling me a liar?" Jacob asked, his fingers wrapped around nothing.

"You're boxing at shadows, Mr. Bloch."

Jacob turned to Julia. "Yes, the n-word is clearly bad. Bad, bad, very bad. But it was one word among many."

"You think the larger context of misogyny, homophobia, and perversion makes it *better*?"

"But he *didn't do it*."

The rabbi shifted in his chair. "If I can speak frankly for a moment." He paused, thumbing the inside of his nostril with plausible deniability. "It can't be easy for Sam—being Irving Bloch's grandson."

Julia leaned back and thought about sand castles, and the Shinto shrine gate that washed up in Oregon two years after the tsunami.

Jacob turned to the rabbi. "Excuse me?"

"For a child's role model—"

"This should be good."

The rabbi addressed Julia. "You must know what I mean."

"I know what you mean."

"We do *not* know what you mean."

"Perhaps if it didn't seem, to Sam, that saying anything, no matter—"

"You've read volume two of Robert Caro's biography of Lyndon Johnson?"

"I have not."

"Well, if you were the worldly kind of rabbi, and *had* read that classic of the genre, you'd know that pages 432 to 435 are devoted to how Irving Bloch did more than anyone else in Washington, or *anywhere*, to ensure the passage of the Voting Rights Act. A kid could not *find* a better role model."

"A kid shouldn't have to look," Julia said, facing forward.

"Now . . . did my father blog something regrettable? Yes. He did. It was regrettable. He regrets it. An all-you-can-eat buffet of regret. But for you to suggest that his righteousness is anything but an inspiration to his grandchildren—"

"With all due respect, Mr. Bloch—"

Jacob turned to Julia: "Let's get out of here."

"Let's actually get what Sam needs."

"Sam doesn't need anything from this place. It was a mistake to force him to have a bar mitzvah."

"What? Jacob, we didn't force him. We might have *nudged* him, but—"

"We nudged him to get circumcised. With the bar mitzvah, it was proper force."

"For the last two years, your grandfather has been saying that the only reason he hangs on is to make it to Sam's bar mitzvah."

"All the more reason not to have it."

"And we wanted Sam to know that he's Jewish."

"Was there any chance of him not knowing that?"

"To *be* Jewish."

"Jewish, yes. But *religious*?"

Jacob never knew how to answer the question "Are you religious?" He'd never not belonged to a synagogue, never not made some gesture toward kashruth, never not assumed—not even in his moments of greatest frustration with Israel, or his father, or American Jewry, or God's absence—that he would raise his children with some degree of Jewish literacy and practice. But double negatives never sustained a religion. Or as Sam's brother Max would put it in his bar mitzvah speech three years later,

"You only get to keep what you refuse to let go of." And as much as Jacob wanted the continuity (of history, culture, thought, and values), as much as he wanted to believe that there was a deeper meaning available not only to him but to his children and their children—light shone between his fingers.

When they had started dating, Jacob and Julia often spoke about a "religion for two." It would have felt embarrassing if it hadn't felt ennobling. Their Shabbat: every Friday night, Jacob would read a letter he had written for Julia over the course of the week, and she would recite a poem from memory; and without overhead lighting, the phone unplugged, the watches stowed under the cushion of the red corduroy armchair, they would slowly eat the dinner they'd slowly prepared together; and they would draw a bath and make love while the waterline rose. Wednesday sunrise strolls: the route became unwittingly ritualized, traced and retraced week after week, until the sidewalk bore an impression of their path— imperceptible, but there. Every Rosh Hashanah, in lieu of going to services, they performed the ritual of tashlich: casting breadcrumbs, meant to symbolize the past year's regrets, into the Potomac. Some sank, some were carried to other shores by the current, some regrets were taken by gulls to feed their still-blind young. Every morning, before rising from the bed, Jacob kissed Julia between the legs—not sexually (the ritual demanded that the kiss never lead to anything), but religiously. They started to collect, when traveling, things whose insides had an aspect of being larger than their outsides: the ocean contained in a seashell, a depleted typewriter ribbon, the world in a mercury-glass mirror. Everything seemed to move toward ritual—Jacob picking Julia up from work on Thursdays, the morning coffee in shared silence, Julia replacing Jacob's bookmarks with small notes—until, like a universe that has expanded to its limit and then contracts toward its beginning, everything was undone.

Some Friday nights were just too late, and some Wednesday mornings were just too early. After a difficult conversation there would be no kiss between the legs, and if one isn't feeling generous, how many things really qualify as being larger on the inside than on the outside? (You can't put resentment on a shelf.) They held on to what they could, and tried not to acknowledge how secular they had become. But every now and then, usually in a moment of defensiveness that, despite the pleas of every better angel, simply could not resist taking the form of blame, one of them would say, "I miss our Shabbats."

Sam's birth felt like another chance, as did Max's and Benjy's. A religion for three, for four, for five. They ritualistically marked the children's heights on the doorframe on the first day of every year—secular and Jewish—always first thing in the morning, before gravity did its work of compression. They threw resolutions into the fire every December 31, took Argus on a family walk every Tuesday after dinner, and read report cards aloud on the way to Vace for otherwise forbidden aranciatas and limonatas. Tuck-in happened in a certain order, according to certain elaborate protocols, and on anyone's birthday everyone slept in the same bed. They often observed Shabbat—as much in the sense of self-consciously witnessing religion as fulfilling it—with a Whole Foods challah, Kedem grape juice, and the tapered wax of endangered bees in the silver candleholders of extinct ancestors. After the blessings, and before eating, Jacob and Julia would go to each of the children, hold his head, and whisper into his ear something of which they were proud that week. The extreme intimacy of the fingers in the hair, the love that wasn't secret but had to be whispered, sent tremors through the filaments of the dimmed bulbs.

After dinner, they performed a ritual whose origin no one could remember and whose meaning no one questioned: they closed their eyes and walked around their house. It was fine to speak, to be silly, to laugh, but their blindness always became silent. Over time, they developed a tolerance for the dark quiet and could last for ten minutes, then twenty. They would meet back at the kitchen table, and then open their eyes together. Each time it was revelatory. Two revelations: the foreignness of a home the children had lived in their entire lives, and the foreignness of sight.

One Shabbat, as they drove to visit their great-grandfather Isaac, Jacob said, "A person gets drunk at a party, and hits and kills a kid on the way home. Another person gets equally drunk, and makes it home safely. Why does the first one go to jail for the rest of his life, while the second gets to wake up the next morning as if nothing happened?"

"Because he killed a kid."

"But in terms of what they did wrong, they are equally guilty."

"But the second one didn't kill a kid."

"Not because he was innocent, but because he was lucky."

"But still, the first one killed a kid."

"But when we think about guilt, shouldn't we think about actions and intentions, in addition to outcomes?"

"What kind of party was it?"

"What?"

"Yeah, and what was the kid doing out that late, anyway?"

"I think the point—"

"His parents should have kept him safe. *They* should be sent to jail. But I guess then the kid wouldn't have parents. Unless he lived in jail with them."

"You're forgetting he's dead."

"Oh, right."

Sam and Max became enthralled by intention. Once, Max ran into the kitchen crying, holding his stomach. "I punched him," Sam said from the living room, "but not on purpose." Or when, in retaliation, Max stomped on Sam's half-finished Lego chalet and said, "It wasn't on purpose; I only meant to stomp on the rug beneath it." Broccoli was fed to Argus under the table, "by accident." Quizzes weren't studied for, "on purpose." The first time Max told Jacob "Shut up"—in response to a poorly timed suggestion that he take a break from some Tetris derivative on which he was about to crack the top ten scores of the day but wasn't supposed to be playing in the first place—he put down Jacob's phone, ran to him, hugged him, and with fear-glazed eyes, said, "I didn't mean it."

When the fingers of Sam's left hand were crushed in the hinge of the heavy iron door and he screamed, "Why did that happen?" over and over and over, "Why did that happen?" and Julia, holding him against her, blood blooming across her shirt as breast milk used to when she heard a baby cry, said simply, "I love you, and I'm here," and Jacob said, "We need to go to the emergency room," Sam, who feared doctors more than anything any doctor could ever treat, pleaded, "We don't! We don't! It was on purpose! I did this on purpose!"

Time passed, the world exerted itself, and Jacob and Julia began to forget to do things on purpose. They didn't refuse to let go, and like the resolutions, and Tuesday walks, and birthday calls to the cousins in Israel, and three overflowing shopping bags of Jewish deli food brought to Great-Grandpa Isaac on the first Sunday of every month, and skipping school for the Nats' home opener, and singing "Singin' in the Rain" while riding Ed the Hyena through the automated car wash, and the "gratitude journals," and "ear inspections," and annual pumpkin picking and carving and seed roasting and monthlong decomposition, the whispered pride fell away.

The inside of life became far smaller than the outside, creating a cavity, an emptiness. Which is why the bar mitzvah felt so important: it was the final thread of the frayed tether. To snip it, as Sam had so badly wanted, and as Jacob was now suggesting against his own real need, would send not just Sam but the family floating off into that emptiness—more than enough oxygen to last a life, but what kind of life?

Julia turned to the rabbi: "If Sam apologizes—"

"For *what*?" Jacob asked.

"If he apologizes—"

"To *whom*?"

"Everyone," the rabbi said.

"Everyone? Everyone living and dead?"

Jacob assembled that phrase—*everyone living and dead*—not in the light of all that was about to happen, but in the pitch-blackness of the moment: this was before the folded prayers bloomed from the Wailing Wall, before the Japanese Crisis, before the ten thousand missing children and the March of a Million, before "Adia" became the most searched term in the history of the Internet. Before the devastating aftershocks, before the alignment of nine armies and the distribution of iodine pills, before America never sent F-16s, before the Messiah was too distracted or nonexistent to awake the living or the dead. Sam was becoming a man. Isaac was weighing whether to kill himself or move from a home to a Home.

"We want to put this behind us," Julia said to the rabbi. "We want to make it right, and go through with the bar mitzvah as planned."

"By apologizing for everything to everyone?"

"We want to get back to happiness."

Jacob and Julia silently registered the hope and sadness and strangeness of what she'd said, as the word dissipated through the room and settled atop the stacks of religious books and on the stained carpeting. They'd lost their way, and lost their compass, but not their belief that it was possible to get back—even if neither knew exactly what happiness she was referring to.

The rabbi interwove his fingers, just like a rabbi, and said, "There's a Hasidic proverb: 'While we pursue happiness, we flee from contentment.'"

Jacob rose, folded the paper, tucked it in his pocket, and said, "You've got the wrong guy."

HERE I AMN'T

While Sam waited on the bench outside Rabbi Singer's office, Samanta approached the bimah. Sam had built it from digital old-growth elm salvaged from the bottom of a digital freshwater lake that he'd dug and in which he'd submerged a small forest a year ago when, like one of those innocent dogs on one of those existence-of-evil electrified floors, he'd learned helplessness.

"It doesn't matter whether or not you want a bar mitzvah," his dad had said. "But try to think of that as inspiring."

Why was he so obsessed with animal cruelty, anyway? Why was he irrepressibly drawn to videos that he knew would only reinforce his convictions about humankind? He spent enormous amounts of time seeking violence: animal cruelty, but also animal fights (organized by humans, and in nature), animals attacking people, bullfighters getting what they deserved, skateboarders getting what they deserved, athletes' knees bending the wrong way, bum fights, helicopter beheadings, and more: garbage disposal accidents, car antenna lobotomies, civilian victims of chemical warfare, masturbation injuries, Shia heads on Sunni fence posts, botched surgeries, steam-burn victims, instructional videos about cutting away the questionable parts of roadkill (as if there were unquestionable parts), instructional videos about painless suicide (as if that weren't definitionally impossible), and so on, and on and on. The images were sharp objects he used against himself: there was so much in him that he needed to move to the outside, but the process required wounds.

On the silent drive home, he explored the chapel that he'd built around the bimah: the three-toed claw feet of the weightless two-ton pews; the Gordian-knotted fringes at the ends of the rag-rug runner down the aisle; the prayer books, each word of which was continually refreshed with its synonym: *the Lord is One . . . the Sovereign is Alone . . . the Absolute is Abandoned . . .* Left to go long enough, the prayers would, if only for an instant, return to their origins. But even if the average life expectancy continued to increase by one year with each passing year, it would take forever for people to live forever, so probably no one would ever see it.

The pressure of Sam's unreleased insides often took the shape of un-shared, useless brilliance, and while his dad, brothers, and grandparents ate lunch downstairs, while they were *obviously* talking about what he'd been accused of and what to do with him, while he was supposed to be memorizing the Hebrew words and Jewish melody of a haftorah whose meaning no one ever bothered with, he created morphing stained-glass windows. The window to Samanta's right depicted baby Moses being swept down the Nile, between mothers. It was a loop, but stitched to-gether to evoke an endless journey.

Sam thought it would be cool if the chapel's largest window were an ongoing depiction of the Jewish Present, so instead of learning the idiotic and utterly useless Ashrei, he wrote a script that pulled keywords from a Jewish-related Google News feed, ran them through a jury-rigged video search (which combed out redundancies, red herrings, and anti-Semitic propaganda), ran *those* results through a jury-rigged video filter (which scaled the images to best conform to the round frame and color-adjusted for continuity), and projected them onto the window. It was better in his head than in reality, but everything was.

Around the chapel he'd built the synagogue itself: the labyrinth of literally infinitely forking hallways; the aranciata-dispensing water foun-tains, and urinals made of the bones of ivory poachers; the stashes of genuinely loving, nonmisogynistic face-sitting porn in the storage closet in the Men's Club social hall; the ironic handicapped spot in the stroller parking lot; the Memorial Wall with tiny, never-working bulbs beside the names of those upon whom he wished quick and painless death, but death (former best friends, the people who made acne pads sting on pur-pose, etc.); various make-out grottoes where tenderhearted and legiti-mately funny girls, who dressed like American Apparel advertisements and wrote Percy Jackson fan fiction, allowed klutzes to suck their perfect boobs;

chalkboards that delivered 600-volt electrical pulses when scratched by
the fingernails of smart-ass, dumb-fuck bullies who were so obviously—
except to everyone besides Sam—fifteen short years from being paunchy
schmucks with tedious jobs and dumpy wives; small plaques on every
surface letting everyone know that it was because of Samanta's benefi-
cence, her fundamental goodness, her love of mercy and fairness and the
benefit of the doubt, her decency, her inherent value, her nontoxic un-
shittiness, that the ladder to the roof existed, that the roof existed, that
the perpetually buffering God existed.

The synagogue was originally at the edge of a community that had
developed around a shared love of videos in which guilty dogs express
shame. He could watch such videos all day—more than once he *did*—
without going too deep into what he found so appealing about them. The
obvious explanation would be that he empathized with the dog, and there
was obviously some truth in that. ("Did you do that, Sam? Did you write
those words? Were you bad?") But he was also drawn to the owners. Every
single one of the videos was made by someone who loved his dog more
than himself; the "shaming" was always funnily overdramatized and
good-spirited, and they all ended with reconciliation. (He'd tried making
his own such videos, but Argus was too old and tired to do anything other
than shit himself, for which no shaming could be good-spirited.) So it
had something to do with the sinner, and something with the judge, and
the fear of not being forgiven, and the relief of being loved again. Maybe
in his next life, his feelings would be less than all-consuming and some
portion of him would remain for understanding.

There was nothing exactly wrong with the original location, but life
was for good-enough, and Other Life was for putting things in the places
they longed to be. Sam secretly believed that everything was capable of
longing, and more, that everything was always longing. So after the shame-
inducing chew-out he got from his mom later that day, he paid some digital
movers some digital currency to disassemble the synagogue into the largest
parts that would fit into the largest trucks, move them, and reassemble
them according to screen grabs.

"*We're going to have to talk when Dad comes home from his meeting,
but I need to say something. It is* required."

"*Fine.*"

"*Stop saying 'fine.'*"

"Sorry."

"Stop saying 'sorry.'"

"I thought the whole point was that I was supposed to be apologizing?"

"For what you did."

"But I didn't—"

"I'm very disappointed in you."

"I know."

"That's it? You don't have anything else to say? Like maybe, 'I did it and I'm sorry'?"

"I didn't do it."

"Clean up this mess. It's disgusting."

"It's my room."

"But it's our house."

"I can't move that board. We're only halfway done with the game. Dad said we could finish after I'm not in trouble anymore."

"You know why you always beat him?"

"Because he lets me win."

"He hasn't let you win in years."

"He goes easy."

"He doesn't. You beat him because it excites him to capture pieces, but you're always thinking four moves ahead. It makes you good at chess, and it makes you good at life."

"I'm not good at life."

"You are when you're thoughtful."

"Is Dad bad at life?"

It went almost perfectly, but movers are less almost-perfect than the rest of humankind, and there were mishaps, hardly any of them noticeable—who but Sam would know that a Jewish star was dinged and hung upside down?—especially when hardly any of it was noticed in the first place. The tiny distance from perfect rendered it shit.

Sam's dad had given him an article about a boy in a concentration camp who observed his bar mitzvah by digging an imaginary synagogue and filling it with upright twigs to serve as a silent congregation. Of course, his dad never would have guessed that Sam actually read it, and they never spoke about it, and does it count as recalling something if you are thinking of it constantly?

It was all for the occasion—the entire edifice of organized religion conceived of, built, and tended to simply for a brief ritual. Despite the incomprehensible vastness of Other Life, there was no synagogue. And despite his profound reluctance ever to step foot in an actual synagogue, there had to be a synagogue. He didn't long for one, he needed one: you can't destroy what doesn't exist.

HAPPINESS

All happy mornings resemble one another, as do all unhappy mornings, and that's at the bottom of what makes them so deeply unhappy: the feeling that this unhappiness has happened before, that efforts to avoid it will at best reinforce it, and probably even exacerbate it, that the universe is, for whatever inconceivable, unnecessary, and unjust reason, conspiring against the innocent sequence of clothes, breakfast, teeth and egregious cowlicks, backpacks, shoes, jackets, goodbye.

Jacob had insisted that Julia take her car to the meeting with Rabbi Singer so she could leave straight from there and still get her day off. The walk through the school to the parking lot was severely quiet. Sam had never heard of Miranda rights, but he intuited them. Not that it mattered—his parents didn't want to talk in front of him before talking behind his back. So they left him at the entrance, among the mustached man-children playing Yu-Gi-Oh!, while they went to their cars.

"Did you want me to pick anything up?" Jacob asked.

"When?"

"Now."

"You have to get home for brunch with your parents."

"I'm just trying to take some load off your shoulders."

"We could use sandwich bread."

"Any particular kind?"

"The particular kind we always get."

"What?"

"What what?"

"You seem bothered."

"You aren't bothered?"

Had she found the phone?

"We're not going to talk about what just happened in there?"

She hadn't found the phone.

"Of course we are," he said. "But not in this parking lot. Not with Sam waiting on the steps for us and my parents waiting at the house."

"So when?"

"Tonight?"

"Tonight? With a question mark? Or, *tonight*."

"*Tonight*."

"You promise?"

"Julia."

"And don't just let him sulk in his room with his iPad. He should know we're upset."

"He knows."

"Yes, but I want him to know even when I'm not there."

"He'll *know*."

"You promise?" she asked, this time letting the question descend rather than rise.

"Cross my heart and hope against hope to die."

She could have said more—given examples from recent history, or explained why it wasn't the punishment she was worried about, but the reinforcement of their nearly calcified and completely miscast parental roles—but chose instead to offer a gentle, sustained squeeze of the arm.

"I'll see you this afternoon."

Touch had always saved them in the past. No matter the anger or hurt, no matter the depth of the aloneness, a touch, even a light and passing touch, reminded them of their long togetherness. A palm on a neck: it all flooded back. A head leaned upon a shoulder: the chemicals surged, the memory of love. At times, it was almost impossible to cross the distance between their bodies, to reach out. At times, it *was* impossible. Each knew the feeling so well, in the silence of a darkened bedroom, looking at the same ceiling: If I could open my fingers, my heart's fingers could open. But I can't. I want to reach across the distance, and I want to be reached. But I can't.

"I'm sorry about this morning," he said. "I wanted you to have the whole day."

"You're not the one who wrote those words."

"Neither is Sam."

"Jacob."

"What?"

"It cannot, it will not, be the case that one of us believes him and one doesn't."

"So believe him."

"He clearly did it."

"Believe him anyway. We're his parents."

"That's right. And we need to teach him that actions have consequences."

"Believing him is more important," Jacob said, the conversation happening too quickly for him to catch up to his own meaning. Why was he choosing this battle?

"No," Julia said, "loving him is more important. And on the other side of punishment, he'll know that our love, which requires causing him pain every now and then, is the ultimate consequence."

Jacob opened Julia's car door for her and said, "To be continued."

"Yes, to be continued. But I need you to tell me we're on the same page here."

"That I don't believe him?"

"That whatever you believe, you're going to help me make clear that we are disappointed, and that he has to apologize."

Jacob hated this. He hated Julia for forcing him to betray Sam, and he hated himself for not standing up to her. If there had been any hatred left, it would have been for Sam.

"OK," he said.

"Yes?"

"Yes."

"Thank you," she said, getting into the car. "To be continued tonight."

"OK," he said, shutting the door. "And take as long as you want today."

"What if as long as I want doesn't fit in a day?"

"And I have that HBO meeting."

"What meeting?"

"But not until seven. I mentioned it. You probably would've come back by then, anyway."

"We'll never know."

"It's annoying that it's on a weekend, but it'll only be an hour or two."

"That's fine."

He gave her arm a squeeze and said, "Take what's left."

"What?"

"The day."

The drive home was silent, save for NPR, whose omnipresence took on the character of silence. Jacob glanced at Sam in the rearview mirror.

"I went and done ate a can of your tuna fish, Ms. Daisy."

"Are you having a stroke or something?"

"Movie reference. And might've been salmon."

He knew he shouldn't let Sam use his iPad in the backseat, but the poor kid had been through enough that morning. A little self-soothing seemed fair. And it deferred the conversation that he didn't feel like having right then, or ever.

Jacob had planned on preparing an elaborate brunch, but when the call from Rabbi Singer came at nine fifteen, he asked his parents, Irv and Deborah, to come over early to watch Max and Benjy. Now there would be no ricotta-stuffed brioche french toast. There would be no lentil salad, no shaved brussels sprout salad. There would be calories.

"Two pieces of rye with creamy peanut butter, cut diagonally," Jacob said, handing a plate to Benjy.

Max intercepted the food: "That's actually mine."

"Right," Jacob said, handing a bowl to Benjy, "because *you* have Honey Nut Cheerios with a splash of rice milk."

Max examined Benjy's bowl: "Those are plain Cheerios with honey on them."

"Yes."

"So why did you lie to him?"

"Thanks, Max."

"And I said *toasted*, not *immolated*."

"*Imlated?*" Benjy asked.

"Destroyed by fire," Deborah said.

"What's with Camus?" Irv asked.

"Leave him alone," Jacob said.

"Hey, Maxy," Irv said, pulling his grandson into him, "someone once told me about the most incredible zoo . . ."

"Where's Sam?" Deborah asked.

"Lying is bad," Benjy said.

Max let out a laugh.

"Good one," Irv said. "Right?"

"He got into a little trouble at Hebrew school this morning and is doing time up in his room." And to Benjy: "I didn't lie."

Max peered into Benjy's bowl and told him, "You realize that's not even honey. It's agave."

"I want Mom."

"We're giving her a day off."

"A day off from *us*?" Benjy asked.

"No, no. She never needs time off from you guys."

"Time off from *you*?" Max asked.

"One of my friends, Joey, has two dads. But babies come out of vagina holes. Why?"

"Why what?"

"Why did you lie to me?"

"No one lied to anyone."

"I want a frozen burrito."

"The freezer's broken," Jacob said.

"For breakfast?" Deborah asked.

"Brunch," Max corrected.

"*Sí se puede*," Irv said.

"I could run out and get you one," Deborah offered.

"Frozen."

Over the previous months, Benjy's eating habits had veered toward what might be called unrealized foods: frozen vegetables (as in, still frozen when eaten), uncooked oatmeal, unboiled ramen noodles, dough, raw quinoa, dry macaroni with unreconstituted cheese powder sprinkled on top. Beyond adjusting shopping lists, Jacob and Julia never talked about it; it felt too psychological to touch.

"So what did Sammy do?" Irv asked, his mouth full of gluten.

"I'll tell you later."

"Frozen burrito, please."

"There might not be a later."

"Apparently, he wrote some bad words on a piece of paper in class."

"Apparently?"

"He says he didn't do it."

"Well, did he?"

"I don't know. Julia thinks so."

"Whatever the reality, and whatever each of you believes, you guys have to approach it together," Deborah said.

"I know."

"And remind me what a bad word is?" Irv said.

"You can imagine."

"In fact I can't. I can imagine bad *contexts*—"

"The words and the context of Hebrew school definitely didn't jibe."

"Which words?"

"Does it really matter?"

"Of course it really matters."

"It doesn't matter," Deborah said.

"Let's just say the n-word was featured."

"I want a frozen— What's the n-word?"

"Happy now?" Jacob asked his father.

"He used it actively or passively?" Irv asked.

"I'll tell you later," Max said to his little brother.

"There's no passive use of that word," Jacob said to Irv. "And no, you won't," he said to Max.

"There might not be a later," Benjy said.

"Did I really raise a son who refers to a word as *that word*?"

"No," Jacob said, "you didn't raise a son."

Benjy went to his grandma, who never said no: "If you love me you'll get me a frozen burrito and tell me what the n-word is."

"And what was the context?" Irv asked.

"It doesn't matter," Jacob said, "and we're done talking about it."

"Nothing could matter more. Without context, we'd all be monsters."

"N-word," Benjy said.

Jacob put down his fork and knife.

"OK, since you asked, the context is Sam watching you make a fool of yourself on the news every morning, and watching you being made a fool of on late shows every night."

"You let your kids watch too much TV."

"They watch hardly any."

"Can we go watch TV?" Max asked.

Jacob ignored him and went back at Irv: "He's suspended until he agrees to apologize. No apology, no bar mitzvah."

"Apologize to whom?"

"Premium cable?" Max asked.

"Everyone."

"Why not go all the way and extradite him to Uganda for some scrotal electrocution?"

Jacob handed a plate to Max and whispered something in his ear. Max nodded and left the table.

"He did something wrong," Jacob said.

"Exercising his freedom of speech?"

"Freedom of *hate* speech."

"Have you even banged a teacher's desk yet?"

"No, no. Absolutely not. We had a talk with the rabbi, and now we're fully in salvage-the-bar-mitzvah mode."

"You had a *talk*? You think *talk* got us out of Egypt or Entebbe? Uh-uh. Plagues and Uzis. Talk gets you a good place in line for a shower that isn't a shower."

"Jesus, Dad. Always?"

"Of course always. 'Always' so 'never again.'"

"Well, what do you say you leave this one to me?"

"Because you're doing such a great job?"

"Because he's Sam's father," Deborah said. "And you're not."

"Because it's one thing to pick up your dog's shits," Jacob said, "and it's another to pick up your dad's."

"Shits," Benjy echoed.

"Mom, could you go read to Benjy upstairs?"

"I want to be with the adults," Benjy said.

"I'm the only adult here," Deborah said.

"Before I blow my top," Irv said, "I want to be sure I'm understanding. You're suggesting that there's a line to be drawn from my misread blog to Sam's First Amendment problem?"

"No one misread your blog."

"Radically misconstrued."

"You wrote that Arabs hate their children."

"Incorrect. I wrote that Arab hatred for Jews has transcended their love for their own children."

"And that they are animals."

"Yes. I wrote that, too. They're animals. Humans are animals. This is definitional stuff."

"Jews are animals?"

"It's not that simple, no."

"What's the n-word?" Benjy whispered to Deborah.

"Noodle," she whispered back.

"No it's not." She lifted Benjy in her arms and carried him out of the room. "The n-word is *no*," he said, "isn't it?"

"Yes."

"No it's not."

"One Dr. Phil is already one too many," Irv said. "What Sammy needs is a fixer. This is a bone-dry freedom of speech issue, and as you do or should know, I am not only on the national board of the ACLU, its members tell my story every Passover. If you were *me*—"

"I'd kill myself to spare my family."

"—you'd chum the Adas Israel waters for an insanely smart, autistically monomaniacal lawyer who has sacrificed worldly rewards for the pleasure of defending civil liberties. Look, I appreciate the pleasure of bitching about injustice as much as anyone, but you're capable, Jacob, and he's your son. No one would condemn you for not helping yourself, but no one would forgive you for not helping your son."

"You're romanticizing racism, misogyny, and homophobia."

"Have you even *read* Caro's—"

"I saw the movie."

"I'm trying to get my grandson out of a bind. That's so wrong?"

"If he shouldn't get out of it."

Benjy trotted back into the room: "Is it *married*?"

"Is what married?"

"The n-word."

"That begins with an *m*."

Benjy turned and trotted back out.

"What your mother said before, about you and Julia needing to approach this together? That was wrong. You need to defend Sam. Let everyone else worry about what actually happened."

"I believe him."

And then, as if noticing her absence for the first time: "Where is Julia, anyway?"

"Taking the day off."

"Off from what?"

"*Off.*"

"Thank you, Anne Sullivan, but in fact I heard you. Off from *what?*"

"From *on.* Can you just let it be?"

"Sure," Irv said, nodding. "That's an option. But let me speak some words of wisdom that not even Mother Mary knows."

"Can't wait."

"Nothing goes away. Not on its own. You deal with it, or it deals with you."

"This too shall—?"

"Solomon wasn't perfect. In all of human history, nothing has ever gone away on its own."

"Farts do," Jacob said, as if to honor Sam's absence.

"Your house stinks, Jacob. You just can't smell it, because it's yours."

Jacob could have pointed out that there was Argus shit somewhere within a three-room radius. He'd known it as soon as he opened the front door.

Benjy came back into the room. "I remembered my question," he said, despite having given no indication of trying to remember anything.

"Yes?"

"The sound of time. What happened to it?"

A HAND THE SIZE OF YOURS,
A HOUSE THE SIZE OF THIS ONE

Julia liked the eye being led where the body can't go. She liked irregular brickwork, when one can't tell if the craftsmanship is careless or masterly. She liked the feeling of enclosure, with the suggestion of expansiveness. She liked it when the view wasn't centered in the window, but also liked remembering that views are, by nature's nature, centered. She liked doorknobs that one wants to keep holding. She liked steps up, and steps down. She liked shadows laid upon other shadows. She liked breakfast banquettes. She liked light woods (beech, maple), and didn't like "masculine" woods (walnut, mahogany), and didn't care for steel, and hated stainless steel (until it was thoroughly scratched), and imitations of natural materials were intolerable, unless their fakeness was declared, was the point, in which case they could be quite beautiful. She liked textures that the fingers and feet know, even if the eye doesn't. She liked fireplaces centered in kitchens centered on the main living floor. She liked more bookshelves than are necessary. She liked skylights over showers, but nowhere else. She liked intentional imperfections, but she couldn't bear nonchalance, but she also liked to remember that there could be no such thing as an intentional imperfection. People are always mistaking something that looks good for something that feels good.

you're begging me to fuck your tight pussy, but you don't deserve it yet

She didn't like uniform textures—they aren't how things *are*. She didn't like rugs centered in rooms. Good architecture should make one feel as if one is in a cave with a view of the horizon. She didn't like double-height ceilings. She didn't like too much glass. The function of a window is to bring in light, not to frame a view. A ceiling should be just out of reach of the extended fingers of a raised hand of the tallest occupant standing on tiptoes. She didn't like carefully placed trinkets—things belong where they don't. An eleven-foot ceiling is too high. It makes one feel lost, forsaken. A ten-foot ceiling is too high. She felt that everything was out of reach. Nine feet is too high. Something that feels good—safe, comfortable, designed for living—can always be made to look good. She didn't like recessed lighting, or lamps controlled by wall switches—so sconces, chandeliers, and effort. She didn't like concealed functions— refrigerators behind panels, toiletries behind mirrors, TVs that descend into cabinets.

> *you don't need it enough yet*
> *i want to see you dripping onto your asshole*

Every architect has fantasies of building her own home, and so does every woman. For as long as she could remember, Julia had felt a secret thrill whenever she passed a small parking lot or an undeveloped slice of land: *potential.* For what? To build something beautiful? Intelligent? New? Or simply for a home that might feel like home? Her joys were shared, not fully hers, but her thrills were private.

She had never wanted to become an architect, but she always wanted to make a home for herself. She disposed of the dolls to free the boxes they came in. She spent a summer furnishing the space under her bed. Her clothes covered every surface in her room, because closets shouldn't be wasted with utility. It wasn't until she started designing homes for herself— all on paper, each a source of pride and shame—that she came to understand what was meant by "herself."

"This is so great," Jacob said while being led through a floor plan. Julia never shared her personal work with him unless he explicitly asked. It wasn't a secret, but the experience of sharing always seemed to leave her feeling humiliated. He was never enthusiastic enough, or not in the right ways. And when his enthusiasm came, it felt like a gift with too precious a bow. (The *so* ruined everything.) He was filing away his enthusiasm for future retrieval the next time she said he was never enthusiastic about her work. And it humiliated her, also, to need his enthusiasm, even to want it.

What's wrong with such wanting and needing? Nothing. And the yawning distance from where you are to what you'd always imagined does not have to suggest failure. Disappointment need not be disappointing. The wanting, the needing, the distance, the disappointment: growing, knowing, committing, aging beside another. Alone, one can live perfectly. But not a life.

"It's great," he said, so close his nose almost touched the two-dimensional rendering of her fantasy. "Amazing, actually. How do you think of these things?"

"I'm not sure I do think of them."

"This is what, an interior garden?"

"Yeah, the stairs will rise around a light shaft."

"Sam would say, 'Shaft . . .'"

"And you would laugh, and I would ignore it."

"Or we'd both ignore it. Anyway, this is really, really nice."

"Thank you."

Jacob touched his finger to the floor plan, moved it through a series of rooms, always through the doors. "I know I'm no good at reading these things, but where would the kids sleep?"

"What do you mean?"

"Unless I'm misunderstanding something here, which is probably the case, there's only one bedroom."

Julia tilted her head, squinted.

Jacob said, "You know the one about the couple who get divorced after eighty years of marriage?"

"No."

"Everyone asks, 'Why now? Why not decades ago, when there was still life to live? Or why not just see it through to the end?' And they respond, 'We were waiting for the grandchildren to die.'"

Julia liked calculators that printed—the Jews of the office store, having stubbornly out-survived so many more-promising business machines— and while the kids assembled school supplies, she would tap out feet of numbers. Once, she calculated the minutes until Benjy went to college. She left it there, as evidence.

Her homes were just stupid little exercises, a hobby. She and Jacob would never have the money, nor the time and energy, and she'd done enough residential architecture to know that the desire to wring out a few more drips of happiness almost always destroyed the happiness you were so lucky to have, and so foolish never to acknowledge. It happens every time: a forty-thousand-dollar kitchen remodel becomes a seventy-five-thousand-dollar kitchen remodel (because everyone comes to believe that small differences make big differences), becomes a new exit to the garden (to bring more light into the enhanced kitchen), becomes a new bathroom (if you're already sealing off the floor for work . . .), becomes stupidly rewiring the house to be smart (so you can control the music in the kitchen with your phone), becomes passive-aggression over whether the new bookshelves should be on legs (to reveal the inlaid floor borders), becomes aggressive-aggression whose origin can no longer be remembered. One can build a perfect home, but not live in it.

> *do you like my tongue pushing its way between your tight lips?*
> *show me*
> *cum on my mouth*

There was a night, early in their marriage, at a Pennsylvania inn. She and Jacob shared a joint—the first time either had smoked since college—and lay in bed naked, and promised to share everything, everything without exception, regardless of the shame or discomfort or potential for hurt. It felt like the most ambitious promise two people could make to each other. Basic truth telling felt like a revelation.

"No exceptions," Jacob said.

"Even one would undermine everything."

"Bed-wetting. That kind of thing."

Julia took Jacob's hand and said, "Do you know how much I'd love you for sharing something like that?"

"I don't happen to bed-wet, by the way. I'm just establishing boundaries."

"No boundaries. That's the point."

"Past sexual encounters?" Jacob asked, because he knew it was the address of his greatest vulnerability, and so the place such sharing would have to go. Always, even after he'd lost the desire to touch or be touched by her, he abhorred the thought of her touching or being touched by another man. People she'd been with, pleasure she'd given and received, things she'd moaned. He was not an insecure person in other contexts, but his brain was compelled, with the magnetism of someone unable to escape the perpetual reliving of a trauma, to imagine her being sexually intimate with others. What did she say to them that she also said to him? Why would such repetitions feel like the ultimate betrayal?

"Of course they would be painful," she said. "But the point isn't that I want to know everything about you. It's that I don't want anything about you withheld."

"So I won't."

"And I won't."

They passed the joint back and forth a few times, feeling so brave, so still-young.

"What are you withholding right now?" she asked, almost giddily.

"Right now, nothing."

"But you *have* withheld?"

"Therefore I am."

She laughed. She loved his quickness, the oddly comforting warmth of his mind's connections.

"What's the last thing you withheld from me?"

He thought about it. Being stoned made it harder to think, but easier to share thoughts.

"OK," he said. "It's a little one."

"I want all of them."

"OK. We were in the apartment the other day. It was Wednesday, maybe? And I made breakfast for you. Remember? The goat cheese frittata."

"Yeah," she said, resting her hand on his thigh, "that was nice."

"I let you sleep in, and I secretly made breakfast."

She exhaled a column of smoke that held its form for longer than seemed possible, and said, "I could eat a lot of that right now."

"I made it because I wanted to take care of you."

"I felt that," she said, moving her hand up his thigh, making him hard.

"And I made it look really nice on the plate. That little salad beside it."

"Like a restaurant," she said, taking his cock in her hand.

"And after your first bite—"

"Yes?"

"There's a reason people withhold."

"We're not people."

"OK. Well, after your first bite, instead of thanking me, or saying it was delicious, you asked me if I'd salted it."

"So?" she asked, moving her fist up and down.

"So that felt like shit."

"That I asked if it was salted?"

"Maybe not felt like shit. It annoyed me. Or disappointed me. Whatever I felt, I didn't share it."

"But I was just asking a matter-of-fact question."

"That feels good."

"Good, love."

"But can you see how, in the context of the effort I was making for you, asking if it was salted conveyed criticism rather than gratefulness?"

"It feels like an effort to cook breakfast for me?"

"It was a special breakfast."

"Does this feel good?"

"It feels amazing."

"So in the future, if I think a food needs more salt, I should keep that to myself?"

"Or it sounds like I should keep my hurt to myself."

"Your *disappointment*."

"I could already come."

"So come."

"I don't want to come yet."

She slowed down, slowed to a grip.

"What are you withholding right now?" he asked. "And don't say that you're slightly hurt, annoyed, and disappointed by my hurt, annoyance, and disappointment, because you're not withholding that."

She laughed.

"So?"

"I'm not withholding anything," she said.

"Dig."

She shook her head and laughed.

"What?"

"In the car, you were singing 'All Apologies' and you kept singing, 'I can see from shame.'"

"So?"

"So that's not what it is."

"Of course that's what it is."

"Aqua seafoam shame."

"What!"

"Yup."

"Aqua. Seafoam. Shame?"

"My hand upon the Jewish Bible."

"You're telling me that my perfectly sensical phrase—sensical on its own, *and* in its context—is actually just a subconscious expression of my repressed whatever, and that Kurt Cobain intentionally strung together the words *aqua seafoam shame?*"

"That is what I'm telling you."

"Well, I cannot believe that. But at the same time, I'm extremely embarrassed."

"Don't be."

"That usually works when someone's embarrassed."

She laughed.

"That shouldn't count," he said. "Hobbyist withholding. Give me something good."

"Good?"

"Something really difficult."

She smiled.

"What?" he asked.

"Nothing."

"What?"

"Nothing."

"Sure sounds like something."

"OK," she said. "I'm withholding something. Something really difficult."

"Excellent."

"But I don't think I'm evolved enough to share."

"So went the dinosaurs."

She pressed a pillow over her face and scissored her legs.

"It's just me," he said.

"OK," with a sigh. "OK. Well. Lying here, stoned, our bodies naked, I just had a desire."

He instinctively reached his hand between her legs, and found that she was already wet.

"Tell me," he said.

"I can't."

"I bet you can."

She laughed.

"Close your eyes," he said. "It will make it easier."

She closed her eyes.

"Nope," she said. "Not easier. Maybe if you close yours?"

He closed his eyes.

"I'm having this desire. I don't know where it comes from. I don't know why I'm having it."

"But you're having it."

"I am."

"Tell me."

"I'm having this desire." She laughed again, and nuzzled her face into his armpit. "I want to spread my legs, and I want you to move your head down and look at me until I come."

"Only look?"

"No fingers. No tongue. I want your eyes to make me come."

"Open your eyes."

"And you open yours."

He didn't say a word or make a sound. With enough but not too much force, he rolled her onto her stomach. He intuited that what she wanted involved her inability to see him looking at her, for that final safety to be given over. She moaned, letting him know he was right. He moved his body down her body. He parted her legs, then spread them farther. He tucked his face close enough to smell her.

"You're looking at me?"

"I am."

"Do you like what you see?"

"I want what I see."

"But you can't touch it."

"I won't."

"But you can jerk yourself off while you look at me."

"I am."

"You want to fuck what you're looking at."

"I do."

"But you can't."

"No."

"You want to feel how wet I am."

"I do."

"But you can't."

"But I can see."

"But you can't see how tight I get when I'm about to come."

"I can't."

"Tell me what I look like and I'll come."

They came together, without touching, and it could have ended there. She could have rolled onto her side, put her head on his chest. They could have fallen asleep. But something happened: she looked at him, held his gaze, and once again closed her eyes. Jacob closed his eyes. And it could have ended there. They could have explored each other in the bed, but Julia rose and explored the room. Jacob didn't see her—he knew not to open his eyes—but he heard her. Without saying anything, he also got up. They each touched the bench at the foot of the bed, the desk and the cup with its pens, the tassels on the curtain tiebacks. He touched the peephole, she touched the dial that controlled the ceiling fan, he pressed his palm against the mini-fridge's warm top.

She said, "You make sense to me."

He said, "You, too."

She said, "I really love you, Jacob. But please just say 'I know.'"

He said, "I know," and felt along the walls, along the mounted quilts, until he came to the light switch. "I think I just made it dark."

Julia became pregnant with Sam a year later. Then Max. Then Benjy. Her body changed, but Jacob's desire didn't. It was their volume of withholding that changed. They continued to have sex, although what had always arisen spontaneously came to require either an impetus (drunkenness, watching *Blue Is the Warmest Color* on Jacob's laptop in bed, Valentine's Day) or muscling through the self-consciousness and fear of embarrassment, which usually led to big orgasms and no kissing. They still occasionally said things that, the moment after coming, felt humiliating to the point of needing to physically remove oneself to get an unwanted glass of water. Each still masturbated to thoughts of the other, even if those fantasies bore no blood relationship to lived life and often included another other. But even the memory of that night in Pennsylvania had to be withheld, because it was a horizontal line on a doorframe: *Look at how much we've changed.*

There were things Jacob wanted, and he wanted them from Julia. But the possibility of sharing desires diminished as her need to hear them increased. It was the same for her. They loved each other's company, and would always choose it over either aloneness or the company of anyone else, but the more comfort they found together, the more life they shared, the more estranged they became from their inner lives.

In the beginning, they were always either consuming each other or consuming the world together. Every child wants to see the marks ascend the doorframe, but how many couples are able to see progress in simply staying the same? How many can make more money and not contemplate what could be bought with it? How many, approaching the end of child-bearing years, can know that they already have the right number of children?

Jacob and Julia were never ones to resist convention on principle, but neither could they have imagined becoming quite so conventional: they got a second car (and second-car insurance); joined a gym with a twenty-page course offering; stopped doing their taxes themselves; occasionally sent back a bottle of wine; bought a house with side-by-side sinks (and house insurance); doubled their toiletries; had a teak enclosure built for their garbage bins; replaced a stove with one that looked better; had a child (and bought life insurance); ordered vitamins from California and mattresses from Sweden; bought organic clothing whose price, amortized over the number of times it was worn, all but required them to have another child. They had another child. They considered whether a rug would hold its value, knew which of everything was best (Miele vacuum, Vitamix blender, Misono knives, Farrow and Ball paint), consumed Freudian amounts of sushi, and worked harder so they could pay the very best people to care for their children while they worked. They had another child.

Their inner lives were overwhelmed by all the living—not only in terms of the time and energy required by a family of five, but of which muscles were forced to strengthen and which withered. Julia's unwavering composure with the children had grown to resemble omnipatience, while her capacity to express urgency to her husband had shrunk to texted Poems of the Day. Jacob's magic trick of removing Julia's bra without his hands was replaced by the depressingly impressive ability to assemble a Pack 'n Play as he carried it up the stairs. Julia could clip newborn fingernails with her teeth, and breast-feed while making a lasagna, and remove splinters without tweezers or pain, and have the kids begging for the lice comb, and compel sleep with a third-eye massage—but she had forgotten how to touch her husband. Jacob taught the kids the difference between *farther* and *further*, but no longer knew how to talk to his wife.

Their inner lives were nurtured in private—Julia designed houses for herself; Jacob worked on his bible, and bought a second phone—and a destructive cycle developed between them: with Julia's inability to express urgency, Jacob became even less sure that he was wanted, and more afraid of risking foolishness, which furthered the distance between Julia's hand and Jacob's body, which Jacob had no language to address. Desire became a threat—an enemy—to their domesticity.

When Max was in kindergarten, he used to give everything away. Any friend who would come over for a playdate would inevitably leave with a plastic car or stuffed animal. Any money that he somehow acquired—change found on the sidewalk, a five-dollar bill from his grandfather for having made a persuasive argument—would be offered to Julia in a check-out line, or to Jacob at a parking meter. He invited Sam to take as much of his dessert as he liked. "Go on," he would say when Sam demurred. "Take, take."

Max wasn't responding to the needs of others, which he seemed as capable of ignoring as any child. And he wasn't being generous—that would require the knowledge of giving, which was precisely what he lacked. Everyone has a pipeline through which he pushes what he is willing and able to share of himself out into the world, and through which he takes in all of the world that he is willing and able to bear. Max's conduit wasn't bigger than anyone else's, it was simply unclogged.

What had been a source of pride for Jacob and Julia became a source of concern: Max will be left with nothing. Careful not to suggest that there was anything wrong with the way he lived, they gently introduced notions of worth, and the finitude of resources. At first he resisted— "There's always more"—but as children do, he came to understand that there was something wrong with the way he lived.

He became obsessed with comparative value. "Could you get one house for forty cars?" ("It depends on the house and the cars.") Or, "Would you rather have a handful of diamonds or a houseful of silver? A hand the size of yours, a house the size of this one." He started trading compulsively: toys with friends, belongings with Sam, deeds with his parents. ("If I eat half of this kale, will you let me go to bed twenty minutes later?") He wanted to know if it was better to be a FedEx driver or a music teacher, and became frustrated when his parents challenged his use of *better*. He wanted to know if it was OK that his dad had to pay for an extra ticket when they took his friend Clive to the zoo. "I'm wasting my life!"

he would often exclaim when not engaged in an activity. He crawled into bed with them, too early one morning, wanting to know if that's what being dead is.

"What's that, baby?"

"Having nothing."

The withholding of sexual needs between Jacob and Julia was the most primitive and frustrating kind of withdrawal, but hardly the most damaging. The movement toward estrangement—from each other, and from themselves—took place in far smaller, subtler steps. They were always becoming closer in the realm of doing—coordinating the ever-expanding routines, talking and texting more (and more efficiently), cleaning together the mess made by the children they made—and farther in feeling.

Once, Julia bought some lingerie. She'd placed her palm atop the soft stack, not because she had any interest, but because, like her mother, she couldn't control the impulse to touch merchandise in stores. She took five hundred dollars out of an ATM so it wouldn't show up on the credit card bill. She wanted to share it with Jacob, and tried her best to find or create the right occasion. One night, after the kids were asleep, she put on the panties. She wanted to descend the stairs, cap Jacob's pen, not say a word, but communicate: *Look how I can look*. But she couldn't. Just as she couldn't bring herself to put them on before bed, fearing his not noticing. Just as she couldn't even lay them on the bed for him to come upon and ask about. Just as she couldn't return them.

Once, Jacob wrote a line he thought was the best he'd ever written. He wanted to share it with Julia—not because he was proud of himself, but because he wanted to see if it was still possible to reach her as he used to, to inspire her to say something like "You're my writer." He took the pages into the kitchen, laid them facedown on the counter.

"How's it going?" she asked.

"It's going," he said, in precisely the way he most hated.

"Progress?"

"Yes, just not clear it's in the right direction."

"Is there a right direction?"

He wanted to say, "Just say, 'You're my writer.'"

But he couldn't cross the distance that didn't exist. The vastness of their shared life made sharing their singularity impossible. They needed a distance that wasn't a withdrawal, but a beckoning. And when Jacob returned to the line the next morning, he was surprised and saddened to see that it was still great.

Once, Julia was washing her hands at the bathroom sink, after having cleaned up yet another Argus shit, and as she observed the soap forming webs between her fingers, the sconce flickered but persisted, and she was unexpectedly overwhelmed by a kind of sadness that didn't refer to or mean anything, but whose weight was punishing. She wanted to bring that sadness to Jacob—not with the hope of his understanding something that she couldn't understand, but with the hope that he might help carry something that she couldn't carry. But the distance that didn't exist was too great. Argus had shit on his bed, and either didn't realize it or couldn't be bothered to move; it got all over his side and tail. While Julia scrubbed it off with human shampoo and a damp T-shirt from some forgotten soccer team that once broke hearts, she told him, "Here we go. It's OK. Almost finished."

Once, Jacob considered buying a brooch for Julia. He had wandered into a store on Connecticut Avenue—the kind of place that sells salad bowls turned from reclaimed wood, and salad tongs with horn handles. He wasn't looking to buy anything, and there was no upcoming occasion for which a gift would have been appropriate. His lunch date had texted that she was stuck behind a garbage truck, he hadn't thought to bring along a book or newspaper, and every chair in Starbucks was occupied by someone who would finish his thinning life before finishing his thinly veiled memoir, leaving Jacob no place to go deep into his very thin phone.

"Is that one nice?" he asked the woman on the other side of the case. "Dumb question."

"I love it," she said.

"Right, of course you do."

"I don't like that," she said, pointing at a bracelet in the case.

"It's a brooch, right?"

"It is. A silver cast of an actual twig. One-of-a-kind."

"And those are opals?"

"They are."

He walked to another section, pretended to examine an inlaid cutting board, then returned to the brooch. "It's nice, though, right? I can't tell if it looks costumey."

"Not at all," she said, taking it from the case and putting it on a velvet-lined tray.

"Maybe," Jacob said, not picking it up.

Was it nice? It was risky. Did people wear brooches? Was it cornily figurative? Would it end up in a jewelry box, never to be seen again until it was bequeathed as an heirloom to one of the boys' brides so that she could put it in a jewelry box until it was one day passed down again? Was seven hundred fifty dollars an appropriate price for such a thing? It wasn't the money that concerned him, it was the risk of getting it wrong, the embarrassment of trying and failing—an extended limb is far easier to break than a bent one. After lunch, Jacob went back to the store.

"Sorry if I'm being ridiculous," he said, returning to the woman who had been helping him, "but would you mind putting it on?"

She took it back out of the case and pinned it to her sweater.

"And it's not heavy? It doesn't pull on the fabric?"

"It's quite light."

"Is it fancy?"

"You could wear it with a dress, or on a jacket, or sweater."

"And you would be happy if someone gave it to you?"

Distance begets distance, but if the distance is nothing, what is its origin? There was no transgression, no cruelty, not even indifference. The original distance was closeness: the inability to overcome the shame of subterranean needs that no longer had a home aboveground.

give me your cum
then you can have my cock

Only in the privacy of her own mind could Julia wonder what her own home would look like. What she would gain, and what she would lose. Could she live without seeing the kids every morning and evening? And what if she were to admit that she could? In six and a half million minutes, she would have to. No one judges a mother for letting her children go to college. Letting go wasn't the crime. The crime was choosing to let go.

you don't deserve to get fucked in the ass

If she built a new life for herself, so would Jacob. He would remarry. Men do. They get over it, and get on with it. Every time. It was easy to imagine him marrying the first person he dated. He deserved someone who didn't build imaginary homes for one. He didn't deserve Julia, but he deserved better than Julia. He deserved someone who stretched upon waking, rather than recoiled. Someone who didn't sniff food before eating it. Someone who didn't see pets as burdens, who had a pet name for him, and made jokes in front of friends about how much she liked being fucked by him. Some new, unclogged pipeline to a new person, and even if it were doomed to ultimately fail, at least the failure would be preceded by happiness.

now you deserve to get fucked in the ass

She needed a day off. She would have loved the feeling of not knowing how to fill the time, of wandering without a destination in Rock Creek Park, of actually savoring a meal of the kind of food that her kids would never tolerate, and reading something longer and of more substance than a sidebar about how better to organize emotions or spices. But one of her clients needed help selecting door hardware. Of course it had to be a Saturday, because when else could someone who was able to afford bespoke hardware have time to sample it? And of course no one needs help to look at door hardware, but Mark and Jennifer were unusually helpless when it came to negotiating their incompatible lacks of taste, and a doorknob was exactly unimportant and symbolic enough to require mediation.

Compounding Julia's irritation was the fact that Mark and Jennifer were the parents of one of Sam's friends, and thought of Jacob and Julia as *their* friends, and wanted to have a coffee after to "catch up." Julia liked them and, insofar as she could muster enthusiasm for extrafamilial relations, considered them friends. But she couldn't muster much. At least not until she could catch up with herself.

Someone needed to invent a way to be close to people without having to see them, or talk to them on the phone, or write (or read) letters, or e-mails, or texts. Was it only mothers who understood the preciousness of time? That there was none of it, ever? And you can't just have coffee, even and especially not with people you rarely see, because it takes half an hour to reach the café (if you're lucky), and half an hour to return home (if you're lucky again), not to mention the twenty-minute tax you pay just to get out the door, and a quick coffee ends up being forty-five minutes in the Olympic scenario. And there was the horrible rigmarole at Hebrew school that morning, and the Israelis were coming in less than two weeks, and the bar mitzvah was saying its goodbyes in the ICU, and while it's entirely possible to get help, help feels bad, help shames. One can order groceries online and have them delivered, but that feels like a failure, an abdication of motherly duty—motherly privilege. Driving farther to the store with good produce, selecting the avocado that will be perfectly ripe at its moment of use, making sure it doesn't get crushed in the grocery bag and that the grocery bag doesn't get crushed in the cart . . . it's a mother's job. Not job, but joy. What if she could accomplish the job but not the joy?

She never knew what to do with the feeling of wanting more for herself: time, space, quiet. Maybe girls would have been different, but she had boys. For a year she held them against her, but after that sleepless holiday she was at the mercy of their physicality: their screaming, wrestling, table drumming, competitive farting, and endless explorations of their scrotums. She loved it, all of it, but needed time, space, and quiet. Maybe if she'd had girls, maybe they'd have been more contemplative, less brutish, more constructive, less animalistic. Even approaching such thoughts made her feel unmotherly, although she always knew she was a good mother. So why was it so complicated? There were women who would spend their last pennies to do the things she resented. Every blessing that was promised the barren heroines of the Bible had fallen into her open hands like rain. And through them.

i want to lick the cum out of your asshole

She met Mark at the hardware gallery. It was elegant, and it was obnoxious, and in a world where the bodies of Syrian children washed up on beaches, it was unethical, or at least vulgar. But her commissions added up.

Mark was already handling samples when she arrived. He looked good: a tightly cropped, gray-dusted beard; clothes that were intentionally snug and not bought in sets of three. He had the physical confidence of someone who doesn't know within one hundred thousand dollars the contents of his bank account at any given moment. It wasn't attractive, but it wasn't ignorable.

"Julia."

"Mark."

"We seem not to have Alzheimer's."

"What's Alzheimer's?"

Innocent flirtation was so revitalizing—the gentle tickling of language that gently tickled one's ego. She was good at it, and loved it, always had, but grew to feel guilty about it in the course of her marriage. She knew there was nothing wrong with such playfulness; she wanted Jacob to have it in his life. But she also knew of his irrational, uncontainable jealousy. And frustrating as it could be—she never dared to mention a romantic or sexual experience from her past, and needed to overclarify any remotely misinterpretable experience in the present—it was part of him, and so something she wanted to care for.

And it was a part of him that drew her in. His sexual insecurity was so profound, it could only have sprung from a profound source. And even when she felt that she knew everything about him, she never knew what created his insatiable need for reassurance. Sometimes, after deliberately omitting something innocent that she knew would upset his brittle peace, she would look at her husband with love and think, *What happened to you?*

"Sorry I'm late," she said, adjusting her collar. "Sam got in some trouble at Hebrew school."

"Oy vey."

"Indeed. Anyway, I'm here. Physically and mentally."

"Maybe we should go get that coffee first?"

"I'm trying to quit."

"Why?"

"Too dependent on it."

"That's only a problem if there isn't coffee around."

"And Jacob says—"

"That's only a problem if Jacob's around."

Julia giggled at that, unsure if she was giggling at his joke or her girlish inability to resist his boyish charm.

"Let's earn the caffeine," she said, taking a too-distressed bronze knob from his hand.

"So I have some news," Mark said.

"Me, too. Should we wait for Jennifer?"

"We shouldn't. And that's my news."

"What do you mean?"

"Jennifer and I are getting divorced."

"*What?*"

"We've been separated since May."

"You said *divorced*."

"We've been separated. We're getting divorced."

"No," she said, squeezing the knob, further distressing it, "you haven't."

"Haven't what?"

"Been separated."

"I would know."

"But we've been together. We went to the Kennedy Center."

"Yes, we were at a play."

"You laughed, and touched. I *saw*."

"We're friends. Friends laugh."

"They don't touch."

Mark extended his hand and touched Julia's shoulder. She reflexively recoiled, eliciting a laugh from each of them.

"We're friends who were married," he said.

Julia organized her hair behind her ear and said, "Who still *are* married."

"Who are about not to be."

"I don't think this is right."

"*Right?*"

"Happening."

He held up his ringless hand: "It's been happening for at least long enough to erase a tan line."

A skinny woman approached.

"Anything I can help with today?"

"Maybe tomorrow," Julia said.

"I think we're OK for now," Mark said, with a smile that appeared, to Julia, as flirtatious as the one he'd given her.

"I'll just be over there," the woman said.

Julia put down the knob with a bit too much force and picked up another, a stainless octagon—ridiculously effortful, repulsively masculine.

"Well, Mark . . . I don't know what to say."

"Congratulations?"

"*Congratulations?*"

"Sure."

"That doesn't feel right at all."

"But it's *my* feelings we're talking about here."

"Congratulations? Really?"

"I'm young. Just barely, but still."

"Not just barely."

"You're right. We're resolutely young. If we were seventy it would be different. Maybe even if we were sixty or fifty. Maybe then I'd say, *This is who I am. This is my lot.* But I'm forty-four. A huge portion of my life hasn't happened. And the same is true for Jennifer. We realized we would be happier living other lives. That's a good thing. Certainly better than pretending, or repressing, or just being so consumed with the responsibility of playing a part that you never question if it's the part you would choose. I'm still young, Julia, and I want to choose happiness."

"Happiness?"

"Happiness."

"*Whose* happiness?"

"My happiness. Jennifer's, too. Our happiness, but separately."

"While we pursue happiness, we flee from contentment."

"Well, neither my happiness nor contentment is with her. And her happiness definitely isn't with me."

"Where is it? Under a sofa cushion?"

"In fact, under her French tutor."

"Holy *shit*," Julia said, bringing the knob to her forehead harder than she'd intended.

"I don't know why you're having this reaction to good news."

"She doesn't even *speak* French."

"And now we know why."

Julia looked for the anorexic clerk. Anything to look away from Mark.

"And *your* happiness?" she asked. "What language are you not learning?"

He laughed. "For now, I'm happy to be alone. I've spent my whole life with others—my parents, girlfriends, Jennifer. Maybe I want something different."

"Loneliness?"

"Aloneness isn't loneliness."

"This doorknob is very ugly."

"Are you upset?"

"Too little distress, too much distress, it isn't rocket science."

"That's why they save rocket scientists for rocket science."

"I can't believe you haven't even mentioned the kids."

"It's painful."

"What this is going to do to them. What seeing them half the time is going to do to you."

She pressed into the display case, angled herself a few degrees. No amount of adjusting could make this conversation comfortable, but it would at least deflect the blow. She put down the knob and picked up one whose only honest comparison would be the dildo she was given at her bachelorette party, sixteen years before. It had resembled a penis as little as this knob resembled a knob. Her girlfriends laughed, and she laughed, and four months later she came upon it while searching her closet with the hopes of regifting an unopened matcha whisk, and she found herself bored or hormonal enough to give it a shot. It accomplished nothing. Too dry. Too unwillful. But holding the ridiculous doorknob, then, she could think of nothing else.

"I lost my interior monologue," Mark said.

"Your *interior monologue*?" Julia asked with a dismissive grin.

"That's right."

She handed him the knob: "Mark, it's your interior monologue calling. He was mugged by your id in Nigeria and needs you to wire it two hundred fifty thousand dollars by the end of the day."

"Maybe it sounds silly. Maybe I sound selfish—"

"Yes and yes."

"—but I lost what made me *me*."

"You're an adult, Mark, not a Shel Silverstein character contemplating emotional boo-boos on the stump of a tree whose trunk he used for a dacha, or whatever."

"The harder you push back," he said, "the more sure I am that you agree."

"Agree? Agree with what? We're talking about *your* life."

"We're talking about the endless clenched-jaw worrying about the kids all day, and the endless replaying of unhad fights with your spouse all night. You wouldn't be a happier, more ambitious and productive architect if you were alone? You wouldn't be less *weary*?"

"What, me weary?"

"The more you joke, the more sure—"

"Of course I would."

"And vacations? You wouldn't enjoy them more alone?"

"Not so loud."

"Or someone would hear that you're human?"

She ran her thumb over the head of the knob.

"Of course I'd miss my kids," she said. "You wouldn't?"

"That's not what I asked."

"Yes, I'd prefer to have them with me and them on vacation."

"Tough sentence to assemble?"

"I would choose their presence. If it were a choice."

"Is it the never sleeping in, the never enjoying a meal, or the hyper-vigilance at the edge of a beach chair that your back will never touch?"

"It's the fulfillment that has no other source. The first thought I have every morning, and the last thought every night, is about my kids."

"That's my point."

"It's *my* point."

"When do you think about yourself?"

"When I think that one day, a few decades from now, which will feel like a few hours from now, I'll be facing death all alone, except that I won't be all alone, because I'll be surrounded by my family."

"Living the wrong life is far worse than dying the wrong death."

"No shit! I got the same fortune cookie last night!"

Mark leaned closer to Julia.

"Just tell me," he said, "you wouldn't like to have your time and mind back? I'm not asking you to speak badly of your husband or kids. Let's take it for granted that you've never cared about anything half as much, and couldn't care about anything more. I'm not asking for the answer you want to give, or feel you have to. I know this is hard to think about, much less talk about. But honestly: you wouldn't be happier alone?"

"You're assuming happiness is the ultimate ambition."

"I'm not. I'm just asking if you would be happier alone."

Of course it wasn't the first time she'd confronted the question, but it was the first time that it had been posed by someone else. It was the first time she didn't have the ability to evade it. Would she be happier alone? *I am a mother*, she thought—not an answer to the question being asked, and no more her ultimate ambition than happiness, but her ultimate identity. She had no lives to compare with her life, no parallel aloneness to measure against her aloneness. She was simply doing what she thought was the right thing to do. Living what she thought was the right life.

"No," she said. "I would not be happier alone."

He ran his finger around a platonically spherical knob and said, "Then you have it all. Lucky you."

"Yes. Lucky me. I do feel lucky."

A long few seconds of touching cold metal in silence, and then Mark asked, "So?" and placed the knob back on the counter.

"What?"

"So what's your news?"

"What are you talking about?"

"You said you had news."

"Oh, right," she said, shaking her head. "No, it isn't news."

And it wasn't. She and Jacob had been talking about thinking about looking for a place in the country. Something dinky that could be re-imagined. Not even *talking about*, really, but allowing the joke to linger for long enough to become unfunny. It wasn't news. It was process.

The morning after their night in the Pennsylvania inn, a decade and a half before, Julia and Jacob went on a hike through a nature preserve. An unusually chatty welcome sign at the entrance explained that the existing paths weren't original but were "desire lines," shortcuts people took that trampled the growth and over time appeared deliberate.

Julia and Jacob's family life became characterized by process, endless negotiation, tiny adjustments. Maybe we should throw caution to the wind and take off the window screens this year. Maybe fencing is one ac-tivity too many for Max, and too conspicuously bourgeois for his parents. Maybe if we replaced the metal spatulas with rubber spatulas, we wouldn't need to replace all the nonstick pans that are giving us cancer. Maybe we should get a car with a third row of seats. Maybe one of those projection things would be nice. Maybe Sam's cello teacher was right and he should just be playing songs he loves, even if that means "Watch Me (Whip/Nae Nae)." Maybe more nature is part of the answer. Maybe hav-ing groceries delivered would encourage better cooking, which would re-lieve the unnecessary but unshakable guilt of having groceries delivered.

Their family life was the sum of nudges and corrections. Infinite tiny increments. News happens in emergency rooms and lawyers' offices and, apparently, the Alliance Française. It is to be sought and avoided with everything one has.

"Let's look at hardware another day," Julia said, slipping the knob into her handbag.

"We're not going to do the renovation."

"You're not?"

"No one even lives there anymore."

"Right."

"I'm sorry, Julia. Of course we'll pay you for—"

"No, right. Of course. I'm just a little slow today."

"You put in so much work."

After a snowfall, there are only desire lines. But it always warms, and even if it takes longer than it should, the snow inevitably melts, revealing what was chosen.

i don't care if you cum, but i'll make you cum anyway

For their tenth anniversary, they went back to the Pennsylvania inn. They'd stumbled upon it the first time—before GPS, before TripAdvisor, before the rareness of freedom spoiled freedom.

The anniversary visit involved a week of preparations, which began with the most difficult task of locating the inn. (Somewhere in Amish country, quilts on the bedroom walls, red front door, rough-hewn banisters, wasn't there a tree-lined drive?) They had to find a night when Irv and Deborah could stay over to watch the kids, when neither Jacob nor Julia had any pressing work obligations, when the boys didn't have anything—teacher conference, doctor's visit, performance—that would require parental presence, and when that specific room was available. The first night to thread all the needles in the pincushion was three weeks out. Julia didn't know if that felt near or far.

Jacob made the reservation, and Julia made the itinerary. They wouldn't arrive until sundown, but they would arrive *for* sundown. The following day, they would have breakfast at the inn (she called ahead to ask about the menu), repeat the first half of their hike through the nature preserve, visit the oldest barn and the third-oldest church in the northeast, check out a few antiques shops—who knows, maybe find something for the collection.

"Collection?"

"Things with insides larger than their outsides."

"Great."

"And then lunch at a small winery I read about on *Remodelista*. You'll note I didn't mention finding a place for tchotchkes to bring home for the boys."

"Noted."

"And we'll make it back for a family dinner."

"We'll have time for all of that?"

"Better to have too many options," Julia said.

(They never made it to the antiques shops, because their vacation's insides were larger than its outsides.)

As they'd promised themselves, they didn't write out instructions for Deborah and Irv, didn't precook dinner or prepack lunches, didn't tell Sam that he would be the "man of the house" while they were gone. They made clear to everyone that they would not be calling to check in—but that, of course, should any need arise, they'd have their cell phones close and charged the whole time.

On the drive up, they talked—not about the kids—until they had nothing to say. The quiet wasn't awkward or threatening, but shared, comfortable, and safe. It was the edge of autumn, as it had been a decade before, and they drove north along a color spectrum—a few miles farther, a few degrees colder, a few shades brighter. A decade of autumn.

"Mind if I put on a podcast?" Jacob asked, embarrassed by his desire for both distraction and Julia's permission.

"That sounds great," she said, relieving the embarrassment she sensed in him, without knowing its source.

A few seconds in, Jacob said, "Ah, I've heard this one."

"So put on another."

"No, it's really great. I want you to hear it."

She put her hand on his hand on the gearshift and said, "You're kind," and the distance from the expected *that's kind* to *you're kind* was a kindness.

The podcast began with a description of the 1863 World Championship of Checkers, at which every game of the forty-game series ended in a draw and twenty-one of the games were identical, move for move.

"Twenty-one identical games. Every single move."

"Incredible."

The problem was that checkers has a relatively limited number of possible combinations, and since some moves are definitively better than others, one could know and remember the "ideal" game. The narrator explained that the term *book* refers to the sum history of all preceding games. A game is "in book" when the configuration of the board has occurred before. A game is "out of book" or "off book" when the configuration is unprecedented. The book for checkers is relatively small. The 1863 championship demonstrated that checkers had been, in essence, perfected, and its book memorized. So there was nothing left besides monotonous repetition, every game a draw.

Chess, however, is almost infinitely complex. There are more possible chess games than atoms in the universe.

"Think about that. More than *atoms in the universe!*"

"How could they know how many atoms there are in the universe?"

"Count them, I guess."

"Think of how many fingers that would take."

"You make me laugh."

"Apparently not."

"On the inside, I am. Silently."

Jacob slid his five fingers between Julia's.

The book for chess was created in the sixteenth century, and by the middle of the twentieth century it occupied an entire library in the Moscow Chess Club—hundreds of boxes filled with cards documenting every professional chess game ever played. In the 1980s, chess's book was put online—many mark that as the beginning of the end of the game, even if the end would never be reached. After that, when two players faced each other, they had the ability to search their opponent's history: how he responded in different situations, his strengths and weaknesses, what he would be likely to do.

Access to the book has made whole portions of chess games checkers-like—sequences that follow an idealized, memorized pattern— particularly openings. The first sixteen to twenty moves can be hammered out simply by "reciting" the book. Still, in all but the rarest chess games a "novelty" is reached—a configuration of pieces that has never been seen in the history of the universe. In the notation of a chess game, the next move is marked "out of book." Both sides are now on their own, without history, no dead stars to navigate by.

Jacob and Julia arrived at the inn as the sun was dipping below the horizon, as they had a decade before. "Slow down just a bit," she'd told Jacob when they were about twenty minutes away. He thought she wanted to hear the rest of the podcast, which touched him, but she wanted to give him the same arrival they'd had last time, which would have touched him if he'd known.

Jacob brought the car almost all the way into the parking space and left it in neutral. He turned off the stereo and looked at Julia, his wife, for a long time. Earth's rotation brought the sun under the horizon, and the space fully under the car. It was dark: a decade of sunset.

"Nothing has changed," Jacob said, running his hand along the dry-stone wall as they walked the mossy path to the entrance. Jacob wondered, as he'd wondered ten years before, how the hell such a wall was made.

"I remember everything but us," Julia said with an audible laugh.

They checked in, but before taking the duffel to the room, went to the fire and eased into the coma-inducing leather armchairs that they hadn't remembered but then couldn't stop remembering.

"What did we drink when we sat here last time?" Jacob asked.

"I actually remember," Julia said, "because I was so surprised by your order. Rosé."

Jacob let out a hearty laugh and asked, "What's wrong with rosé?"

"Nothing," Julia laughed. "It was just unexpected."

They ordered two glasses of rosé.

They tried to remember everything about the first visit, every smallest detail: what was worn (what clothes, what jewelry), what was said when, what music was playing (if any), what was on the TV over the honesty bar, what complimentary appetizers were offered, what jokes Jacob told to impress her, what jokes Jacob told to deflect a conversation he didn't want to have, what each had been thinking, who had the courage to nudge the still-new marriage onto the invisible bridge between where they were (which was thrilling, but untrustworthy) and where they wanted to be (which would be thrilling and trustworthy), across a chasm of so much potential hurt.

They ran their hands along the rough-hewn banister of the stairs to the dining room and had a candlelit dinner, almost all the food sourced from the property.

"I think it was on that trip that I explained why I don't fold my glasses before putting them on the bedside table."

"I think you're right."

Another glass of rosé.

"Remember when you came back from the bathroom and it took you like twenty minutes to see the note I'd written in butter on your plate?"

"'You're my butter half.'"

"Yeah. I really choked. Sorry about that."

"If we'd been sitting closer to the fire, you might have been spared."

"Although hard to explain the puddle. Ah, well. Next time I'll do butter."

"Next time is right now," she said—an offering and a summoning.

"And I'm supposed to just churn them out?" With a wink: "Churn?"

"Yes, I get it."

"Your stoicism is a butter pill to swallow."

"So give me something good."

"I know what you're thinking: *Bad butter puns, how dairy!*"

That got a chuckle. She reflexively tried to withhold her laughter (not from him, but herself) and felt an unexpected desire to reach across the table and touch him.

"What? You can't believe it's not better?"

Another chuckle.

"Butter precedes essence."

"That one I don't get. What do you say we move on to bread puns, or maybe even dialogue?"

"Have I milked it too much?"

"Relent, Jacob."

"Who ya gonna call? Goat's Butter!"

"Best yet. *Definitely* the one to end it on."

"Just to clear the dairy air, I'm the funniest man you've ever known?"

"Only because Benjy isn't yet a man," she said, but the combination of her husband's overwhelming quickness and his overwhelming need to be loved brought waves of love, pulled her into its ocean.

"Guns don't kill people, people kill people. Toasters don't toast toast, toast toasts toast."

"Toasters toast bread."

"The margarine for error is too small!"

What if she'd given him the love he needed, and she needed to give, if she'd said, "Your mind is making me want to touch you"?

What if he'd been able to make the right joke at the right time, or better still, be still?

Another glass of rosé.

"You stole a clock from the desk! I just remembered that!"

"I did not steal a clock."

"You did," Julia said. "You totally did."

The only time in his life he impersonated Nixon: "I am not a crook!"

"Well, you definitely *were*. It was a tiny, folding, cheap nothing. After we made love. You went to the desk, stopped the clock, and put it in your jacket pocket."

"Why would I have done that?"

"I think it was supposed to be romantic? Or funny? Or you were trying to show me your spontaneity credentials? I have no idea. Go back and ask yourself."

"You're sure you're thinking of me? And not some other man? Some other romantic night at an inn?"

"I've never had a romantic night at an inn with anyone else," Julia said, which shouldn't have required saying, and wasn't true, but she wanted to care for Jacob, especially right then. Neither knew, only a few steps onto that invisible bridge, that it never ended, that the rest of their life together would require steps of trust, which only led to the next step of trust. She wanted to care for him then, but she wouldn't always.

They stayed at their table until the waiter, in splutters of profuse apology, explained that the restaurant was shutting down for the night.

"What was the name of that movie we didn't watch?"

They would have to go to the room.

Jacob put the duffel on the bed, just as he had. Julia moved it to the bench at the foot of the bed, just as she had. Jacob removed the toiletry bag.

Julia said, "I know I shouldn't, but I wonder what the kids are doing right now."

Jacob chuckled. Julia changed into her "fancy" pajamas. Jacob watched her, unaware of anything that had changed about her body in the decade since they'd last been there, because he'd seen her body nearly every day since. He still stole peeks, like a teenager, at her breasts and ass, still fantasized about what was both real and his. Julia felt herself being watched, and liked it, so took her time. Jacob changed into boxers and a T-shirt. Julia went to the sink and ritually craned her neck back, a worn habit, examining herself as she gently pulled on a lower eyelid—as if she were about to insert a contact lens. Jacob produced both toothbrushes and applied toothpaste to each, resting hers, bristles up, on the sink.

"Thanks," Julia said.

"Do. Not. Mention. It," Jacob replied in a funny robot voice whose utterly random arrival could only have been an expression of anxiety about the emotions and actions now expected of them. Or so Julia thought.

Jacob brushed his teeth and thought, *What if I don't get hard?* Julia brushed her teeth, searching the mirror for something she didn't want to see. Jacob applied five seconds of Old Spice to each armpit (despite being an inert and sweatless sleeper), washed his face with Cetaphil Daily Facial Cleanser for Normal to Oily Skin (despite having Normal to Dry Skin), then applied Eucerin Daily Protection Moisturizing Face Lotion, Broad Spectrum SPF 30 (despite the sun having disappeared hours ago, and despite sleeping under a ceiling). He gave an extra squirt of Eucerin to his trouble spots: around the alas (a word he knew only from neurotic Google searches—*Alas, poor Yorick, the alas of your missing nose*), and between the eyebrows and the tops of the upper eyelids. Julia's regimen was more complex: a face wash with S.W. Basics Cleanser, application of Skin-Ceuticals Retinol 1.0 Maximum Strength Refining Night Cream, application of Laneige Water Bank Moisture Cream, gentle tapping application of Lancôme Rénergie Lift Multi-Action Night cream around her eyes. Jacob went to the bedroom and did the stretches that everyone in the family made fun of, despite the chiropractor's insistence that they were necessary for someone with such a sedentary lifestyle, and the fact that they actually helped. Julia flossed with an Oral-B Glide 3D Floss Pick, which, despite being both an environmental nightmare and a rip-off, spared her from gagging. Jacob returned to the bathroom and flossed with the cheapest thing he could find at CVS, string being string.

"You already brushed?" Julia asked.

Jacob said, "Beside you. Just a minute ago."

Julia made a dollop of hand cream disappear in her palms.

They moved to the bedroom, and Jacob said, "I have to pee," as he always did at that moment. He went back into the bathroom, locked the door, performed his nightly solitary ritual, and flushed the unused toilet to complete the charade. When he reentered the bedroom, Julia was propped against the headboard, applying L'Oreal Collagen Re-Plumper Night Cream across the thigh of her bent leg. Jacob often wanted to tell her that it wasn't necessary, that he would love her as she was, just as she would love him; but wanting to feel attractive was who she was, just as it was who he was, and that, too, should be loved. Julia tied back her hair.

Jacob touched a tapestry, a depiction of a naval battle beneath the bannered words "The American Situation: War of 1812," and said, "Nice." Did she remember?

Julia said, "Please tell me not to call the kids."

"Not to call the kids."

"Of course I shouldn't."

"Or call them. We're not vacation fundamentalists."

Julia laughed.

Jacob was never immune to her laughter.

"Come," she said, patting the bed beside her.

Jacob said, "We have a big day tomorrow," illuminating several emergency exit paths at once: they needed rest; tomorrow was more important than tonight; it wouldn't be a disappointment if she acknowledged her tiredness.

"You must be beat," Julia said, redirecting things slightly by putting the onus on him.

"I am," he said, almost as a question, almost accepting his role. "And you must be, too," asking her to accept hers.

"Come," she said, "hold me."

Jacob turned off the lights, placed his unfolded glasses on the bedside table, and got into bed, beside his wife of a decade. She turned onto her side, bringing her head into her husband's armpit. He kissed the North Pole of her head. Now they were on their own, without history, no dead stars to navigate by.

If they'd said what they were thinking, Jacob would have said, "To be honest, it's not as nice as I remembered."

And she would have said, "It couldn't have been."

"When I was a boy, I used to ride my bike down a hill behind the house. I'd narrate each run. You know, 'Jacob Bloch, set to attempt a new land speed record. He grips his handlebars. Can he do it?' I called it 'The Huge Hill.' More than anything else in my childhood, it made me feel brave. I went back the other day. It was on the way to a meeting, and I had a few minutes. I couldn't find it. I found where it was, or should have been, but it wasn't there. Only the gentlest slope."

"You grew," she would have said.

If they'd said what they were thinking, Jacob would have said, "I'm thinking about how we're not having sex. Are you?"

And without defensiveness or hurt, Julia would have said, "Yeah, I am."

"There's nothing I'm asking you to say here. I promise. I just want to tell you where I am. OK?"

"OK."

And risking another step onto the invisible bridge, Jacob would have said, "I'm worrying that you don't want to have sex with me. That you don't desire me."

"You don't need to worry," Julia would have said as she would have brought her hand to the side of his face.

"I always desire you," he would have said. "I was watching you undress—"

"I know. I felt it."

"You look every bit as beautiful as you did ten years ago."

"That's plainly untrue. But thank you."

"It's true to me."

"Thank you."

And Jacob would have found himself in the middle of the invisible bridge, above the chasm of potential hurt, at the farthest point from safety: "Why do you think we aren't having sex?"

And Julia would have stood beside him and, without looking down, said, "Maybe because the expectation is so great?"

"Could be. And we're genuinely tired."

"I know I am."

"I'm going to say something that isn't easy to say."

"You're safe," she would have promised.

He would have turned to her and said, "We never talk about how I can't get hard sometimes. Do you ever think it's you?"

"I do."

"It isn't you."

"Thank you for saying that."

"Julia," he would have said, "it isn't you."

But he didn't say anything, and neither did she. Not because the words were deliberately withheld, but because the pipeline between them was too occluded for such bravery. Too many small accumulations: wrong words, absences of words, imposed quiet, plausibly deniable attacks on known vulnerabilities, mentions of things that needn't be mentioned, misunderstandings and accidents, moments of weakness, tiny acts of shitty retribution for tiny acts of shitty retribution for tiny acts of shitty retribution for an original offense that no one could remember. Or for no offense at all.

They didn't recede from each other that night. They didn't roll to opposite sides of the bed, or withdraw into two silences. They held each other and shared a silence in the darkness. But it was silence. Neither suggested they explore the room with their eyes closed, as they'd done the last time they were there. They explored the room independently, in their minds, beside each other. And in Jacob's jacket pocket was the stopped clock—a decade of 1:43—which he'd been waiting for just the right moment to reveal.

i'll keep making you cum after you beg me to stop

In the hardware gallery parking lot, she sat in her car—her Volvo like everybody else's, in a color she knew was wrong the second after it was impossible to change her mind—not knowing what to do with herself, knowing only that she had to do something. She wasn't sufficiently adept with her phone to waste the kind of time she needed to waste. But she could squander at least a little. She found the company that made her favorite architectural model trees. They weren't the most realistic, they weren't even well made. She didn't like them because they evoked trees but because they evoked the sadness that trees evoke—the way an out-of-focus photograph might best capture its subject's essence. It was extremely unlikely that the manufacturer intended any of that, but it was possible, and it didn't matter.

They were featuring a new line of autumn trees. Who could be the market for such things? Orange Maple, Red Maple, Yellow Maple, Autumn Sycamore, Light Orange Aspen, Yellowing Aspen, Turning Maple, Turning Sycamore. She imagined a tiny, younger Jacob, and a tiny, younger Julia, in a tiny, scratched and dinged Saab, driving shoelace roads bordered by an infinity of tiny, turning trees, under an infinity of tiny, massive stars, and like the trees, the tiny young couple weren't realistic, or well made, and they didn't evoke their bigger, older selves, but they evoked the sadness that they would grow to evoke.

Mark tapped her window. She tried rolling it down and realized the car needed to be on, but the key wasn't in the ignition or in her hand, and she didn't have it in her to go through her bag, so she clumsily opened the door.

"I'll see you at the Model UN trip."

"What?"

"In a couple of weeks. I'm the male chaperone."

"Oh. I didn't know that."

"So we can continue our talk then."

"I don't know how much more there is to say."

"There's always more to say."

"Sometimes not."

And then, on her day off, wanting only to get as far away from her life as possible, she found herself trampling a desire line home.

it's enough when i say it's enough

HERE I AMN'T

> Anyone know how to take a picture of stars?
> Like in the sky, or with their hands in wet sidewalk?
> My phone's flash makes everything white. I turned it off, but the shutter stays open for so long my tiny movements blur everything. I tried bracing my arm with my other hand, but it was still a blur.
> Phones are useless at night.
> Unless you need to go down a dark hallway.
> My phone is dying.
> Or call someone.
> Just try to make it comfortable.
> Samanta, this place is fucking lit!
> Insane.
> Where are you that there are stars out?
> The guy told me there was nothing wrong with it. I said, "If there's nothing wrong with it, why is it broken?" And he said, "Why is it broken if there's nothing wrong with it?" And I tried, again, to show him, but of course it worked again. I almost cried, or killed him.
> What happens at a bat mitzvah, anyway?

At any given time, there are forty times in the world. Another interesting fact: China used to have five time zones, but now it has only one, and for some Chinese people the sun doesn't rise until after ten. Another: long before man traveled into space, rabbis debated how one would observe Shabbat there—not because they anticipated space travel but because

Buddhists strive to live with questions and Jews would rather die. On Earth, the sun rises and sets once each day. A spaceship orbits Earth once every ninety minutes, which would require a Shabbat every nine hours. One line of thinking held that Jews simply shouldn't be in a place that raises doubts about prayer and observance. Another, that one's earthly obligations are earthbound—what happens in space stays in space. Some argued that a Jewish astronaut should observe the same routine he would on Earth. Others, that Shabbat should be observed by the time set on his instruments, despite the city of Houston being about as Jewish as the Rockets' locker room. Two Jewish astronauts have died in space. No Jewish astronaut has observed Shabbat.

Sam's dad gave him an article about Ilan Ramon, the only Israeli ever to go into space. Before leaving, Ramon went to the Holocaust Museum, to find an artifact to take with him. He chose a drawing of Earth by a young, anonymous boy who died in the war.

"Imagine that sweet child scribbling away," Sam's dad said. "If an angel had landed on his shoulder and told him, 'You're going to be killed before your next birthday, and in sixty years a representative of the Jewish state is going to carry your drawing of Earth as seen from space *into space*—"

"If there were angels," Sam said, "he wouldn't have been killed."

"If the angels were good angels."

"Do we believe in bad angels?"

"We probably don't believe in any angels."

Sam enjoyed knowledge. The accumulation and distribution of facts gave him a feeling of control, of utility, of the opposite of the powerlessness that comes with having a smallish, underdeveloped body that doesn't dependably respond to the mental commands of a largish, overstimulated brain.

It was always dusk in Other Life, so once every day the "other time" corresponded to the "real time" of its citizens. Some referred to that moment as "The Harmony." Some wouldn't miss it. Some didn't like to be at their screens when it happened. Sam's bar mitzvah was still a ways off. Samanta's bat mitzvah was today. Did the drawing simply immolate when the space shuttle exploded? Are any small pieces of it still orbiting? Did they fall to the water, descend, over hours, to the ocean floor, and veil one of those deep-sea creatures that are so alien they look like they came from outer space?

The pews were filled with everyone Samanta knew, people Sam had never met. They came from Kyoto, Lisbon, Sacramento, Lagos, Toronto, Oklahoma City, and Beirut. Twenty-seven dusks. They were sitting together in the virtual sanctuary of Sam's creation—they saw the beauty; Sam saw all that was wrong with it, all that was wrong with him. They came for Samanta, a community of her communities. As far as they knew, it was a happy occasion.

> Just take it to someone else. Insist that they open it up.
> Just fucking throw your phone from a bridge.
> Can someone explain to me what's going to happen here?
> Funnily enough, I'm crossing a bridge right now, but I'm on an Amtrak and you can't open the windows.
> Send us a picture of the water.
> Today Samanta becomes a woman.
> There's more than one way to open a window.
> She's having her period?
> Imagine thousands of phones washed up on the beach.
> Love letters in digital bottles.
> Why imagine? Go to India.
> Today she's becoming a Jewish woman.
> I'm on an Amtrak, too!
> A Jewish woman how?
> More like hate mail.
> Let's not figure out if we're on the same train, OK?
> Israel is the fucking worst.
> Wiki: "When a girl reaches 12 years old she becomes 'bat mitzvah'—daughter of commandment—and is recognized by Jewish tradition as having the same rights as an adult. She is now morally and ethically responsible for her decisions and actions."
> Set your camera's phone on timer and then rest it on the ground, facing up.
> Jewish people are the worst.
> Knock knock.
> Why would you even want to take a picture of stars?
> Who's there?
> To remember them.
> Not six million Jews!

> ?
> Dying laughing.
> Anti-Semite!
> Dying, anyway.
> I'm Jewish!

No one ever asked Sam why he took a Latina as an avatar, because no one, other than Max, knew that he had. The choice might have seemed odd. Some might even have thought it was offensive. They would be wrong. Being Sam was odd and offensive. Having such prolific salivary and sweat glands. Being unable not to think about walking while walking. Backne and buttne. There was no experience more humiliating or existentially dispiriting than shopping for clothes. But how to explain to his mom that he would rather have nothing that properly fit than have it confirmed to him, in a mirrored torture chamber, that nothing ever *would* fit? Sleeves would never end at the right place. Collars would never not be too pointy, or rise too high, or angle improperly. The buttons of every button-down shirt would always be spaced such that the penultimate one from the top made the neck opening either too constrictive or too revealing. There was a point—literally a single location in space—where a button might be positioned to create the natural feel and effect. But no shirt had ever been made with such button placement, probably because no one's upper-body proportions were as disproportionate as his.

Because his parents were technological fucktards, Sam knew that they periodically checked his search history, the regular sweeping of which only rubbed his blackheaded nose in the patheticness of being a preteen with a Y chromosome who watched button-sewing tutorials on YouTube. And in those evenings behind his locked bedroom door, when his parents worried that he was researching firearms, or bisexuality, or Islam, he took to moving the penultimate buttons and slits of his loathsome shirts to the only endurable position. Half the things he did were stereotypically gay. In fact, probably a far greater proportion, if you were to remove the activities, such as walking an average-size dog and sleeping, that had no quality of straightness or gayness. He didn't care. He had not even the smallest issue with gay people, not even aesthetically. But he would have liked to correct the record, because he had the largest of all issues with being misunderstood.

One morning at breakfast, his mom asked if he'd been removing and resewing the buttons on his shirts. He denied it with nonchalant vehemence.

She said, "I think it's neat."

And so from then on, the upper half of his daily, all-seasons uniform shifted to American Apparel T-shirts, even though they broadcast the tits mysteriously sprouting from his otherwise collapsed torso.

It felt odd to have hair that never once, despite repeated and generous applications of product, rested properly. It felt odd to walk, and he often found himself slipping into an over- (or under-) stylized catwalk stride, whereby he swung his ass out to each side and pounded his feet into the ground as if trying not only to kill insects but to perpetrate an insect genocide. Why did he walk like that? Because he wanted to walk like nothing, and the extreme effort to do so generated a horrible spectacle of horrible perambulation by someone who was such a human cowlick he actually used the word *perambulation*. It felt odd to have to sit in chairs, to have to make eye contact, to have to speak with a voice that he knew to be his own but did not recognize, or only recognized as belonging to yet another self-appointed Wikipedia sheriff who would never possess a biographical entry visited, much less edited, by someone who wasn't him.

He assumed that there were times, other than while masturbating, when he felt at home in his body, but he couldn't remember them—maybe before he smashed his fingers? Samanta wasn't his first Other Life avatar, but she was the first whose logarithmic skin fit. He never had to explain the choice to anyone else—Max was wide-eyed or righteous enough not to care—but how did he explain it to himself? He didn't wish he were a girl. He didn't wish he were a Latina. Then again, he didn't *not* wish he were a Latina girl. Despite the near-constant regret he felt about being himself, he never confused himself for the problem. The problem was the world. It was the world that didn't fit. But how much happiness has ever resulted from correcting the record on the culpability of the world?

> I was up until 3:00, cruising the Google Street View of my neighborhood, and I saw myself.
> Is there going to be some sort of party after this?
> Does anyone know how to manipulate a PDF? I'm too lazy to figure it out.
> My celebrity memoir title: It Was the Worst of Times, It Was the Worst of Times.

> What kind of PDF?

> We're going to run out of maple syrup in three years?

> Is this going to be in Hebrew? If so, can someone less lazy than me write a script to stream it through a translator?

> I read that, too.

> Why do I find it so incredibly sad?

> Anyone have a NexTek thumb drive?

> Because you love waffles.

> My celebrity memoir title: "I Did It Your Way."

> I skipped right over the article about Syrian refugees. I know that shit is horrible, and I know it in theory makes me sad, but I can't find a way to have an actual emotion about it. But the syrup made me want to hide under my bed.

> They only work for a few weeks.

> So hide and cry your maple tears.

> Samanta, I got you something you're going to love, if you don't already have it, which you probably do. Anyway, transferring now.

> I can hear the most beautiful song coming from the earphones of the girl sitting across the aisle from me.

> Today's most-watched: some kids in Russia with a homemade bungee jump, an alligator biting an electric eel, an old Korean grocer beating the shit out of a burglar, quintuplets laughing, two black girls beating the shit out of each other on a playground . . .

> What song?

> I want to do something massive, but what?

> Forget it, I figured it out.

> Shit, I didn't know you're supposed to bring a gift to a bat mitzvah.

> Transfer is taking forever.

Sam thought about texting Billie, seeing if she might want to join him at a modern dance performance (or show, or whatever they're called) on Saturday. It sounded cool, as she'd written about it in her diary, which he'd removed from her unattended backpack while she was in gym, concealed behind his far larger, far less interesting chemistry textbook, and perused—a word that means the exact opposite of what most people think it means. He didn't like texting, because he had to look at his thumb—

the finger that got it worst, or healed least well. The one people tried not to notice. Weeks after the other fingers had regained their color and approximate shape, the thumb was black, and askew at the knuckle. The doctor said it wasn't taking, and would have to be amputated to protect the rest of the hand from infection. He said this in front of Sam. Sam's dad said, "You're sure?" His mom insisted they get another opinion. The second opinion was the same, and his dad sighed, and his mom insisted they get another. The third doctor said there was no immediate risk of infection, and kids are almost superhumanly resilient, and "almost always these things just find a way to heal themselves." His dad didn't trust the sound of that, but his mom did, and within two weeks, the darkness was receding toward the thumb's tip. Sam was nearly eight. He doesn't remember any of the doctors, or even the physical therapy. He barely remembers the accident itself, and sometimes wonders if he's just remembering his parents' memories.

Sam doesn't remember screaming, "Why did that happen?" as loud as he could, not out of terror, or anger, or confusion, but because of the size of the question. There are stories of mothers lifting cars off their trapped children, he remembers that, but he doesn't remember his mom's super-human composure when she met his wild eyes and subdued them, promising, "I love you, and I'm here." He doesn't remember being pinned while the doctor reattached the ends of his fingers. He doesn't remember waking up from his five-hour post-surgery nap to find that his dad had filled his room with the contents of Child's Play. But he remembers the game they used to play when he was a child: *Where is Thumbkin? Where is Thumbkin? Here I am! Here I am!* They never played it with Benjy after the injury, not once, and never once acknowledged that they had stopped playing it. His parents were trying to spare Sam, not understanding that the shame suggested by the silence was the one thing he could have been spared.

> Here's an app that should exist: You point your phone at something and it streams video of what that thing looked like a few seconds before. (Obviously this would depend on pretty much everyone filming and uploading pretty much everything pretty much always, but we're already pretty much there.) So you would be experiencing the world as it just happened.

> Cool idea. And you could change settings to increase the lag.
> ?
> You could see the world of yesterday, or a month ago, or your birthday, or—and this won't be possible until the future, once enough video has been uploaded—people could move around their childhoods.
> Imagine a dying person, who hasn't yet been born, one day walking through his childhood home.
> What if it had been torn down?
> And there would be ghosts, too.
> Ghosts how?
> "A dying person who hasn't yet been born."
> Is this thing ever gonna start?

Sam was brought back to the other side of the screen by a knocking.
"Go away."
"Fine."
"What?" he asked, opening the door for Max.
"Just going away."
"What's that?"
"A plate of food."
"No it isn't."
"Toast is food."
"Why the hell would I want toast?"
"To plug your ears?"
Sam gestured for Max to come into the room.
"They're talking about me?"
"*Oh* yeah."
"Bad things?"
"They definitely aren't singing 'For He's a Jolly Good Fellow,' or whatever."
"Is Dad disappointed?"
"I'd say so."
Sam went back to his screen, while Max nonchalantly tried to absorb the details of his brother's room.
"In me?" Sam asked without turning to face his brother.
"What?"

"Disappointed in me?"

"I thought that's what you meant."

"He can be such a pussy."

"Yeah, but Mom can be such a dick."

Sam laughed. "Absolutely true." He logged off and spun to face Max. "They're peeling off the Band-Aid so slowly, new hairs have time to grow and get stuck to it."

"Huh?"

"I wish they'd just get divorced already."

"Divorced?" Max asked, his body rerouting blood to the part of the brain that conceals panic.

"Obviously."

"Really?"

"What are you, ignorant?"

"Is that like stupid?"

"Not-knowing."

"No."

"So," Sam asked, running his finger around the frame of his iPad, around the rectangular tear in the physical world, "who would you choose?"

"For what?"

"*Choose.* To live with."

Max didn't like this.

"Don't kids just, like, split time, or whatever?"

"Yeah, it would begin like that, but then, you know, it always becomes a choice."

Max hated this.

"I guess Dad's more fun," he said. "And I'd get in trouble a lot less. And probably have more cool stuff and screen time—"

"To enjoy before you die of scurvy, or melanoma from never putting on sunscreen, or just get sent to jail for getting to school late every single day."

"Do they send you to jail for that?"

"It's definitely the law that you have to go."

"I'd also miss Mom."

"What about her?"

"That she's her."

Sam didn't like this.

"But I'd miss Dad if I went with Mom," Max said, "so, I guess I don't know. Who would you choose?"

"For you?"

"For yourself. I'd just want to be where you are."

Sam hated this.

Max tilted his head up and looked at the ceiling, encouraging the tears to roll back under his eyes. It appeared almost robotic, but his inability to directly face such direct human emotion was what made him human. Or at least his father's son.

Max put his hands in his pockets—a Jolly Rancher wrapper, a stubby pencil from a mini golf outing, a receipt whose type had vanished—and said, "So I went to a zoo once."

"You've been to the zoo a lot of times."

"It's a joke."

"Ah."

"So I went to a zoo once, because I'd heard it was like the greatest zoo in the world. And, you know, I wanted to see it for myself."

"Must have been pretty spectacular."

"Well, the weird thing is, there was only one animal in the entire zoo."

"No kidding."

"Yeah. And it was a dog."

"Argus?"

"You just screwed up my timing."

"Do the last line again."

"I'll just start from the beginning."

"OK."

"So I went to a zoo once, because I'd heard it was the greatest zoo in the world. But the thing is, there was only one animal in the entire zoo. And it was a dog."

"Jeez!"

"Yeah, turns out it was a shih tzu. Get it?"

"Really funny," Sam said, unable to laugh, despite finding it genuinely really funny.

"You get it, though, right? Shih tzu?"

"Yeah."

"Shih. Tzu."

"Thanks, Max."

"Am I being annoying?"

"Not at all."

"I am."

"Just the opposite."

"What's the opposite of annoying?"

Sam tilted his head up, darted his eyes toward the ceiling, and said, "Thanks for not asking if I did it."

"Oh," Max said, rubbing the erased receipt between his thumb and forefinger. "It's because I don't care."

"I know. You're the only one who doesn't care."

"Turns out it was a shit family," Max said, wondering where he would go after leaving the room.

"That's not funny."

"Maybe you don't get it."

EPITOME

"Dad?" Benjy said, entering the kitchen yet again, his grandmother in tow. He always said *Dad* with a question mark, as if asking where his father was.

"Yeah, buddy?"

"When you made dinner last night, my broccoli was touching my chicken."

"And you were just thinking about that?"

"No. All day."

"It mixes in your stomach anyway," Max said from the threshold.

"Where'd you come from?" Jacob asked.

"Mom's vagina hole," Benjy said.

"And you're going to die anyway," Max continued, "so who cares what touches the chicken, which is dead anyway."

Benjy turned to Jacob: "Is that true, Dad?"

"Which part?"

"I'm going to die?"

"Why, Max? In what way was this necessary?"

"I'm going to die!"

"Many, many years from now."

"Does that really make a difference?" Max asked.

"It could be worse," Irv said. "You could be Argus."

"Why would it be worse to be Argus?"

"You know, one paw in the oven."

Benjy let out a plaintive wail, and then, as if carried on a light beam from wherever she'd been, Julia opened the door and rushed in.

"What happened?"

"What are you doing back?" Jacob asked, hating everything about the moment.

"Dad says I'm gonna die."

"In fact," Jacob said with a forced laugh, "what I *said* was, you're going to live a very, very, *very* long life."

Julia brought Benjy onto her lap and said, "Of course you aren't going to die."

"Then make that *two* frozen burritos," Irv said.

"Hi, darling," Deborah said to Julia. "It was beginning to feel a bit estrogen-starved in here."

"Why did I get a boo-boo, Mama?"

"You don't have a boo-boo," Jacob said.

"On my knee," Benjy said, pointing at nothing. *"There."*

"You must have fallen," Julia said.

"Why?"

"There is literally no boo-boo."

"Because falling is part of life," Julia said.

"It's the epitome of life," Max said.

"Nice vocab, Max."

"Epitome?" Benjy asked.

"Essence of," Deborah said.

"Why is falling the epitome of life?"

"It isn't," Jacob said.

"The earth is always falling toward the sun," Max said.

"Why?" Benjy asked.

"Because of gravity," Max said.

"No," Benjy said, addressing his question to Jacob. "Why isn't falling the epitome of life?"

"Why *isn't* it?"

"Yes."

"I'm not sure I understand your question."

"Why?"

"Why am I not sure that I understand your question?"

"Yeah, that."

"Because this conversation has become confusing, and because I'm just a human with severely limited intelligence."

"Jacob."

"I'm dying!"

"You're overreacting."

"No I amn't!"

"No you *aren't*."

"I amn't."

"Aren't, Benjy."

Deborah: *"Kiss it*, Jacob."

Jacob kissed Benjy's nonexistent boo-boo.

"I can carry our refrigerator," Benjy said, not quite sure if he was ready to be done with his crying.

"That's wonderful," Deborah said.

"Of course you can't," Max said.

"Max said of course I can't."

"Give the kid a break," Jacob whispered to Max at conversational volume. "If he says he can lift the fridge, he can lift the fridge."

"I can carry it far away."

"I've got it from here," Julia said.

"I can control the microwave with my mind," Max said.

"No *way*," Jacob said to Julia, too casually to be believable. "We're doing great. We've been having a great time. You walked in at a bad moment. Unrepresentative. But everything is cool, and this is your day."

"Off from *what*?" Benjy asked his mother.

"What?" Julia asked.

"What do you need a day off from?"

"Who said I needed a day off?"

"Dad just did."

"I said we were giving you a day off."

"Off from *what*?" Benjy asked.

"Exactly," Irv said.

"Us, obviously," Max said.

So much sublimation: domestic closeness had become intimate distance, intimate distance had become shame, shame had become resignation, resignation had become fear, fear had become resentment, resentment had become self-protection. Julia often thought that if they could just trace the string back to the source of their withholding, they might actually find their openness. Was it Sam's injury? The never-asked question of how it happened? She'd always assumed they were protecting each other with that silence, but what if they were trying to injure, to transfer the wound from Sam to themselves? Or was it older? Did the withholding from each other predate meeting each other? Believing that would change everything.

The resentment that was fear, that was resignation, that was shame, that was distance, that was closeness, was too heavy to carry all day, every day. So where to put it down? On the kids, of course. Jacob and Julia were both guilty, but Jacob was guiltier. He'd become increasingly snippy with them, because he knew they would take it. He pushed, because they wouldn't push back. He was afraid of Julia, but he wasn't afraid of them, so he gave them what was hers.

"Enough!" he said to Max, his voice rising to a growl. "Enough."

"Enough yourself," Max said.

Jacob and Julia met eyes, registering that first act of talking back.

"Excuse me?"

"Nothing."

Jacob let it rip: "I'm not discussing things with you, Max. I'm tired of discussion. We discuss *too much* in this family."

"Who's discussing?" Max asked.

Deborah went to her son and said, "Take a breath, Jacob."

"I take too many breaths."

"Let's go upstairs for a second," Julia said.

"No. That's what *we* do with *them*. Not what *you* do with *me*." Then, turning back to Max: "Sometimes, in life, in a family, you have to just do the right thing without endlessly parsing and negotiating. You get with the program."

"Yeah, get with the pogrom," Irv said, imitating his son.

"Dad, just stop. OK?"

"I can lift the whole kitchen," Benjy said, touching his father's arm.

"Kitchens aren't liftable," Jacob said.

"They are."

"No, Benjy. They are not."

"You're so *strong*," Julia said, her fingers wrapped around each of Benjy's wrists.

"Immolated," Benjy said. And then, in a whisper: *"I can lift our kitchen."*

Max looked to his mother. She closed her eyes, unwilling or unable to protect him as she did his little brother.

A godsent dogfight on the street brought everyone to the window. It wasn't actually a fight, just two dogs barking at a smug squirrel on a branch. Still, godsent. By the time the family reassumed positions in the kitchen, the previous ten minutes felt ten years old.

Julia excused herself and went up to the shower. She never showered in the middle of the day, and was surprised by the force of the hand that guided her there. She could hear sound effects coming from Sam's room— he was obviously ignoring the first commandment of his exile—but she didn't stop.

She closed and locked the door of the bathroom, put down her bag, undressed, and examined herself in the mirror. Reaching her arm to the sky, she could follow a vein as it traversed the underside of her right breast. Her chest had sunk, her belly had protruded. These things had happened in tiny, imperceptible increments. The wisps of pubic hair reaching to her belly had darkened—the skin itself seemed to have. None of it was news, but process. She had observed, and felt, the unwanted renovation of her body, at least since Sam was born: the expansion and ultimate shrinking of her breasts, the settling and pockmarking of her thighs, the relaxing of all that was firm. Jacob had told her, on their second visit to the inn, and on other occasions, that he loved her body exactly as it was. But despite believing him, some nights she felt a need to apologize to him.

And then she remembered it. Of course she did: it was put there for her to remember at this moment. She didn't know it at the time. She didn't know why she, who had never stolen anything in her life, was stealing. This was why.

She raised one foot onto the sink and held the doorknob to her mouth, warming and wetting it with her breathing. She parted the lips of her pussy and pressed it there, gentle at first, then less so, starting to spin the knob. She felt the first wave of something good go through her, and her legs weakened. She squatted, pulled down the neck of her shirt, and exposed one breast. Then she re-wet the knob with her tongue and found its place between her lips again, pressing tiny circles against her clit, then just tapping it there, liking how the warm metal began to stick to her skin, to pull at it a little each time.

She was on her hands and knees. No. She was standing. Where was she? Outside. Yes. Leaning against her car. In a parking lot. In a field. No, bent, the top half of her body across the car's backseat, her feet on the earth. Her pants and underwear were pulled down only far enough to expose her ass. She pressed her face into the seat and pushed her ass out. She spread her legs as wide as the pants would allow. She wanted them held together. She wanted it to be difficult. They could be discovered at any moment. You have to be fast, she told him. Him? Just fuck me hard. It was Jacob. Just make me come. Just fuck me how you want, Jacob, and walk away. Just leave me here with your cum dripping down my thighs. Fuck me and go. No. It shifted. Now she was in the bespoke hardware showroom. No men. Only doorknobs. She ground the knob into her clit, licked three fingers, and slid them inside to feel the contractions as she came.

She felt a sudden thud, like the violent landing that would sometimes jerk her from near-sleep. But it wasn't that—she wasn't crashing onto the floor; something was crashing onto her. What the hell was going on? Had too much blood rushed to her waist too quickly, causing some kind of neurological event? Masturbation was about mental exertion, but she was suddenly at the mercy of her mind.

Through the ceiling of her pine coffin she could see Sam standing above her, so handsome in his suit, a shovel in hand. She didn't choose this. It didn't bring her pleasure. What a beautiful boy. What a beautiful man. It's OK, love. OK, OK, OK. She moaned, and he wailed, both of them animals. He scooped another shovelful of dirt and tipped it onto her. So this is what it's like. Now I know, and nothing will be different.

And then Sam left.

And Jacob and Max and Benjy left.

All her men left.

And then more dirt, this time from the shovels of strangers, four at a time.

And then they left.

And she was alone, in the tiniest house of her life.

She was brought back to the world, back to life, by a buzzing—it shook her free from her unchosen fantasy, and she was hit by the full absurdity of what she was doing. Who did she think she was? Her in-laws downstairs, her son down the hall, her IRA bigger than her savings account. She didn't feel ashamed; she felt stupid.

Another buzz.

She couldn't place its source.

It was a phone, but not a buzz she'd ever heard before.

Did Jacob get Sam a smartphone to replace the hand-me-down flip phone on which he'd been texting at Joseph Mitchell speed for the last year? They'd discussed the possibility of doing so for his bar mitzvah, but that was still weeks off, and before Sam had gotten into trouble, and anyway, they'd rejected the idea. Too much already pulling everyone too far into the noisy elsewhere. The experiment with Other Life had all but kidnapped Sam's consciousness.

She heard the buzz.

She searched the wicker basket full of toiletry odds and ends, the medicine cabinet: small and huge bottles of Advil, nail polish remover, organic tampons, Aquaphor, hydrogen peroxide, rubbing alcohol, Benadryl, Neosporin, Polysporin, children's ibuprofen, Sudafed, Purell, Imodium, Colace, amoxicillin, aspirin, triamcinolone acetonide cream, lidocaine cream, Dermoplast spray, Debrox drops, saline solution, Bactroban cream, floss, vitamin E lotion . . . all the things bodies might have a need for. When did bodies develop so many needs? For so many years she needed nothing.

She heard the buzz.

Where was it? She might have been able to convince herself that it was coming from the neighbors', on the other side of the wall, or even that she'd imagined it, but it buzzed again, and this time she could place the sound in the corner, by the floor.

She got on her hands and knees. In the basket of magazines? Behind the toilet? She reached her hand around the bowl, and no sooner had she touched it than it buzzed again, as if touching her back. Whose phone was this? One final buzz: a missed call from JULIA.

Julia?

But *she* was Julia.

what happened to you?

T-H-I-S-2-S-H-A-L-L-N-'-T-P-A-S-S

Sam knew that everything would collapse, he just didn't know exactly how or when. His parents were going to get divorced and ultimately hate each other and spread destruction like that Japanese reactor. That much was clear, if not to them. He tried not to notice their lives, but it was impossible to ignore how often his dad fell asleep in front of the absence of news, how often his mom retreated into pruning the trees of her architectural models, how his dad started serving dessert every night, how his mom told Argus she "needed space" whenever he licked her, how devoted his mom had become to the Travel section, how his dad's search history was all real estate sites, how his mom would put Benjy on her lap whenever his dad was in the room, the violence with which his dad began to hate *spoiled* athletes who *don't even try*, how his mom gave three thousand dollars to the fall NPR drive, how his dad bought a Vespa in retaliation, the end of appetizers in restaurants, the end of the third bedtime story for Benjy, the end of eye contact.

He saw what they either couldn't see or couldn't allow themselves to see, and that only made him more pissed, because being less stupid than one's parents is repulsive, like taking a gulp from a glass of milk that you thought was orange juice. Because he was less stupid than his parents, he knew it would one day be suggested to him that he wouldn't have to choose, even though he would. He knew he would begin to lose the desire or ability to fake it in school, and his grades would roll down an inclined plane according to some formula he was supposed to be proficient with, and the expressions of his parents' love would inflate in response to their sadness about his sadness, and he would be rewarded for falling apart. His parents' guilt about asking so much of him would get him off the hook for organized sports, and he'd be able to favorably renegotiate his screen time, and dinners would start to look a lot less organic, and soon enough he'd be steering toward the iceberg while his parents played dueling violins at each other.

He loved interesting facts, but was almost always troubled by his strange recurrent thoughts. Like this one: What if he witnessed a miracle? How would he convince anyone that he wasn't joking? If a newborn told him a secret? If a tree walked away? If he met his older self and learned about all the avoidable catastrophic mistakes he would be unable to avoid? He imagined his conversations with his mom, with his dad, with fake friends at school, with real friends in Other Life. Most of them would just laugh. Maybe one or two could be nudged to a gesture of belief. Max would at least want to believe him. Benjy would believe him, but only because he believed everything. Billie? No. Sam would be alone with a miracle.

There was a knock on his door. Not the sanctuary door, but his bedroom door.

"Scram, fucker."

"Excuse me?" his mom said, opening and entering.

"Sorry," Sam said, flipping the iPad facedown on his desk. "I thought you were Max."

"And you think that's a good way to talk to your brother?"

"No."

"Or to anybody?"

"No."

"So why?"

"I don't know."

"Maybe take a moment to question yourself."

He didn't know if the suggestion was rhetorical, but he knew this wasn't the time to take her anything less than literally.

After a moment of questioning himself, the best he could muster was "I guess I'm someone who says things he knows he shouldn't say."

"I guess so."

"But I'll get better at that."

She scanned the room. God, did he hate her little stolen surveys: of his homework, his belongings, his appearance. Her constant judgment carved through him like a river, creating two shores.

"What have you been doing up here?"

"Not e-mailing, or texting, or playing Other Life."

"OK, but what *have* you been doing?"

"I don't really know."

"I'm not sure how that could be possible."

"Isn't this your day off?"

"No, it's not my day *off*. It's my day to get some things done that I've been *putting* off. Like breathing and thinking. But then we had to make an unscheduled visit to Adas Israel this morning, as you might remember, and then I had to meet with a client—"

"Why did you have to?"

"Because it's my job."

"But why today?"

"I felt that I had to, OK?"

"OK."

"And then in the car it occurred to me that even though you have almost certainly thwarted it, we should probably continue to act as if your bar mitzvah is going to happen. And among the many, many things that only I would remember to remember is your suit."

"What suit?"

"Exactly."

"It's true. I don't have a suit."

"Obvious once stated, isn't it?"

"Yes."

"I continually find it amazing how many things are like that."

"Sorry."

"Why are *you* apologizing?"

"I don't know."

"So, we need to get you a suit."

"Today?"

"Yes."

"Really?"

"The first three places we go aren't going to have what we need, and should we find something passable, it's not going to fit, and the tailor is going to get it wrong twice."

"Do I have to be there?"

"Where?"

"The suit place."

"No, no, of course you don't have to be there. Let's make things easy and build our own 3-D printer out of popsicle sticks and macaroni, and render a perfectly accurate anatomical model of you that I can schlep to the *suit place* alone on my day off."

"Could we teach it my haftorah?"

"I'm not laughing at your jokes right now."

"That didn't require saying."

"Excuse me?"

"You don't have to say you aren't laughing for someone to know you aren't laughing."

"That didn't require saying, either, Sam."

"Fine. Sorry."

"We're going to have to talk when Dad comes home from his meeting, but I need to say something. It is *required*."

"Fine."

"Stop saying 'fine.'"

"Sorry."

"Stop saying 'sorry.'"

"I thought the whole point was that I was supposed to be apologizing?"

"For what you did."

"But I *didn't*—"

"I'm very disappointed in you."

"I know."

"That's it? You don't have anything else to say? Like maybe, 'I did it and I'm sorry'?"

"I didn't do it."

She put her hands on her waist, forefingers through belt loops.

"Clean up this mess. It's disgusting."

"It's my room."

"But it's our house."

"I can't move that board. We're only halfway done with the game. Dad said we could finish after I'm not in trouble anymore."

"You know why you always beat him?"

"Because he lets me win."

"He hasn't let you win in years."

"He goes easy."

"He doesn't. You beat him because it excites him to capture pieces, but you're always thinking four moves ahead. It makes you good at chess, and it makes you good at life."

"I'm not good at life."

"You are when you're thoughtful."

"Is Dad bad at life?"

"That's not the conversation we're having right now."

"If he focused, he could beat me."

"That might very well be true, but we'll never know."

"What conversation *are* we having?"

She took the phone from her pocket. "What is this?"

"That's a cellular telephone."

"Is it yours?"

"I'm not allowed to have a smartphone."

"Which is why it would upset me if it were yours."

"So you don't need to be upset."

"Whose is it?"

"No idea."

"Phones aren't like dinosaur bones. They don't just show up."

"Dinosaur bones aren't like that, either."

"If I were you, I'd tone down the intelligence." She turned the phone over. And over. "How do I look through it?"

"I assume it has a password."

"It does."

"So you're out of luck."

"I might as well try *this2shallpass*, right?"

"I guess."

Every adult member of the Bloch family used that ridiculous password for everything—from Amazon to Netflix to home alarm systems to phones.

"Nope," she said, showing Sam the screen.

"Worth a shot."

"Should I take it to the store, or something?"

"They don't even open the phones of terrorists."

"Maybe I'll try the same password, but with caps."

"You could."

"How do you capitalize a letter?"

Sam took the phone. He typed like rain hitting a skylight, but Julia saw only the disfigured thumb, and in slow motion.

"Nope," he said.

"Try spelling it out."

"What?"

"*T-o-o.*"

"That would be pretty stupid."

"It would be brilliant compared with using the same password that's used for everything."

"*T-h-i-s-t-o-o-s-h-a-l-l-p-a-s-s* . . . Nope. Sorry. I mean, I'm not sorry."

"Try spelling it out and capitalizing the first letter."

"Huh?"

"Capital *T*, and *t-w-o* for the numeral."

This he typed more slowly, carefully. "Hm."

"It's open?"

She reached to take the phone, but he held it for just a fraction of a second, enough to create an awkward stutter. Sam looked at his mother. Her enormous, ancient thumb pushed words up the tiny glass mountain. She looked at Sam.

"What?" he asked.

"What what?"

"Why are you looking at me?"

"Why am I looking at you?"

"Like that?"

Jacob couldn't fall asleep without a podcast. He said the information soothed him, but Julia knew it was the company. She was usually asleep by the time he came to bed—unacknowledged choreography—but every now and then she'd find herself listening alone. One night, her husband snoring beside her, she heard a sleep scientist explain lucid dreaming—a dream in which one is aware that one is dreaming. The most common technique for bringing on a lucid dream is to get in the habit, in waking life, of looking at texts—a page of a book or magazine, a billboard, a screen—and then looking away, and looking back. In dreams, texts don't remain constant. If you exercise the habit, it becomes a reflex. And if you exercise the reflex, it slips into dreams. The discontinuity of the text will indicate that you're dreaming, at which point you will not only be aware, but also in control.

She looked away from the phone, and looked back.

"I know you don't *play* Other Life. What is it you do?"

"Huh?"

"What's the word for what you do?"

"Live?" he said, trying to understand the change that was coming over his mother's face.

"I mean in Other Life."

"Yeah, I know."

"You *live* Other Life?"

"I don't usually have to describe what I'm doing there, but sure."

"You can live Other Life."

"Right."

"No, I mean you are allowed to."

"Now?"

"Yes."

"I thought I was grounded."

"You are," she said, putting the phone in her pocket. "But you can live that now, if you want."

"We can go get the suit."

"Another day. There's time."

Sam looked away from his mother, and looked back.

He'd checked all the devices. He wasn't angry, he just wanted to say what needed to be said, and then flatten the synagogue to rubble. It didn't fit, wasn't home. He'd wired everything double-redundantly, and placed three times as many explosives as were necessary: under each pew, out of sight atop the bookshelf that held the siddurim, buried beneath the hundreds of yarmulkes in their waist-high, octagonal wooden container.

Samanta removed the Torah from the ark. She chanted some memorized nonsense, undressed the Torah, and spread it out in front of her on the bimah. All of those beautiful pitch-black letters. All of those beautiful minimalist sentences, combining to tell all of those beautiful, endlessly echoing stories that should have been lost to history and still might be. The detonator was inside the Torah pointer. Samanta grasped it, found her place on the scroll, and started to chant.

> Bar'chu et Adonai Ham'vorach.
> Say what?

> I took my little brother to the zoo and these rhinos started fucking and it was insane. He just stood there looking. He didn't even know it was funny, which was the funniest part.
> Pay attention!
> It's funny when someone doesn't know it's funny.
> How can I miss someone I never met?
> Baruch Adonai Ham'vorach l'olam va'ed.
> I will always, always, always take dishonesty over faux honesty.
> App: Everything you say will one day be used against you.
> Baruch Atah, Adonai . . .
> Got it: We praise You . . .
> I've been having this weird thing where I can't remember what people I know look like. Or I convince myself I can't. I'll find myself trying to imagine my brother's face, and can't. It's not that I couldn't pick him out of a crowd, or that I wouldn't recognize him. But when I try to think of him, I can't.
> Eloheynu melech ha'olam . . .
> Download a program called VeryPDF. It's pretty straightforward.
> Eternal God, King of the Universe . . .
> Sorry, I was just eating dinner. I'm in Kyoto. The stars have been out for hours.
> Did anyone see the video of that Jewish reporter getting decapitated?
> asher bachar banu mikol ha'amim . . .
> VeryPDF has a million bugs.
> You have called us to Your service . . .
> My iPhone is making me seasick.
> v'natan lanu et Torato . . .
> You need to lock rotation. Double click on the Home button to bring up the multitasking bar. Swipe right until you get to something that looks like a circular arrow—it enables and disables rotation lock.
> Could you go blind from staring at a movie of the sun?
> Does anybody know anything about this new telescope that the Chinese are talking about building? It's supposed to see twice as far back in time as any telescope has before.
> Baruch Atah, Adonai . . .
> I know I sound like I'm high, but shouldn't we acknowledge the weirdness of what you just said? It can see twice as far back in time?

> I could fit every word I've ever written in my life onto a thumb drive.
> Which means?
> We praise You . . .
> Imagine if they put a massive mirror in space, really far away from us. Couldn't we, by aiming a telescope at it, see ourselves in the past?
> Meaning?
> The farther away it was, the deeper into our past we could see: our births, our parents' first kiss, cavemen.
> The dinosaurs.
> My parents never kissed, and fucked exactly once.
> Life crawling out of the ocean.
> notein haTorah.
> And if it were lined up straight, you could look at yourself not being there.
> Giver of the Torah.

Samanta looked up.

What on earth would it take for a fundamentally good human being to be seen? Not noticed, but seen. Not appreciated, not cherished, not even loved. But fully seen.

She looked out upon the congregation of avatars. They were trustworthy, generous, fundamentally nice unreal people. The most fundamentally nice people she would ever meet were people she would never meet.

She looked simultaneously at and through the stained-glass Jewish Present.

Sam had overheard every word from the other side of Rabbi Singer's door. He knew that his father believed him, and that his mother didn't. He knew that his mother was trying to do what she thought was best, and that his father was trying to do what he thought was best. But best for whom?

He'd found the phone a full day before his mother had.

Many apologies were due, but he didn't owe any apology to anyone.

With no throat to clear, Samanta began to speak, to say what needed to be said.

EPITOME

The older one gets, the harder it is to account for time. Children ask: "Are we there yet?" Adults: "How did we get here so quickly?"

Somehow, it was late. Somehow, the hours had gone somewhere. Irv and Deborah had gone home. The boys had eaten an early dinner, taken an early bath. Jacob and Julia had managed to collaborate in avoidance: You walk Argus, while I help Max with his math, while you fold laundry, while I search for the Lego piece on which everything depends, while you pretend to know how to fix a running toilet, and somehow, the day that began as Julia's to have to herself ended with Jacob ostensibly out at drinks with someone-or-other from HBO and Julia definitively cleaning up the day's mess. So much mess made by so few people in such little time. She was doing the dishes when Jacob entered the kitchen.

"That went later than I thought," he said preemptively. And to further compact his guilt: "Very boring."

"You must be drunk."

"No."

"How do you have drinks for four hours without getting drunk?"

"Just a drink," he said, draping his jacket over the counter stool, "not drinks. And only three-and-a-half."

"That's some awfully slow sipping." Her tone was pointed, but it could have been sharpened by a number of things: her lost day off, the stress from the morning, the bar mitzvah.

She wiped her brow with the first part of her forearm that wasn't soapy, and said, "We were supposed to talk to Sam."

Good, Jacob thought. Of the conflicts available, this was the least terri-fying. He could apologize, make it right, get back to happiness.

"I know," he said, tasting the alcohol on his teeth.

"You say 'I know,' and yet it's night and we're not talking to him."

"I just walked in. I was going to have a glass of water and then go talk to him."

"And the plan was to talk to him together."

"Well, I can spare you from having to be bad cop."

"Spare him from having a bad cop, you mean."

"I'll be both cops."

"No, you'll be a paramedic."

"I don't know what that means."

"You'll apologize for having to correct him in any way, and the two of you will end up laughing, and I'll be left as the annoying, nitpicking mother again. You get your seven-minute wink, and I get a month of resentment."

"None of what you just said is true."

"Right."

She scrubbed at the charred residue on a burnt pan.

"Max is asleep?" he asked, aiming his lips at hers and his eyes to the side.

"It's *ten thirty.*"

"Sam's in his room?"

"One drink for four hours?"

"Three and a half. Someone else showed up halfway through, and it just—"

"Yes, Sam is up in his emotional bomb shelter."

"Playing Other Life?"

"Living it."

They'd grown so afraid of not having the kids to fill the void. Some-times Julia wondered if she let them stay up only to protect herself against the quiet, if she called Benjy onto her lap to be a human shield.

"How was Max's night?"

"He's depressed."

"Depressed? No he's not."

"You're right. He must just have mono."

"He's only *eleven.*"

"He's only *ten.*"

"*Depressed* is a strong word."

"It does a good job of describing a strong experience."

"And Benjy?" Jacob asked while looking through a drawer.

"Missing something?"

"What?"

"You're searching around."

"I'll go give Benjy a kiss."

"You'll wake him up."

"I'll be a ninja."

"It took him an hour to fall asleep."

"Literally an hour? Or it felt like an hour?"

"Literally sixty minutes thinking about death."

"He's an amazing kid."

"Because he's obsessed with dying?"

"Because he's sensitive."

Jacob looked through the mail while Julia filled the washer: Restoration Hardware's monthly Yellow Pages of gray furniture, the ACLU's weekly infringement of privacy, a never-to-be-opened financial appeal from Georgetown Day, a flyer from some broker with orthodontics broadcasting how much he just sold the neighbor's house for, various paper confirmations of paperless utilities payments, a catalog from a children's clothing manufacturer whose marketing algorithm wasn't sophisticated enough to realize that toddlerhood is a temporary state.

Julia held up the phone.

Jacob held up his body, although everything inside fell—like one of those bottom-weighted inflatable clowns that keep coming back for more punches.

"Do you know whose this is?"

"It's mine," he said, taking it. "I got a new one."

"When?"

"A few weeks ago."

"Why?"

"Because . . . people get new phones."

She put too much soap in the machine and closed it too firmly.

"There's a password on it."

"Yeah."

"Your old phone didn't have a password."

"Yes it did."

"No it didn't."

"How do you know?"

"Because why wouldn't I?"

"I guess so."

"Is there something you need to tell me?"

Jacob was busted for plagiarism in college. This was before computer programs that could search for it, so getting caught required flamboyant stealing, which his was. But he wasn't caught; he accidentally confessed. He'd been called into his "American Epic" professor's office, asked to take a seat, made to ferment in the halitosis while waiting for the professor to finish reading the last three pages of a book and then clumsily shuffle through papers on his desk in search of Jacob's work.

"Mr. Bloch."

Was that a statement? A confirmation that he had the right guy?

"Yes?"

"Mr. Bloch"—shaking the pages like a lulav—"where do these ideas come from?"

But before the professor was given a chance to say, "Because they're sophisticated far beyond your years," Jacob said, "Harold Bloom."

Despite his failing grade, and despite the academic probation, he was grateful to have made the blunder—not because honesty was so important to him in this case, but because there was nothing he hated more than exposed guilt. It made a terrified child out of him, and he would do anything to relieve it.

"New phones ask for a password," Jacob said. "I think they require one."

"That's a funny way of saying no."

"What was the question?"

"Is there something you need to tell me?"

"There's always a lot of things I want to tell you."

"I said *need*."

Argus moaned.

"I don't understand this conversation," Jacob said. "And what the hell is that smell?"

So many days in their shared life. So many experiences. How had they managed to spend the previous sixteen years unlearning each other? How had all the presence summed to disappearance?

And now, their first baby on the brink of manhood, and their last asking questions about death, they found themselves in the kitchen with things finally worth not talking about.

Julia noticed a small stain on her shirt and starting rubbing at it, despite knowing it was old and permanent.

"I'm guessing you didn't bring home the dry cleaning."

The only thing she hated more than feeling like she was feeling was sounding like she was sounding. As Irv had told her Golda Meir had told Anwar Sadat: "We can forgive you for killing our children, but we will never forgive you for making us kill yours." She hated the person Jacob forced her to sound like: pissy and aggrieved, unfun, the nagging wife she would have killed herself to avoid becoming.

"I have a bad memory," he said. "I'm sorry."

"I have a bad memory, too, but I don't forget things."

"I'm sorry, OK?"

"That would be easier to accept without the *OK*."

"You act as if I only ever make mistakes."

"Help me out," she said. "What, in this house, do you do well?"

"You're serious?"

Argus let out a long moan.

Jacob turned to him and gave a bit of what he wasn't capable of giving to Julia: "Chill the fuck out!" And then, not appreciating the joke he was making at his own expense: "I never raise my voice."

She appreciated it: "Isn't that right, Argus?"

"Not at you or the kids."

"Not raising your voice—or not beating me or molesting the children, for that matter—doesn't qualify as something you *do well*. It qualifies as basic decency. And anyway, you don't raise your voice, because you're repressed."

"No I'm not."

"If you don't say so."

"Even *if* that's why I don't raise my voice, and I don't think it is, it's still a good thing. A lot of men scream."

"I'm jealous of their wives."

"You want me to be an asshole?"

"I want you to be a person."

"What's that supposed to mean?"

"Are you sure there isn't something you need to tell me?"

"I don't understand why you keep asking me that."

"I'll rephrase the question: What's the password?"

"To what?"

"To the phone you're clenching."

"It's my new phone. What's the big deal?"

"I'm your wife. *I'm* the big deal."

"You're not making sense."

"I don't have to."

"What do you want, Julia?"

"Your password."

"Why?"

"Because I want to know what it is you can't tell me."

"Julia."

"Once again, you have correctly identified me."

Jacob had spent more waking hours in his kitchen than in any other room. No baby knows when the nipple is pulled from his mouth for the last time. No child knows when he last calls his mother "Mama." No small boy knows when the book has closed on the last bedtime story that will ever be read to him. No boy knows when the water drains from the last bath he will ever take with his brother. No young man knows, as he first feels his greatest pleasure, that he will never again not be sexual. No brinking woman knows, as she sleeps, that it will be four decades before she will again awake infertile. No mother knows she is hearing the word *Mama* for the last time. No father knows when the book has closed on the last bedtime story he will ever read: *From that day on, and for many years to come, peace reigned on the island of Ithaca, and the gods looked favorably upon Odysseus, his wife, and his son.* Jacob knew that whatever happened, he would see the kitchen again. And yet his eyes became sponges for the details—the burnished handle of the snack drawer; the seam where the slabs of soapstone met; the Special Award for Bravery sticker on the underside of the island's overhang, given to Max for what no one knew was his last pulled tooth, a sticker Argus saw many times every day, and only Argus ever saw—because Jacob knew he would one day wring them out for the last drops of these last moments; they would come as tears.

"Fine," Jacob said.

"Fine what?"

"Fine, I'll tell you the password."

He put the phone on the counter with a righteous force that might, just *might*, have jarred loose the workings, and said, "But know that this lack of trust will always be between us."

"I can live with that."

He looked at the phone.

"I'm just trying to remember what the password even *is*. I lost it right after I got it. I don't even think I've *used* it yet."

He picked up the phone and stared at it.

"Maybe the password the Blochs use for everything?" she suggested.

"Right," he said. "That's definitely what I would have used: *t-h-i-s-2-s-h-a-l-l-p-a-s-s. And* . . . nope."

"Hm. I guess not."

"I can probably have the store unlock it."

"Maybe, and this is just a stab in the dark, you could capitalize the first letter, and type *t-w-o* instead of the numeral?"

"I wouldn't do it like that," he said.

"No?"

"No. We always do it the same way."

"Give it a try."

He wanted to escape this childish terror, but he wanted to be a child.

"But I wouldn't do it like that."

"Who really knows what one would do? Just try it."

He examined the phone, and his fingers around it, and the house around them, and with an unmediated impulse—as reflexive as the kicked leg of a hammered knee—he hurled it through the window, shattering the glass.

"I thought it was open."

And then a silence that struck bedrock.

Julia said, "You think I don't know how to get to our lawn?"

"I—"

"And why wouldn't you just create a sophisticated password? One Sam wouldn't be able to guess?"

"Sam looked at the phone?"

"No. But only because you're incredibly lucky."

"You're sure?"

"How could you have *written* those things?"

"What things?"

"It's *way* too late in this conversation for that."

Jacob knew it was too late, and absorbed the gouges in the cutting board, the succulents between the sink and window, the kids' drawings blue-taped to the backsplash.

"They didn't mean anything," he said.

"I feel sorry for someone who is capable of saying so much and meaning nothing."

"Julia, give me a chance to explain."

"Why can't you mean nothing to *me*?"

"What?"

"You tell someone who isn't the mother of your children that you want to lick your cum out of her asshole, and the only person who makes me feel beautiful is the fucking Korean florist at the back of the deli, who isn't even a *florist*."

"I'm disgusting."

"Don't you dare do that."

"Julia, this might be hard to believe, but they were only texts. That's all that ever happened."

"First of all, that's easy to believe. No one knows better than I do that you're incapable of an actually brave transgression. I know that you're too big a pussy to actually lick anyone's asshole, cum-filled or not."

"Julia."

"But more important, how much *needs* to happen? You think you can go around saying and writing whatever you want without consequence? Maybe your father can. Maybe your mother is weak enough to tolerate that kind of piggishness. But I'm not. There's decency and indecency, and they're *different*. Good and bad are *different*. Do you not know this?"

"Of course I—"

"No, of course you *don't*. You wrote to a woman who isn't your wife that her tight pussy doesn't deserve you?"

"That's not really what I wrote. And it was in the context of—"

"And you're not really a good person, and there is no context that could make such a thing OK to say."

"It was a moment of weakness, Julia."

"Are you forgetting that you never deleted any of them? That there is a history to refer to? It wasn't a *moment* of weakness, it was a *person* of weakness. And will you *please* stop saying my name."

"It's over."

"Do you want to know the worst part? I don't even *care*. The saddest thing about this has been confronting my own lack of sadness."

Jacob didn't believe that, but neither could he believe that she would say it. The pretense of a loving relationship had made the absence of a loving relationship bearable. But now she was letting go of appearances.

"Listen, I think—"

"Lick the cum out of her asshole?" She laughed. *"You?* You're a coward and a germ freak. You just wanted to write it. Which is fine. Which is even great. But acknowledge the make-believe. You *want* to want some kind of sexually supercharged life, but you *actually* want the gate-checked stroller, and the Aquaphor, and even your desiccated, blowjobless existence, because it spares you worrying about erections. Jesus, Jacob, you carry a packet of wipes so you'll never have to use toilet paper. That's not the behavior of a man who wants to lick cum from anyone's asshole."

"Julia, stop."

"And by the way, even if you found yourself in that situation, with an *actual* woman's *actual* asshole filled with your *actual* cum and beckoning your tongue? You know what you'd do? You'd get your ridiculous hand tremors, sweat through your shirt, lose the one-quarter, Jell-O mold erection you would have been lucky to achieve in the first place, and probably shuffle off to the bathroom to check the *Huffington Post* for puerile, unfunny videos or relisten to the Radiolab in praise of tortoises. *That's* what would happen. And she'd know you were the joke that you are."

"I wouldn't be wearing a shirt."

"What?"

"I wouldn't sweat through my shirt, because I wouldn't be wearing a shirt."

"That's a fucking mean thing to say."

"Stop pushing me."

"You're serious? You can't be. You cannot be serious." She turned on the sink faucet, for no obvious reason. "And you think you're the only one who wants to act recklessly?"

"You want to have an affair?"

"I want to let things fall apart."

"I'm not having an affair, and I'm not letting things fall apart."

"I saw Mark today. He and Jennifer are getting divorced."

"Great. Or terrible. What am I supposed to say?"

"And Mark was flirting with me."

"What are you doing?"

"I've protected you so much. Cared for your pathetic, baby-bird insecurity. Spared you innocent things that you would have had no right to be upset by, but would be crushed by. And you think I've never had fantasies? You think every time I masturbate I'm imagining you? Do you?"

"This isn't going anywhere."

"Did some part of me want to fuck Mark today? Yes. In fact, every part below the brain. But I didn't, because I wouldn't, because I'm not like you—"

"I didn't fuck anybody, Julia."

"—but I wanted to."

Jacob raised his voice for the second time in the conversation: "God-*damn* it, what's that smell?"

"Your dog took another shit in the house."

"*My* dog?"

"Yes, the dog that *you* brought home, despite our explicit agreement *not* to get a dog."

"The kids wanted it."

"The kids want their arms connected to IV drip bags filled with melted Chunky Monkey and their brains in vats of Steve Jobs's cum. Good parenting has nothing to do with satisfying your children's wants."

"They were sad about something."

"*Everybody* is sad about something. Stop blaming the kids, Jacob. You needed to be a hero, and you needed to make me a villain—"

"That's not fair."

"Not even close to fair. You brought home a dog that we *agreed* it would be a mistake to get, and you were the superhero and I was the supervillain, and now there's a stale shit-bâtard on our living room floor."

"And it didn't occur to you to clean it up?"

"No. Just like it didn't occur to you to house-train it—"

"*Him.* House-train *him.* And the poor guy can't help it. He's—"

"Or walk it, or take it to the vet, or wash its bed, or remember its heart-worm pills, or check it for ticks, or buy it food, or feed it. I pick up his shit every single day. Twice a day. Or more. Jesus, Jacob, I *hate* dogs, and hate *this* dog, and didn't and don't want this dog, but if it weren't for me, this dog would have been dead years ago."

"He understands you when you say that."

"And yet you don't. Your dog—"

"*Our* dog."

"—is smarter than my husband."

And then he screamed. It was the first time he'd ever raised his voice at her. It was a scream that had been building in him for sixteen years of marriage, and four decades of life, and five millennia of history—a scream that was directed at her, but also at everyone living and dead, but primarily at himself. For years he'd always been elsewhere, always underground behind a twelve-inch door, always taking refuge in an interior monologue to which no one—including himself—had access, or in dialogue trapped in a locked drawer. But this was *him*.

He took four steps toward her, bringing the lenses of his glasses as close to her eyes as to his own, and screamed: *"You are my enemy!"*

A few minutes before, she'd told Jacob that the saddest thing had been confronting her own lack of sadness. It was true then, but it wasn't true anymore. Through the prism of tears, she saw her kitchen: the cracked rubber gasket of the faucet, the casement windows that still looked good but whose frames would crumble if gripped. She saw her dining room and living room: they still looked good, but were two layers of paint over a layer of primer over a decade and a half of slow decay. Her husband: not her partner.

Sam came home from third grade one day and excitedly told Julia, "If Earth were the size of an apple, the atmosphere would be thinner than the apple's skin."

"What?"

"If Earth were the size of an apple, the atmosphere would be thinner than the apple's skin."

"I might not be smart enough to understand why that's interesting. Can you explain?"

"Look up," he said. "Does it seem thin to you?"

"The ceiling?"

"If we were outside."

The shell was so thin, but she had always felt safe.

They got a dartboard at a yard sale, dozens of Sundays before, and hung it on the door at the end of the hall. The boys missed the board as often as they hit it, and each dart pulled from the door held the door's previous color on its tip. Julia took the board down after Max came into the living room, blood dripping from his shoulder, saying, "It was nobody's fault." What remained was a circle, defined and surrounded by hundreds of holes.

As she stared at the shell of her kitchen, the saddest thing was her knowledge of what was beneath, what a tiny scratch, in a vulnerable place, would reveal.

"Mom?"

They turned to see Benjy standing in the doorway, leaning against the growth chart, his hands searching for pajama pockets that didn't exist. For how long had he been there?

"Mom and I were just—"

"You mean *epitome*."

"What, love?"

"You said *enemy*, but you meant *epitome*."

"You can have your kiss now," Julia told Jacob as she wiped away her tears, replacing them with soap suds.

Jacob got down on his knees, took Benjy's hands into his.

"Bad dream, buddy?"

"I'm OK with dying," Benjy said.

"What?"

"I'm OK with dying."

"You are?"

"As long as everyone else dies with me, I'm actually OK with dying. I'm just afraid of everyone else not dying."

"You had a bad dream?"

"No. You were fighting."

"We weren't fighting. We—"

"And I heard glass break."

"We were fighting," Julia said. "Humans have feelings, sometimes very difficult ones. But it's OK. Now go on back to bed."

Jacob carried him, Benjy's cheek resting on his shoulder. How light he still was. How heavy he was getting. No father knows that he is carrying his son up the stairs for the final time.

Jacob tucked Benjy back under the covers and stroked his hair.

"Dad?"

"Yes?"

"I agree with you that heaven probably doesn't exist."

"I didn't say that. I said there's no way to know for sure, and so it's probably not a great idea to organize our lives around it."

"Yeah, that's what I agree with."

He could forgive himself for withholding his own comfort, but why did he withhold everyone else's as well? Why couldn't he just let his kinder-gartener feel happy and safe in a just and beautiful and unreal world?

"So what do you think we *should* organize our lives around?" Benjy asked.

"Our families?"

"I think so, too."

"Good night, buddy."

Jacob went to the door, but didn't walk away.

After a few long moments in that silence, Benjy called out: "Dad? I need you!"

"I'm here."

"Squirrels evolved to have bushy tails. Why?"

"Maybe for balance? Or to keep them warm? Time for sleep."

"We'll google it in the morning."

"OK. But now sleep."

"Dad?"

"Right here."

"If the world goes on for long enough, will there be fossils of fossils?"

"Oh, Benjy. That's a great question. We can talk about it in the morning."

"Yeah. I need my sleep."

"Right."

"Dad?"

Now Jacob was losing his patience: *"Benjy."*

"Dad?"

"I'm here."

He stood in the doorway until he heard his youngest son's heavy breathing. Jacob was a man who withheld comfort but stood at thresholds long after others would have walked away. He always stood at the open front door until the car pool drove off. Just as he stood at the window until the back wheel of Sam's bike disappeared around the corner. Just as he watched himself disappear.

HERE I AMN'T

> It is with a sense of history and extreme annoyance that I stand at this bimah today, prepared to fulfill the so-called rite of passage into adulthood, whatever that is. I want to thank Cantor Fleischman, for helping transform me, over the past half year, into a Jewish automaton. On the extreme off chance that I remember any of this a year from now, I still won't know what it means, and for that I am grateful. I also want to thank Rabbi Singer, who is a sulfuric acid enema. My only living great-grandparent is Isaac Bloch. My dad said that I had to go through with this for him, something my great-grandfather has never, himself, asked of me. There are things he *has* asked, like not to be forced to move into the Jewish Home. My family cares very much about caring for him, but not enough to actually care, and I didn't understand a word of my chanting today, but I understand that. I want to thank my grandparents Irv and Deborah Bloch, for being inspirations in my life and always urging me to try a little bit harder, dig a little bit deeper, become rich, and say whatever I want whenever I feel like it. Also my grandparents Allen and Leah Selman, who live in Florida, and whose mortal status I am only aware of thanks to the Hanukkah and birthday checks that haven't been adjusted for cost-of-living increases since my birth. I want to thank my brothers, Benjy and Max, for requiring great portions of my parents' attention. I cannot imagine surviving an existence in which I bore the

undivided brunt of their love. Also, when I threw up on Benjy on a plane, he said, "I know how bad it feels to throw up." And Max once offered to get a blood test so I wouldn't have to. Which brings me to my parents, Jacob and Julia Bloch. The truth is, I didn't want to have a bat mitzvah. No part of me, not even a little. There aren't enough savings bonds in the world. We had conversations about it, as if my opinions were of consequence. It was all a charade, a charade to set in motion this charade, itself only a stepping-stone in the charade of my Jewish identity. Which is to say, in the most literal sense, without them this wouldn't have been possible. I don't blame them for being who they are. But I do blame them for blaming me for being who I am. That's enough thanking. So, my Torah portion is Vayeira. It is one of the most well-known and studied portions in the Torah, and I've been told it is a great honor to read it. Given my total lack of interest in the Torah, it would have been better to give this to a kid who actually gives a Jewish shit, should such a kid exist, and to give me one of the throwaway portions about rules governing menstruating lepers. Joke's on everyone, I guess. One more thing: portions of the interpretation that follows were blatantly ripped off. Good thing Jews only believe in collective punishment. OK . . God's test of Abraham is written like this: "Sometime later, God tested Abraham. He said to him, 'Abraham!' 'Here I am,' Abraham replied." Most people assume that the test is what follows: God asking Abraham to sacrifice his son, Isaac. But I think it could also be read that the test was when He called to him. Abraham didn't say, "What do you want?" He didn't say, "Yes?" He answered with a statement: "Here I am." Whatever God needs or wants, Abraham is wholly present for Him, without conditions or reservations or need for explanation. That word, *hineni*—here I am—comes up two other times in the portion. When Abraham is taking Isaac up Mount Moriah, Isaac becomes aware of what they are doing, and how fucked up it is. He knows that he is about to be the sacrifice, in the way that all kids always do when it's about to happen. It says: "And Isaac said to Abraham, his father, 'My father!' and he said, 'Here I am, my son.' And Isaac said, 'Here is the fire and the wood but where is the sheep for the offering?' And Abraham said, 'God will see to the sheep for the offering, my son.'" Isaac doesn't say, "Father," he says, "My father."

Abraham is the father of the Jewish people, but he is also Isaac's father, his personal father. And Abraham doesn't ask, "What do you want?" He says, "Here I am." When God asks for Abraham, Abraham is wholly present for God. When Isaac asks for Abraham, Abraham is wholly present for his son. But how can that be possible? God is asking Abraham to kill Isaac, and Isaac is asking his father to protect him. How can Abraham be two directly opposing things at once? *Hineni* is used one more time in the story, at the most dramatic moment. "And they came to the place that God had said to him, and Abraham built there an altar and laid out the wood and bound Isaac, his son, and placed him on the altar on top of the wood. And Abraham reached out his hand and took the cleaver to his son. And the Lord's messenger called out to him from the heavens, and said, 'Abraham, Abraham!' and he said, 'Here I am.' And he said, 'Do not reach out your hand against the boy, and do nothing to him, for now I know that you fear God and you have not held back your son, your only one, from me.'" Abraham does not ask, "What do you want?" He says, "Here I am." My bat mitzvah portion is about many things, but I think it is primarily about who we are wholly there for, and how that, more than anything else, defines our identity. My great-grandfather, who I mentioned before, has asked for help. He doesn't want to go to the Jewish Home. But nobody in the family has responded by saying, "Here I am." Instead, they have tried to convince him that he doesn't know what is best, and doesn't even know what he wants. Really, they haven't even tried to convince him; they've just told him what he's going to do. I was accused of having used some bad language in Hebrew school this morning. I'm not even sure *used* is the right word—making a list is hardly making *use* of anything. Anyway, when my parents showed up to speak with Rabbi Singer, they didn't tell me, "Here we are." They asked, "What did you do?" I wish I had been given the benefit of the doubt, because I deserve it. Everyone who knows me knows that I make a shitload of mistakes, but also that I am a good person. But it's not because I'm a good person that I deserve the benefit of the doubt, it's because I'm their child. Even if they didn't believe me, they should have acted as if they did. My dad once told me that before I was born, when the only proof of my life was sonograms, he had to believe in me. In other words, being

born allows your parents to stop believing in you. OK, thanks for
coming, everybody out.
> That's it?
> No. Not exactly. I'm going to blow this place up.
> What the fuck?
> I set up a reception on the roof of the old color film factory
across the street. We'll watch.
> Run!
> Color film?
> You don't need to run. No one is going to get hurt.
> Trust her.
> Film for old-fashioned cameras.
> You don't even need to trust me. Think about it: if you'd needed
to run, you'd already be dead.
> That's some fucked-up logic.
> Last thing, before we go: Does anybody know why airplanes dim
their lights at takeoff and landing?
> What the fuck?
> So the pilot can see better?
> Let's just go, OK?
> To save power?
> I don't want to die.
> Good guesses, but no. It's because those are the most critical
moments of the flight. More than eighty percent of accidents happen during takeoff and landing. They dim the lights to give your
eyes time to adjust to the darkness of a smoke-filled cabin.
> There should be a word for things like that.
> You can follow the lighted path out of the synagogue. It will show
you the way. Or you can follow me.

SOMEONE! SOMEONE!

Julia was at her bathroom sink, Jacob at his. Side-by-side sinks: a much-sought-after feature in old Cleveland Park houses, like intricate borders framing the parquet floors, original mantels, and converted gas chandeliers. There were so few differences between the houses that the small differences had to be celebrated, otherwise everyone was working too hard for too little. On the other hand, who actually wants side-by-side sinks?

"You know what Benjy just asked me?" Jacob said, facing the mirror above his sink.

"If the world goes on for long enough, will there be fossils of fossils?"

"How did you—?"

"The monitor knows all."

"Right."

Jacob almost always flossed when there was a witness. Forty years of sometimes flossing, and he'd had only three cavities—all that saved time. Tonight, his wife his witness, he flossed. He wanted to spend a little time at those side-by-side sinks. Or spare a little time in that one bed.

"When I was a kid, I created my own postal system. I made a post office out of a refrigerator box. My mom sewed a uniform for me. I even had stamps with my grandfather's face on them."

"Why are you telling me this?" she asked.

"I don't know," he said, a thread between his two front teeth. "I just thought of it."

"*Why* did you just think of it?"

He chuckled: "You sound like Dr. Silvers."

She didn't chuckle: "You love Dr. Silvers."

"I had nothing to deliver," he said, "so I started writing letters to my mom. It was the system I was drawn to; I didn't care about the messages. Anyway, the first one said, 'If you're reading this, our postal system works!' I remember that."

"*Our*," she said.

"What?"

"*Our. Our* postal system. Not *my* postal system."

"Maybe I wrote *my*," he said, unwinding the thread from his fingers, revealing the impressions of rings. "I can't remember."

"You can."

"I don't know."

"You *can*. And that's why you're telling it to me."

"She was a great mom," he said.

"I know that. I've always known that. She manages to make the boys feel that no one in the world is better than them, and that they aren't better than anyone. That's a hard balance."

"My dad doesn't strike it."

"There is no balance that he strikes."

The impressions were already gone.

Julia picked up a toothbrush and handed it to her husband.

Jacob tried to force something that wouldn't come, and said, "We're out of toothpaste."

"There's another in the cabinet."

A moment of quiet while they brushed. If they spent ten minutes every night getting ready for bed—and surely they did, surely at least that much—it would be sixty hours a year. More hours getting ready for bed together than being awake on vacation together. They had been married for sixteen years. In that time, they had spent the equivalent of forty full days getting ready for bed, almost always at the sought-after and lonely side-by-side sinks, almost always quietly.

A few months after moving out, Jacob would create a postal system with the boys. Max was receding. He laughed less, scowled more, always sought the seat closest to the window. Jacob could deny it to himself, but then others started to notice and mention it—Deborah took him aside one brunch and asked, "How does Max seem to you?"

Jacob found vintage hanging mailboxes on Etsy and affixed one to each kid's bedroom door, and one to his own. He told them they would have their own secret postal system, to be used for those messages that felt impossible to say aloud.

"Like how people used to leave notes in the Wailing Wall," Benjy suggested.

No, Jacob thought, but he said, "Yes. Kind of like that."

"Except you're not God," Max said, which, although plainly obvious, and the position Jacob would want his children to take (as atheists, and people who don't fear their parents), still stung.

He checked his mailbox every day. Benjy was the only one who ever wrote: "World peace"; "Snow day"; "Bigger TV."

So much about parenting alone was difficult: the logistics of getting three kids ready for school with only two hands, the Heathrow control-tower volume of transportation to coordinate, having to multitask the multitasking. But most challenging was finding time to talk intimately with the kids. They were always together, there was always commotion, something always needed to get done, and there was no one with whom to share the load. So when one-on-one situations arose, he felt both a need to make use of them (however unnatural it might be at the time) and a concentrated dose of the old fear of saying too much or too little.

One night a few weeks after the creation of the postal system, Sam was reading to Benjy before bed, and Max and Jacob found themselves peeing into the same toilet.

"Don't cross the streams, Ray."

"Huh?"

"From *Ghostbusters*."

"I know that's a movie, but I've never seen it."

"You're kidding."

"No."

"But I remember watching with—"

"I haven't seen it."

"OK. Well, there's a great scene in which they fire their proton-whatevers for the first time, and Egon says, 'Don't cross the streams, Ray,' because it would result in some sort of apocalyptic moment, and ever since, I've always thought about it when peeing in the same toilet with someone. But we both seem to be finished, so now it really makes no sense."

"Whatever."

"I noticed you haven't put anything in my mailbox."

"Yeah. I will."

"It's not an assignment. I just thought it might be a helpful way to get some things off your chest."

"OK."

"Everyone holds things in. Your brothers do. I do. Mom does. But it can make life really difficult."

"I'm sorry."

"No, I meant for you. I've spent my life making huge efforts to protect myself from the things I most fear, and in the end it wouldn't be right to say that there was nothing to fear, but maybe the realization of my worst fears wouldn't have been so bad. Maybe all of my efforts were worse. I remember the night I left for the airport. I kissed you guys like it was any other trip, and said something like 'See you in a week or two.' As I was getting ready to go, Mom asked me what I was waiting for. She said it was a big deal so I must be feeling big things, and you guys must be, too."

"But you didn't come back and say anything else."

"I was too afraid."

"What were you afraid of?"

"There was nothing to be afraid of. That's what I'm trying to tell you."

"I know there was nothing actually to be afraid of. But what were you afraid of?"

"Making it real?"

"Going?"

"No. What we had. What we have."

Julia tucked her toothbrush deep in her cheek and brought her palms to the sink. Jacob spit, and said, "I'm failing my family just like my father failed us."

"You're not," she said. "But it's not enough to avoid his mistakes."

"What?"

She removed the brush and said, "You're not. But it's not enough to avoid his mistakes."

"You're a great mom."

"What made you say that?"

"I was thinking about how my mom was a great mom."

She closed the vanity, paused, as if considering whether to speak, then spoke: "You aren't happy."

"What made you say *that*?"

"It's the truth. You seem happy. Maybe you even think you're happy. But you aren't."

"You think I'm depressed?"

"No. I think you put enormous emphasis on happiness—your own and others'—and find unhappiness so threatening that you would rather go down with the ship than acknowledge a leak."

"I don't think that's true."

"And yes, I think you're depressed."

"It's probably just mono."

"You're tired of writing a TV show that isn't yours, and that everyone loves but you."

"Not everyone loves it."

"Well, *you* definitely don't."

"I like it."

"And you hate only liking what you do."

"I don't know."

"But you *do* know," she said. "You know there's something inside of you—a book, or show, or movie, whatever—and if it could only be released, all of the sacrifices you feel you've made wouldn't feel like sacrifices anymore."

"I don't feel that I've had to make—"

"See how you changed the grammar? I said, the sacrifices you feel you've *made*. You said, *had to make*. See the difference?"

"Jesus, you should really get some accreditation and a couch."

"I'm not kidding."

"I know."

"And you're tired of pretending to be happily married—"

"Julia."

"—and you hate only liking the most important relationship in your life."

Jacob often resented Julia, sometimes even hated her, but there was never a moment when he wanted to hurt her.

"That isn't true," he said.

"You're too kind or scared to admit it, but it's true."

"It's not."

"And you're tired of being a dad and a son."

"Why are you trying to hurt me?"

"I'm not trying to. And there are worse things than hurting each other." She arranged the various anti-aging and anti-dying products on the shelf and said, "Let's go to bed."

Let's go to bed. Those four words differentiate a marriage from every other kind of relationship. We aren't going to find a way to agree, but let's go to bed. Not because we want to, but because we have to. We hate each other right now, but let's go to bed. It's the only bed we have. Let's go to our sides, but the sides of the same bed. Let's retreat into ourselves, but together. How many conversations had ended with those four words? How many fights?

Sometimes they would go to bed and make one more effort, now horizontal, to work it through. Sometimes going to bed made things possible that weren't possible in the infinitely large room. The intimacy of being under the same sheet, two furnaces contributing to the shared warmth, but at the same time not having to see each other. The view of the ceiling, and all that ceilings make one think about. Or perhaps it was at the back of the brain, where all the blood then pooled, that the generosity lobe was located.

Sometimes they would go to bed and roll to the edges of the mattress that they independently wished were a king, and independently wish it would all just go away, without having enough bones in their forefingers to hold down the word *it*. *It* the night? *It* the marriage? *It* the entire predicament of this family's family life? They went to bed together not because they didn't have a choice—*kein briere iz oich a breire*, as the rabbi would say at the funeral in three weeks; *not to have a choice is also a choice.* Marriage is the opposite of suicide, but is its only peer as a definitive act of will.

Let's go to bed . . .

Just before easing himself onto the bed, Jacob gave a puzzled look, patted his boxer briefs' nonexistent pockets, as if suddenly realizing he didn't know where his key was, and said, "I'm just going to pee." Exactly as he did every night at that moment.

He closed and locked the door, opened the middle drawer of the medicine cabinet, lifted the stack of *New Yorkers*, and removed the box of hydrocortisone acetate suppositories. He laid out a bath towel on the floor, rolled another into a pillow, rested himself on his left side with his right knee bent, thought about Terri Schiavo, or Bill Buckner, or Nicole Brown Simpson, and gently pushed it in. He suspected that Julia knew what he did every night, but he couldn't bring himself to ask her, because that would first require admitting to having an entire human body. Almost all of his body was sharable almost all of the time, as was almost all of hers almost always, but sometimes some parts had to be hidden. They had spent countless hours parsing the bowel movements of their children; directly applied Desitin with bare forefingers; twirled rectal thermometers, at Dr. Donowitz's instruction, to stimulate the sphincter in an effort to relieve a baby's constipation. But when it came to each other, some denial was required.

you don't deserve to get fucked in the ass

The asshole, with which every member of the Bloch family was, in his or her own way, obsessed, was the epicenter of Jacob and Julia's denial. It was necessary for life, but never to be spoken of. It was what one had, but had to hide. It was where everything came together—the cinch of the human body—and nothing, especially not attention, and *especially* not a finger or cock, and *especially, especially* not a tongue, could go. There were enough matches by the toilet to both light and fuel a bonfire.

Every night, Jacob excused himself to pee, and every night Julia waited for him, and she knew he hid the suppository wrappers in balls of toilet paper at the bottom of the lidded can, and she knew that when he flushed he flushed nothing. Those minutes of hiding, of silent shame, had walls and a ceiling. Just as their Shabbats, and those whispered confessions of pride, had made architecture of time. Without having hired any men with lumbar braces, or sent change-of-address cards, or even replaced one key on their heart's ring with another, they had moved from one house to another.

Max used to love playing hide-and-seek, and no one, not even Benjy, could tolerate it. The house was too well known, too thoroughly explored, the game was as done as checkers. So it was only on special occasions (a birthday, as a reward for an act of extreme menschiness) that Max was able to force a game. And they were always as boring as everyone anticipated: someone was holding his breath behind Julia's blouses in the closet, someone was flat in the bath or crouched under the sink, someone was hiding with his eyes closed, unable to overcome the instinct that it made him less visible.

Even when the boys weren't hiding, Jacob and Julia were seeking them—out of fear, out of love. But hours could pass without Argus's absence being noticed. He'd always turn up when the front door was opened, or the bath was run, or food was put on the table. His return was taken for granted. Jacob tried to stimulate heated discussion at dinner, to help the boys become eloquent, critical thinkers. In the middle of one such debate—should Jerusalem or Tel Aviv be Israel's capital?—Julia asked if anyone had seen Argus. "His dinner is just sitting there."

After only a few minutes of gentle calling for him and casual searching, the boys began to panic. They rang the doorbell. They put out a bowl of human food. Max played through Suzuki Book I, which always elicited a whine. Nothing.

The screen door was closed, but the front door was open, so it was conceivable he had gone outside. (*Who left the door open?* Jacob wondered—angry, but at no one.) They searched the neighborhood, calling for Argus, lovingly then desperately. Some neighbors joined the search. Jacob couldn't help but wonder—only to himself, of course— if Argus had gone off to die, as some dogs apparently do. It became dark, hard to see.

As it turned out, he'd been in the upstairs guest bathroom. Somehow he'd closed himself in, and was too old, or good, to bark. Or maybe, at least until he became hungry, he preferred it in there. He was allowed to sleep in the bed that night. As were the kids. Because they'd thought they'd lost him, and because he'd been so close all along.

At dinner the next night, Jacob said: "Resolved: Argus should be allowed to sleep in the bed every night." The boys whooped. Smiling, Jacob said, "I take it you'll be arguing the affirmative."

Not smiling, Julia said, "Wait, wait, wait."

It was the last time those six animals slept under the same cover.

Jacob and Julia hid themselves inside the work that they hid from each other.

They sought happiness that didn't have to be at the expense of anyone else's happiness.

They hid behind the administration of family life.

Their purest seeking was on Shabbat, when they closed their eyes and made their home, and themselves, new.

That architecture of minutes, when Jacob excused himself to the bathroom and Julia didn't read the book she held, was their purest hiding.

now you deserve to get fucked in the ass

They went to bed, Julia in her nightgown, Jacob in his T-shirt and boxers. She slept with a bra on. She said the support made her more comfortable, and maybe that was the entire truth. He said the warmth of the shirt made it easier to sleep, and maybe that was entirely true as well. They turned off the lights, took off their glasses, and stared through the same ceiling, the same roof, with two pairs of flawed eyes that could be compensated for but were never going to get better on their own.

"I wish you'd known me when I was a kid," Jacob said.

"A kid?"

"Or just . . . *before*. Before I became *this*."

"You wish I'd known you before you knew me."

"No. You don't understand."

"Find another way to say it."

"Julia, I am not . . . myself."

"Then who are you?"

Jacob wanted to cry, but couldn't. But he also couldn't hide his hiding. She stroked his hair. There was nothing that she forgave him for. Nothing. Not the texts, not the years. But she couldn't not respond to his need. She didn't want to, but she couldn't not. It was a version of love. But double negatives never sustained a religion.

He said, "I've never said what I feel."

"Never?"

"No."

"That's quite an indictment."

"It's true."

"Well," she said, with her first chuckle since finding the phone, "there are so many other things you do well."

"That's the sound of all not being lost."

"What is?"

"Your chuckle."

"That? No, that was the sound of appreciated irony."

Fall asleep, he implored himself. *Fall asleep.*

"What do I do well?" he asked.

"You're serious?"

"Just one thing."

He was hurting. And no matter how much she felt he deserved the hurt, she couldn't tolerate it. She'd devoted so much of herself—forfeited so much of herself—to protecting him. How many experiences, how many subjects of conversation, how many words, were sacrificed in order to soothe his profound vulnerability? They couldn't go to a city that she'd been to with a boyfriend twenty years before. She couldn't make gentle observations about the lack of boundaries at his parents' house, much less his own parenting choices, which often resembled the absence of choices. She picked up Argus's shits because Argus couldn't help it, and because, even if she didn't choose or want him, and even if it was an unfair burden, Argus was hers.

"You're kind," she told her husband.

"No. I'm really not."

"I could give you a hundred examples . . ."

"Three or four would be extremely helpful right now."

She didn't want to do this, but she couldn't not. "You always return your grocery cart to the right place. You fold up your *Post* and leave it for another reader on the Metro. You draw maps for lost tourists . . ."

"Is that *kindness*, or *conscientiousness*?"

"So you're conscientious."

Could he tolerate her hurt? She wanted to know, but didn't trust him to tell her.

She asked, "Does it make you sad that we love the kids more than we love each other?"

"I wouldn't put it that way."

"No, you would say I'm your enemy."

"I was worked up."

"I know."

"I wasn't meaning what I was saying."

"I know," she said. "But you were saying it."

"I don't believe that anger reveals truth. Sometimes you just say something."

"I know. But I don't believe that any something comes from nowhere."

"I don't love the kids more than I love you."

"You do," she said. "*I* do. Maybe we're supposed to. Maybe evolution forces us to."

"I love you," he said, turning to her.

"I know you do. I've never doubted that, and I don't doubt it now. But it's a different kind of love than the kind I need."

"What does that mean for us?"

"I don't know."

Fall asleep, Jacob.

He said, "You know how novocaine leaves you unsure of where your mouth ends and the world begins?"

"I suppose I do."

"Or how sometimes you think there's going to be another stair when there isn't, and your foot falls through an imaginary stair?"

"Sure."

Why was it so hard for him to cross the physical space? It shouldn't have been, but it was.

"I don't know what I was saying."

She could feel him struggling.

"What?"

"I don't know."

He tucked his hand behind her hair, cupping the back of her neck.

"You're tired," he said.

"I'm really exhausted."

"We're tired. We've run ourselves into the ground. We need to find ways to rest."

"I would understand if you were having an affair. I'd be angry, and I'd be hurt, and I'd probably be moved to do something I don't even want to do—"

"Like what?"

"I would hate you, Jacob, but at least I'd understand you. I always understood you. Remember how I would tell you that? That you were the only person who made sense to me? Now everything you do confuses me."

"Confuses you?"

"Your obsession with real estate."

"I'm not obsessed with real estate."

"Every time I walk past your laptop, the screen is filled with a house listing."

"Just curious."

"But why? And why won't you tell Sam he's better than you at chess?"

"I do."

"You don't. You let him believe that you let him win. And why are you such a completely different person in different situations? You become passive-aggressively quiet with me, but you snap at the boys, but you let your father walk all over you. You haven't written me a Friday letter in a decade, but you spend all of your free time working on something that you love but won't share with anyone, and then you write those texts that you say mean nothing. I walked seven circles around you when we got married. I can't even find you now."

"I'm not having an affair."

"You're not?"

"I'm not."

She started to cry.

"I exchanged some horribly inappropriate texts with someone at work."

"An actress."

"No."

"Who?"

"Does it matter?"

"If it matters to me, it matters."

"One of the directors."

"Who has my name?"

"No."

"Is it that woman with the red hair?"

"No."

"You know, I don't even care."

"Good. You shouldn't. There's no reason—"

"How did it start?"

"It just . . . evolved. As things do. It took on a—"

"I don't even care."

"It never became anything other than words."

"For how long?"

"I don't know."

"Of course you do."

"Maybe four months."

"You're asking me to believe that for four months you've been exchanging sexually explicit texts with someone you work with every day and it never led to anything physical?"

"I'm not asking you to believe me. I'm telling you the truth."

"The sad thing is, I believe you."

"That's not sad. It's hope."

"No, it's sad. You are the only person I know, or could even imagine, who would be capable of writing such bold sentences while living so meekly. I actually do believe that you could write to someone that you want to lick her asshole, and have that bluff called, and then sit beside her every day for an entire four months without allowing your hand to wander the six necessary inches to her thigh. Without mustering that bravery. Without even sending the signal that it's OK for her to take up the slack of your cowardice and move her hand onto your thigh. Think about the signals you must have been sending to keep her pussy wet and her hand away."

"That's too far, Julia."

"*Too far?* You're serious? *You* are the person in this room who doesn't know what *too far* means."

"I know that I went too far in what I wrote."

"I'm telling you, you didn't go far enough in what you lived."

"What's that supposed to mean? You want me to have an affair?"

"No, I want you to write Shabbat letters to me. But if you're going to write pornographic texts to someone else, then yes, I want you to have an affair. Because then I could respect you."

"You're not making sense."

"I'm making perfect sense. I would have respected you so much more if you'd fucked her. It would have proven something to me that I have found harder and harder to believe."

"Which is?"

"That you're a human being."

"You don't believe I'm human?"

"I don't believe you're there at all."

Jacob opened his mouth, without knowing what would come out. He wanted to return everything she'd given to him, to catalog her neuroses, and irrationalities, and weaknesses, and hypocrisies, and ugliness. He also wanted to acknowledge that everything she'd said was true, but contextualize his monstrousness—not all of it was his fault. He wanted to mortar bricks with one hand while taking a hammer to them with the other.

But instead of his voice, they heard Benjy's: "I need you! I really need you!"

Julia released a burst of laughter.

"Why are you laughing?"

"It has nothing to do with things not being lost."

It was the nervous laughter of oppositions. The dark laughter of the knowledge of the end. The religious laughter of scale.

Benjy called out again through the monitor: *"Someone! Someone!"*

They fell silent.

Julia searched the darkness for her husband's eyes, wanting to search them.

"Someone!"

THE N-WORD

Julia had fallen asleep by the time Jacob came back down from calming Benjy. Or she did a perfectly believable impression of a sleeping person. Jacob was restless. He didn't want to read—not a book or a magazine, not even a real estate blog. He didn't want to watch TV. Writing wasn't going to happen. Neither was masturbation. No activity appealed to him, anything would feel like an act, an impersonation of a person.

He went to Sam's room, hoping for a few moments of peace, observing his first child's sleeping body. A shifting light spread from under the door onto the hallway, then pulled back: waves from the digital ocean on the other side. Sam, ever vigilant of his privacy, heard his father's heavy steps.

"Dad?"

"The one and lonely."

"So . . . Are you standing there? Do you need something?"

"Can I come in?"

Without waiting for an answer he opened the door.

"You were being rhetorical?" Sam asked, not looking away from the screen.

"What are you doing?"

"I'm watching TV."

"You don't have a TV."

"On my computer."

"So aren't you watching your computer?"

"Sure."

"What's on?"

"Everything."

"What are you watching?"

"Nothing."

"You have a second?"

"Yes: one . . ."

"I was being rhetorical."

"*Ah.*"

"How's it going?"

"Is this a conversation?"

"Just checking in."

"I'm fine."

"Does it feel great to feel fine?"

"What?"

"I don't know. I think I heard it somewhere. So . . . Sam."

"The one and bony."

"Nice one. Anyway, listen. I'm sorry to have to get into this. But. The thing at Hebrew school this morning."

"I didn't do it."

"Right. It's just."

"Don't you believe me?"

"It's not even a question of that."

"Yes it is."

"It would be a whole lot easier to get you out of this if you had some other explanation."

"I don't."

"A bunch of those words are really no big deal. Between us, it wouldn't even bother me if you *had* written them."

"I didn't."

"But the n-word."

Sam finally turned his attention to his father.

"What, *divorce*?"

"What?"

"Never mind."

"Why did you say that?"

"I didn't."

"Are you talking about Mom and me?"

"I don't know. I can't even hear myself over the fighting and glass-breaking."

"Earlier? No, what you heard—"

"It's OK. Mom came up and we had a talk."

Jacob glanced at the TV on the computer. He thought about how Guy de Maupassant ate lunch at the Eiffel Tower's restaurant every day because it was the only place in Paris without a view of the tower. The Nats were playing the Dodgers, extra innings. With a sudden burst of excitement, he clapped his hands. "Let's go to the game tomorrow!"

"What?"

"So fun! We could get there early for batting practice. Eat tons of shit."

"Eat tons of shit?"

"Shitty food."

"Would it be OK if I just watched this?"

"But I'm having an awesome idea."

"Are you?"

"Aren't I?"

"I have soccer, and cello, and bar mitzvah lessons, assuming that's still on, God forbid."

"I can get you out of that."

"My life?"

"I'm afraid I can only bring you into that."

"And they're playing in L.A."

"Right," Jacob said, and quieter, "I should have realized that."

That quietness made Sam wonder if maybe he'd hurt his father. He experienced a tremor of a feeling that, despite knowing it was utterly foolish, he would grow to experience more often and more strongly in the coming year: that maybe everything was at least a little bit his fault.

"Finish the chess game?"

"Nah."

"You're OK with money?"

"Yeah."

"And this thing at Hebrew school. It obviously isn't because of Grandpa, right?"

"Not unless he's also the grandfather of whoever did it."

"That's what I thought. Anyway—"

"Dad, Billie's black, so how could I be a racist?"

"Billie?"

"The girl I'm in love with."

"You have a girlfriend?"

"No."

"I'm confused."

"She's the girl *I'm in love with*."

"OK. And you said *Billie*? But a girl, right?"

"Yes. And she's black. So how could I be racist?"

"I'm not sure that logic quite works."

"It does."

"You know who points out that some of his best friends are black? Someone who isn't comfortable with black people."

"None of my best friends are black."

"And for whatever it's worth, I'm pretty sure *African American* is the preferred nomenclature."

"Nomenclature?"

"Terminology."

"Shouldn't the guy who's in love with a black girl be the one establishing the nomenclature?"

"Isn't that the pot calling the kettle African American?"

"Pot?"

"I'm joking around. It's an interesting name, that's all. Not a judgment. You know you were named for a great-great-uncle who perished in Birkenau. With Jews there always has to be some significance attached."

"Some suffering, you mean."

"Gentiles pick names that sound nice. Or they just make them up."

"Billie was named after Billie Holiday."

"So she's the exception that proves the rule."

"Who are you named after?" Sam asked, his interest a small concession in response to the guilt of having forced his dad's voice into quiet sadness.

"A distant relative named Yakov. Supposedly an amazing, larger-than-life guy. Story goes he crushed a Cossack's head in his hand."

"Cool."

"I'm obviously not strong like that."

"We don't even *know* any Cossacks."

"And at most, I'm the size of life."

One of their stomachs grumbled, but neither knew whose.

"Well, bottom line, I think it's awesome that you have a girlfriend."

"She's not my girlfriend."

"Nomenclature strikes twice. I think it's awesome that you're in love."

"I'm not in love. I love her."

"Whatever's going on, this obviously stays between us. You can count on me."

"I've already talked to Mom about it."

"Really? When?"

"I don't know. Couple of weeks ago?"

"This is old news?"

"It's all relative."

Jacob stared at Sam's screen. Was this what drew Sam to it? Not the ability to be elsewhere, but to be nowhere?

"What did you tell her?" Jacob asked.

"Who?"

"Your mother?"

"You mean *Mom*?"

"That's the one."

"I don't know."

"You don't know, as in you don't feel like talking about it with me right now?"

"As in that."

"It's strange, because she's convinced you wrote those words."

"I didn't."

"OK. I'm becoming annoying. I'll go."

"I didn't say you were annoying."

Jacob moved to the door to leave, but paused. "Wanna hear a joke?"

"No."

"It's dirty."

"Then *definitely* no."

"What's the difference between a Subaru and an erection?"

"No means no."

"Seriously. What's the difference?"

"Seriously, not interested."

Jacob leaned forward and whispered, "I don't have a Subaru."

Despite himself, Sam released a huge laugh, the kind involving snorting and saliva. Jacob laughed, not at his own joke but at his son's laughter. They laughed together, vigorously, hysterically.

Sam struggled, without success, to regain his composure, and said, "The funny thing . . . the really funny thing . . . is . . . you *do* have a Subaru."

And then they laughed more, and Jacob spit a little, and teared up, and remembered how horrible it was to be Sam's age, how painful and unfair.

"It's true," Jacob said. "I totally have a Subaru. I should have said Toyota. What was I thinking?"

"What were you thinking?"

What was he thinking?

They calmed down.

Jacob gave the sleeves of his shirt another roll—a bit tight, but he wanted them over the elbow.

"Mom feels that you need to apologize."

"Do *you*?"

In his pocket, he closed his hand around nothing, around a knife, and said, "I do."

The one and phony.

"OK, then," Sam said.

"It won't be that bad."

"Yes it will."

"Yeah," Jacob said, kissing Sam on the top of his head—the last kissable place. "It's gonna suck."

At the threshold, Jacob turned.

"How's it going in Other Life?"

"Eh."

"What are you working on?"

"Building a new synagogue."

"Really?"

"Yeah."

"Can I ask why?"

"Because I destroyed the old synagogue."

"Destroyed? Like with a wrecking ball?"

"Like that."

"So now you're going to build one for yourself?"

"I built the old one, too."

"Mom would love that," Jacob said, understanding the brilliance and beauty of what Sam never shared. "And she would probably have a million ideas."

"Please don't mention it to her."

That gave Jacob a spike of pleasure that he didn't want. He nodded and said, "Of course," then shook his head and said, "I would never."

"OK," Sam said, "so, unless there's something else?"

"And the old synagogue? Why did you build it?"

"So I could blow it up."

"Blow it up? You know, if I were a different dad, and you were a different kid, I'd probably feel obligated to report you to the FBI."

"But if you were a different dad, and I were a different kid, I wouldn't have needed to blow up a virtual synagogue."

"Touché," Jacob said. "But isn't it possible that you weren't building it to destroy? Or at least not only to destroy?"

"No, that isn't possible."

"Like, maybe you were trying to get something exactly right, and when it wasn't, you needed to destroy it?"

"Nobody believes me."

"I do. I believe that you want things to be right."

"You just don't get it," Sam said, because there was no way he was going to concede any understanding to his father. But his father got it. Sam hadn't built the synagogue to destroy it. He wasn't one of those Tibetan sand-mandala whatevers he'd been forced to hear about during a drive—five silent guys working for thousands of hours on an arts and crafts project whose function was to be functionless. ("And I used to think *Nazis* were the opposite of Jews," his dad had said, disconnecting his phone from the car stereo.) No, he built the synagogue with the hope of feeling, finally, comfortable somewhere. It wasn't simply that he could create it to his own esoteric specifications; he could be there without being there. Not unlike masturbating. But as with masturbating, if it wasn't exactly right, it was completely and irretrievably wrong. Sometimes, at the worst possible moment, his drunken id would suddenly veer, and in his mental headlights would be Rabbi Singer, or Seal (the singer), or his mom. And there was never any coming back from that. With the synagogue, too, the slightest imperfection—an infinitesimally asymmetrical rotunda, stairs with risers too high for short kids, an upside-down Jewish star—and it all had to go. He wasn't being impulsive. He was being careful. Couldn't he simply have fixed what wasn't right? No. Because he would always know that it had been wrong: "That's the star that once hung upside down." To another person, the correction would have made it more perfect than if it had been right the first time. Sam was not another person. Neither was Samanta.

Jacob sat on Sam's bed and said, "When I was young, maybe in high school, I used to like to write out the lyrics of all of my favorite songs. I don't know why. I guess it gave me that feeling of things being in the right place. Anyway, this was long before the Internet. So I'd sit with my boom box—"

"Your *boom box*?"

"A tape player with speakers."

"I was being dismissive."

"All right . . . well . . . I'd sit with my *boom box* and play a second or two of a song, then write down what I'd heard, then rewind and play it again to make sure I'd gotten it right, then let it play again, and write down a bit more, then rewind for the parts I didn't quite hear, or wasn't sure I'd heard, then write them down. Rewinding a tape is really imprecise, so I'd inevitably go back too far, or not far enough. It was incredibly laborious. But I loved it. I loved how careful it felt. I loved the feeling of getting it right. I spent who knows how many thousands of hours doing that. Sometimes a lyric would really stump me, especially when grunge and hip-hop came along. And I wouldn't accept guessing, because that would undermine the entire point of writing the lyrics out—to get it right. Sometimes I'd have to listen to the same little bit over and over and over, dozens of times, hundreds. I would literally wear through that part of the tape, so that when I listened to the song later, the part I most wanted to get right wasn't there anymore. I remember a phrase in 'All Apologies'— you know that song, right?"

"Nope."

"Nirvana? Great, great, *great* song. Anyway, Kurt Cobain's marbles seemed to have migrated to his mouth, and there was one phrase I had a particularly hard time making out. My best guess, after hundreds of listenings, was 'I can see from shame.' I didn't realize I was wrong until many years later, when I sang it, at the top of my lungs, like an idiot, with Mom. Not long after we got married."

"She pointed out that you were wrong?"

"Yeah."

"That's so Mom."

"I was grateful."

"But you were singing."

"Singing wrongly."

"Still. She should have let it go."

"No, she did the right thing."

"So what was the real lyric?"

"Fasten your seat belt. It was: 'aqua seafoam shame.'"

"No way."

"Right?"

"What's that even supposed to *mean*?"

"It doesn't mean anything. That was my mistake. I thought it had to mean something."

II

LEARNING
IMPERMANENCE

ANTIETAM

Neither Jacob nor Julia knew what, exactly, was happening in those first two weeks after Julia discovered the phone: what had been agreed to, implied, broached hypothetically, asked for. Neither knew what was real. It felt like there were so many emotional land mines; they moved through the hours and rooms on their hearts' tiptoes, with large earphones connected to sensitive metal detectors that could pick up traces of buried feeling—if at the expense of blocking out the rest of life.

At a breakfast that might, to a television audience, have seemed in every way happy, Julia said into the fridge, "We're always running out of milk," and through his earphones Jacob heard "You have never taken good enough care of us," but he didn't hear Max say, "Don't come to the talent show tomorrow."

And the next day, at Max's school, forced to share the small space of the elevator alone together, Jacob said, "The Door Close button isn't even attached to anything. Purely psychological." Through her earphones, Julia heard "Let's get this over with." But she didn't hear herself say, "I thought everything was purely psychological." Which, through Jacob's earphones, sounded like "All of those years of therapy and no one knows less about happiness." And he didn't hear himself say, "There's pure, and there's pure." A probably content parent in a probably unbroken family entered and asked Jacob if he meant to be pressing Door Open.

All that tiptoeing, all that precious overinterpreting and evading, and it wasn't a minefield at all. It was a Civil War battlefield. Jacob had taken Sam to Antietam, just as Irv had taken Jacob. And he had given a similar speech about what a privilege it is to be American. Sam found a half-buried bullet. The weapons in Jacob and Julia's earth were as harmless as that—artifacts of old battles, safe to be examined, explored, even valued. If they'd known not to fear them.

The domestic rituals were sufficiently ingrained as to make avoidance fairly easy and inconspicuous. She showered, he got breakfast going. She served breakfast, he showered. He supervised teeth brushing, she laid clothes out on beds, he confirmed the contents of the backpacks, she checked the weather and responded to it with appropriate outer clothing, he got Ed the Hyena going (warmed in the six months of too cold, cooled in the six months of too hot), she brought the boys out and stepped into Newark to look for cars coming down the hill, he reversed.

They found two seats near the front of the auditorium, but after depositing his bag, Jacob said, "I'll go grab us some coffees." Which he did. And then waited at the school entrance with them until three minutes of curtain. Halfway through a girl's talentless rendition of "Let It Go," Jacob whispered, "I wish she would," into Julia's ear. No response. A group of boys reenacted a scene from *Avatar*. What was probably a girl used different kinds of pasta to explain how the euro works. Neither Jacob nor Julia wanted to admit to not knowing what Max was going to do. Neither could bear the shame of having been too preoccupied with personal hurt to be present for their child. And neither could bear the shame of the other having been a better parent. Each privately guessed that Max would perform the card trick that the magician had taught him after Julia's fortieth. Two girls did that cup thing while singing "When I'm Gone," and Jacob whispered, "So go already."

"*What?*"

"No. Her. The singer."

"Be nice."

For the finale, the drama and music teachers teamed up for a sanitized version of the opener from *The Book of Mormon*—living out their dreams while reconfirming why they were dreams. Lots of applause, a brief thank-you from the principal, and the kids filed out and back to class.

Jacob and Julia walked back to their cars in silence. And the talent show wasn't mentioned at home that night. Had Max chickened out? Did he consider himself talentless? Was his abstention an act of aggression or a call for help? If they'd brought any of these questions to him, he would have pointed out that he told them not to go.

Three nights later, when Jacob came to bed, after having waited the requisite hour, Julia was still reading, so he said, "Oh, I forgot something," and headed back down to not read the paper while not watching another episode of *Homeland* and regretting, as he often did, that Mandy Patinkin wasn't ten years older—he'd have made a great Irv.

Two days after that, Julia walked into the pantry, where Jacob was checking to see if a few hundred billion atoms had spontaneously organized themselves into an unhealthy snack in the ten minutes since he last checked. She walked back out. (Unlike Jacob, she never gave an ostensible explanation for moving away from him, she never "forgot something.") The pantry wasn't among the unofficially claimed spaces—as the TV room was Jacob's, and the small sitting room was Julia's—but it was too small to be shared.

On the tenth day, Jacob opened the bathroom door to see Julia drying off after a bath. She covered herself. He had seen her come out of hundreds of baths, seen three children come out of her body. He had watched her dress and undress thousands and thousands of times, and twice at the inn in Pennsylvania. They'd made love in every position, offering every view of every body part. "Sorry," he said, not knowing what the word referred to, only that his foot had half depressed a mine's trigger.

Or stumbled upon an artifact of old battle, which might have been safe to examine, explore, even value.

What if, instead of apologizing and turning, he'd asked her if the need to conceal herself was new, or old with a new justification?

When Robert E. Lee's defensive line at Petersburg had been broken and the evacuation of Richmond was imminent, Jefferson Davis ordered the Confederate treasury be moved. It went by train, and then wagon, under many eyes and between many hands. The Union pressed forward, the Confederacy crumbled, and the whereabouts of the five tons of gold bars remain a mystery, although they are assumed buried.

What if, instead of apologizing and turning, he'd gone to her, touched her, shown her not only that he still wanted to make love to her, but that he was still capable of risking rejection?

On Jacob's first visit to Israel, his cousin Shlomo took the family to the Dome of the Rock, which at the time could be entered by non-Muslims. Jacob was as deeply moved by the devotion of the men on the prayer rugs as he was by the Jews below. He was more moved, because the devotion was less self-conscious: at the Wailing Wall the men merely bobbed; here they wailed. Shlomo explained that they were standing atop a cave carved into the Foundation Stone. And in the floor of that cave was a slight depression, thought to be above another cave, often referred to as the Well of Souls. It was there that Abraham answered God's call, and prepared to sacrifice his beloved son; there that Muhammad ascended to heaven; there that the Ark of the Covenant was buried, full of broken and whole tablets. According to the Talmud, the stone marks the center of the world, serving as a cover for the abyss in which the waters from the Flood still rage.

"We are standing atop the greatest archaeological site that will never be," Shlomo said, "filled with the most valuable objects in the world, the place where history and religion meet. All underground, never to be touched."

Irv was adamant that Israel should dig, come what may. It was a cultural, historical, and intellectual obligation. But to Jacob, until those things were unearthed—until they could be seen and touched—they would be unreal. So it was better to keep them out of sight.

What if, instead of apologizing and turning, Jacob had gone to Julia and lifted the towel, as he'd lifted her veil before the wedding, confirming that she was still the woman she said she was, the woman he still wanted?

Jacob tried to keep the conversations with Julia underground, but she needed the end of their family to be seen and touched. She expressed her continued respect for Jacob, her desire to be friends, *best* friends, and good co-parents, the *best*, and to use a mediator and not get lost in all that was not to be cared about, and to live around the corner from each other and go on vacations together, and to dance at each other's second weddings—although she swore that she would never marry again. Jacob agreed, without believing that any of what she said was either happening or would happen. They'd experienced so many necessary passages—sleep-training the boys, teething, falls from small bicycles, Sam's physical therapy. This, too, would probably pass.

They could navigate the house to avoid each other, and they could navigate conversations to maintain the illusion of safety, but there was no underground when a child was in the room or the conversation. Many times, Julia would catch sight of one of the boys—Benjy looking up in thought from a drawing of Odysseus facing the Cyclops, Max examining the hairs on his forearm, Sam carefully applying reinforcements as needed in his binder—and think, *I can't.*

And Jacob would think, *We won't.*

DAMASCUS

The day before the beginning of the destruction of Israel, Julia and Sam were scrambling to get their things together before the Uber driver, Mohammed, was moved to give them a one-star rating, thereby sealing their fate as *haram* passengers. Jacob was preparing Benjy, who was dressed like a pirate, for a day with his grandparents.

"You have everything?" Julia asked Sam.

"*Yes*," he said, unable to muster the herculean effort to conceal his annoyance at nothing.

"Don't *yes* Mom," Jacob said, for Julia's benefit and his own. Camaraderie had been hard to find in the past two weeks—not because there was cruelty, just the absence of direct interaction. There had been a few moments, usually triggered by a shared reflexive wonder at something one of the boys had said or done, when it felt like Jacob and Julia were once again wearing the same uniform. The day Oliver Sacks died, Jacob shared some of his hero's life with the boys, explaining the range of his interests, his closeted homosexuality, his famous use of L-dopa with human produce, and how perhaps the most curious and engaged person of the last fifty years spent more than thirty of those years celibate.

"Celibate?" Max asked.

"Not having sex."

"So?"

"So he was eager to take in everything the world had to offer, but he didn't want to, or couldn't, share himself."

"Maybe he was impotent," Julia suggested.

"No," Jacob said, feeling the wound open, "he just—"

"Or maybe he was patient."

"I'm celibate," Benjy said.

"You?" Sam said. "You're Wilt Chamberlain."

"I'm not whoever that is, and I haven't stuck my penis into another person's vagina hole."

The defense of his celibacy was kind of funny. Referring to "another person's vagina hole" was kind of funny. But he said funnier, more precocious things every few minutes. It didn't feel like a metaphor, or accidental wisdom. It didn't scratch any exposed nerves. But for the first time since she discovered the phone, it forced Julia's eyes to meet Jacob's. And in that moment, he felt sure that they would find their way back.

But there wasn't a lot of camaraderie now.

"What did I say?" Sam asked.

"It's how you said it," Jacob said.

"How did I say whatever I said?"

"Like this," Jacob said, imitating Sam's *Yes.*

"I can handle my half of a conversation with my son," Julia told Jacob. Then she asked Sam, "Did you remember your toothbrush?"

"Of course he has his toothbrush," Jacob said, making a small allegiance correction.

"Shit," Sam said, turning and hustling upstairs.

"He wanted you to chaperone," Julia said.

"No. I don't think that's true."

She picked up Benjy and said, "I'm going to miss you, my little man."

"Opi said I can say bad words at his house."

"In his house, it's his rules," Jacob said.

"Well, no," Julia corrected.

"Shit, or *penis . . ."*

"Penis isn't a bad word," Jacob said.

"I doubt Omi would like you talking like that."

"Opi said it didn't matter."

"You misheard him."

"He said, 'Omi doesn't matter.'"

"He was *joking,"* Jacob said.

"Asshole is a bad word."

Sam came back down the stairs with his toothbrush.

"Dress shoes?" Julia asked.

"Fuuuuuuck."

"*Fuck*, too," Benjy said.

Sam hustled back up the stairs.

"Maybe give him a bit more space?" Jacob suggested in the form of a question ostensibly addressed to the collective consciousness.

"I don't think I was being annoying."

"Of course you weren't. I just meant that Mark can play the bad guy on the trip. If necessary."

"Hopefully it won't be."

"Forty pubescents away from home?"

"I wouldn't describe Sam as *pubescent*."

"Pubescent?" Benjy asked.

"I'm glad Mark will be there," Jacob said. "You know, you might not even remember, but you said something about him, a couple of weeks ago, in the context of—"

"I remember."

"We said a lot of things."

"We did."

"I just wanted to say that."

"I'm not sure what you just said."

"Just that."

"Take the opportunity to get to know him a bit," Julia said, moving right along.

"Max?"

"Don't just go off to your separate worlds."

"I don't have a world, so that shouldn't be a problem."

"It'll be fun picking up the Israelis tomorrow."

"Will it?"

"You and Max can be Team America."

Max came down the stairs. "Why are you talking about me?"

"We weren't talking about you," Jacob said.

"I was just saying to Dad that you guys should try to find things to do together while everyone's away."

The doorbell rang.

"My folks," Jacob said.

"*Together* together?" Max whispered to Julia.

Jacob opened the door. Benjy wrestled himself free of Julia's arms and ran to Deborah.

"Omi!"

"Hey, Omi," Max said.

"I've got Ebola?" Irv asked.

"Ebola?"

"Hey, Opi."

"Cool Moshe Dayan outfit."

"I'm a *pirate*."

Irv lowered himself to Benjy's level and performed what might very well have been a perfect Dayan impression, if anyone had known what Dayan sounded like: "The Syrians will soon learn that the road from Damascus to Jerusalem also goes from Jerusalem to Damascus!"

"Arrrgggg!"

"I wrote up his schedule," Julia said to Deborah. "And put together a bag with a few prepared meals."

"I've prepared a meal or two million in my day."

"I know," Julia said, trying to reciprocate Deborah's obvious affection. "I just want to make it as easy as possible."

"I have a freezer full of very frozen foods," Deborah told Benjy.

"Morningstar Farms veggie bacon strips?"

"Hm."

"Fuuuuuuck."

"Benjy!"

Sam came running down the stairs with his shoes, paused, said, "Goddamn it!" and turned back around.

"Language," Julia said.

"Dad says there's no bad language."

"I said there's bad *usage*. And that was bad usage."

"Are we gonna burn the midnight oil?" Irv asked Benjy.

"I don't know."

"Not *too* late," Julia told Deborah.

"And tomorrow we'll fetch the Israelis?"

"I'm taking him to the zoo," Deborah said. "Remember?"

Irv held up his phone: "Siri, do I remember what this woman is talking about?"

Sam came running back down the stairs with a belt.

"Hey, kid," Irv said.

"Hey, Opi. Hey, Omi."

"All's copacetic with your hate speech?"

"I didn't do it."

"You know, I once chaperoned your dad's class on a Model UN trip."

"No you didn't," Jacob said.

"Sure I did."

"Believe me, you didn't."

"You're right," Irv said, winking at Sam. "I'm thinking of the time I took you to the *actual* UN." And then, slapping his own hand: "Bad father."

"You *forgot* me there."

"Obviously not permanently." And then, to Sam: "Ready to give 'em hell?"

"I guess so."

"Remember, if they seat a delegate from so-called Palestine, you tell them what's what, then get up and walk out. You hear me? Punch with your mouth, and talk with your feet."

"We're representing Micronesia—"

"Siri, what is Micronesia?"

"And we, you know, debate resolutions, and respond to whatever crisis they manufacture."

"*They* the Arabs?"

"The facilitators."

"He knows what he's doing, Dad."

Three full honks, followed by nine rapid blasts—*Shevarim, Teruah.*

"Mohammed is losing patience," Julia said.

"And it was never his forte," Irv said.

"We'll go, too," Deborah said. "We have a big day planned: story time, arts and crafts, a nature walk—"

"—eat jelly fruit slices, make fun of Charlie Rose . . ."

"Come on, Argus!" Jacob called.

"I want to marry jelly fruit slices."

"We're going to the vet," Max explained to Deborah.

"Everything's fine," Jacob said, alleviating concern that belonged to no one.

"Except he poops in the house twice every day," Max said.

"He's old. It's convention."

"Does Great-Grandpa poop in the house twice every day?" Benjy asked.

Silence as everyone privately acknowledged that, as their visits had become so rare, it was impossible to rule out the possibility that Isaac pooped in the house twice a day.

"Actually, doesn't *everyone* poop in the house twice a day?" Benjy asked.

"Your brother means in the house, but not in the bathroom."

"He has a colostomy bag," Irv said. "Wherever he goes, there his poop is."

"What's a whatever bag?" Benjy asked.

Jacob cleared his throat and began: "Great-Grandpa's intestines—"

"Like a doggie bag for his crap," Irv said.

"But why would he want to eat it later?" Benjy asked.

"Maybe someone could check in on him while we're away," Julia said. "You could even bring the Israelis by on the way home."

"That's what I was planning," Jacob lied.

Mohammed honked again, this time with the sustain pedal.

Everyone headed out together: Deborah, Irv, and Benjy off to a marionette *Pinocchio* at Glen Echo; Julia and Sam to catch the bus from school; Jacob, Max, and Argus to the vet. Julia hugged Max and Benjy, and didn't hug Jacob, but told him: "Don't forget to—"

"*Go*," he said. "Have fun. Make world peace."

"A lasting peace," Julia said, the words having organized themselves.

"And say hi to Mark for me. Really."

"Not now, OK?"

"You're hearing something I didn't say."

A curt "Goodbye."

Halfway down the stoop, Benjy called back: "What if I don't miss you?"

"You can call us," Jacob said. "My phone will always be on, and I'll never be more than a short drive away."

"I said what if I *don't* miss you?"

"What?"

"Is that OK?"

"Of course it's OK," Julia said, giving Benjy a last kiss. "Nothing would make me happier than for you to have so much fun you don't think about us at all."

Jacob came down the stairs to give Benjy the last, last kiss.

"And anyway," he said, "you'll miss us."

And then, for the first time in his life, Benjy chose not to voice a thought.

THE SIDE THAT FACES AWAY

They stopped at McDonald's on the way. It was a vet visit ritual, something Jacob started doing after hearing a podcast about a shelter in L.A. that euthanized more dogs than anywhere else in America. The woman who ran it put down each and every dog herself, sometimes a dozen a day. She called each by its name, gave each as good a walk as it could handle, talked to it, stroked it, and, as a final gesture before the needle, fed it McNuggets. As she put it, "It's the last meal they would ask for."

Argus's visits in the past couple of years had been for joint pain, eye cloudiness, fatty lumps on the belly, and incontinence. They weren't suggestive of an imminent end, but Jacob knew how nervous the vet's office made him and felt that he owed his pal a reward, which might also serve as a positive association. Whether or not he would have chosen them as his last meal, Argus tore through the McNuggets, swallowing most of them whole. For as long as he'd been a member of the Bloch family, he had eaten Newman's Own twice a day without any variation. (Julia militantly banned table scraps, as they would "force Argus to become a beggar.") The McNuggets always led to diarrhea, sometimes vomiting. But that usually took a few hours, which could be timed to coincide with a walk in the park. And it was worth it.

Jacob and Max got McNuggets for themselves, too. They almost never ate meat in the house—again, Julia's decision—and fast food ranked just below cannibalism on the list of things not to be done. Neither Jacob nor Max missed McNuggets, but sharing something Julia disapproved of was a bonding experience. They pulled over at Fort Reno Park and made an impromptu picnic. Argus was loyal enough, and lethargic enough, to be trusted off-leash. Max stroked him as he swallowed McNugget after McNugget, telling him, "You're a good dog. You're good. You're good."

Pathetic as it felt, Jacob was jealous. Julia's cruel comments—however accurate, however deserved—lingered painfully in his mind. He kept returning to the line "I don't believe you're there at all." It was among the least specific, least pointed things she'd said in the course of their first fight about the phone, and a different person's mind would probably have attached itself to something else. But that was what echoed: "I don't believe you're there at all."

"I used to come here a lot when I was younger," Jacob said to Max. "We'd sled down that hill."

"Who was *we*?"

"Usually friends. Grandpa might have taken me a couple times, though I don't remember it. When it was warm, I'd come here to play baseball."

"Games? Or just goofing around?"

"Mostly goofing. It was never easy to get a minyan. Sometimes. Maybe the last day of school before a break."

"You're good, Argus. So good."

"When I got older, we'd buy beer from the Tenleytown Grocery—just over there. They never carded us."

"What's that mean?"

"You have to be twenty-one to buy beer legally, so usually places will ask for ID, like a driver's license, to see how old you are. Tenleytown never did. So we all bought beer there."

"You were breaking the law."

"It was a different time. And you know what Martin Luther King said about just and unjust laws."

"I don't."

"Basically, it was our moral responsibility to buy the beer."

"Good Argus."

"I'm kidding, of course. It is not good to buy beer before you're of age, and please don't tell Mom that I told you that story."

"OK."

"Do you know what a minyan is?"

"No."

"Why didn't you ask?"

"I don't know."

"It's ten men over the age of thirteen. That's what's required for prayers to count at synagogue."

"Sounds sexist and ageist."

"Definitely both," Jacob said, pulling a wildflower. "Fugazi used to play a free show here every summer."

"What's *Fugazi*?"

"Only the greatest band ever to have existed, by any definition of great. Their music was great. Their ethos was great. They were just great."

"What's *ethos*?"

"Guiding belief."

"What was their ethos?"

"Don't price-gouge your fans, don't tolerate violence at shows, don't make videos or sell merchandise. *Do* make music with anticorporate, anti-misogynist, class-conscious messaging, and make it make your face melt."

"You're a good dog."

"We should probably get going."

"My ethos is 'Find light in the beautiful sea, I choose to be happy.'"

"That's a great ethos, Max."

"It's a line from a Rihanna song."

"Well, Rihanna is wise."

"She didn't write the song."

"Whoever wrote it."

"Sia."

"So Sia's wise."

"And I was just kidding."

"Right."

"What's yours?"

"What?"

"Ethos."

"Don't price-gouge your fans, don't tolerate violence at shows—"

"No, seriously."

Jacob laughed.

"Seriously," Max said.

"Let me think about it."

"That's probably your ethos."

"That's Hamlet's ethos. You know Hamlet, right?"

"I'm ten, I'm not unborn."

"Sorry."

"Also, Sam's reading it in class."

"I wonder where Fugazi is now. I wonder if they're still idealistic, whatever they're doing."

"You're good, Argus."

When they got to the vet's office, they were led to an examining room in the back.

"In a weird way this reminds me of Great-Grandpa's house."

"That *is* weird."

"All the photos of the dogs are kind of like the pictures of me, Sam, and Benjy. And the jar of treats is like the jar of hard candies."

"And it smells like . . ."

"What?"

"Nothing."

"*What?*"

"I was going to say death, but it didn't feel like a nice thing to say, so I tried to keep it to myself."

"What does death smell like?"

"Like this."

"How do you even know?"

Jacob had never smelled a dead person. His three dead grandparents had died either before he was born or early enough in his childhood for him to have been protected from it. None of his colleagues or friends, or former colleagues or former friends, had died. Sometimes it amazed him that he'd managed to live forty-two years without proximity to mortality. And that amazement was always followed by the fear that the statistics would catch up with him and offer a lot of death at once. And he wouldn't be ready.

The vet took half an hour to see them, and Max gave Argus treat after treat.

"Might not mix well with the McNuggets," Jacob warned.

"You're good. You're so good."

Argus brought out a different side of Max, a sweetness, or vulnerability, that usually faced away. Jacob thought about a day he spent with his father at the National Museum of Natural History when he was Max's age. He had so few memories of time alone with his father—Irv worked long hours at the magazine, and when he wasn't writing, he was teaching, and when he wasn't teaching, he was socializing with important people, to confirm that he was an important person—but Jacob remembered that day.

They were facing a diorama. A bison.

"Nice," Irv said, "right?"

"Really nice," Jacob said, moved—shaken, even—by the extreme presence of the animal, how self-contained it was.

"None of this is by accident," Irv said.

"What do you mean?"

"They go to lengths to re-create an accurate nature scene. That's the point. But there are a lot of accurate scenes they could have chosen, right? The bison could have been galloping instead of standing still. He could have been battling, or hunting, or eating. There could have been two instead of one. They could have perched a small bird on his back. A lot of choices."

Jacob used to love being taught by his father. It felt intoxicating, and safe. And it confirmed that Jacob was an important person in his father's life.

"But the choices aren't always made freely," Irv said.

"Why not?"

"Because they have to hide what brought the animals here."

"What do you mean?"

"Where do you think the animals come from?"

"Africa, or something?"

"But how do they end up in dioramas? Do you think they volunteer to be taxidermied? Are they roadkill that lucky scientists stumble upon?"

"I guess I don't know."

"They're hunted."

"Really?"

"And hunting isn't clean."

"It isn't?"

"No one ever got something that didn't want to be gotten without making a mess."

"Oh."

"Bullets leave holes, sometimes big ones. Arrows, too. And you don't bring down a bison with a little hole."

"I guess not."

"So when they position the animals in the dioramas, they turn the holes and gashes and tears away from the viewer. Only the animals painted into the landscape get to see them. But remembering they're there changes everything."

Once, after hearing Jacob recount an example of Julia's subtle belittling, Dr. Silvers said, "Most people behave badly when wounded. If you can remember the wounds, it is far more possible to forgive the behavior."

Julia was in the bath when he'd come home that night. He tried—with gentle knocking, calling into the room, and unnecessarily loud shuffling—to make her aware of his presence, but the water was too loud, and opening the door, he startled her. After catching her breath, and laughing at her fear, she rested her chin on the tub's lip. They listened to the water together. A seashell brought to the ear becomes an echo chamber for one's circulatory system. The ocean you hear is your own blood. The bathroom that night was an echo chamber for their shared life. And behind Julia, where the towels and hanging robe should have been, Jacob saw a painted landscape, a flat forever occupied by a school, a soccer field, the Whole Foods bulk section (a grid of plastic bins filled with painted split peas and brown rice, dried mango and raw cashews), a Subaru and a Volvo, a home, their home, and through a second-story window there was a room, so tiny and precisely painted, only a Master could have made it, and on a table in that room, which became her office once there was no more need for a nursery, was an architectural model, a house, and in that house in that house in the house in which life happened was a woman, carefully positioned.

Finally, the vet came. She wasn't what Jacob was anticipating, or hoping for: some gentle, gentile, grandfather figure. To begin with, she was a she. In Jacob's experience, vets were like airplane pilots: virtually always male, gray (or graying), and calming. Dr. Shelling looked too young to buy Jacob a drink—not that the situation would ever arise—was fit, firm, and wearing what appeared to be a tailored lab coat.

"What brings you here today?" she asked, riffling through Argus's chart.

Did Max see what Jacob saw? Was he old enough to pay any attention? To be embarrassed?

"He's been having some problems," Jacob said, "probably just normal stuff for a dog of his age: incontinence, some joint issues. Our previous vet—Dr. Hazel at Animal Kind—put him on Rimadyl and Cosequin, and said we should consider adjusting the dosage if things didn't improve. They didn't improve, and we doubled the dosage, and added a dementia pill, but nothing happened. So I thought we'd seek another opinion."

"OK," she said, putting down the clipboard. "And this dog has a name?"

"Argus," Max offered.

"Great name," she said, lowering herself onto a knee.

She held the sides of Argus's face, and looked into his eyes while she stroked his head.

"He's in pain," Max said.

"He has occasional discomfort," Jacob clarified. "But it's not constant, and it's not pain."

"Are you in pain?" Dr. Shelling asked Argus.

"He whines when he gets up and down," Max said.

"That doesn't sound good."

"But he'll also whine if we don't drop enough popcorn during movies," Jacob said. "He's a catholic whiner."

"Can you think of other times he whines out of discomfort?"

"Again, almost all of his whining is for food or a walk. But that's not pain, or even discomfort. Just desire."

"He whines when you and Mom fight."

"That's Mom's whining," Jacob said, trying to relieve the shame he felt in front of the veterinarian.

"Does he get enough walks?" she asked. "He shouldn't be whining for a walk."

"He gets a lot of walks," Jacob said.

"Three," Max said.

"A dog of Argus's age needs five walks. At least."

"Five walks a day?" Jacob asked.

"And the pain you've witnessed. For how long has it been going on?"

"Discomfort," Jacob corrected. "*Pain* is too strong a word."

"A long time," Max said.

"Not that long. Maybe half a year?"

"It's gotten bad in the last half a year," Max said, "but he's been whining since Benjy was like three."

"Same could be said of Benjy."

The vet looked into Argus's eyes for another few moments, now in silence. Jacob wanted to be looked at like that.

"OK," she said. "Let's take a temperature, I'll check his vitals, and if it feels right, we can do some blood work."

She pulled a thermometer from a glass bottle on the counter, squeezed some lube onto it, and positioned herself behind Argus. Did it thrill Jacob? Did it depress him? It depressed him. But why? Because of Argus's stoicism whenever this happened? How it reminded him of his own unwillingness, or inability, to show discomfort? No, it had to do with the vet—her youthful beauty (she seemed to be reverse-aging as the visit progressed), but more, her tender care. She inspired fantasizing in Jacob, but not about a sexual encounter. Not even about her guiding in a suppository. He imagined her pressing a stethoscope to his chest; her fingers gently exploring the glands of his neck; how she would extend and bend his arms and legs, listening for the difference between discomfort and pain with the closeness and quietness and care of someone trying to crack a safe.

Max got down on a knee, placed his face in front of Argus's, and said, "That's my boy. Look at me. There you go, boy."

"OK," she said, removing the thermometer. "A little high, but within the healthy range."

She then ran her hands over Argus's body, examining the insides of his ears, lifting his lip to look at the teeth and gums, pressing Argus's belly, rotating his thigh until he whined.

"Sensitive on that leg."

"He had both of his hips replaced," Max said.

"Total hip replacements?"

Jacob shrugged.

"The left was a femoral head osteotomy," Max said.

"That's an interesting choice."

"Yeah," Max went on, "he was on the border in terms of weight, and the vet thought we could spare him the THR. But it was a mistake."

"Sounds like you were paying pretty close attention."

"He's my dog," Max said.

"OK," she said, "he's obviously got some tenderness. Probably a bit of arthritis."

"He's been pooping in the house for about a year," Max said.

"Not a year," Jacob corrected.

"Don't you remember Sam's slumber party?"

"Right, but that was unusual. It didn't become a consistent problem until several months after that."

"And is he also urinating in the house?"

"Mostly just defecating," Jacob said, "some peeing more recently."

"Does he still squat to poop? Often it's really an arthritic problem, rather than an intestinal or rectal one—the dog can no longer assume the position, and so poops while walking."

"He often poops while walking," Jacob said.

"But sometimes he'll poop in his bed," Max said.

"As if he doesn't realize he's pooping," the vet suggested. "Or simply has no control."

"Right," Max said. "I don't know if dogs get embarrassed, or sad, but."

Jacob received a text from Julia: *made it to the hotel.*

"We'll never know," the vet said, "but it definitely doesn't sound pleasant."

That's it? Jacob thought. *Made it to the hotel?* As if to a tolerated colleague, or the most minimal communication required to satisfy a legal obligation. And then he thought, *Why does she always give me so little?* And that thought surprised him, not just the flash flood of anger it rode in on, but how comfortable it felt—and that word, *always*—despite his never before having consciously thought it. *Why does she always give me so little?* So little of the benefit of the doubt. So few compliments. Such rare appreciation. When was the last time she didn't stifle a laugh at one of his jokes? When did she last ask to read what he was working on? When did she last initiate sex? So little to live off. He'd behaved badly, but only after a decade of wounds from arrows too blunt to get the job done.

He often thought of that piece by Andy Goldsworthy, for which he lay flat on the ground as a storm came in, and remained there until it passed. When he stood up, his dry silhouette remained. Like the chalk outline of a victim. Like the unpunctured circle where the dartboard used to be.

"He still enjoys himself at the park," Jacob said to the vet.

"What's that?"

"I was just saying that he still enjoys himself at the park."

And with that seeming non sequitur, the conversation rotated 180 degrees, so that the other side faced front.

"Sometimes he does," Max said. "But mostly he just lies there. And he has such a hard time with the stairs at home."

"He ran the other day."

"And then limped for like the next three days."

"Look," Jacob said, "obviously his quality of life is diminishing. Obviously he's not the dog he used to be. But he has a life worth living."

"Says who?"

"Dogs don't want to die."

"Great-Grandpa does."

"Whoa, wait. What did you just say?"

"Great-Grandpa wants to die," Max said matter-of-factly.

"Great-Grandpa isn't a dog." The full strangeness of that comment started to creep up the walls of the room. Jacob tried to cut it back with the obvious amendment: "And he doesn't want to die."

"Says who?"

"Would you two like a little time?" the vet asked, crossing her arms and taking a long backward stride toward the door.

"Great-Grandpa has hopes for the future," Jacob said. "Like living to see Sam's bar mitzvah. And he takes pleasure in memories."

"Same as Argus."

"You think Argus is looking forward to Sam's bar mitzvah?"

"No one is looking forward to Sam's bar mitzvah."

"Great-Grandpa is."

"Says who?"

"Dogs take all kinds of very subtle pleasure in life," the vet said. "Lying in a patch of sun. The occasional bit of tasty human food. It's hard to say how far their mental experience extends beyond that. It's left to us to make assumptions."

"Argus feels like we forgot him," Max said, making his assumption clear.

"Forgot him?"

"Just like Great-Grandpa."

Jacob gave the vet a ruffled smile and said, "Who said Great-Grandpa feels forgotten?"

"He does."

"When?"

"When we talk."

"And when is that?"

"When we skype."

"He doesn't mean it."

"So how do you know Argus means it when he whines?"

"Dogs can't not mean things."

"Tell him," Max said to the vet.

"Tell him what?"

"Tell him that Argus should be put to sleep."

"Oh. That's not for me to say. It's a very personal decision."

"OK, but if you thought he shouldn't be put to sleep, you would have just said he shouldn't be put to sleep."

"He runs in the park, Max. He watches movies on the sofa."

"Tell him," Max said to the vet.

"My job, as a vet, is to care for Argus, to help keep him healthy. It isn't to offer advice about end-of-life decisions."

"So in other words, you agree with me."

"She didn't say that, Max."

"I didn't say that."

"Do you think my great-grandfather should be put to sleep?"

"No," the vet said, immediately regretting the credence her response lent the question.

"Tell him."

"Tell him what?"

"Tell him that you think Argus should be put to sleep."

"That's really not for me to say."

"See?" Max said to his father.

"You realize Argus is in the room, Max?"

"He doesn't understand."

"Of course he understands."

"So hold on. You think Argus understands, but Great-Grandpa doesn't?"

"Great-Grandpa understands."

"Really?"

"Yes."

"Then you're a monster."

"*Max.*"

"*Tell him.*"

Argus vomited a dozen almost perfectly formed McNuggets at the vet's feet.

"How do they keep the glass clean?" Jacob had asked his father, three decades before.

Irv gave a puzzled look and said, "Windex?"

"I mean the *other* side. People can't walk in there. They'd ruin all the stuff on the ground."

"But if no one ever goes in, it stays clean."

"It doesn't," Jacob said. "Remember when we came back from Israel and everything was dirty? Even though no one had been there for three weeks? Remember how we wrote our names in Hebrew in the dust on the windows?"

"A house isn't a closed environment."

"Yes it is."

"Not as closed as a diorama."

"It is."

The only thing Irv loved more than teaching Jacob was being challenged by him: the intimations of one day being surpassed by his child.

"Maybe that's why they face that side of the glass away," he said, smiling, but hiding his fingers in his son's hair, which, given enough time, would grow to bury them.

"I don't think glass works like that."

"No?"

"You can't hide the other side."

"Do animals work like that?"

"What do you mean?"

"Look at the face of that bison."

"What?"

"Look closely."

NOT YET

Sam and Billie sat in the back of the bus, several empty rows behind the rest.

"I want to show you something," she said.

"OK."

"On your iPad."

"I left it at home."

"Seriously?"

"My mom made me," Sam said, wishing he'd invented a less infantilizing explanation.

"Did she read an op-ed, or something?"

"She wants me to be 'present' on the trip."

"What uses ten gallons of gas but doesn't move?"

"What?"

"A Buddhist monk."

Sam laughed, not getting it.

"You've seen the one where the alligator bites the electric eel?" she asked.

"Yeah, it's fucking nuts."

Billie took out the generic, lamer-than-an-adult-on-a-scooter tablet her parents got her for Christmas, and started typing. "Have you seen the weatherman with the hard-on?"

They watched together and laughed.

"The best part is when he says, 'We're looking at a hot one.'"

She loaded a new video and said, "Check out the syphilis on this guinea pig."

"I think that's a hamster."

"You're missing the genital sores for the trees."

"I hate to sound like my dad, but isn't it insane that we have access to this shit?"

"It's not insane. It's the world."

"Well, then isn't the world insane?"

"Definitionally it can't be. Insane is what other people are."

"I really, really like how you think."

"I really, really like that you would say that."

"I'm not saying it; it's true."

"And another thing I really, really like is that you can't bring yourself to say the l-word, because you're afraid I'll think you're saying something you aren't."

"Huh?"

"Really, really, *really* like."

He loved her.

She put the tablet in a coma and said, *"Emet hi hasheker hatov beyoter."*

"What's that?"

"Hebrew."

"You speak Hebrew?"

"As Franz Rosenzweig famously responded when asked if he was religious, 'Not yet.' But I figured one of us should learn a bit in honor of your bar mitzvah."

"Franz *who*? And wait, what's it mean?"

"Truth is the safest lie."

"Ah. Well: *Anata wa subete o rikai shite iru baai wa, gokai suru hitsuyo ga arimasu.*"

"What's that supposed to mean?"

"'If you understand everything, you must be misinformed.' Japanese, I think. It was the epigraph to Call of Duty: Black Ops."

"Yeah, I study Japanese on Thursdays. I just didn't understand your usage."

Sam wanted to show her the new synagogue he'd been working on for the past two weeks. He wondered if it was the best expression of the best of him, and he wondered if she'd like it.

The bus pulled up to the Washington Hilton—the hotel at which Sam's bar mitzvah party would theoretically take place in two weeks, if an apology could be wrested from him—and the kids disembarked and scattered.

Inside the lobby hung a large banner: WELCOME 2016 MODEL UNITED NATIONS. A few dozen suitcases and duffels were piled in the corner, nearly every one containing something it wasn't supposed to. While Mark struggled to do a head count, Sam pulled his mother aside.

"Don't make a big deal when you talk to everyone, OK?"

"A big deal about what?"

"About anything. Just don't make a big deal."

"You're worried that I'm going to embarrass you?"

"Yes. You made me say it."

"Sam, we're here to have a blast—"

"Don't say *blast*."

"—and the absolute last thing I'd want to be is a drag."

"Or *drag*."

Mark gave Julia a thumbs-up, and she addressed the group: "Can I have everyone's attention?"

Everyone withheld his attention.

"Yoo-hoo!"

"Or *yoo-hoo*," Sam whispered to no one.

Mark unleashed a baritone that made charm bracelets into wind chimes: "Mouths shut, eyes up here, *now!*"

The kids silenced.

"OK," Julia said. "Well, as you probably know, I'm Sam's mom. He told me not to make a big deal, so I'll keep this to the essentials. First, I want to let you all know how totally psyched I am to be here with you."

Sam closed his eyes, willing himself to unlearn object permanence.

"This is going to be interesting, challenging, and awesome."

Julia saw Sam's closed eyes but didn't know what she'd done.

"So . . . just a bit of housekeeping before passing out room keys, which I believe are cards and not keys, but we'll call them keys. You'll find that I'm a very laid-back person. But laid-backness is a two-way street. I know you guys are here to enjoy yourselves, but remember that you're also representatives of Georgetown Day School, not to mention our archipelago home, the Federated States of Micronesia!"

She waited for applause. Or anything. Billie filled the silence with a single clap, and then *she* was holding the hot potato of awkwardness.

Julia continued: "So, I'm sure it goes without saying, but recreational drug use isn't going to happen."

Sam lost muscle control of his neck, his head slumping forward.

"If you have a prescription for something, of course that's fine, so long as it isn't used recreationally or otherwise abused. Now, I realize most of you aren't even thirteen, but I also want to broach the subject of sexual relations."

Sam walked to the side. Billie followed him.

Mark saw what was happening and intervened: "I think what Mrs. Bloch is trying to say is, don't do anything you wouldn't want us to tell your parents about. Because we'll tell your parents about it, and then you'll be in deep shit. Got it?"

The students collectively affirmed.

"My mother is why Kurt Cobain killed himself," Sam whispered to Billie.

"Cut her some slack."

"Why?"

As Mark handed out key cards, he said, "Take your stuff to your rooms, unpack, and don't turn on the TV, and don't have anything to do with the minibar. We'll meet at my room, eleven twenty-four, at two o'clock. If you have a device, input it: eleven twenty-four at two. If you don't have a device, try your brain. Now, being smart and motivated young people, you will use this time to go over position papers so you're sharp for this afternoon's minisessions. You have my cell number in case, and only in case, something comes up. Know that I am omniscient. Which is to say, even without being physically present, I can see and hear everything. Goodbye."

The kids took their key cards and dispersed.

"And for you," Mark said, handing Julia her key card.

"Presidential Suite, I assume?"

"That's right. But president of Micronesia, I'm afraid."

"Thanks for saving me back there."

"Thanks for making me an icon of cool."

Julia laughed.

"Wanna grab a drink?" he asked.

"Really? A *drink* drink?"

"An imbibable relaxant. Yes."

"I should check in with Jacob's parents. They've got Benjy for the weekend."

"Cute."

"Until he comes back a latency-phased Meir Kahane."

"Huh?"

"He was a deranged right-wing—"

"You *need* need a *drink* drink."

And then, suddenly, there was nothing logistical to go over, no small talk to indulge in, only the inching shadow of their conversation at the bespoke hardware gallery, and all that Julia knew but wouldn't share.

"Go make your call."

"It will only be five minutes."

"Whatever it is, it is. Text me when you're ready and I'll meet you at the bar. We have plenty of time."

"It isn't too early for a drink?"

"In the millennium?"

"In the day."

"In your life?"

"In the *day*, Mark. You're already drunk on your bachelorhood."

"A drunk person wouldn't point out that a bachelor is someone who has never been married."

"Then you're drunk on your freedom."

"Don't you mean aloneness?"

"I was imagining what you might say."

"I'm drunk on my new sobriety."

She thought of herself as being unusually astute about the motivations of others, but she couldn't parse what he was doing. Flirting with someone he desired? Bolstering someone he felt sorry for? Innocently bantering? And what was *she* doing? Any guilt she might have felt about flirting was now so far beyond the horizon it might well have been right behind her. If anything, she wished Jacob were there to watch.

They used to have their own secret lines of communication, ways of smuggling messages: spelling in front of the young children; whispering in front of Isaac; writing notes to each other about a phone conversation in progress; hand and facial gestures organically developed over years, like when, in Rabbi Singer's office, Julia pressed two fingers to her brow and gently shook her head while flaring her nostrils, which meant: *Let it go.* They could find a way of reaching each other around any obstacle. But they needed the obstacle.

Her mind leaped: Jacob had forced Sam to listen to a podcast about messenger birds in World War I, and it captured Sam's imagination—he asked for a homing pigeon for his eleventh birthday. Delighting in the originality of the request and, as always, wanting not only to go to any length to provide for her children, but also to be seen as having gone to any length to provide for her children, she took him seriously.

"They make wonderful indoor pets," he promised. "There's a—"

"Indoor?"

"Yeah. They need a big cage, but—"

"What about Argus?"

"With a little conditioning—"

"Great word."

"*Mom*. With a little conditioning, they can totally be friends. And once—"

"What about pooping?"

"They wear pigeon pants. Basically a diaper. You change it every three hours."

"No burden there."

"I would do it."

"Your school day is longer than three hours."

"Mom, it would be *so fun*," he said, shaking his fists in the way that once inspired Jacob to wonder if he might have a sprinkle of Asperger's. "We could take it to the park, or to school, or Omi and Opi's, or wherever, attach a message to its collar, and it would just fly home."

"Can I ask what's fun about that?"

"Really?"

"In your own words."

"If it isn't obvious, I don't know how to explain it."

"And is it difficult to train them?"

"It's super easy. You basically just give them a great home, and they'll want to come back."

"What makes a home great?"

"It's spacious, in direct sunlight, and the chicken wire enclosing it is too tightly meshed for his head to fit through and get stuck."

"That does sound nice."

"And the bottom is lined with grassy sod, which is changed regularly. And he has a bath, which is cleaned regularly."

"Right."

"And lots of tasty treats, like endive, berries, buckwheat, flax, mung bean sprouts, vetch."

"Vetch?"

"I don't know, I read it."

"How spacious a cage are we talking about?"

"Really great would be six by nine."

"Six by nine *what?*"

"Feet. Six-foot width and length, nine-foot height."

"And where would we put such a spacious cage?"

"In my room."

"We'd have to raise the ceiling."

"Is that something we could do?"

"No."

"So it could be a bit less tall and still OK."

"And what if it doesn't like its home?"

"It will."

"But what if it doesn't?"

"Mom, it *will*, because I'm going to do all of the things you're supposed to do to create a great home that it loves."

"I'm just asking what if."

"*Mom.*"

"I can't ask a question?"

"I guess it doesn't come back. OK? It goes and keeps going."

It took only a week for Sam to forget that there were such things as homing pigeons in the world—he learned that there were such things as Nerf guns in the world—but Julia never forgot what he said: *It goes and keeps going.*

"Why not," she said to Mark, wishing there were a nearby surface to rap her knuckles against. "Let's have a *drink* drink."

"Only one?"

"You're right," she said, preening the underside of her wing before a flight that would reveal the comfort of her cage. "It's probably too late for that."

SOMEONE ELSE'S OTHER LIFE

It had been more than eight hours since they'd driven home in silence from the vet's office, four hundred ninety minutes of avoiding each other in the house. There were ingredients, but there was no will, so Jacob microwaved burritos. He arranged a dozen baby carrots that had no chance of being eaten, and a heaping dollop of hummus so Julia could see the amount missing from the container when she returned. He brought the food up to Max's room, knocked, and entered.

"I didn't say come in."

"I wasn't asking for permission. Just giving you time to take your finger out of your nose."

Max put his finger into his nose. Jacob put the plate on the desk.

"Wat'cha doin'?"

"I'cha not doin' nothin'," Max said, turning the iPad facedown.

"Seriously, what?"

"Seriously, nothing."

"What, dirty movies? Buying stuff on my credit card?"

"No."

"Looking up home euthanasia recipes?"

"Not at all funny."

"Then what?"

"Other Life."

"I didn't know you played that."

"No one plays it."

"Right. I didn't know you *did* it."

"I don't, really. Sam won't let me."

"But the cat's away."

"I guess so."

"I won't rat you out."

"Thanks."

"Get it? Cat's away? Rat you out?"

"Sure."

"What's the deal with that, anyway? It's a game?"

"It's not a game."

"No?"

"It's a community."

"Well, I don't know about *that*," Jacob said, unable to resist using his most belittling voice.

"No," Max said, "you don't."

"But isn't it more—to my understanding, anyway—more like a bunch of people who pay a monthly membership to gather and explore an, I don't know, *imagined landscape* together?"

"No, it's not like synagogue."

"Well played."

"Thanks for the food. See ya."

"Whatever it is," Jacob said, trying again, "it looks cool. From what I've been able to see. From a distance."

Max plugged his speech orifice with a burrito.

"Really," Jacob said, sidling up. "I'm curious. I know Sam plays—I mean, *does*—this all the time, and I want to see what it's all about."

"You wouldn't understand."

"Try me."

"You wouldn't understand."

"You realize I won a National Jewish Book Award at the age of twenty-four?"

Max turned the iPad faceup, swiped it bright, and said, "I'm currently recruiting work valences for a resonance promotion. Then I can barter for some psychic upholstery and—"

"*Psychic upholstery?*"

"I wonder if the winner of an *actual* National Book Award would need to ask."

"And that's you?" Jacob asked, touching an elflike creature.

"No. And don't touch the screen."

"Which one is you?"

"None of them is me."

"Which one is Sam?"

"None."

"Which is Sam's person?"

"His avatar?"

"OK."

"There. By the vending machine."

"What? The tan girl?"

"She's a Latina."

"Why is Sam a Latina?"

"Why are you a white man?"

"Because I didn't have a choice."

"Well, he did."

"Can I take her for a spin?"

Max hated the feeling of his father's hand on his shoulder. It was repulsive to him—an experience somewhere near the middle of the spectrum whose opposing poles were runny eggs and thirty thousand people demanding gratification when the Nationals Park Kiss Cam imprisoned his mom and him in the Jumbotron.

"No," he said, shaking his shoulder free, "you can't."

"What's the worst that could happen?"

"You could kill her."

"Obviously I won't. But even if I *did*, which I won't, can't you just put in some more quarters and continue?"

"It took Sam four months to develop her skill set, bounty of armaments, and psychic resources."

"It's taken me forty-two years."

"Which is why you shouldn't let anyone take your controls."

"Maxy . . ."

"*Max* is fine."

"Max. He who gave you life is begging you."

"No."

"I command you to let me partake in Sam's community."

Max let out a deep, dramatic sigh.

"Two minutes," he said. "And only aimless wandering."

"Aimless Wandering is my middle name."

With great reluctance, Max handed Jacob the iPad.

"To move, just slide your thumb in the direction you want to go. To pick something up—"

"My thumb is the squat one on the end, right?"

Max didn't respond.

"I'cha *kidding*, dude."

"Keep your eyes on the road."

When Jacob was a kid, games had one button. They were simple, and fun, and no one felt that they were in any way lacking. No one felt a need to crouch, to pivot, to switch weapons. You had a gun, you shot the bastards, you high-fived your friends. Jacob didn't want all these options—the more control available, the less control he felt.

"You kinda suck at this," Max said.

"Maybe it's this game that kinda sucks."

"It's not a game, and it made more money in one day than every book published in America that entire year combined."

"I'm sure that isn't true."

"I'm sure it is, because there was an article about it."

"Where?"

"The Arts section."

"The *Arts* section? Since when do you read the Arts section, and since when were video games art?"

"It's not a game."

"And even if it did make all that money," Jacob said, sliding his feet into the stirrups of his high horse, "so what? What is that even a measure of?"

"How much money it made."

"Which is a measure of what?"

"I don't know, how important it is?"

"There's a difference, I'm sure you realize, between *prevalence* and *importance*."

"I'm sure you realize that I don't even know what *prevalence* means."

"Kanye West is not more culturally important than—"

"Yes he is."

"—than Philip Roth."

"First of all, I've never even heard of that person. Second, Kanye might not be valuable to you, but he's definitely more important to the world."

Jacob remembered the period when Max was obsessed with relative values—*Would you rather have a handful of diamonds or a houseful of silver?* For a moment, which disappeared as it emerged, he saw the smaller Max.

"I guess we look at things differently," Jacob said.

"That's right," Max said. "I look at things correctly. You don't. That's a difference. How many people watch your TV show every week?"

"It's not my show."

"The show that you write for."

"That's not a simple question. There's people who watch it when it's first on, then people who watch other showings, and DVR—"

"A few million?"

"Four."

"Seventy million people play this game. And they had to *buy* it, not just turn on the TV when they didn't feel like spending time with their kids or making out with their wives."

"How old are you?"

"Basically eleven."

"When I was your age—"

Max pointed at the screen.

"Pay attention to what you're doing, Dad."

"Of course I am."

"Just don't—"

"Under control."

"Dad—"

"Yeah, yeah, yeahs," he said, then turned his attention from the iPad to Max. "They're a band."

"Dad!"

"You really inherited Mom's talent for worrying."

And then there was a sound Jacob had never heard before—a cross between a screeching tire and the dying animal it just ran over.

"Oh shit!" Max screamed.

"What?"

"Oh *shit!*"

"Hold on, is that blood mine?"

"It's *Sam's!* You killed him!"

"No I didn't. I just smelled some flowers."

"You just inhaled a Bouquet of Fatality!"

"Why would there be a *bouquet of fatality?*"

"So assholes have a stupid way to die!"

"*Easy*, Max. It was an honest mistake."

"Who cares if it was honest!"

"And with all due respect—"

"Oh shit, shit, shit!"

"—it's a game."

Jacob shouldn't have said that. Clearly he shouldn't have.

"With all due respect," Max said with scary composure, "fuck you."

"What did you just say?"

"I said"—Max was unable to look his father in the eye, but he had no trouble repeating himself—"*fuck you*."

"Don't you *ever* speak to me like that."

"Too bad I didn't inherit Mom's talent for eating shit."

"What's that supposed to mean?"

"Nothing."

"Didn't sound like nothing."

"Nothing, *OK*?"

"No, *not* OK. Mom does a lot of things, and eating shit is not one of them. And yes, I know you weren't speaking literally."

Had Max also heard them fighting? The broken glass? Or was he merely fishing, seeing what kind of response he might get? What kind of response did he want? And what was Jacob prepared to give?

Jacob stamped to the door, then turned back and said, "When you're ready to apologize, I'll be—"

"I'm *dead*," Max said. "The dead don't apologize."

"You aren't *dead*, Max. There are *actual* dead people in the world, and you aren't one of them. You are upset. Upset and dead are different states."

The phone rang—a reprieve. Jacob was expecting it to be Julia; when away, she always checked in before the kids went to bed.

"Hello?"

"Hi."

"Benjy?"

"Hey, Dad."

"Is everything OK?"

"Yeah."

"It's late."

"I'm in my pj's."

"Do you need anything, buddy?"

"No. Do you?"

"I'm fine."

"You just wanted to say hi before bed?"

"*You* called *me*."

"Actually, I wanted to talk to Max."

"Now? On the phone?"

"Yeah."

"Benjy wants to talk to you," Jacob said, handing the phone to Max.

"Could we have a little privacy?" Max asked.

The absurdity of it, the agony and beauty of it, almost brought Jacob to his knees: these two independent consciousnesses, neither of which existed ten and a half years ago, and existed only because of him, could now not only operate free of him (that much he'd known for a long time), but demand freedom.

Jacob picked up the iPad and left his offspring to talk. While he fiddled, he accidentally maximized the window behind Other Life. It was a discussion board, with the heading "Can You Humanely Euthanize a Dog at Home?" The first comment his eyes fell upon read: "I had the same problem, but with a grown dog. It's so sad. My mum took Charlie to our friend, a farmer down the way, who said he would be able to shoot him. It was much easier for us. He took him for a walk, talked to him, and shot him while they were walking."

THE ARTIFICIAL EMERGENCY

Instead of calling to check on Benjy, who was obviously fine, Julia fussed with her hair, sucked in her cheeks, tugged down her shirt, scrutinized her makeup, pressed her belly, squinted. She texted Mark, if only to create a hard stop to her self-loathing: *confirmed kid is alive. ready whenever.* By the time she got to the hotel bar, he was already at a table.

"Spacious accommodations?" he asked as she took the seat across from him.

"A room of my own? An *oven* would feel spacious."

"Sounds like you were born seventy-five years too late." And then, with a faux wince: "Too soon?"

"Let's see, my father-in-law would say it's absolutely fine, so long as the person making the joke doesn't have a cell of goyish blood. Then Jacob would disagree. Then they'd switch positions and fight with twice the energy."

The waiter approached.

"A couple of glasses of white?" Mark suggested.

"Sounds great," Julia said. "Are you going to have one, too?"

Mark laughed and held up two fingers.

"How is Irv? Seems like he's stirred up a lot of shit."

"He's a human plunger. But it beats being ignored."

"Being universally reviled?"

"Talking about him is exactly what he'd want us to be doing right now. Let's not give him the satisfaction."

"Moving along."

"So how's it going?"

"What? The divorce?"

"The divorce, your rediscovered interior monologue, the whole thing."

"It's a process."

"Isn't that how Cheney described torture?"

"You know that old joke: 'Why are divorces so expensive?'"

"Why?"

"Because they're worth it."

"I thought that's what they said about chemo."

"Well, both make you bald," he said, holding back his hair.

"You aren't bald."

"Please, God, not *distinguished*."

"Not even distinguished."

"Just taller than my hair."

"You're all the same: endlessly experimenting with facial hair configurations, obsessed with thinning hair where there isn't any. And yet indifferent to the paunch spilling over your belt."

"I am a very bald man. But that's not the point. The point is, divorce is profoundly expensive—emotionally, logistically, financially—and it's worth it. But just."

"Just?"

"It's no landslide. It just barely ekes it out."

"But you eke it out with your life, right?"

"Better to get out of the building with burns over ninety percent of your body than perish inside. But best to have left before the fire."

"Yeah, but it's cold outside."

"Where's your burning house? Nunavut?"

"I always imagine house fires in winter."

"And you?" Mark asked. "What's the news on Newark Street?"

"You're not the only one in a process."

"What's going on?"

"Nothing," she said, unfolding the napkin.

"Nunavut?"

"What?"

"You'll be sharing none of it?"

"It's truly nothing," she said, refolding it.

"So, fine."

"I shouldn't talk about it."

"You probably shouldn't."

"But even though we haven't started drinking, I've got a psychosomatic buzz."

"This is going to be a bomb, isn't it?"

"I can trust you, right?"

"I suppose it depends."

"Seriously?"

"Only a trustworthy person would admit to his unreliability."

"Forget it."

"I cheated on my taxes last year, OK? Badly. I deducted an office I don't even have. Now you can blackmail me, if it comes to that."

"Why would you cheat on your taxes?"

"Because it's an honor to contribute to our functioning society, but only to a point. Because I'm a schmuck. Because my accountant is a schmuck and told me I could. I don't know why."

"The other day I was at home and heard a buzzing. There was a cell phone on the floor."

"Oh shit."

"What?"

"There is not a single story about a cell phone that ends well."

"I opened it up and there were some pretty sexually explicit messages."

"Texts, or images?"

"Does it make a difference?"

"An image is what it is. A text could be anything."

"Licking cum out of assholes. That kind of stuff."

"Image?"

"Words," Julia said. "But if you ask for the context, I'm going to call the IRS."

The drinks arrived, and the waitress scurried off. Julia wondered how much, if anything, she had heard, what she might tell the hostess, what young, unencumbered women might have a laugh that night at the expense of the Bloch family.

"I confronted Jacob about it, and he said it was just talk. Just some seriously overheated flirting."

"Overheated? Licking cum out of assholes is Dresden."

"It's not good."

"And who was at the other end of them?"

"A director he works with."

"Not Scorsese . . ."

"*That's* too soon."

"Seriously, Julia, I am so very sorry to hear this. And shocked."

"Maybe it's for the best. Like you said, the door has to open to light up the dark room."

"I didn't say that."

"Didn't you?"

"Do you believe him?"

"In what sense?"

"That it was just words."

"I do."

"And does the distinction matter to you?"

"Between talking and doing? Sure it matters."

"How much does it matter?"

"I don't know."

"He cheated on you, Julia."

"He didn't *cheat* on me."

"Too big a word for having had sex with another woman?"

"He didn't have sex with another woman."

"Of course he did. And even if he didn't, he did. And you know it."

"I'm not excusing, or minimizing, what he did. But there's a difference."

"Writing to another woman like that is a betrayal, no hairs to split. I'm sorry, but I can't sit here and allow you to think you don't deserve better."

"It was only words."

"And if you'd written those 'only words'? How do you think he'd have reacted?"

"If he knew that we were having this drink, he'd have a grand mal seizure."

"Why?"

"Because that's how insecure he is."

"In a marriage with three children?"

"He's the fourth."

"I don't get it."

"What?"

"If he were only pathologically insecure, OK. He is who he is. And if he'd only cheated, I suppose I can see the way back from that. But the combination? How can you accept it?"

"Because of the boys. Because I'm forty-three years old. Because I have almost twenty years of history with him, almost all of which is good history. Because regardless of the stupidity or evil of his mistake, he's a fundamentally good person. He is. Because I've never sexted with anyone, but I've done my share of flirting and fantasizing. Because I often haven't been a good wife, often on purpose. Because I'm weak."

"Only the weakness is persuasive."

A thought walked in, a memory: checking the boys for ticks on the porch of the rental in Connecticut. They passed the kids back and forth—looking in armpits, through the hair, between toes—she and Jacob double-checking each other's work, always finding ticks the other missed. She was good at removing them in their entirety, and he was good at distracting the boys with funny impressions of their mother shopping in the super-market. Why that memory right then?

"What do you fantasize about?" Mark asked.

"What?"

"You said you've done your share of fantasizing. About what?"

"I don't know," she said, taking a drink. "I was just talking."

"I know. And I'm just asking. What do you fantasize about?"

"That's not of your business."

"*Not* of my business?"

"*None.*"

"Drunk on your weakness?"

"I don't find you cute."

"Of course not."

"Or charming. Despite all of the effort."

"It's effortless to be this charmless."

"Or sexy."

Mark took a long drink, draining the remaining half of his glass, then said, "Leave him."

"I'm not going to *leave* him."

"Why not?"

"Because marriage is the thing you don't give up on."

"No, life is."

"And because I'm not you."

"No, but you're *you.*"

"There is not a part of me that wishes I were alone."

But as the words entered the world, she knew they were false. She thought about her one-bedroom dream homes, the subconscious blueprints for her departure. They predated the sexting, by years.

"And I'm not going to destroy my family," she added, at once a non sequitur and the logical conclusion to the line of thought.

"By fixing your family?"

"By ending it."

Just then, at the best, or worst, possible moment, Billie came running up, giddy or asthmatic.

"I'm sorry to interrupt—"

"Is everything OK?"

"Micronesia has a n—"

"Slow down."

"Micronesia has a nu—"

"Breathe."

She reached for one of the glasses and took a gulp.

"That's not water," she said, her hand to her chest.

"It's chardonnay."

"I just broke the law."

"We'll testify to your character," Mark said.

"Micronesia has a nuclear weapon!"

"What?"

"Last year Russia invaded Mongolia. The year before was bird flu. Usually they wait until the second afternoon, but. We have a nuke! Isn't that cool! So lucky!"

"What do you mean we have a nuke?" Mark asked.

"We need to convene the delegation."

"What?"

"Pay for your drinks and keep up with me."

Mark put some cash on the table and the three race-walked toward the elevators.

"The program facilitators released a statement that a weapons dealer was caught attempting to smuggle an armed suitcase bomb through Yap Airport."

"Yap Airport?"

"Yeah, I don't know, that's what it's called."

"Why through Micronesia?" Mark asked.

"*Precisely,*" Billie said, although not one of the three knew even approximately what that meant. "We've already started to get offers from Pakistan, Iran, and, weirdly, Luxembourg."

"Offers?" Mark asked.

"They want us to sell them the bomb." And then, to Julia: "You understand, right?"

Julia gave an uncertain nod.

"So explain it to him later. It's a whole new ball game!"

"Let's round up the kids," Julia said to Mark.

"I'll get the ones on eleven, you get the ones on twelve. Meet in your room?"

"Why mine?"

"Fine, mine."

"No, mine is fine, I just—"

"Mark's room," Billie said.

Mark got on the elevator. Billie held Julia back for a moment.

"Is everything OK?" Billie asked when the elevator doors closed.

"It's confusing to have a nuclear weapon."

"I meant you."

"What about me?"

"Are you OK?"

"Why do you ask?"

"You look like you're about to cry."

"Me? No."

"Oh, OK."

"I don't think I am?"

But maybe she was. Maybe the artificial emergency released trapped feelings about the real emergency. There was a trauma center in her brain—she had no Dr. Silvers to explain that to her, but she had the Internet. The most unexpected situations would set it off, and then all thoughts and perception rushed toward it. At the center was Sam's injury. And at the center of that—the vortex into which all thoughts and perceptions were pulled—was the moment when Jacob carried him into the house, saying, "Something happened," and she saw more blood than there was but couldn't hear Sam's screaming, and for a moment, no longer than a moment, she lost control. For a moment she was untethered from rationality, from reality, from herself. The soul departs the body at the moment of death, but there is a yet more complete abandoning: *everything* departed her body at the moment she saw her child's flowing blood.

Jacob looked at her, sternly, hard-hearted, godlike, and made each word a sentence: "Get. Yourself. Together. *Now*." The sum of everything she hated him for would never surpass her love for him in that moment.

He put Sam in her arms and said, "We'll call Dr. Kaisen on the way to the emergency room."

Sam looked at Julia with a prehuman terror and screamed, "Why did that happen? Why did that happen?" And pleaded, "It's funny. It's funny, right?"

She gripped Sam's eyes with her eyes, held them hard, and didn't say, "It will be OK," and didn't say nothing. She said, "I love you, and I'm here."

The sum of everything she hated herself for would never surpass her knowledge that in the most important moment of her child's life, she'd been a good mother.

And then, as quickly as it had seized control, Julia's trauma center relented. Maybe it was tired. Maybe it was merciful. Maybe she had looked away and looked back, and remembered that she was in the world. But how had the last thirty minutes passed? Had she taken the elevator or the stairs? Had she knocked on the door of Mark's room or was it open?

The debate was under way and roiling. Did anyone notice her absence? Her presence?

"A stolen nuclear weapon is not an occasion for bartering," Billie said. "We want this thing disarmed, pronto, period."

"*We* didn't steal it. But I totally agree with what you just said."

"We should just bury it."

"Can't we turn it into energy somehow?"

"We should give it to the Israelis," said a boy in a yarmulke.

"Screw that, let's *bury* it in Israel."

"If I can butt in for just a moment," Mark said. "My role here isn't to suggest conclusions but to help you ask provocative questions, so try this one on for size: Is it possible that there's an important option we haven't yet entertained? What if we kept the bomb?"

"*Kept the bomb?*" Julia said, making her presence unignorable. "No, we can't *keep the bomb.*"

"Why not?" Mark asked.

"Because we're responsible people."

"Let's just play this out."

"*Play* is *not* the right word for a discussion about a nuclear bomb."

"Let him talk," Sam said.

Mark talked: "Maybe this is a chance to finally control our destiny? For most of our history, we've been at the mercy of others: overrun by the Portuguese and Spanish trading goliaths, sold to Germany, conquered by Japan and the United States . . ."

"I don't suppose anyone brought an extremely small violin?" Julia said to the kids. Nobody understood the joke.

Mark lowered his volume, asserting calm: "I'm just saying, we have never been fully self-reliant."

"There hasn't been a fully self-reliant country in the history of the world," Julia said.

"Oh, you just got *served*," a boy said to Mark.

"Iceland is fully self-reliant," Mark said.

"Oh, *you* just got served!" the same boy said to Julia.

"No one's getting served," Mark said. "We're thinking our way through a very complicated issue."

"Iceland is a Hooverville," Julia said.

"Look," Mark said, "if I'm being an idiot, the only thing my blathering will have cost us is three minutes."

"I just got a text from Liechtenstein," Billie said, holding her phone as if it were the torch and she were the Statue of Liberty. "They're offering us a deal."

"Now, clearly we have no nuclear program of any kind—"

"Liechtenstein is a country?"

"—and wouldn't have the means or motives to acquire a nuclear weapon on the black market."

"Jamaica wants in," Billie said, holding up another text. "They're offering three hundred billion dollars."

"They know we're talking about a *bomb*, right? Not a nuclear *bong*? Can I get a hallelujah!"

"Xenophobic," someone muttered.

"And yet," Mark went on, "we suddenly find ourselves nuclear, with the ability, should we choose to exercise it, of entering the league of functionally autonomous nations, nations capable of dictating their own terms, nations that aren't subservient to other nations, or to the predicaments of their histories."

"Right," Julia said, her famous composure now in witness protection. "So we have some gripes, so life hasn't been a trip to Epcot, and hey hey, as it turns out, we just click our uranium heels and *boom*, life's bouncer lets us into the greatest of all parties."

"That's not what he was suggesting," Sam said.

"He's an unclear suggester." And then, turning to Mark: "You're an un-cle-ar bomb, that's what you are."

"I was *trying* to suggest that we explore, if only to dismiss, the potential upsides of having a bomb."

"Let's bomb someone!" someone said.

"Let's!" Julia echoed. "Who? Or does it even matter?"

"Of course it matters," Billie said, puzzled and upset by Julia's behavior.

"Mexico?" a girl asked.

"Iran, obviously," Yarmulke Boy said.

"*Maybe*," Julia said, "we should bomb some war-torn, famine-ravaged African country where orphans are so skinny they're fat?"

That killed the buzz.

"Why would we do that?" Billie asked.

"Because we can," Julia said.

"*Jesus*, Mom."

"Don't '*Jesus*, Mom' me."

"We're not going to bomb anyone," Mark said.

"But you see, we *are*," Julia said. "That's how the story always ends. You're either a country that *never* bombs, or you're a country that is open to bombing. And once you make yourself open to bombing, you will bomb."

"That doesn't make any sense, Julia."

"Only because you're a man, Mark."

The kids looked at one another. A few giggled nervously, Sam not among them.

"OK," Mark said, calling and raising Julia, "so here's another idea: let's bomb ourselves."

"Why?" Billie asked, confused to the point of anguish.

"Because Julia—"

"Mrs. Bloch."

"—would rather die than save her life. So why draw it out?"

"See what you did?" Sam said to his mother.

"Jamaica went up to four hundred billion," Billie said, holding up her phone.

Someone said: "Yah, mon."

Someone said: "Jamaica doesn't have four *hundred* dollars."

Someone said: "We should be asking for real money. The kind we can take home and buy real stuff with."

Sam pulled his mother into the hallway by her wrist, as she'd many times pulled him.

"What are you *doing*?" he said.

"What am *I* doing?"

"I *told* Dad I didn't want you to come on this trip, and you made a big deal when I said don't make a big deal, and you're more worried about coming off as a cool mom than actually being a good mom."

"Excuse me?"

"You make everything about *you*. Everything is always *you*."

"I have no idea what you're talking about, and neither do you."

"You're making me apologize for words I didn't write, so I can have a bar mitzvah that only you want me to have. You not only check my online search history, you try to hide the fact that you don't trust me. And do you think I think the pencils on my desk sharpen themselves?"

"I take care of you, Sam. Believe me, it brings me no pleasure to be shamed in front of the rabbi, or to organize your pigsty desk."

"You're a *nag*. And it *does* bring you pleasure. The only thing that makes you happy is controlling every last tiny detail of our lives, because you have no control over your own."

"Where'd you learn that word?"

"What word?"

"*Nag*."

"Everyone knows that word."

"It's not a kid word."

"I'm not a kid."

"You're *my* kid."

"It's annoying enough when you treat your kids like kids, but Dad—"

"Be careful, Sam."

"He says you can't help yourself, but I don't see why that makes any difference.".

"Be *careful*."

"Or what? I'll realize there's Internet porn, or break a pencil tip and die?"

"Stop *now*."

"Or I'll accidentally say something that everybody already knows?"

"And what would that be?"

"Be *careful*, Mom."

"What does everybody know?"

"Nothing."

"You don't know as much as you think you do."

"That we're all just scared of you. We're unhappy because we can't live our lives, because you're a nag and we're scared of you."

"We?"

Billie came into the hallway and approached Sam.

"Are you OK?"

"Go away, Billie."

"What did I do?"

"You didn't do anything," Julia said.

Sam continued to lay into his mother, but now through Billie: "Will you please just mind your own business for three consecutive seconds?"

"Did I say something?" she asked Julia.

"You aren't wanted," Sam told her. "Go away."

"Sam?"

Tears brimming, Sam scurried off. Julia stayed there, an ice sculpture of frozen tears.

"It's kind of funny, right?" Billie said, her eyes overflowing with the tears neither mother nor son could release.

Julia thought about her injured baby pleading, *It's funny. It's funny.*

"What's funny?"

"Babies kick you from the inside, and then they come out and kick you some more."

"It's been my experience," Julia said, her hand moving to her belly.

"I read it in one of my parents' parenting books."

"Why on earth do you read those?"

"To try to understand them."

SOMEONE ELSE'S OTHER DEATH

Jacob went online and didn't scan for breaking news in the worlds of real estate porn, design porn, or porn, and didn't scan for the good fortune of people he envied and would have preferred dead, and didn't spend a soothing half hour in Bob Ross's happy little womb. He found the tech support number for Other Life. No great surprise, he had to navigate his way through an automated service—a sedentary Theseus with only a phone cord.

"Other Life . . . iPad . . . I don't know . . . I really don't know . . . I don't know . . . Help . . . Help . . ."

After a few minutes of saying "I don't know" and "Help" like an alien impersonating a human, he was connected to someone with an almost impenetrable accent who did everything possible to conceal the fact that he was an Indian impersonating an American.

"Yes, hi, my name is Jacob Bloch and I'm calling on behalf of my son. We had an accident with his avatar . . ."

"Good evening, Mr. Bloch. I see that you are calling from Washington, D.C. Are you enjoying the unseasonably nice weather this late evening?"

"No." Jacob had no patience to lose, but being asked to pretend that the phone call wasn't international found him some nastiness.

"I'm sorry, Mr. Bloch. Good evening. My name is John Williams."

"No kidding! I loved what you did with *Schindler's List*."

"Thank you, sir."

"*Jurassic World*, not as much."

"How can I assist you tonight?"

"As I said, there was an accident with my son's avatar."

"What kind of accident?"

"I accidentally sniffed a Bouquet of Fatalism."

"Fatality?"

"Whatever. I sniffed it."

"And can I ask why would you do that?"

"I don't know. Why does anyone want to smell anything?"

"Yes, but a Bouquet of Fatality offers instant death."

"Right, no, I get that—I get that *now*. But I was new to the game."

"It is not a game."

"Fine. Can we just fix this?"

"Were you trying to kill yourself, Mr. Bloch?"

"Of course not. And it's not me. It's my son."

"Your son sniffed it?"

"I sniffed it on my son's behalf."

"Yes, I see."

"Isn't there some kind of Other Life mulligan, or something?"

"*Mulligan*, sir?"

"Do-over."

"If there were no consequences, it would only be a game."

"I'm a writer, so I really do understand the gravity of mortality, but—"

"You can reincarnate, but without any of your psychic upholstery. So it will be as if you are beginning again."

"So what do you suggest I do?"

"You could reacquire psychic upholstery on your son's behalf."

"But I don't know how to play."

"It's not play."

"I don't know how to *do* it."

"Simply graze for low-hanging resilience fruit."

"Graze *what*?"

"Apothecary vineyards."

"I wouldn't know how."

"It's extremely time-consuming, but not difficult."

"How time-consuming are we talking about?"

"Assuming you became proficient fairly quickly, I would estimate six months."

"Only six months? Well, that's fantastic news, because I was sitting here worrying you were talking about something *really* time-consuming. But this is great, because I don't have time to get the manifest-destined mole on my breast looked at, but I can certainly spend a thousand hours clamping shut my carpal tunnels while committing brain cell genocide as I scour apothecary vineyards for low-hanging resilience fruit, whatever the fuck that means."

"Or you could purchase a complete rebirth."

"A what?"

"It is possible to revert your avatar's profile to a designated moment in time. In your case, to immediately before sniffing the Bouquet of Fatality."

"Why the hell didn't you lead with that?"

"Some people find the option offensive."

"Offensive?"

"Some believe that it undermines the spirit of Other Life."

"Well, I doubt that many fathers in my position would feel that way. This is something we can do right now? Over the phone?"

"Yes, I can process your payment and remotely initiate the complete rebirth."

"Well, this is just the best news I've heard . . . maybe ever. Thank you. Thank you. And really, I'm sorry about being such an asshole earlier. A lot is on the line here."

"Yes, I understand, Mr. Bloch."

"Call me Jacob."

"Thank you, Jacob. I will have to obtain some information about the avatar, and the reversion date and time. But to confirm, you are purchasing the twelve-hundred-dollar complete rebirth."

"Sorry, did you say twelve hundred dollars?"

"Yes."

"As in: a one, followed by a two, followed by consecutive zeroes, with no decimal?"

"Plus tax. Yes."

"How much did the game cost?"

"It is not a game."

"Cut the shit, Williams."

"Other Life is free."

"Is this some kind of joke? Twelve hundred dollars?"

"It is not a joke, Jacob."

"You realize we live in a world with starving children and cleft pal-ates, right?"

"I do realize that."

"And you still think it's ethical to charge twelve hundred dollars to correct an accident in a video game?"

"It is not a game, sir."

"Giving twelve hundred to you requires me making twenty-four hun-dred. You know this, right?"

"I do not set the prices, sir."

"Is anyone *not* the messenger?"

"Would you like to process a complete rebirth, or has the price made this option unappealing?"

"Unappealing? *Leukemia* is unappealing. This is fucking *criminal*. And you should be ashamed."

"I take it that you no longer want to purchase a complete rebirth."

"Take it as a class-action suit I'm going to bring against your depraved company. I know people that your people should be very afraid of. I know serious lawyers who would do this for me as a favor. And I'm going to write about this for *The Washington Post*—Style section, or maybe Outlook—and they'll publish it, you'll see, and then you'll be sorry. You have fucked with the wrong guy!"

Jacob smelled Argus shit, but then he often smelled Argus shit when raging.

"Before ending this call, Jacob, would you say that I have responded to your needs in a satisfactory manner?"

Mr. Bloch hung up the phone, then growled, "Fuck my needs."

He took a breath that he hated, picked the phone back up, but didn't dial any number.

"Help . . . ," he said to no one. "Help . . ."

A COMPLETE REBIRTH

Julia was sitting on the edge of her bed. The TV was set to an advertisement for the hotel in which she was already captive. The lithograph on the wall was in an edition of five thousand—five thousand perfectly identical, perfectly unique, utterly corny snowflakes. She started to dial Jacob. She considered looking for Sam. There were always too many things to do when she had no time. But in need of a way to fill minutes, she never knew how.

The wilderness was interrupted by a knock.

"Thank you for opening the door," Mark said when it was only cracked.

"The peephole was smudgy," Julia said, opening it farther.

"I was out of line."

"You were off the map."

"I'm trying to apologize here."

"You found your interior monologue, and it told you you were being an asshole?"

"That's exactly what happened."

"Well, allow my exterior monologue to echo the sentiment."

"Duly noted."

"Now isn't a good time."

"I know."

"I just had a terrible fight with Sam."

"I know."

"You know everything."

"I wasn't lying when I told the kids I'm omniscient."

Julia rubbed her temple and turned, creating a space for Mark to enter.

"Whenever Sam would cry as a baby, we'd say, 'I know, I know,' and give him his pacifier. So he started calling it his 'I-know.' Your omniscience just reminded me of that. I haven't thought about it for years." And with a disbelieving shake of the head: "Was that even this life?"

"Same life, different person."

With a voice like a window that knows it's about to be broken, she said, "I'm a good mother, Mark."

"You are. I know."

"I'm a really good mother. It's not just that I try hard. I'm *good*."

The distance between them closed by a step, and Mark said, "You're a good wife, and good mother, and good friend."

"I try so hard."

When Jacob brought Argus home, Julia felt betrayed—she showed fury to Jacob, and delight to the boys. And yet it was she who actually bothered to read a book on dog training and care. Most of it was intuitively obvious, but one thing that struck her was the advice that one shouldn't say no to a dog, as it would process the *no* as an existential assessment—a negation of the animal's worth. It would hear *no* as its name: "You are No." Instead, you should make a little clicking sound, or say, "Uh-uh," or clap your hands. How anyone could know this much about a dog's mental life, or why it would be so much better to be named "Uh-uh," was beyond Julia, but something about it seemed plausible, even significant.

Julia needed an existential assessment of goodness. She needed to be renamed, to hear: "You are Good."

Mark put his hand on her cheek.

She took a half step back.

"What are you doing?"

"I'm sorry. Did that feel wrong?"

"Of course it did. You *know* Jacob."

"Yes."

"And you know my kids."

"I do."

"And you know that I'm going through something very difficult. And you know that Sam and I had a terrible fight."

"Yes."

"And your response is to try to kiss me?"

"I didn't try to kiss you."

Could she have misinterpreted? She couldn't have. But neither could she prove that he was trying to kiss her. Which made her feel small enough to go hide in the closet by walking under its closed door.

"OK, so what *were* you trying to do?"

"I wasn't trying to do anything. You obviously needed comforting, and reaching for you felt natural."

"Natural to *you*."

"I'm sorry."

"And I don't need comforting."

"I thought it would be welcomed. And everyone needs comforting."

"You thought touching my face would be welcomed?"

"I did. The way you angled your body to suggest I enter the room. How you looked at me. When you said, 'I'm good,' and took a step closer."

Had she done that? She remembered the moment, but felt certain that *he* had stepped toward *her*.

"Boy, was I asking for it."

Was it possible she'd been too hard on Jacob, simply because he'd been first to express what she knew she'd been first to feel? There was no balance to be found in cruelty—only in cheating on him, which she wasn't going to do.

"I'm not full of shit, Julia. You think I am—"

"I do."

"—but I'm not. I'm sorry if I put you in an uncomfortable position. That's not at all what I had in mind."

"You're lonely, and I look like a Band-Aid."

"I'm not lonely, and you don't—"

"*You're* the one who needed comforting."

"We both did. We both do."

"You need to leave."

"OK."

"So why aren't you going?"

"Because I believe you don't want me to go."

"How could I prove it?"

"You could push me."

"I'm not going to push you, Mark."

"Why do you think you just used my name?"

"Because it's yours."

"What were you emphasizing? You didn't use my name when telling me to go. Only when telling me what you weren't going to do."

"Jesus. Just go, Mark."

"OK," he said, and turned for the door.

She didn't know what the emergency was, only that the trauma center of her brain was consuming everything. At the margin, still safe, remained the strange joy of finding and removing ticks in Connecticut. But the trauma smelled the pleasure, and attacked it. At the end of every night, she sat in a dry bathtub and checked herself, because if she didn't, no one would.

"No, wait," Julia said. Mark turned back to face her. "I did need comforting."

"Still, I—"

"I'm not finished. I did need comforting, and I'm sure I communicated as much, even if I didn't intend to, or realize it."

"Thank you for telling me that. And while we're in the business of full disclosure: I stepped toward you."

"You lied to me."

"No, I just couldn't find a way to—"

"You lied to me, and made me question myself."

"I couldn't find a way—"

"I knew I was right." She paused. A small memory displaced a small laugh: "Kisses. I just remembered what Sam used to call kisses."

"What?"

"He had a few different names for them, depending on the situation. A 'make-it-better' was a kiss given in response to an injury. A 'sheyna boychick' was a kiss from his great-grandfather. A 'that-face' was from his grandmother. A 'you' was one of those spontaneous, I-need-to-kiss-you-right-now kisses. I guess we'd always say 'You' when going in for one of those."

"Kids are wonderful."

"Before they know anything, they really are."

Mark folded his arms and said, "So, here's the thing, Julia—"

"Uh-oh, emphasis."

"I *was* trying to kiss you."

"You were?" She felt not only relieved of the earlier embarrassment, but, for the first time in her selectively edited memory, wanted.

"Truth be told."

"Why were you trying to kiss me?"

"*Why?*"

"To *make-it-better* me?"

"To *you* you."

"I see."

"So you've chosen not to close your eyes?"

"What?"

"You see."

She stepped toward him, open-eyed, and asked, "Are things about to become bad?"

"No."

She took another half step toward him, and asked, "You promise?"

"No."

There was no more distance to cross.

She asked: "What can you promise?"

He promised: "Things are about to be different."

III

USES OF A JEWISH FIST

HOLDING A PEN,
PUNCHING, SELF-LOVE

"This is a *joke*?" Irv asked as they drove to Washington National—the Blochs would sooner renounce air travel than refer to it as Reagan National. NPR was on, because Irv sought confrontations with what he loathed, and to his extreme revulsion there had been a balanced segment on new settlement construction in the West Bank. Irv loathed NPR. It was not only the wretched politics, but the flamboyantly precious, out-of-no-closet sissiness, the wide-eyed wonder coming from the you-wouldn't-hit-a-guy-with-glasses voices. (And all of them—men, women, young and old—seem to share the same voice, passing it from one throat to another as necessary.) The virtues of "listener-supported radio" don't alter the fact that no one with self-respect uses the word *satchel*, much less an actual satchel, and anyway, how many subscriptions to *The New Yorker* does a person need?

"Well, now I'll have an answer," Irv said, with a self-satisfied nod that resembled davening or Parkinson's.

"To what?" Jacob asked, unable to swim past the bait.

"When someone asks me what was the most factually erroneous, morally repugnant, and also just boring radio segment I've ever heard."

Irv's knee-jerk response triggered a reflex in Jacob's brain's knee, and within a few exchanges they were rhetorical Russian wedding dancers—arms crossed, kicking at everything but anything.

"And anyway," Jacob said, feeling that they'd taken things far enough, "it was a self-described *opinion piece*."

"Well, that stupid idiot's opinion is *wrong*—"

Without looking up from his iPad, Max defended National Public Radio—or semantics, in any case—from the backseat: "Opinions can't be wrong."

"So here's why that idiot's opinion is idiotic . . ." Irv ticked off each "because" on the fingers of his left hand: "Because only an anti-Semite can be *provoked to anti-Semitism*—a hideous phrase; because the mere *suggestion* of a willingness to talk to these freaks would just be throwing Manischewitz on an oil fire; because—not for nothing—*their* hospitals are filled with rockets aimed at *our* hospitals, which are filled with *them*; because at the end of the day, *we* love kung pao chicken and *they* love death; because—and this really should have been my first point—the simple and undeniable fact is . . . we're *right!*"

"Jesus, watch your lane!"

Irv removed his other hand—balancing the wheel on his knees—to acquire another rhetorical finger: "And because anyway, why should *our* yarmulkes bunch over a troop of Goy Scouts earning protest patches in front of the Berkeley Co-op, or simians in keffiyehs doing a little urban stone-skipping in Gaza so-called City?"

"At least *one* hand on the wheel, Dad."

"I'm getting in an accident?"

"And find a better word than *simians*."

Irv turned to face his grandson while continuing to drive with his knees: "You gotta hear this. You put a million monkeys in front of a million typewriters and you get *Hamlet*. Two billion in front of two billion and you get—"

"Watch the *road!*"

"The Koran. Funny, right?"

"Racist," Max muttered.

"Arabs aren't a *race*, bubeleh. They're an *ethnicity*."

"What's a typewriter?"

"Let me also say this," Irv said, turning to Jacob and pointing his spare index finger while continuing to hold up the other six fingers. "People in glass houses shouldn't throw stones, but people with no homeland *really* shouldn't. Because when those stones of theirs start breaking Chagall windows, don't expect to see us on our knees with a dustpan. Just because we're smarter than those lunatics doesn't mean they have a monopoly on insanity. The Arabs have to understand that *we've* got some stones, too, but *our* slingshot's in Dimona, and the finger on the button is connected to an arm with a string of numbers tattooed on it!"

"You're finished?" Jacob asked.

"With what?"

"If I can host you back on the Blue Planet for just a second, I was thinking we should take Tamir around to see Isaac on the way back."

"Why?"

"Because he's obviously depressed about the move and—"

"If he were capable of depression, he would have killed himself seventy years ago."

"Fucking shitcock!" Max said, shaking his iPad like an Etch A Sketch.

"He's not *depressed*," Irv said. "He's *old*. Age presents like depression, but isn't."

"Sorry," Jacob said, "I forgot: no one is depressed."

"No, *I'm* sorry, I forgot: *everyone* is depressed."

"I assume that's a dig at my therapy?"

"What belt are you up to, anyway? Brown? Black? And you win when it's around your neck?"

Jacob was weighing whether to give it back or let it go. Dr. Silvers would call that binary thinking, but Dr. Silvers's reliance on the binary critique was, itself, binary. And this was too demanding a morning to become nuanced with his anvil of a father. So, as always, he let it go. Or rather, he absorbed it.

"It's a tough change for him," Jacob said. "It's ultimate. I'm just saying we should be sensitive—"

"He's a human callus."

"He's an internal bleeder."

Max pointed to the light: "Green is for go."

But instead of driving, Irv turned to press the point from which he'd strayed: "Here's the deal: the world population of Jews falls within the margin of error of the Chinese census, and everyone hates us." Ignoring the honking coming from behind him, he continued: "Europe . . . now, *there's* a Jew-hating continent. The French, those spineless vaginas, would shed *no* tears of sadness over our disappearance."

"What are you talking about? Remember what the French prime minister said after the attack on the kosher market? 'Every Jew who leaves France is a piece of France that is gone.' Or something like that."

"Bull-*merde*. You know he had a bottle of Château Sang de Juif 1942 airing out backstage to toast France's missing piece. The English, the Spanish, the Italians. These people live to make us die." He stuck his head out the window and hollered at the honking driver: "I'm an *asshole*, asshole! I'm not deaf!" And then back to Jacob: "Our only reliable friends in Europe are the Germans, and does anyone doubt that they'll one day run out of guilt and lampshades? And does anyone really doubt that one day, when the conditions are right, America will decide we're noisy, and smelly, and pushy, and way too smart for anybody else's good?"

"I do," Max said, opening up a pinch to zoom in on something.

"Hey, Maxy," Irv said, trying to catch his eye in the rearview mirror, "you know why paleontologists look for bones and not anti-Semitism?"

"Because they're paleontologists and not the ADL?" Jacob suggested.

"Because they like to dig. Get it?"

"No."

"Even if everything you say is true," Jacob said, "which it *isn't*—"

"Resolutely is."

"It *isn't*—"

"*Is.*"

"But even if it *were*—"

"The world hates Jews. I know you think the prevalence of Jews in culture is some kind of counterargument, but that's like saying the world loves pandas because crowds come to see them in zoos. The world *hates* pandas. Wants them dead. Even the cubs. And the world hates Jews. Always has. Always will. Yeah, there are more polite words to use, and political contexts to cite, but the hatred is always hatred and always because we're Jewish."

"I like pandas," Max chimed in.

"You don't," Irv corrected.

"I would be psyched to have one as a pet."

"It would eat your face, Maxy."

"Awesome."

"Or at least occupy our house and subject us to its sense of entitlement," Jacob added.

"The Germans murdered one and a half million Jewish children because they were Jewish children, and they got to host the Olympics thirty years later. And what a job they did with that! The Jews win *by a hair* a war *for our survival* and are a permanent pariah state. *Why?* Why, only a generation after our near-destruction, is the Jewish will to survive considered a will to conquer? Ask yourself: *Why?*"

His *why* wasn't a question, not even a rhetorical one. It was a shove. A stiff arm in a time of forced hands. Everything had an aspect of coercion. Isaac didn't want to move; they were forcing him to. The singular sense in which Sam wanted to become a man was sexual relations with a person who wasn't himself, but they were forcing him to apologize for words he said he didn't write, so that he could be forced to chant memorized words of unknown meaning before family he didn't believe in, and friends he didn't believe in, and God. Julia was being forced to shift her focus from ambitious buildings that would never be built to the bathroom and kitchen renovations of disappointed people with resources. And the phone incident was forcing an examination that the marriage might not survive—their relationship, like all relationships, dependent on willful blindness and forgetting. Even Irv's descent into bigotry was guided by an invisible hand.

Nobody wants to be a caricature. Nobody wants to be a diminished version of herself. Nobody wants to be a Jewish man, or a dying man.

Jacob didn't want to coerce or be coerced, but what was he supposed to do? Sit on his hands waiting for his grandfather to shatter his hip and die in a hospital room as every abandoned old person is destined to do? Allow Sam to snip a ritualistic thread that reached back to kings and prophets, simply because Judaism as they practiced it was boring as hell and overflowed with hypocrisy? Maybe. In the rabbi's office he'd felt ready to use the scissors.

Jacob and Julia had batted about the notion of having the bar mitzvah in Israel—the Jewish coming-of-age version of eloping. Perhaps that would be a way to do it without *doing* it. Sam objected on the grounds of it being a terrible idea.

"Terrible why?" Jacob asked, knowing full well why.

"You really don't see the irony?" Sam said. Jacob saw many ironies, and was curious to hear which one Sam was thinking of. "Israel was created as a place for Jews to escape persecution. We would be going to escape Judaism." Nicely put.

So the bar mitzvah would be at the synagogue they paid twenty-five hundred dollars per visit to be members of, and officiated by the hip young rabbi who wasn't, by any reasonable definition, hip, young, or a rabbi. The party would be at the Hilton where Reagan was *this close* to being put out of our misery, and where Julia and Sam were representing Micronesia. The band would be capable of playing both a good horah and good rock. Of course, such a band has never existed in the history of live music, but Jacob knew that at a certain point you just crunch the capsule you've been hiding in your cheek and hope not to feel too much. The theme—handled with delicacy and taste—would be Sam's Family's Diaspora. (This was Julia's idea, and insofar as a bar mitzvah theme could ever be a good idea, it was sufficiently OK.) They would have tables representing each of the countries the family had been dispersed to—America, Brazil, Argentina, Spain, Australia, South Africa, Israel, Canada—and instead of seating cards, each guest would receive a "passport" to one of the nations. The tables would be designed to reflect regional culture and landmarks—this is where delicacy and taste were most severely challenged—and the centerpieces would include a family tree, and photographs of relatives currently living in those places. The buffet would feature stations of regionally specific foods: Brazilian feijoada, Spanish tapas, Israeli falafel, whatever they eat in Canada, and so on. The party favors would be snow globes of the various locales. There are more wars than snowfalls in Israel, but the Chinese are smart enough to know that Americans are dumb enough to buy anything. Especially Jewish Americans, who will go to any length, short of practicing Judaism, to instill a sense of Jewish identity in their children.

"I asked you a question," Irv said, bringing Jacob back to the argument that only Irv was having.

"Did you?"

"Yes: *Why?*"

"Why *what?*"

"The *what* doesn't even matter. The answer is the same to every question about us: *Because the world hates Jews.*"

Jacob turned to face Max. "You realize that genetics aren't destiny, right?"

"Whatever you say . . ."

"In much the same way that I escaped the baldness that ravaged your grandfather's head, you have a fighting chance of dodging the insanity that transformed a passable human into the man who married my mother."

Irv gave a deep, dramatic exhale, and then, with the full force of his faux sincerity: "Would it be all right if I offered an opinion?"

Both Jacob and Max laughed at that. Jacob liked that feeling, that spontaneous father-son camaraderie.

"Listen, don't listen, it's up to you. But I want to get this off my chest. I think you're wasting your life."

"Oh, *that's* all?" Jacob said. "I was bracing for something big."

"I think you are an immensely talented, deeply feeling, profoundly intelligent person."

"The zayde doth protest too much, methinks."

"And you have made some very bad choices."

"I'm guessing you have a specific choice in mind."

"Yes, writing for that dumb TV show."

"That dumb TV show is watched by four million people."

"A: So what? B: *Which* four million?"

"And is critically acclaimed."

"Those who can't teach gym, acclaim."

"And it's my *job*. It's how I support the family."

"It's how you make money. There are other ways to support a family."

"I should be a dermatologist? That would be a good use of my talent, feeling, and intellect?"

"You should make something that befits your abilities and expresses your definition of substance."

"I *am*."

"No, you're dotting the *i*'s and crossing the *t*'s of the epic dragon adventure of someone who isn't fit to spit shine your hemorrhoids. You weren't put on earth to do that."

"And now you're going to tell me what I was put on earth to do?"

"That's exactly what I'm going to do."

Jacob sang: *"Somewhere in my youth, or childhood, I must have done something very bad."*

"As I was about to say—"

"High on his horse was my lonely dad, Irv, lay ee old lay ee old lay hee hoo."

"You're witty—we get it, Fraukenstein."

"Bad advice, bad advice, bless my homeland for never."

This time leaving no room to fill: "Jacob, you should forge in the smithy of your soul the uncreated conscience of your race."

An underwhelmed "Wow."

"Yes: wow."

"Would you mind saying that once more, and projecting, for the cheap seats in my brain?"

"You should forge in the smithy of your soul the uncreated conscience of your race."

"Didn't the ovens at Auschwitz do that?"

"They destroyed. I'm talking about forging."

"I appreciate your sudden vote of confidence in me—"

"I just stuffed the ballot box."

"—but my soul's smithy doesn't get that hot."

"That's because you're so desperate to be loved. Friction generates heat."

"I don't even know what that means."

"It's the same with the n-word business at Sam's school."

"We should probably leave Sam out of this," Max suggested.

"It's the same everywhere you look in your life," Irv said. "You're making the same mistake we've been making for thousands of years—"

"*We?*"

"—believing that if we can only be loved, we'll be safe."

"My conversation GPS is on the fritz. We're back to the hatred of the Jews?"

"*Back to?* No. You can't return to something you've never left."

"The show is *entertainment*."

"I don't believe that you believe that."

"Well, that sounds like the end of our road."

"Because I'm ready to give you more credit than you're ready to give yourself?"

"Because as you're often the first to point out, you can't negotiate without a negotiating partner."

"Who's negotiating?"

"You can't *converse*."

"Really, Jacob. Let down your guard for a second and ask yourself: What is it with the ravenous need for love? You used to write such honest books. Honest and emotionally ambitious. Maybe they weren't finding millions of readers. Maybe they weren't making you rich. But they were making the *world* rich."

"And you hated them."

"Yes, that's right," he said, switching lanes without checking any of his mirrors, "I hated them. God forbid you should see my marginalia. But do you know who hates your show?"

"It isn't *my* show."

"Nobody. You've passed a lot of time for a lot of grateful zombies."

"So this is an argument against television?"

"That's another argument I could make," he said, taking the airport exit. "But this is an argument against your show."

"It isn't *my* show."

"So get a show."

"But I have nothing left to offer the tooth fairy in exchange."

"Have you tried?"

"Have I *tried*?"

No one had tried harder. Not to *get* a show—it wasn't yet the time for that—but to write one. For more than a decade Jacob had been breaking his soul's back shoveling coal into the smithy. He'd devoted himself to the secret, utterly futile task of redeeming his people through language. His people? His family. His family? Himself. What self? And *redeeming* might not be quite the right word.

Ever-Dying People was exactly what his father thought he was hoping for—a shofar blast from a mountaintop. Or at least a silent cry from a basement. But if Irv had ever been given the chance to read it, he would have hated it—a far more expansive hatred than the one he felt for the novels. Jacob's definition of substance could get pretty ugly, but more, there were some essential disagreements about whom the sharp point of the forged conscience should be turned on.

And there was a far bigger problem: the show would kill Jacob's grandfather. Not metaphorically. It would literally commit grand-patricide. He who could survive anything would never survive a mirror. So Jacob held it close to his chest in a locked desk drawer. And the less able he was to share it, the more devoted he felt to it.

The show began with the beginning of the writing of the show. The characters in the show were the characters in the real Jacob's life: an unhappy wife (who didn't want to be described that way); three sons: one on the brink of manhood, one on the brink of extreme self-consciousness, one on the brink of mental independence; a terrified, xenophobic father; a quietly weaving and unweaving mother; a depressed grandfather. Should he one day share it and be asked how autobiographical it was, he would say, "It's not my life, but it's me." And if someone—who else but

Dr. Silvers?—were to ask how autobiographical his life was, he would say, "It's my life, but it's not me."

The writing kept pace with the changing events in Jacob's life. Or his life kept pace with the writing. Sometimes it was hard to tell. Jacob wrote about the discovery of his phone months before he even bought a second phone—psychology so double-left-handed it didn't justify even one six-dollar minute with Dr. Silvers and was given several dozen hours. But it wasn't just psychological. There were times when Julia would say or do things so eerily similar to what Jacob had written that he had to wonder if she'd read it. The night she discovered the phone, she asked, "Does it make you sad that we love the kids more than we love each other?" That exact line—those words in that order—had been in the script for months. Although they were Jacob's.

Save for the moments that most people would do anything to avoid, life is pretty slow and uninteresting and undramatic and uninspiring. Jacob's solution to that problem, or blessing, wasn't to alter the drama of the show—the authenticity of his work was the only antidote to the inauthenticity of his life—but to generate more and more paraphernalia.

Twenty-four years earlier, around the time that his lack of patience overwhelmed his passion for guitar, Jacob started designing album covers for an imaginary band. He wrote track lists, and lyrics, and liner notes. He thanked people who didn't exist: engineers, producers, managers. He copied copyright language from *Steady Diet of Nothing*. An atlas at his side, he created a U.S. tour, and then a world tour, giving thought to the limits of his physical and emotional endurance: Is Paris, Stockholm, Brussels, Copenhagen, Barcelona, Madrid too much for one week? Especially after eight months on the road? And even if it were endurable, what good would come from pushing the band toward an irritability that would only jeopardize everything they believed in and worked so hard to achieve? The dates were printed on the backs of T-shirts he designed, and actually produced, and actually wore. But he couldn't play barre chords.

His relationship to the show was something like that—the more stunted the reality, the more expansive the related materials.

He created, and perpetually added to, a "bible" for the show—a kind of user's manual for those who would one day work on it. He generated an ever-adjusting dossier of background information on each of the characters—

SAM BLOCH

On the brink of 13. The eldest of the Bloch brothers. Spends virtually all of his time in the virtual world of Other Life. Hates the fit of all clothing. Loves watching videos of bullies getting knocked out. Incapable of ignoring, or even not perceiving, sexual double entendres. Would take a body covered with acne scarring in the future for a clear forehead in the present. Longs for his positive qualities to be universally recognized but never mentioned.

GERSHOM BLUMENBERG

Long dead. Son of Anshel, father of Isaac. Grandfather of Irving. Grandson of someone whose name has been lost forever. Great Rabbi of Drohobycz. Died in a burning synagogue. Namesake of a small park with cool marble benches in Jerusalem. Appears only in nightmares.

JULIA BLOCH

43. Wife of Jacob. Architect, although secretly ashamed of referring to herself as such, given that she's never built a building. Immensely talented, tragically overburdened, perpetually unappreciated, seasonally optimistic. Often wonders if all it would take to completely change her life would be a complete change of context.

—and a catalog of settings, which included short (if always expanding) descriptions of place, hundreds of photographs for a future props department, maps, floor plans, real estate listings, anecdotes—

2294 NEWARK STREET

Bloch House. Nicer than many, but not the nicest. But nice. If not as nice as it could be. Thoughtful interiors, within the working limits. Some good midcentury furniture, mostly through eBay and Etsy. Some IKEA furniture with cool hacks (leather pulls, faceted cabinet fronts). Pictures hung in clusters (equitably distributed between Jacob's and Julia's families). Almond flour in a Williams-Sonoma glass jar on a soapstone counter. A too-beautiful-to-use Le Creuset Dutch Oven in Mineral Blue on the back right burner of a double-wide Lacanche range whose potential is wasted on veggie chili. Some books that were bought to be read (or at least dipped into); others to give the impression of a very specific kind of very broad-minded curiosity; others, like the two-volume slipcased edition of The Man Without Qualities, *because of their beautiful spines. Hydrocortisone acetate suppositories beneath a stack of* New Yorkers *in the middle drawer of the medicine cabinet. A vibrator in the foot of a shoe on a high shelf. Holocaust books behind non-Holocaust books. And running up the kitchen doorframe, a growth chart of the Bloch boys.*

When it was time for me to move, I lingered at this threshold. The doorframe was the only thing I couldn't let go of. Forget the Papa Bear Chair and forget its ottoman. Forget the candlesticks and lamps. Forget Blind Botanist, *the drawing we bought together, attributed to one of my heroes, Ben Shahn, lacking any provenance. Forget the moody orchid. While Julia was out one afternoon, I jimmied the doorframe loose from the wall with the aid of a flathead screwdriver, slid it down the length of the Subaru (one end against the glass of the hatchback, the other touching the windshield), and drove the record of my children's growth to a new house. Two weeks later, a house-painter painted over it. I redid the lines to the best of my sorry memory.*

—and most ambitiously (or neurotically, or pathetically): the notes to the actors, striving to convey what the scripts on their own could not, because more words were needed: HOW TO PLAY LATE LAUGHTER; HOW TO PLAY "WHAT IS YOUR NAME?"; HOW TO PLAY SUICIDE GROWTH RINGS . . . Each episode was only twenty-seven pages, give or take. Each season only ten episodes. There was room for a little background, a few flashbacks and tangents and clumsy insertions of information that didn't drive the plot but filled out the motivation. So many more words were needed: HOW TO PLAY THE NEED FOR DISSATISFACTION; HOW TO PLAY LOVE; HOW TO PLAY THE DEATH OF LANGUAGE . . . The notes were Jewish-motherly in their irrepressibly naggy didacticism, Jewish-fatherly in their need to obscure every emotion in metaphor and deflection. HOW TO PLAY AMERICAN; HOW TO PLAY THE GOOD BOY; HOW TO PLAY THE SOUND OF TIME . . . The bible quickly surpassed the scripts themselves in length and depth—the explanatory material overwhelmed what it attempted to explain. So Jewish.

Jacob wanted to make something that would redeem everything, and instead he was explaining, explaining, explaining . . .

HOW TO PLAY THE SOUND OF TIME

The morning Julia found the phone, my parents were over for brunch. Everything was falling apart around Benjy, although I'll never know what he knew at the time, and neither will he. The adults were talking when he reentered the kitchen and said, "The sound of time. What happened to it?"

"What are you talking about?"

"You know," he said, waving his tiny hand about, "the sound of time."

It took time—about five frustrating minutes—to figure out what he was getting at. Our refrigerator was being repaired, so the kitchen lacked its omnipresent, nearly imperceptible buzzing sound. He spent virtually all his home life within reach of that sound, and so had come to associate it with life happening.

I loved his misunderstanding, because it wasn't a misunderstanding.

My grandfather heard the cries of his dead brothers. That was the sound of his time.

My father heard attacks.

Julia heard the boys' voices.

I heard silences.

Sam heard betrayals and the sounds of Apple products turning on.

Max heard Argus's whining.

Benjy was the only one still young enough to hear home.

Irv lowered all four windows and told Jacob, "You lack strength."

"And you lack intelligence. Together we make a fully incomplete person."

"Seriously, Jacob. What is the ravenous need for love?"

"Seriously, Dad. What is the ravenous need for that diagnosis?"

"I'm not diagnosing you. I'm explaining yourself to you."

"And *you* don't need love?"

"As a grandfather, yes. As a father and son, yes. As a Jew? No. So some fifth-tier British university won't let us participate in their ridiculous conference on recent advances in marine biology? Who *cares*? Stephen

Hawking won't come to Israel? I'm not one to punch a quadriplegic with glasses, but I'm sure he won't mind if we ask for his voice back—you know, the one that was created by *Israeli* engineers. And while we're at it, I'll happily lose my seat at the United-Against-Israel Nations if it means I can keep my ass. Jews have become the smartest weakest people in the history of the world. Look, I'm not always right. I realize that. But I'm always strong. And if our history has taught us anything, it's that it's more important to be strong than right. Or *good*, for that matter. I would rather be alive and wrong and evil. I don't need Bishop Wears-a-Tutu, or that hydrocephalic peanut farmer president, or the backseat-driving pseudo-sociologist eunichs from the *New York Times* op-ed page, or *anyone*, to give me their blessing. I don't need to be a Light unto the Nations; I need to not be on fire. Life is long when you're alive, and history has a short memory. America had its way with the Indians. Australia and Germany and Spain . . . They *did what had to be done*. And what was the big deal? Their history books have a few regrettable pages? They have to issue weak-tea apologies once a year and pay out some reparations to the unfinished parts of the job? They did what had to be done, and life went on."

"What are you saying?"

"Nothing. I'm just *saying*."

"What? That Israel should commit genocide?"

"That word is yours."

"It's what you meant."

"I said, and *meant*, that Israel should be a self-respecting, self-defending country like any other."

"Like Nazi Germany."

"Like Germany. Like Iceland. Like America. Like every country that's ever existed and not stopped existing."

"Sounds inspiring."

"Wouldn't be pretty while it was happening, but twenty years from now, with fifty million Jews filling the Land of Israel, from the Suez Canal all the way to the oil fields, with the largest economy between Germany and China—"

"Israel isn't between Germany and China."

"—with the Olympics in Tel Aviv and more tourists in Jerusalem than Paris, you think anyone is going to be going on about how the kosher sausage was made?"

Irv took a deep breath and nodded his head, as if in agreement with something only he had access to.

"The world will always hate Jews. On to the next thought, which is: What to do with that hatred? We can deny it, or try to overcome it. We could even choose to join the club and hate ourselves."

"The *club*?"

"You know the membership: Jews who would sooner fix their so-called deviated septums than break a nose for their survival; Jews who refuse to acknowledge that Tina Fey isn't Jewish, or that the IDF is; ersatz-quote Jews like Ralph Lauren (né Lifshitz), Winona Ryder (née Horowitz), George Soros, Mike Wallace, pretty much all Jews living in the United Kingdom, Billy Joel, Tony Judt, Bob Silvers—"

"Billy Joel isn't Jewish."

"Of course he is."

"'Scenes from an Italian Restaurant'?"

"Chinese restaurant, no?"

"No."

"Point is, a Jewish fist can do more than masturbate and hold a pen. Slide out the writing implement, you've got a punching implement. You understand? We don't need another Einstein. We need a Koufax who pitches at the head."

"Did it ever occur to you—" Jacob began.

"Yes, it probably did."

"—that I don't include myself in your *we*?"

"Did it ever occur to you that the meshuggener mullah with the nuclear codes *does*?"

"So our identity is at the mercy of crazy strangers?"

"If you can't generate it yourself."

"What do you want from me? To spy for Israel? To blow myself up in a mosque?"

"I want you to write something that matters."

"First of all, what I write matters to a lot of people."

"No, it entertains them."

Jacob remembered the previous night's conversation with Max, and considered pointing out that his show generated more revenue than every book published in America that entire year combined. That might not have been true, but he would know how to play false authority.

"I take your silence to mean you understand me," Irv said.

"How about *you* stick to the bigoted blogging, and *I'll* take care of award-winning television?"

"Hey, Maxy, you know who made the award-winning entertainment in the time of the Maccabees?"

"Pray tell," he said, blowing dust from his screen.

"I can't, because we only remember the Maccabees."

What Jacob really thought: his father was an ignorant, narcissistic, self-righteous pig, too anal-retentive and pussy-whipped to grasp the extreme reaches of his hypocrisy, emotional impotence, and mental infancy.

"So we're in agreement, then?"

"No."

"So we're agreed?"

"No."

"I'm glad you agree with me."

But there were arguments for forgiving him, too. There were. Good ones. Beautiful intentions. Wounds.

Jacob's phone rang. His real phone. It was Julia. The real Julia. He would have leaped through any open or closed window to escape the conversation with his father, but he was afraid of answering.

"Hi?"

"   "
" . . . "

"I bet."

"   "
" . . . "

"Do they even have room for it?"

"   "
" . . . "

"I figured. Not the bomb part, but—"

"   "
" . . . "

"I'm in the car."

"   "
" . . . "

"Their flight is arriving early."

"   "
" . . . "

"Max did."

"   "
" . . . "

"Max, do you want to say hi to Mom?"

"   "
" . . . "

"Are you in the hotel? I hear nature."

"   "
· · ·
"Tell her hi."
"My dad says hi."
"   "
· · ·
"She says hi."
"And that Benjy had a great time at our house, and didn't die."
"He wants you to know that Benjy had a great time at his house."
"   "
· · ·
"She says thanks."
"Tell her I say hi."
"Max says hi."
"   "
· · ·
"She says hi."
"   "
· · ·
"Let's see. Argus is very old. That was reconfirmed. We got some new pills for joint pain, and they upped the dosage on the other one. He'll live to bark another day."
"   "
· · ·
"Nothing to be done. The vet gave the spiel about what an honor it is to care for loved ones, how it only happens once."
"No she didn't," Max said.
Jacob shrugged his shoulders.
"And tell her the vet thinks we should put Argus down."
"Hold on," Jacob told Julia, then muted the phone.
"That's not what the vet said, Max."
"Tell her."
Jacob unmuted the phone and said, "Max wants me to communicate that the vet thinks we should put Argus down, although the vet said no such thing."
"She did, Mom!"
"   "
· · ·
"She did."
"   "
· · ·
"We had a nice conversation about quality of life and so on."
"   "
· · ·
"I took him to Fort Reno on the way, told him some stories about when I was a kid."
"   "
· · ·

"Ate McDonald's."

"..."

"Burritos."

"..."

"No, microwaved."

"..."

"Of course. Carrots. Hummus, too."

With a few movements of his hand, Jacob communicated to Max that Julia had asked if he'd eaten vegetables.

"..."

"Will do."

"..."

"One other thing is that last night we had a little snafu with Sam's avatar."

"..."

"In Other Life. His avatar. We were messing around with it."

"*You* were," Max corrected.

"..."

"No, probably not. Max was fiddling with it—"

"What? Dad, that's just not true. Mom, it's not true!"

"And I wanted to, you know, display interest, and we ended up doing it together. Nothing dramatic. Just walking around and exploring. Anyway, we killed her."

"*We* didn't. *You* did. Mom: Dad killed her!"

"..."

"His avatar. Yes."

"..."

"Unintended."

"..."

"You can't fix death, Julia."

"..."

"I spent a couple of months on the phone with tech support last night. I can probably get it back to more or less where it was, but it's going to require sitting at his computer until the Messiah calls me away."

"..."

"I haven't spoken to Cory in at least a year."

"..."

"It would be shitty to call him like this after not having returned his calls."

" . . . "

"And I don't think a computer genius is what we need. I'll figure it out. But enough about the sickness and death over here. How are you guys? Having fun?"

" . . . "

"You've met the infamous Billie?"

"Infamous Billie?" Irv asked Max in the rearview mirror.

"Sam's girlfriend," Max said.

" . . . "

"And?"

" . . . "

"What's he like around her?"

" . . . "

"I wouldn't take it personally."

" . . . "

"And Mark?"

" . . . "

"Is it good having him there?"

" . . . "

"Has he had to flush any pot down the toilet, or break up a French-kissing session?"

"French kissing is with tongues, right?" Max asked Irv.

"*Mais oui.*"

" . . . "

"What's wrong?"

" . . . "

"What?"

" . . . "

"Something's wrong. I can hear it."

" . . . "

"Now I *know* something's wrong."

"What's wrong?" Max asked.

" . . . "

"OK, but can you at least tell me what it has to *do* with, so my mind doesn't spiral wildly for the next six hours?"

"..."
"That's not what I meant."
"..."
"Julia. What's going on?"
"Seriously, what *is* going on?" Irv said, finally interested.
"..."
"If it were nothing we wouldn't still be talking about it."
"..."
"OK, I get it."
"..."
"Wait, what?"
"..."
"Julia?"
"..."
"Mark did?"
"..."
"Why the fuck did he do that?"
"Language," Max said.
"..."
"He's *married*."
"..."
"But he *was*."
"..."
"What do you want me to do? Stab a voodoo doll of myself?"

Jacob turned up the radio to make his conversation harder for his father and son to listen in on. An English grammarian was sharing her infatuation with auto-antonyms: words that are their own opposites. *Oversight* means both "to oversee" and "to fail to see." You dust a cake with sugar, dust crops with pesticides; but when furniture is dusted, something is being removed. The house weathered the storm, but the shingles were weathered.

"..."
"That isn't fair."
"..."
"Perhaps. But it's also what people say when something isn't fair."
"..."
"Of course it is."
"..."

"So this is just the most hysterical coincidence of timing since—"

" . . . "

"Ah."

" . . . "

"So please tell me what it's about. If not balance, then—?"

" . . . "

"Great."

" . . . "

"Great."

" . . . "

"The way I do it, yes."

" . . . "

"Both."

"What happened?" Max asked.

"Nothing," Jacob said. And then, to Julia: "Max asked me what happened."

" . . . "

"But you're upset," Max said.

"Life is upsetting," Irv said. "Like blood is wet."

"Scabs," Max pointed out.

Jacob turned the volume yet louder, to the point of aggression. He was fast until his feet were held fast in concrete. The earth was held up by Atlas, and the earth held Atlas up on his way to elsewhere. After she left, no one was left.

" . . . "

"There is no *of course* anymore."

" . . . "

"Are you coming home?"

" . . . "

"I don't understand, Julia. I really don't."

" . . . "

"But you told me, in bed the other night, that it *was* something you—"

" . . . "

"You just said you didn't stop it. I can't believe this. I can't believe you."

"Maybe you guys should get a room?" Irv said to Jacob in a whisper.

" . . . "

"Now I get it. Why you didn't call last night."

"..."

"Does Micronesia even *have* a bomb?"

"..."

Jacob hung up.

They were in battle against each other, and they had served together in battle.

"Jesus," Irv said. "What the hell was *that* about?"

"That was about—"

"Dad?"

For only long enough to be able to dismiss it, Jacob considered telling his father and son everything. That would feel good, but at the price of his goodness.

"That. That was about a whole bunch of logistical crap, having to do with when they're coming home later, and where the Israelis will sleep, and what they'll eat, and so on."

Of course Irv didn't believe him. And of course Max didn't, either. But Jacob almost believed himself.

He cleaved to the life from which he cleaved himself.

THE L-WORD

Billie was preparing her remarks for the General Assembly—after the unproductive caucus of the Pacific Islands Forum, the Micronesian delegation reconvened in Mark's room and argued well past their scheduled curfew, narrowly voting to hand the bomb over to whatever competent and trustworthy third party could safely disarm it and dispose of the nuclear material—when her phone sang the first two words of Adele's "Someone Like You," just enough to unleash a Charybdis of feelings without revealing to others that she didn't find the song totally cheesy. It was the special tone for Sam's texts; she had been holding her phone in her hand since the night before, wanting and not wanting to hear *I heard*.

are you working on your speech?

what makes you think i want to talk to you?

that you just wrote that

someone should invent an emoji
for the word someone should invent
for how hurt i am

i'm sorry

actually, it's guernica

. . .

where'd you go?

had to look up guernica

you could have just asked

nobody is like you, and you are never
like anybody else

did you get that off the side of a tampon box?

???

try harder

emet hi hasheker hatov beyoter

what truth? and what lie?

really, really like . . .
that's the lie

and the truth?

love

did you just say the hardest thing?

no, that was the easiest

why were you so mean to me?

can i tell you something?

ok

when i was eight, my left hand got smashed
in the hinge of a heavy iron door
three of my fingers were severed
and had to be reattached
the nails are all mangled
when my hand stops growing i'm going
to have fake nails attached
anyway, i keep my hand in my pocket a lot
and when i'm sitting i'll
slide it under my thigh

                                        i know

a few times i've wanted
to touch your face

                                        really?

many, many times

                              then why didn't you?

my hand

                        you were afraid of me seeing it?

yes
and also of me seeing it

                        you could have used your other hand

i want to touch you with that hand
that's the point

                  that's the hand i want you to touch me with

really?

. . .

where'd you go?

                 i just pressed my phone to my heart

i could hear it beating

                 even though we're not on the phone?

yes

                 you can touch my face if you want to

i text like achilles
but i'm a pussy in real life

                 i'm a feminist in real life

you know i meant that idiomatically

                 yes, i know you are not a vagina

then i really have you fooled

                 i will never write lol

i'm sorry i hurt you

                 why did you do it?

because it was a cowardly
way to hurt myself

                 what was so hard about it was that
                 i always feel like i understand you
                 but last night i didn't
                 it scared me

do you accept my apology?

                as franz rosenzweig famously responded
                    when asked if he was religious . . .

"not yet"

                          impressive memory

not yet?

                                  not yet

but you will

                did you ever wonder why it even mattered
                    if achilles was wounded in the heel

because that was the only part of him
that wasn't immortal

                so? so he'd be an immortal with a limp

i'm guessing you know why

                                      i do

i'd really, really, really like to know

                    really, really, really, really, really
                    until you broke the word "like"

into a million pieces

                              into love

so tell me

it's not just that his heel was
the only mortal part of him
ALL of his mortality was in his heel
—like moving everyone in a skyscraper
into the basement, and then it floods

and people who work on different floors,
and never otherwise would have met,
talk, and decide to go out to dinner,
and keep going out to dinner,
and meet each other's family,
and celebrate holidays together,
and get married, and have
kids, who have kids, who have kids

but they drowned

so?

MAYBE IT WAS THE DISTANCE

Jacob was the only one who referred to the Israeli cousins as *our* Israeli cousins. To everyone else in the house, they were *the* Israeli cousins. Jacob felt no desire for ownership of them, and too much association made him itchy, but he felt that they were owed familial warmth commensurate with the thickness of blood. Or he felt that he should feel that. It would have been easier if they'd been easier.

He'd known Tamir since they were children. Jacob's grandfather and Tamir's were brothers in a Galician shtetl of such minuscule size and importance that the German people didn't get to it until their second pass through the Pale to wipe up Jewish crumbs. There had been seven brothers. Isaac and Benny avoided the fate of the other five by hiding together in a hole for more than two hundred days, and then living in forests. Every story Jacob overheard about this period—Benny could have killed a Nazi; Isaac could have saved a Jewish boy—suggested a dozen stories that he would never overhear.

The brothers spent a year in a displaced persons camp, where they met their wives, who were sisters. Each couple had a child, each a boy: Irv and Shlomo. Benny moved his family to Israel, and Isaac moved his to America. Isaac never understood Benny. Benny understood Isaac, but never forgave him.

Within two years, Isaac and his wife, Sarah, had opened a Jewish bodega in a schwartze neighborhood, learned enough English to begin working the system, and started saving. Irv learned the infield fly rule, learned the alphabetic/syllabic logic of D.C. street naming, learned to be ashamed of his house's look and smell, and one morning his forty-two-year-old mother went downstairs to open the store, but instead collapsed and died. Died of what? Of a heart attack. Of a stroke. Of surviving. A silence so high and thick was built around her death that not only did no one know any significant details, no one even knew what others knew. Many decades later, at his father's funeral, Irv would allow himself to wonder if his mother had killed herself.

Everything was something never to remember, or never to forget, and what America had done for them was retold and retold. As Jacob grew, his grandfather would regale him with stories of America's glory: how the army had fed and clothed him after the war; how at Ellis Island they never asked him to change his name (it was his own choice); how one was limited only by one's willingness to work; how he'd never experienced anything that carried even the faintest whiff of anti-Semitism—only indifference, which is greater than love, because it's more reliable.

The brothers would visit each other every few years, as if the performance of familial intimacy would retroactively defeat the German people and save everyone. Isaac would lavish Benny and his family with expensive-looking tchotchkes, take them to the "best" second-tier restaurants, close the market for a week to show them the sights of Washington. And when they left, he'd spend twice as long as their visit bemoaning how big-headed and tiny-minded they were, how American Jews were Jews and these Israeli crackpots were Hebrews—people who, given their way, would sacrifice animals and serve kings. Then he'd reiterate how necessary it was to maintain closeness.

Jacob found the Israeli cousins—*his* Israeli cousins—curious, at once alien and familiar. He saw his family's faces in their faces, but also something different, something that could equally well be described as ignorant or unself-conscious, phony or free—hundreds of thousands of years of evolution crammed into one generation. Perhaps it was existential constipation, but the Israelis didn't seem to give a shit about anything. All Jacob's family ever did was give shits. They were shit-givers.

Jacob first visited Israel when he was fourteen—an overdue present that he didn't want for a bar mitzvah he didn't went. The next generation of Blumenbergs took the next generation of Blochs to the Wailing Wall, into whose cracks Jacob inserted prayers for things he didn't actually care about but knew he ought to, like a cure for AIDS and an unbroken ozone layer. They floated in the Dead Sea together, among the ancient, elephantine Jews reading half-submerged newspapers bleeding Cyrillic. They climbed Masada early in the morning and pocketed rocks that might have been held in the palms of Jewish suicides. They watched the wind-mill break the sunset from the perch of Mishkenot Sha'ananim. They went to the small park named after Jacob's great-grandfather Gershom Blumenberg. He had been a beloved rabbi, and his surviving disciples remained loyal to his memory, choosing never to have another rabbi, choos-ing their own demise. It was 105 degrees. The marble bench was cool, but the metal plaque with his name was too hot to touch.

One morning, while they were driving to a hike along the sea, an air-raid siren went off. Jacob's eyes opened to half dollars and found Irv's. Shlomo stopped the car. Right there, where it was, on the highway. "Did we break down?" Irv asked, as if the siren might have been indicating a cracked catalytic converter. Shlomo and Tamir got out of the car with the vacant determination of zombies. Everyone on the highway got out of cars and cargo trucks, off motorcycles. They stood, thousands of Jewish undead, perfectly silent. Jacob didn't know if this was the end, a kind of proud greeting of nuclear winter, or a drill, or some national custom. Like dupes in a grand social psychology experiment, Jacob and his par-ents did as everyone else was doing, and stood by the car in silence. When the siren stopped, life reanimated. Everyone got back in the car and they were on their way.

Irv was apparently too afraid of revealing ignorance to resolve his igno-rance, so Deborah was left to ask what had just happened.

"Yom HaShoah," Shlomo said.

"That's the one for the trees?" Jacob asked.

"For the Jews," Shlomo said, "the ones that were chopped down."

"*Shoah*," Irv said to Jacob, as if he'd known everything all along, "means 'Holocaust.'"

"But why does everyone stop and stand in silence?"

Shlomo said, "Because it feels less wrong than anything else we might do."

"And what is everyone facing?" Jacob asked.

Shlomo said, "Himself."

Jacob was both mesmerized and repulsed by the ritual. The Jewish American response to the Holocaust was "Never forget," because there was a possibility of forgetting. In Israel, they blared the air-raid siren for two minutes, because otherwise it would never stop blaring.

Shlomo was as over-the-top a host as Benny had been. He was further over, untethered as he was from the dignity of survival. And dignity was never Irv's problem. So there were many scenes, especially when the check came at the end of a meal.

"Don't touch that!"

"Don't *you* touch that!"

"Don't insult me!"

"*Me* insult *you?*"

"You're our guests!"

"You're our hosts!"

"I'll never eat with you again."

"Count on it."

More than once this competitive generosity escalated to genuine insult. More than once—twice—perfectly good money was ripped up. Did everyone win, or did everyone lose? Why so binary?

What Jacob remembered most sharply and tenderly was the time they spent in the Blumenbergs' home, a two-story Art Deco–ish construction perched on a Haifan hill. Every surface was made of stone and cool enough to be felt through socks at every time of day—an entire house like the bench in Blumenberg Park. There were diagonally sliced cucumbers and cubes of cheese for breakfast. Jaunts to weirdly specific two-room "zoos": a snake zoo, a small-mammal zoo. Tamir's mother would make huge spreads of side dishes for lunch—half a dozen salads, half a dozen dips. At home, the Blochs made a point of trying not to turn on the TV. The Blumenbergs made a point of trying not to turn it off.

Tamir was obsessed with computers and had a library of RGB porn before Jacob had word processing. In those days, Jacob concealed dirty magazines inside reference books at Barnes & Noble, searched lingerie catalogs for nipples and pubes with the dedication of a Talmudist searching for God's will, and listened to the moans of the visually blocked but aurally exposed Spice channel. The greatest of lewd treats was the three minutes of preview that hotels used to offer for all movies: family, adult, *adult.* Even as a teenager, Jacob recognized the masturbatory tautology: if three minutes of the adult film convinced you that it was a worthy adult film, you would no longer have need of it. Tamir's computer took half a day to download a titty fuck, but what else was time made for?

Once, while they watched a pixelated woman jerkily spread and close her legs—an animation composed of six frames—Tamir asked if Jacob felt like beating off.

Jacob gave an ironic, Tom Brokaw–voiced "No," assuming his cousin was joking.

"Suit yourself," Tamir said, and proceeded to suit himself, pumping a glob of shea butter moisturizer into his palm.

Jacob watched him remove his hard penis from his pants and begin to stroke it, transferring the cream to its length. After a minute or two of this, Tamir got up onto his knees, bringing the head of his penis within inches of the screen—close enough for static shock. His penis was wide, Jacob had to give it that. But he wasn't convinced it was any longer than his own. He wasn't convinced that in the dark one would be able to tell the difference between their penises.

"How does it feel?" Jacob asked, while simultaneously reprimanding himself for voicing such a creepy question.

And then, as if in response, Tamir grabbed a Kleenex from the box on his desk and moaned as he shot a load into it.

Why had Jacob asked that? And why had Tamir come right then? Had Jacob's question made him come? Had that been Jacob's (totally subconscious) intent?

They masturbated side by side a dozen or so times. They certainly never touched each other, but Jacob did wonder if Tamir's quiet moans were always irrepressible—if there wasn't something performative about them. They never spoke about such sessions after—not three minutes after, and not three decades—but they weren't a source of shame for either of them. They were young enough at the time not to worry about meaning, and then old enough to revere what was lost.

Pornography was only one example of the chasm between their life experiences. Tamir walked himself to school before Jacob's parents would leave him at a drop-off birthday party. Tamir cooked his own dinner, while an airplane full of dark green vegetables searched for a landing strip in Jacob's mouth. Tamir drank beer before Jacob, smoked pot before Jacob, got a blowjob before Jacob, got arrested before Jacob (who would never be arrested), traveled abroad before Jacob, had his heart created by having his heart broken before Jacob. When Tamir was given an M16, Jacob was given a Eurail pass. Tamir tried without success to stay out of risky situations; Jacob tried without success to find his way into them. At nineteen, Tamir was in a half-buried outpost in south Lebanon, behind four feet of concrete. Jacob was in a dorm in New Haven whose bricks had been buried for two years before construction so that they would look older than they were. Tamir didn't resent Jacob—he would have *been* Jacob, given the choice—but he had lost some of the lightness necessary to appreciate someone as light as his cousin. He'd fought for his homeland, while Jacob spent entire nights debating whether that stupid *New Yorker* poster where New York is bigger than everything else would look better on this wall or that one. Tamir tried not to get killed, while Jacob tried not to die of boredom.

After his service, Tamir was finally free to live on his own terms. He became hugely ambitious, in the sense of wanting to make shitloads of money and buy loads of shit. He dropped out of Technion after a year and founded the first of a series of high-tech start-ups. Almost all of them were flops, but it doesn't take many nonflops to make your first five million. Jacob was too jealous to give Tamir the pleasure of explaining what his companies did, but it wasn't hard to surmise that, like most Israeli high tech, they applied military technologies to civilian life.

Tamir's homes and cars and ego and girlfriends' breasts got bigger every visit. Jacob put on a respectful face that revealed just the right amount of disapproval, but in the end, all his emotional dog whistles were rendered pointless by Tamir's emotional tone-deafness. Why couldn't Jacob just be happy for his cousin's happiness? Tamir was as good a person as just about anyone, whose great success made his good-enough values increasingly difficult to act on. It's confusing to have more than you need. Who could blame him?

Jacob could. Jacob could because he had less than he needed—he was an honorable, ambitious, near-broke novelist who barely ever wrote—and that wasn't in any way confusing. Nothing was getting bigger in his life—it was a constant struggle to maintain the sizes he'd established—and people without fancy material possessions have their fancy values to flaunt.

Isaac always favored Tamir. Jacob could never figure out why. His grandfather seemed to have serious problems with all his post–bar mitzvah relatives, very much including those who forced their children to skype with him once a week, and took him to doctors, and drove him to distant supermarkets where one could buy six tins of baking powder for the price of five. Everyone ignored Isaac, but no one less than Jacob, and no one more than Tamir. Yet Isaac would have traded six Jacobs for five Tamirs.

Tamir. Now, he's a good grandson.

Even if he wasn't all that good, or in any way his grandson.

Maybe it was the distance Isaac loved. Maybe the absence allowed for a mythology, while Jacob was cursed to be judged by the increments he fell short of perfect menschiness.

Jacob tried to persuade Tamir to come see Isaac before the move to the Jewish Home. There were eighteen months of purgatory as they waited for someone to die and free up a room. But Tamir denied the significance of the event.

"I've moved six times in the last ten years," he e-mailed, although like this: "iv mvd 6 tms n lst 10 yrs," as if English were as vowelless as Hebrew. Or as if there were no possible way for him to give less of a shit about the message.

"Sure," Jacob wrote back, "but never to an assisted-living facility."

"I'll come when he dies, OK?"

"I'm not sure that visit will mean as much to him."

"And we'll be there for Sam's bar mitzvah," Tamir responded, although at that point it was still a year away and definitively happening.

"I hope he makes it that long," Jacob wrote.

"You sound like him."

The year passed, Isaac survived, as was his way, and so did the insolent Jews squatting in the various rooms that were his birthright. But then, *finally*, the exasperating wait was over: someone shattered his hip and died, bringing Isaac to the top of the list. Sam's bar mitzvah was finally upon him. And according to Jacob's phone, the Israelis were in their final descent.

"Listen," Jacob told Max as Irv pulled into a parking spot, "our Israeli cousins—"

"*Your* Israeli cousins."

"Our Israeli cousins are not the easiest people in the world—"

"*We're* the easiest people in the world?"

"I'll tell you the one thing the Arabs get right," Irv said, annoyed by the angle at which a car was parked. "They don't give women licenses."

"We're the second-most-difficult people in the world," Jacob told Max.

"After your Israeli cousins. But the point I'm trying to make is don't judge the State of Israel by the stubbornness, arrogance, and materialism of our cousins."

"Also known as fortitude, righteousness, and ingenuity," Irv said, turning off the car.

"It's not their *Israeliness*," Jacob said, "it's just *them*. And they're ours."

IN THE END,
ONE'S HOME IS PERFECT

There were rolls of bubble wrap in the basement, like rolls of hay in a field in a painting—dozens of liters of trapped air that had been saved for years for an occasion that would never come.

The walls were bare: the bequeathed awards and diplomas had been taken down, the ketubahs, reproductions of posters for Chagall exhibits, wedding photos and graduation photos and bar mitzvah photos and bris photos and framed sonogram images. So many framed pictures, as if he'd been trying to conceal the walls. And in their absence, so many rectangles of discoloration.

The made-in-China tchotchkes had been removed from the china cabinet's shelves and put in its drawers.

On the refrigerator, unbleached rectangles indicated where the gorgeous, genius, tumorless great-grandchildren used to be—all that remained were three class portraits, six closed eyes. The Vishniacs had been touched for the first time in a decade, moved to the floor, and those photos and cards that once covered the fridge now covered the coffee table, each in its own ziplock sandwich bag. It was for this moment that Isaac had saved all those baggies—washed them out after use, slid them over the faucet to dry.

On the bed were more piles of things still to be distributed to loved ones. The last couple of years had been an extended process of giving away everything he owned, and what remained, now, was hardest to let go of—not because of sentimental attachment, but because who would ever want such things? He'd had some genuinely decent silver. Charming porcelain teacups. And if you could imagine going to the trouble and expense of reupholstering, a non-ironic argument could be made to save a few of the chairs. But who would be willing to take home, or even to the nearest dumpster, wrapping paper that still held the creases of the boxes it had once covered?

Who would want the Post-it pads, totes, tiny spiral notebooks, and oversized pens, given as promotional items by pharmaceutical companies and taken because they were there?

That box of petrified jelly beans, pinched from the kiddush honoring the birth of someone who was now an obstetrician. Would anyone want that?

Having no visitors, he had no need for coat storage, so the entry closet was a good place to store more of the bubble wrap he didn't need. In the summer the bubbles expanded and the closet door strained—the hinge pins turning counterclockwise by thousandths of a degree from the pressure.

Who among the living would want what he had left to give?

And what interruption of the stillness, what sudden disturbance, awakened the fizz of the last ginger ale in the fridge?

HERE COME THE ISRAELIS!

Tamir managed to pull three rolling suitcases behind him while carrying two duty-free bags overflowing with—what? What dignity-free doodie could he possibly need enough of to make his cousins wait that much longer? Swatches? Cologne? A massive plastic M&M filled with tiny chocolate M&M's?

The surprise upon seeing him never diminished. Here was someone with whom Jacob shared more genetic material than just about anyone else on earth, and yet how many passersby would even guess they were related? His skin color could be explained by exposure to the sun, and the differences in their builds attributed to diet and exercise and willpower, but what about his sharp jaw, his overhanging brow, the hair on his knuckles and head? What about the size of his feet, his perfect eyesight, his ability to grow a full beard while a bagel toasted?

He went right to Jacob, like an Iron Dome interceptor, took him into his arms, kissed him with his full mouth, then held him at arm's length. He squeezed Jacob's shoulders and looked him up and down, as if he were contemplating eating or raping him.

"Apparently we aren't children anymore!"

"Not even our children are children."

His chest was broad and firm. It would have made a good surface on which someone like Jacob could write about someone like Tamir.

Once again, he held Jacob at arm's length.

"What's your shirt mean?" Jacob asked.

"Funny, no?"

"I think so, but I'm not sure I get it."

"'You look like I need a drink.' You know, *you* look like *I* need a drink."

"What, like, you're so ugly I need a drink? Or, I can see, reflected in your expression, my own need for alcohol?"

Tamir turned to Barak and said, "Didn't I tell you?"

Barak nodded and laughed, and Jacob didn't know what that meant, either.

It had been almost seven years since Tamir's last visit; Jacob hadn't been to Israel since he was married.

Jacob had sent Tamir only good news, much of it embellished, some of it plainly false. As it turned out, Tamir had been doing his own share of embellishing and lying, but it would take a war to make the truth known.

Hugs were exchanged all around. Tamir lifted Irv from the ground, pushing a small fart out of him—an anal Heimlich.

"I made you fart!" Tamir said, pumping a fist.

"Just some gas," Irv said—a distinction without a difference, as Dr. Silvers would say.

"I'm going to make you fart again!"

"I wish you wouldn't."

Tamir wrapped his arms around Irv again, and lifted him back into the air, this time with a firmer squeeze. And again it worked, this time even better—applying a very specific definition of *better*. Tamir put him down, took a deep breath, then opened his arms once more.

"This time you shit."

Irv crossed his arms.

Tamir laughed heartily and said, "Joking, joking!"

Everyone who wasn't Irv laughed. It was the first boisterous laugh that Jacob had heard come from Max in weeks—maybe months.

Then Tamir pulled Barak forward, mussed his hair, and said, "Look at this one. He's a man, no?"

Man was exactly the right word. He was towering, cut from Jerusalem stone and generously garnished with fur—the kind of pecs you could bounce pocket change off, if there hadn't been a forest of thrice-curled hair so dense that all that entered it was deposited for good.

Among his brothers, and between haircuts, Max was boy enough. But Barak made him seem small, weak, ungendered. And everyone seemed to recognize it—no one more than Max, who took a meek half step back, in the direction of his mommy's room at the Washington Hilton.

"Max!" Tamir said, turning his sights on the boy.

"Affirmative."

Jacob gave an embarrassed chuckle: "Affirmative? Really?"

"It just came out," Max said, smelling his own blood.

Tamir gave him a once-over and said, "You look like a vegetarian."

"Pescatarian," Max said.

"You eat meat," Jacob said.

"I know. I *look* like a pescatarian."

Barak gave Max a punch to the chest, for no obvious reason.

"Ouch! What the—"

"Joking," Barak said, "joking."

Max rubbed at his chest. "Your joke fractured my sternum."

"Food?" Tamir asked, slapping his paunch.

"I thought maybe we'd head by Isaac's first," Jacob suggested.

"Let the man eat," Irv said, creating sides by choosing one of them.

"Why the hell not," Jacob said, remembering that Kafka quote: "In the struggle between yourself and the world, side with the world."

Tamir looked around the airport terminal and clapped his hands. "Panda Express! The best!"

He got pork lo mein. Irv did everything he could to conceal his displeasure, but his everything wasn't too formidable. If Tamir couldn't be a character in the Torah, he could at least adhere to it. But Irv was a good host, blood being blood, and bit his tongue until his teeth touched.

"You know where you can get the best Italian food in the world right now?" Tamir asked, stabbing a piece of pork.

"Italy?"

"*Israel.*"

"I'd heard that," Irv said.

Jacob couldn't let such a preposterous statement go.

"You mean the best Italian food *outside of Italy.*"

"No, I'm telling you the best Italian food being cooked right now is being cooked in Israel."

"Right. But you're making the dubious claim that Israel is the country *outside of Italy* that makes the best Italian food."

"*Including* Italy," he said, cracking the knuckles of his forkless hand simply by making a fist and opening it.

"That's definitionally impossible. Like saying the best German beer is Israeli."

"It's called Goldstar."

"Which I love," Irv added.

"You don't even drink beer."

"But when I do."

"Let me ask you something," Tamir said. "Where do they make the best bagels in the world?"

"New York."

"I agree. The best bagels in the world are being made in New York. Now let me ask you: Is a bagel a Jewish food?"

"Depends on what you mean by that."

"Is a bagel a Jewish food in the same way that pasta is an Italian food?"

"In a similar way."

"And let me also ask you: Is Israel the Jewish homeland?"

"Israel is the Jewish *state*."

Tamir straightened in his seat.

"That wasn't the part of my argument you were supposed to disagree with."

Irv shot Jacob a look. "Of course it's the Jewish homeland."

"It depends on what you mean by homeland," Jacob said. "If you mean ancestral homeland—"

"What do *you* mean?" Tamir asked.

"I mean the place my family comes from."

"Which is?"

"Galicia."

"But before that."

"What, Africa?"

Irv let his voice drip like molasses, but not sweet: "*Africa*, Jacob?"

"It's arbitrary. We could go back to the trees, or the ocean, if we wanted. Some go back to Eden. You pick Israel. I pick Galicia."

"You feel Galician?"

"I feel American."

"I feel Jewish," Irv said.

"The truth," Tamir said, popping the last piece of pork into his mouth, "is you feel Julia's titties."

Apropos of nothing, Max asked, "Do you think the bathroom is clean?"

Jacob wondered if Max's question, his desire to be away, was apropos of some knowledge, or intuition, that his father hadn't touched his mother's breasts in months?

"It's a bathroom," Tamir said.

"I'll just wait until we get home."

"If you have to go," Jacob said, "go. It's not good to hold it."

"Says who?" Irv asked.

"Says your prostate."

"You think my prostate speaks to you?"

"I don't have to go," Max said.

"It's good to hold it," Tamir said. "It's like a . . . what do you call it? Not a kugel . . ."

"Give it a shot, OK, Max? Just in case."

"Let the kid not go," Irv said. And to Tamir: "A kegel. And you're absolutely right."

"*I'll* go," Jacob said. "You know why? Because I love my prostate."

"Maybe you should marry it," Max said.

Jacob didn't have to go, but he went. And then he stood there at the urinal, an asshole with an exposed penis, passing a few moments to further his absence of a point, and just in case.

A man his father's age was urinating beside him. His pee came out in bursts, as if from a lawn sprinkler, and to Jacob's unaccredited ear it sounded like a symptom. When the man let out a small grunt, Jacob reflexively glanced over, and they exchanged the briefest of smiles before remembering where they were: a place where exactly one extremely brief moment of acknowledgment was tolerable. Jacob had the strong sensation that he knew this person. He often felt that at urinals, but this time he was sure—as he always was. Where had he seen that face before? A teacher from grade school? One of the boys' teachers? One of his father's friends? He was momentarily convinced that this stranger was a figure in one of Julia's old family photos from Eastern Europe, and that he had traveled through time to deliver a warning.

Jacob returned to thoughts of babbling brooks and the slow death of a lower back whose demise, like so much else, he never considered until forced, and it hit him: *Spielberg.* Once the thought appeared, there was no doubting it. Of course it was him. Jacob was standing, his penis exposed, next to Steven Spielberg, whose penis was exposed. What were the odds?

Jacob had grown up, as had every Jew in the last quarter of the twentieth century, under Spielberg's wing. Rather, in the shadow of his wing. He had seen *E.T.* three times in its opening week, all at the Uptown, each time through his fingers as the bike chase reached a climax so delicious it was literally unbearable. He had seen *Indiana Jones*, and the next one, and the next one. Tried to sit through *Always*. Nobody's perfect. Not until he makes *Schindler's List*, at which point he is not even *he* anymore, but representative of *them*. Them? The murdered millions. No, Jacob thought, representative of *us*. The Unmurdered. But *Schindler* wasn't for us. It was for *them*. Them? Not the Murdered, of course. They couldn't watch movies. It was for all of them who weren't *us*: the goyim. Because with Spielberg, into whose bank account the general public was compelled to make annual deposits, we finally had a way to force them to look at our absence, to rub their noses in the German shepherd's shit.

And God, was he loved. Jacob found the movie schmaltzy, overblown, and flirting with kitsch. But he had been profoundly moved. Irv denounced the choice to tell an uplifting Holocaust story, to give, for all intents and purposes, a statistically negligible happy ending generated by that statistically negligible of species, the good German. But even Irv had been moved to his limits. Isaac couldn't have been more moved: *You see, you see what was done to us, to mine parents, to mine brothers, to me, you see?* Everyone was moved, and everyone was persuaded that being moved was the ultimate aesthetic, intellectual, and ethical experience.

Jacob was going to have to cop a look at Spielberg's penis. The only question was on what pretense.

Every annual physical ended with Dr. Schlesinger kneeling in front of Jacob, cupping Jacob's balls, and asking him to turn his head and cough. That experience seemed to be universal, and universally inexplicable, among men. But coughing and turning one's head had something to do with genitals. The logic wasn't airtight, but it felt right. Jacob coughed and snuck a peek.

The size didn't make an impression—Spielberg was no longer, shorter, wider, or narrower than most doughy Jewish grandfathers. Neither was he particularly bananaed, pendular, reticulated, lightbulb-ish, reptilian, laminar, mushroomed, varicosey, hook-nosed, or cockeyed. What was notable was what wasn't missing: his penis was uncircumcised. Jacob had had precious little exposure to the visual atrocity that is an intact penis, and so wouldn't bet his life on what he saw—and the stakes felt that high—but he knew enough to know that he had to look again. But though urinal etiquette forgives a greeting, and the cough might have been a passable alibi for the glance, there was simply no way to return to the scene without propositioning sex, and even in a world in which Spielberg hadn't made *A.I.*, that wasn't going to happen.

There were four options: (1) he had misidentified him as Steven Spielberg and misidentified his penis as being uncircumcised; (2) he had misidentified him as Steven Spielberg and correctly identified his penis as being uncircumcised; (3) it *was* Steven Spielberg, but he had misidentified his penis as being uncircumcised—*of course* he was circumcised; or (4) Steven Spielberg wasn't circumcised. If he were a betting man, he'd push his mountain of chips onto (4).

Jacob flushed (his face and the urinal), washed too quickly to accomplish anything, and scrambled back out to the others.

"You're never going to guess who I just peed beside."

"*Jesus*, Dad."

"Close. Spielberg."

"Who's that?" Tamir asked.

"You're serious?"

"What?"

"*Spielberg*. Steven Spielberg."

"Never heard of him."

"Give me a break," Jacob said, unsure, as ever, to what extent Tamir was performing. Whatever else could be said about him, Tamir was smart, worldly, and restless. But whatever else could be said about him, he was foolish, solipsistic, and self-satisfied. If he had a sense of humor, it was drier than cornstarch. Which enabled him to practice a kind of psychological acupuncture on Jacob: Did a needle just enter me? Does it hurt? Is this complete bullshit? He couldn't have been serious about Israeli Italian food, could he? About not having heard of Spielberg? Impossible, and entirely possible.

"That's heavy," Irv said.

"And the heaviest part?" Jacob leaned in and whispered, "He's not circumcised."

Max threw his hands into the air. "What did you, kiss his wiener in a bathroom stall?"

"Who is this Spielberg?" Tamir asked.

"We were at *urinals*, Max." And just to be clear: "And of course I didn't kiss his wiener."

"That simply cannot be right," Irv said.

"I know. But I saw it with my own eyes."

"Why were *your own eyes* checking out another man's penis?" Max asked.

"Because he's Steven Spielberg."

"Why won't someone tell me who this person is?" Tamir said.

"Because I don't believe that you don't know who he is."

"Why would I pretend?" Tamir asked, entirely believably.

"Because it's your bizarre Israeli way of diminishing the achievements of American Jews."

"And why would I want to do that?"

"You'd have to tell me."

"OK," Tamir said, calmly wiping the remnants of six packets of duck sauce from the corners of his mouth, "whatever you say." He got up and headed in the direction of the condiments bar.

"You have to go back in and be sure," Irv said. "Introduce yourself."

"You will do no such thing," Max said, exactly as his mother would have.

Irv closed his eyes and said, "My core has been shaken."

"I know."

"What are we to believe?"

"I *know.*"

"All the while we thought his Holocaust schlock was compensating for the *Holocaust.*"

"Now it's schlock?"

"It was always schlock," Irv said. "But it was *our* schlock. Now . . . I have to wonder."

"It's not as if he isn't Jewi—"

But Jacob couldn't finish the sentence. Or he didn't need to. As soon as the fragment of the possibility entered the world, there was no room for anything else.

"I need to sit down," Irv said.

"You are sitting down," Max told him.

"I need to sit on the floor."

"Don't," Jacob said. "It's filthy."

"Everything is now filthy," Irv said.

In silence, they watched dozens of people balancing overstuffed trays weave and dodge and never touch. Presumably, a higher life-form would have its own version of David Attenborough. That "person" could make a great episode of a miniseries about humans featuring such hypnotic observing.

Max whispered something incomprehensible, to no one.

Irv rested his head in his hands and said, "If God had wanted us to be uncircumcised, He wouldn't have invented smegma."

"What?" Jacob asked.

"If God had wanted . . ."

"I'm talking to Max."

"I didn't say anything," Max said.

"What?"

"Nothing."

"Jaws is such a terrible movie," Irv said.

And then Tamir came back. They'd been too preoccupied by their apocalyptic speculations to notice how long he'd been gone.

"So here's the deal," he said.

"What deal?"

"He has problems with urinary retention."

"He?"

"Steve."

Irv clapped his cheeks and squealed like it was his first visit to the American Girl flagship store.

"I can see why you assumed I would know who he is. Very impressive résumé. What can I say? I don't watch a lot of movies. There's no money in watching movies. A lot in making them, though. Do you know that he's worth more than three billion dollars? *Billion* with a *b*?"

"Really?"

"He had no reason to lie to me."

"But why did he have reason to share?"

"I asked."

"How much he's worth?"

"Yeah."

"And you probably asked if he's circumcised, right?"

"I did."

Jacob embraced Tamir. He hadn't meant to. His arms simply reached for him. It wasn't that Tamir had gathered the piece of information. It was that he had all the qualities that Jacob lacked and didn't want but desperately missed: the brashness, the fearlessness where fear was not required, the fearlessness where fear *was* required, the giving of no shits. "Tamir, you are a beautiful human being."

"So . . . ?" Irv begged.

Tamir turned to Jacob.

"He knows you, by the way. He didn't recognize you, but when I mentioned your name, he said he read your first book. He said he considered optioning it, whatever that means."

"He did?"

"That's what he said."

"If Spielberg had made a film out of that book, I'd—"

"Exhume the lede," Irv said. "Is he short-sleeved?"

Tamir jiggled his soda cup, freeing the ice cubes from their group hug.

"Tamir?"

"We agreed it would be funnier if I didn't tell you."

"*We?*"

"Steve and I."

Jacob gave him a shove, as spontaneous as the hug.

"You're bullshitting."

"Israelis never bullshit."

"Israelis *only* bullshit."

"We're mishpuchah," Irv pleaded.

"Yes. And if you can't keep secrets from your family, who can you keep secrets from?"

"So I emancipate myself from the family. Now tell me."

Tamir scraped the remaining lo mein from his bowl and said, "Before I fly back."

"What?"

"I'll tell you before I go."

"You can't be serious."

Could he be serious?

"I can."

Irv banged the table.

"I'll tell Max," Tamir said. "An early bar mitzvah present. What he chooses to do with the information is his own business."

"You know it's Sam's bar mitzvah," Max said. "Not mine."

"Of course," he said with a wink. "This is a very early bar mitzvah present."

He put his hands on Max's shoulders and brought him close. His lips almost touching Max's ear, he whispered. And Max smiled. He laughed.

As they walked to the car, Irv kept signaling for Jacob to take one of Tamir's bags, and Jacob kept signaling that Tamir wouldn't let him. And Jacob signaled to Max that he should talk to Barak, and Max signaled back that his father should—smoke through a stoma? There they were, four men and one almost-man, and yet they were making silly hand gestures that communicated almost nothing and fooled almost no one.

"How's your grandfather?" Tamir asked.

"Compared to what?"

"To how he was last time I saw him."

"That was a decade ago."

"So he's older, probably."

"He's moving in a couple of days."

"Making aliyah?"

"Yup. To the Jewish Home."

"What's he got left?"

"Are you asking me how much longer he is expected to live?"

"You find such complicated ways to say such simple things."

"I can only tell you what his doctor told me."

"So?"

"He's been dead for five years."

"A medical miracle."

"Among other kinds. I'm sure it would mean the world to him to see you."

"Let's go to your house. We'll drop off the bags, see Julia—"

"She won't be back until the late afternoon."

"So we'll nosh, shoot some baskets. I'd like to see your audiovisual setup."

"I don't think we have one. And he usually goes to sleep very early, like—"

"You're our guest," Irv said to Tamir, patting his back. "We'll do whatever you'd like."

"Of course," Jacob said, siding with the world in its struggle against his grandfather. "We can always visit later. Or tomorrow."

"I brought some halvah for him."

"He's diabetic."

"It's from the souk."

"Yeah, his diabetes doesn't really care about sourcing."

Tamir took the halvah from his carry-on bag, opened the wrapping, removed a piece, and tossed it in his mouth.

"I'll drive," Jacob said to Irv as they approached the car.

"Why?"

"Because I'll drive."

"I thought the highway made you anxious?"

"Don't be ridiculous," Jacob said, flashing Tamir a smile of dismissiveness. And then, to Irv, with force: "Give me the keys."

In the car, Tamir pressed the sole of his right foot against the windshield, parachuting his scrotum for any infra-red traffic cameras they might pass. He braided his fingers behind his head—more knuckle cracking—nodded, and began: "To tell you the truth, I'm making a lot of money." *Here we go*, Jacob thought. *Tamir impersonating the bad impersonator of Tamir.* "High tech has gone crazy, and I was smart enough—I was brave enough—to get into a lot of things at the right moment. That's the secret to success: the combination of intelligence and bravery. Because there are a lot of intelligent people in the world, and a lot of brave people in the world, but when you go searching for people who are intelligent *and* brave, you don't find yourself surrounded. And I was lucky. Look, Jake—" Why did he think it was OK to capriciously shear Jacob's name? It was an act of aggression, even if Jacob couldn't parse it, even if he loved it. "I don't believe in luck, but only a fool wouldn't acknowledge the importance of being in the right place at the right time. You make your own luck. That's what I say."

"That's also what everyone says," Jacob pointed out.

"But still, we don't control everything."

"What about Israel?" Irv asked from the backseat.

"Israel?" *Here we go.* "Israel is thriving. Walk down the streets of Tel Aviv one night. There's more culture per square foot than anywhere in the world. Look at our economy. We're sixty-eight years old—younger than you, Irv. We have only seven million people, no natural resources, and are engaged in perpetual war. All of that, and we have more companies on the NASDAQ than any country after America. We have more start-ups than China, India, and the U.K., and file more patents than any country in the world—*including* yours."

"Things are going well," Irv confirmed.

"Things have never been better *anywhere at any time* than they are in Israel right now."

"The height of the Roman Empire?" Jacob felt a need to ask.

"Where are they now?"

"That's what the Romans asked of the Greeks."

"We live in a different apartment than the one you visited. We're always moving. It's good business, and it's good in the general sense, too. We're in a triplex now—three floors. We have seven bedrooms—"

"Eight," Barak corrected.

"He's right. It's eight." *This is performance*, Jacob reminded himself, or tried to convince himself, as he felt a jealousy surfacing. *It's a routine. He's not making you smaller.* Tamir continued: "Eight bedrooms, even though we're only four people now that Noam is in the army. Two bedrooms a person. But I like the space. It's not that we have so many guests, although we have a lot, but I like to stretch out: a couple of rooms for my business ventures; Rivka is insane about meditating; the kids have air hockey, gaming systems. They have a foosball table from Germany. I have an assistant who has nothing to do with my business ventures but just helps with lifestyle things, and I said, 'Go find me the best foosball table in the world.' And she did. She has an amazing body, and she knows how to find *anything*. It's quite amazing. You could leave this foosball table in the rain for a year and it would be fine."

"I thought it never rains in Israel," Jacob said.

"It does," Tamir said, "but you're right, the climate is ideal. Anyway, I rest my drinks on it, and do they ever leave a ring? Barak?"

"No."

"So when we were walking through the new apartment—the most recent apartment—I turned to Rivka and said, 'Eh?' and she said, 'What do we need with an apartment this big?' I told her what I'll tell you now: The more you buy, the more you have to sell."

"You should really write a book," Jacob said to Tamir, taking a tiny needle from his back and placing it in Tamir's.

"So should you," Irv said, taking that tiny needle from Tamir's back and placing it in Jacob's aorta.

"And I told her something else: it's always going to be rich people who have money, so you want to have what the rich people will want to have. The more expensive something is, the more expensive it will become."

"But that's just saying that expensive things are expensive," Jacob pointed out.

"Exactly."

"Well," Jacob's better angel ventriloquized, "I'd love to see it someday."

"You'd have to come to Israel."

With a smile: "The apartment can't come to me?"

"It could, but that would be crazy. And anyway, soon enough it will be another apartment."

"Well, then I'd love to see *that* one."

"And the bathrooms . . . The bathrooms would blow your mind. Everything made in Germany."

Irv groaned.

"You can't *find* this kind of craftsmanship."

"Apparently you can."

"Well, you can't find it in America. My assistant—the personal one, with the body—found me a toilet with a camera that recognizes who is approaching and adjusts to preset settings. Rivka likes a cool seat. I want my ass hairs singed. Yael wants to be practically standing when she shits. Barak faces backwards."

"I don't face backwards," Barak said, punching his father's shoulder.

"You think I'm crazy," Tamir said. "You're probably judging me, even laughing at me in your mind, but I'm the one with a toilet that knows his name, and I'm the one with a refrigerator that does the shopping online, and you're the one driving a Japanese go-kart."

Jacob didn't think Tamir was crazy. He thought his need to exhibit and press the case for his happiness was unconvincing and sad. And sympathetic. That's where the emotional logic broke down. All that should have led Jacob to dislike Tamir brought him closer—not with envy, but love. He loved Tamir's brazen weakness. He loved his inability—his unwillingness—to hide his ugliness. Such exposure was what Jacob most wanted, and most withheld from himself.

"And what about the situation?" Irv asked.

"What situation?"

"Safety."

"What? Food safety?"

"The *Arabs*."

"Which ones?"

"Iran. Syria. Hezbollah. Hamas. The Islamic State. Al-Qaeda."

"The Iranians aren't Arabs. They're Persian."

"I'm sure that helps you sleep at night."

"Things could be better, things could be worse. Beyond that, you know what I know."

"I only know what's in the papers," Irv said.

"Where do you think I get my news?"

"So how does it *feel* over there?" Irv pressed.

"Would I be happier if Noam were a DJ for the army radio station? Sure. But I feel fine. Barak, you feel fine?"

"I feel cool."

"You think Israel's going to bomb Iran?"

"I don't know," Tamir said. "What do you think?"

"Do you think they *should*?" Jacob asked. He wasn't immune to the morbid curiosity, the American Jewish bloodlust at arm's length.

"Of course they should," Irv said.

"If there were a way to bomb Iran without bombing Iran, that would be good. Any other course will be bad."

"So what *do* you think they should do?" Jacob asked.

"He just told you," Irv said. "He thinks they should bomb Iran."

"I think *you* should bomb Iran," Tamir told Irv.

"America?"

"That would be good, too. But I meant you specifically. You could use some of those biological weapons you displayed earlier."

They all laughed at that, especially Max.

"Seriously," Irv pressed, "what do you think should happen?"

"Seriously, I don't know."

"And you're OK with that?"

"Are you?"

"No, I'm not OK with it. I think we should bomb Iran before it's too late."

To which Tamir said, "And I think we should establish who *we* is before it's too late."

All Tamir wanted to talk about was money—the average Israeli income, the size of his own easy fortune, the unrivaled quality of life in that fingernail clipping of oppressively hot homeland hemmed in by psychopathic enemies.

All Irv wanted to talk about was the *situation*—when was Israel going to make us proud by making itself safe? Was there any inside piece of information to be dangled above friends at the dining room at the American Enterprise Institute, or whose pin might be pulled in his blog and thrown? Wasn't it high time we—you—did something about this or that?

All Jacob wanted to talk about was living close to death: Had Tamir killed anyone? Had Noam? Did either have any stories of fellow soldiers torturing or being tortured? What's the worst thing either ever saw with his own eyes?

The Jews Jacob grew up with adjusted their aviator glasses with only the muscles in their faces while parsing Fugazi lyrics while pushing in the lighters of their hand-me-down Volvo wagons. The lighter would pop out, they'd push it back in. Nothing was ever lit. They were miserable at sports, but great at fantasy sports. They avoided fights, but sought arguments. They were the children and grandchildren of immigrants, of survivors. They were defined by, and proud of, their flagrant weakness.

Yet they were intoxicated by muscle. Not literal muscle—they found that suspicious, foolish, and lame. No, they were driven wild by the muscular application of the Jewish brain: Maccabees rolling under the bellies of armored Greek elephants to stab the soft undersides; Mossad missions whose odds, means, and results verged on magic; computer viruses so preternaturally complicated and smart they couldn't not leave Jewish fingerprints. You think you can mess with us, world? You think you can push us around? You can. But brain beats muscle as surely as paper beats rock, and we're gonna learn you; we're gonna sit at our desks and be the last ones standing.

As they sought the parking lot exit, like a marble in one of Benjy's OCD Marble Madness creations, Jacob felt inexplicably peaceful. Despite all that had been spilled, was the cup still half full? Or did a crumb of Wellbutrin just lodge free from between his brain's teeth, offering a morsel of undigested happiness? The cup was half full enough.

Despite his endless smart-ass and legitimate and almost-honorable protestations, Sam showed up for his bar mitzvah lessons. And despite being forced to apologize for a noncrime that he didn't commit, he would show up at the bimah.

Despite being an insufferable, chauvinistic blowhard, Irv was ever present, and, in his own way, ever loving.

Despite his long history of false promises, and despite his older son being on duty in the West Bank, Tamir showed up. He brought his boy. They were family, and they were *being* family.

But what about Jacob? Was he there? His mind kept leaping to the supermagnet of Mark and Julia, though not in the ways he would have expected. He'd often imagined Julia having sex with other men. It very nearly destroyed him, but thrilled what was spared. He didn't want such thoughts, but sexual fantasy wants what is not to be had. He'd imagined Mark fucking her after their meeting at the hardware place. But now that something had happened between them—it was entirely possible they'd already fucked—his mind was released. It's not that the fantasy was suddenly too painful; it suddenly wasn't painful enough.

Now, driving a car full of family, his wife in a hotel with a man she'd at least kissed, his fantasy found the bull's-eye: it was the same car, but different occupants. Julia looks in the rearview mirror and sees Benjy falling asleep in his Benjy way: his body straight, his neck straight, his gaze directly in front of him, his eyes closing so slowly their movement is imperceptible—only by looking away and looking back can you register any change. The physicality of it, the fragility evoked by witnessing such slowness, is perplexing and beautiful. She looks at the road, she looks in the mirror, she looks at the road. Every time she looks at Benjy in the mirror, his eyes have closed another millimeter or two. The process of falling asleep takes ten minutes, the seconds of which have been pulled thin to the translucency of his slowly closing eyelids. And just before his eyes are fully closed, he releases a short puff of breath, as if blowing out his own candle. The rest of the drive is whispering, and each pothole feels like a moon crater, and on the moon is a photograph of a family, left by the Apollo astronaut Charles Duke in 1972. It will remain there, unchanging, for millions of years, outlasting not only the parents and children in the photo, and the grandchildren of the grandchildren of the grandchildren, but human civilization—until the dying sun consumes it. They pull up to the house, cut the engine, unfasten their seat belts, and Mark carries Benjy inside.

That was his new elsewhere, where his mind was as they arrived at the parking lot exit. Tamir reached for his wallet, but Irv was the quicker draw.

"Next time's on me," Tamir said.

"Sure," Irv said. "Next time we're exiting National Airport I'll let you pay for the parking."

The gate rose, and for the first time since they'd gotten in the car, Max spoke up: "Turn on the radio, Dad."

"What?"

"Didn't you hear that?"

"Hear what?"

"In the guy's booth."

"The cashier?"

"Yeah. The radio."

"No."

"Something big happened."

"What?"

"Do I have to do everything?" Tamir asked, turning on the radio.

Entering in the middle of a report, it was impossible to understand at first what had happened, but it was clear that Max was right about its size. NPR's back was straight. Reports were coming in from across the Middle East. It was early. Little was known.

Jacob's mind raced to its place of comfort: the worst possible scenario. The Israelis had launched an attack on Iran, or the other way around. Or the Egyptians had attacked themselves. A bus had exploded. A plane had been hijacked. Someone had sprayed bullets in a mosque or synagogue, swung a knife in a crowded public space. A nuclear blast had vaporized Tel Aviv. But the thing about the worst possible scenario is that by definition it can't be anticipated.

Other Life was happening even when no one was present. Just like Life. Sam was in the Model UN's General Assembly—at that moment, his mom passed him a note: "I can see over the wall. Can you?"—but the ruins of his first synagogue were shimmering beside the foundation of his second synagogue. Scattered among the rubble were the fragments of his stained-glass Jewish Present, each shard illuminated by destruction.

REAL REAL

The Hilton's International Ballroom was arranged in concentric arcs of tables and chairs to resemble the UN General Assembly. Delegations were dressed in regional garb, and some of the students attempted accents before one of the facilitators called a moratorium on that very bad idea.

The Saudi delegation's speech was wrapping up. A young, heavily naturally accented Hispanic girl in a hijab spoke with quivering hands and a weak, trembling voice. Julia hated to see nervous children. She wanted to go to her, give her an inspirational talk—explain that life changes, and what is weak becomes strong, and what is a dream becomes a reality that requires a new dream.

"And so it is our hope," the girl said, clearly grateful to be reaching the end, "that the Federated States of Micronesia comes to its senses and behaves judiciously and with speed to turn over the bomb to the International Atomic Energy Agency. That is all. Thank you. As-salamu alaykum."

There was some light applause, most of it from Julia. At the front of the room, the chairman—a facilitator with a goatee on his face and a Velcro wallet in his back pocket—spoke.

"Thank you, Saudi Arabia. And now we'll hear from the Federated States of Micronesia."

All attention shifted to the Georgetown Day delegation. Billie rose.

"Kind of ironic," she began, asserting her nonchalant dominance by pretending to sort through her papers as she spoke, "for the Saudi delegate to tell us what to do, when *it's illegal for her to swim in her own country.* Just saying."

Kids laughed. The Saudi delegation shriveled. With affected drama, Billie leveled the pages against the desk and continued.

"Fellow members of the United Nations, on behalf of the Federated States of Micronesia, I would like to address what has become known as the nuclear crisis. The Merriam-Webster dictionary defines crisis as"— she swiped her phone into consciousness and read—"'a difficult or danger-ous situation that needs serious attention.' This is not a crisis. There is nothing difficult or dangerous about our situation. What we have here, in fact, is an *opportunity*, which Merriam-Webster defines as . . . just one second . . ."—the Wi-Fi was crappy, and it took her longer than planned to load the bookmarked page—"Here we go: 'an amount of time or a situation in which something can be done.' We didn't choose our fate, but we don't intend to shrink from it. For years, for millennia—or for centuries, anyway—the good people of Micronesia accepted things as they were, understanding our diminished existence as our lot, our bur-den, our fate."

Julia and Sam sat at opposite ends of the delegation. As Julia drew a brick wall on a yellow pad, she replayed the morning's phone call with Jacob: her lot, her burden, her fate. Why did she feel a need to do it right then, like that? Not only had she shot from the hip when she should have spoken from the heart or at least held her tongue, she had risked Max and Irv getting caught in the crossfire. What did they hear and under-stand? What did Jacob have to explain, and how did he do it? Were any of the three going to mention the call to Tamir and Barak? Was that the whole point? Did she want it all to blow up? Her wall now covered three-quarters of the page. Perhaps a thousand bricks.

Billie continued: "Things are about to change, fellow delegates. Mi-cronesia is saying *enough*. Enough being pushed around, enough sub-servience, enough eating scraps. Fellow delegates, things are about to change, beginning, but most certainly not ending, with the following list of demands . . ."

In the remaining space, between the top of the brick wall and the edge of the page, Julia wrote, "I can see over the wall. Can you?" She folded it in half, and folded that in half, and had it passed the length of the delegation. Sam showed no emotion of any kind as he read it. He wrote something on the same page, folded and refolded it, and had it passed back to his mom. She opened it, and at first couldn't see anything he'd written. Nothing in the space above the wall, where she'd written. She searched the bricks themselves—nothing. She looked to him. He put his open hand in front of him, fingers spread, then flipped it palm-up. She turned over the yellow paper, and Sam had written: "The other side of the wall is no wall."

As the rest of the delegation was struggling to catch up with her radical departure from the agreed-upon script, Billie was smashing the rhetorical ceiling: "Micronesia shall, henceforth, have a seat on the UN Security Council; be granted NATO membership—yes, we realize we are in the Pacific—and preferential trading status with EU, NAFTA, UNASUR, AU, and EAEC partners; have an appointed member on the Federal Reserve Open Market Committee—"

A facilitator ran into the room.

"I'm sorry to interrupt the proceedings," he said, "but I have an announcement. There was just a major earthquake in the Middle East."

"This is real?" one of the chaperones asked.

"Real."

"How major?"

"They're calling it historic."

"But real like the nuclear crisis? Or *real* real?"

Julia's phone vibrated with a call; it was Deborah. She shuffled to the corner and answered, while the model crisis gave way to the real real one.

"Deborah?"

"Hi, Julia."

"Is everything OK?"

"Benjy's fine."

"I got scared when I saw your name come up."

"He's fine. He's watching a movie."

"OK. I got scared."

"Julia." She took a long breath, to extend the period of not-knowing. "Something horrible has happened, Julia."

"*Benjy?*"

"Benjy is absolutely fine."

"You're a mother. You would tell me."

"Of course I would. He's fine, Julia. He's happy."

"Let me speak with him."

"This isn't about Benjy."

"Oh my God, did something happen to Jacob and Max?"

"No. They're fine."

"Do you promise me?"

"You need to go home."

VEY IZ MIR

Little was known, which made what little was known terrifying. An earthquake of magnitude 7.6 had struck at 6:23 in the evening, its epicenter deep under the Dead Sea, just outside the Israeli settlement of Kalya. Electricity was out in virtually all of Israel, Jordan, Lebanon, and Syria. It seemed that the most badly damaged areas were Salt and Amman in Jordan, as well as the West Bank city of Jericho, whose walls crumbled thirty-four hundred years before, many archaeologists have argued, not from Joshua's trumpeting but from a massive earthquake.

First accounts were coming in from the Old City of Jerusalem: the Crusader-era Church of the Holy Sepulcher, the traditional burial place of Jesus and the holiest site in Christianity, which was badly damaged in a 1927 earthquake, had partially collapsed with an unknown number of tourists and clergymen inside. Synagogues and yeshivas, monasteries, mosques and madrassas, were in ruins. There was no news about the Temple Mount, either because there was no news or because those bearing it withheld it.

A civil engineer was being interviewed on NPR. The host, a sultry-voiced, probably short-and-bald Jew named Robert Siegel, began:

SIEGEL: We apologize, in advance, for the audio quality of this interview. Normally, when phone lines are down, we use cell phones. But cell service has been disabled as well, so Mr. Horowitz is speaking to us by satellite phone. Mr. Horowitz, are you there?

HOROWITZ: Yes, hello. I am here.

SIEGEL: Can you give us your professional assessment of what's going on right now?

HOROWITZ: My professional assessment, yes, but I can also tell you as a human being standing here that Israel has endured a cataclysmic earthquake. Everywhere you look there is destruction.

SIEGEL: You are safe, though?

HOROWITZ: *Safe* is a relative term. My family is alive, and as you can hear, so am I. Some are safer. Some are less safe.

Why the fuck can't Israelis just answer questions? Jacob wondered. Even then, in the midst of cataclysm—the word itself sounded like classic Israeli hyperbole—the Israeli couldn't just give a straightforward, un-Israeli response.

SIEGEL: Mr. Horowitz, you are an engineer for Israeli civil services, is that correct?

HOROWITZ: An engineer, an adviser on government projects, an academic . . .

SIEGEL: As an engineer, what can you tell us about the potential effects of an earthquake of this magnitude?

HOROWITZ: It is not good.

SIEGEL: Could you elaborate?

HOROWITZ: Of the six hundred fifty thousand structures in Israel, fewer than half are equipped to deal with such an event.

SIEGEL: Are we going to see skyscrapers topple?

HOROWITZ: Of course not, Robert Siegel. They have been engi-neered to withstand even more than this. It's the buildings be-tween three and eight stories I'm most worried about. Many will survive, but few will be habitable. You have to realize that Israel didn't have a building code until the late 1970s, and it's never been enforced.

SIEGEL: Why is that?

HOROWITZ: We've had other things on our minds.

SIEGEL: The conflict.

HOROWITZ: Conflict? We should have been so lucky to have only one conflict. Most buildings are made of concrete—very rigid, unforgiving engineering. Buildings like Israelis, you might say. It's served a booming population well, but couldn't be worse-suited to the current situation.

SIEGEL: What about the West Bank?

HOROWITZ: What about it?

SIEGEL: How will its structures respond to such an earth-quake?

HOROWITZ: You'd have to ask a Palestinian civil engineer.

SIEGEL: Well, we'll certainly try to—

HOROWITZ: But since you're asking me, I have to imagine it has been completely destroyed.

SIEGEL: I'm sorry, *what* has?

HOROWITZ: The West Bank.

SIEGEL: Destroyed?

HOROWITZ: All of the structures. Everything. There's going to be a lot of fatality.

SIEGEL: In the thousands?

HOROWITZ: I'm afraid that as I speak these words, tens of thousands are already dead.

SIEGEL: And I am sure you want to get to your family, but before letting you go, could you offer some possibilities for how this will play out?

HOROWITZ: What time frame are you asking about? Hours? Weeks? A generation?

SIEGEL: Let's start with hours.

HOROWITZ: The next few hours will be pivotal for Israel. It's all about prioritizing now. Electricity is out countrywide, and will likely remain out, even in the major cities, for several days. As you can imagine, military needs will be the first priority.

SIEGEL: I'm surprised to hear you say that.

HOROWITZ: You are Jewish?

SIEGEL: I'm not sure why that's relevant, but yes, I am.

HOROWITZ: I'm surprised that a fellow Jew would be surprised. But then, only an American Jew would question why being Jewish is relevant.

SIEGEL: You're concerned for Israel's safety?

HOROWITZ: You aren't?

SIEGEL: Mr. Horowitz—

HOROWITZ: Israel's tactical superiority is technological, and that has been greatly diminished by the quake. The destruction will cause desperation and unrest. And this will develop—either organically or deliberately—into violence. If it hasn't already happened, we're soon to see masses of people flooding the borders into Israel—from the West Bank, Gaza, Jordan, Lebanon, Syria. I don't have to tell you that Syria already has a refugee problem.

SIEGEL: Why would they come to Israel, a country most in the Arab world view as a mortal enemy?

HOROWITZ: Because their mortal enemy has first-rate medical care. Their mortal enemy has food and water. And Israel is going to be presented with a choice: let them in, or don't. Letting them in will require sharing limited and precious resourses. For others to live, Israelis will have to die. But not letting them in will involve bullets. And of course Israel's neighbors will have a choice, too: take care of their citizens, or take advantage of Israel's sudden vulnerability.

SIEGEL: Let's hope the shared tragedy brings the region together.

HOROWITZ: Yes, but let's not be naïve while we hope.

SIEGEL: And what about the long term? You mentioned the generational view?

HOROWITZ: Of course, no one can know what will happen, but what Israel is facing here is something far more threatening than '67, or '73, or even Iran's nuclear threat. There is the immediate crisis of needing to secure the country, rescue citizens, get food and medical care to those who need it, repair the electricity, gas, water, and other utilities quickly and safely. Then there is also the work of rebuilding the country. This will be a generational challenge. And finally, and perhaps most daunting, will be the work of keeping Jews here.

SIEGEL: Meaning?

HOROWITZ: A young, ambitious, idealistic Israeli has many reasons to leave Israel. You have an expression, "The straw that broke
the camel's back."

SIEGEL: Yes.

HOROWITZ: Thousands of buildings have fallen on the back.

JACOB: *Vey iz mir.*

Jacob hadn't meant to say anything, and he certainly hadn't meant to
say *vey iz mir.* But then, no one ever means to say *vey iz mir.*
"This is bad," Irv said, shaking his head. "Really, really bad in about a
million ways."
Jacob's mind teleported to apocalyptic tableaux: the ceiling collapsed
onto the trundle in Tamir's old bedroom; women in wigs trapped under
slabs of Jerusalem stone, the ruins of the ruins of Masada. He imagined
the marble bench in Blumenberg Park, now shattered stone. It must be a
catastrophe, he thought, but he meant it in two entirely different ways:
that it certainly had to be, and that he wanted it to be. He couldn't acknowledge the second meaning, but he couldn't deny it.
Tamir said, "It's not good. But it's not so bad."
"Do you want to call home?"
"You heard him. The lines are knocked out. And my voice won't help
anyone."
"Are you sure?"
"They're fine. Absolutely. We live in a new construction. Like he said,
it's engineered for this kind of thing—better than any of your skyscrapers,
believe me. The building has a backup generator—two, I think—and in
the bomb shelter there's enough food for months. The shelter is nicer
than that apartment you had in Foggy Bottom. Remember that?"
Jacob remembered the apartment; he had lived there for five years.
But even more clearly he remembered the bomb shelter in Tamir's childhood home, despite having been inside it for less than five minutes. It
was the last day of that first trip to Israel. Deborah and Tamir's mother,
Adina, were on a walk to the market, hoping to find some delicacies to

bring back for Isaac. Over coffee, with what almost looked like a grin, Irv asked Shlomo if the house had a shelter.

"Of course," Shlomo said, "it's the law."

"Underneath the house?"

"Of course."

The second *of course* made clear what should have been clear to Irv with *it's the law*: Shlomo wanted his shelter underground when there was bombing, and underground when there wasn't. But Irv pushed: "Would you show it to us? I'd like Jacob to see." The *I'd like Jacob to see* made clear what should have been clear to Shlomo with *Underneath the house?*: Irv wasn't going to let it go.

Save for the twelve-inch-thick door, the room was slow to reveal its oddness. It was moist, the concrete floor sweating. The light was chalky, in color and texture. Sound seemed to gather in clouds above them. There were four gas masks hanging on the wall, even though there were only three people in Tamir's family. Some sort of four-for-three promotion? Was one for the cleaning lady, or a future child? For Elijah? What would be the protocol if chemical war broke out while Jacob's family was there? Was it like on a plane—adults instructed to care for themselves before attending to their kids? Would Jacob watch himself suffocate in the reflection of his father's mask? His mother would never allow it. But then, she might be suffocating, too. Surely his dad would give it to her, right? Unless she was wearing Tamir's mask, in which case that wouldn't be an issue. Were adults instructed to care for themselves before attending to *their own* children, or *all* children? If the cleaning lady were there, would she really claim one of the masks from Jacob's parents? Tamir was older than Jacob by a few months. Did that make him, relatively speaking, the adult of the two? There was no scenario in which Jacob wouldn't be a victim of chemical warfare.

"Let's get out of this dump," Tamir said to Jacob.

Jacob didn't want to go. He wanted to spend his remaining time in Israel exploring every inch of the room, learning it, learning himself in it, simply being there. He wanted to eat lunch down there, bring down his clothes and suitcase and pack, forgo the last drips of sightseeing in order to spend another couple of hours behind those impenetrable walls. And more: he wanted to hear the air-raid siren—not the false alarm for Yom HaShoah, but a siren signaling a complete destruction from which he would be safe.

"Come on," Tamir said, pulling on Jacob's arm with awkward force.

On the flight back to America, thirty-three thousand feet above the Atlantic, Jacob dreamed of a shelter beneath the shelter, reached by another set of stairs. But this second shelter was enormous, large enough to be confused for the world, large enough to hold enough people to make war inevitable. And when the bombs started to fall in the world on that side of the thick door, the world on the other side became the shelter.

Nearly ten years later, Tamir and Jacob split a six-pack at a kitchen table that couldn't be walked around, in an apartment carved out of an apartment, carved out of a house in Foggy Bottom. "I met someone," Jacob said, saying it aloud for the first time.

And nearly twenty years after that, in a Japanese car bisecting the nation's capital, the Israeli cousin—Jacob's Israeli cousin—said, "Anyway, it's not going to come to that."

"To what?"

"To bomb shelters. To war."

"Who said war?"

"We'll figure it out," Tamir said, as if to himself. "*Israel* is Hebrew for 'contingency plan.'"

They drove the next few minutes without speaking. NPR did its best with unreliable news, and Tamir buried himself in his phone, which might have been a tablet, or even a TV. Despite checking his own with manic constancy, Jacob hated all phones—found them to be even worse than the brain tumors they gave their users. Why? Because he hated that his was ruining his life? Or because he knew that it wasn't ruining his life, but gave him the easy and socially acceptable means to ruin it himself? Or because he suspected that other people were getting more, and more interesting, messages? Or maybe he knew all along that his phone would be his undoing—even if he didn't know how.

Tamir's phone was singularly annoying. Barak's, too. They were phone SUVs. Jacob didn't care how vivid their screens were, or how good the reception, or how easy to link with their other miserable devices. Barak had never even been to America, which, if it wasn't the greatest country in the history of the world, at the very least had a few things to offer eyes that cared to look up. Maybe they were searching for news, although what kind of news site emits *"Boom shakalaka!"* every few seconds?

"What about Noam?" Jacob asked.

"What about him?"

"Where is he now?"

"This moment?" Tamir said. "As we speak? I have no idea. Keeping fathers informed is not of national importance."

"When you last spoke with him?"

"Hebron. But I'm sure they were evacuated."

"By helicopter?"

"I don't know, Jacob. How would I know?"

"And Yael?"

"She's fine. She's in Auschwitz."

Boom shakalaka!

"What?"

"School trip."

They drove the George Washington Parkway in silence, AC battling the humidity that seeped through the invisible points of entry, small talk between Jacob and Irv battling the awkward silence that pressed against the windows—past Gravelly Point, where aviation buffs holding radio scanners, and fathers holding sons, could almost reach up and touch the landing gears of jumbo jets; the Capitol on the right, across the brown Potomac; the inevitable explanation of why the Washington Monument changes shades of white one-third of the way up. They crossed Memorial Bridge, between the golden horses, circled around the backside of the Lincoln Memorial, the steps that seemed to lead to nothing, and slid into the flow of Rock Creek Parkway. After passing under the terrace of the Kennedy Center and beside the teeth of the Watergate balconies, they followed the curves of the creek away from the outposts of the capital's civilization.

"The zoo," Tamir said, looking up from his phone.

"The zoo," Jacob echoed.

Irv leaned forward: "You know, our favorite primates, Benjy and Deborah, are probably there right now."

The zoo was at the epicenter of Tamir and Jacob's friendship, their familialship; it marked the threshold between their youth and adulthood. And it was at the epicenter of Jacob's life. Jacob's mind often traveled to his own deathbed scene, especially when he felt that he was wasting his life. What moments, in his final moments, would he return to? He would remember arriving at the inn with Julia—both times. He would remember carrying Sam into the house after the ER, the tiny hand mummified in layers and layers of bandaging, cartoonishly large: the biggest, most useless fist in the world. He would remember the night at the zoo.

He wondered if Tamir ever thought about it, if he was thinking about it then.

And then Tamir let out a deep, subterranean laugh.

"What's funny?" Jacob asked.

"Me. This feeling."

"What feeling?"

He laughed again—his greatest performance yet?

"Jealousy."

"*Jealousy*? That's not what I was expecting you to say."

"It's not what I was expecting to feel. That's why it's funny."

"I don't understand."

"Noam will finally have better stories than me. I'm jealous. But it's good. It's as it should be."

"As it should be?"

"Having better stories."

Irv said, "Maybe you should call?"

Jacob said, "'Once upon a time there was a man whose life was so good there's no story to tell about it.'"

"I'll try," Tamir said, punching a long string of numbers. "It's not going to work, but for your sake, Irv, I'll try." After a few moments, an automated Hebrew message filled the car. Tamir hung up and, this time without Irv's prompting, tried calling again. He listened. They all listened.

"Circuits busy."

Vey iz mir.

"Try again in a minute?"

"No reason."

"I don't mean to be alarmist," Jacob said, "but do you need to go home?"

Boom shakalaka!

"And how would I do that?"

"We could drive back to the airport and check on flights," Jacob offered.

"All flights in and out of Israel are canceled."
Vey iz mir.
"How do you know?"
Tamir held up his phone and said, "You think I'm playing games?"
Boom shakalaka!

THE SECOND SYNAGOGUE

No synagogue is sentient, but just as Sam believed that all things are capable of longing, so did he believe that all things have some awareness of their imminent end: he would tell fires "It's OK" as the last embers hummed, and apologize to the three-hundred-million-odd sperm before flushing them on their way to wastewater treatment. No synagogue isn't sentient.

When Sam got home from Model UN, he went straight into Other Life, like a smoker racing to get outside Sydney Airport. His iPad awoke with a memo on the screen: Max's explanation of Samanta's death, their father's guilt (as in, culpability), and his own profound guilt (as in, the feeling of culpability). Sam read it twice—for clarification, and to defer the confrontation with reality.

His failure to spaz upon learning that Max wasn't playing a sick joke surprised him. Why wasn't he breaking his iPad over his bedpost, or screaming things that couldn't be taken back at someone who didn't deserve them, or at least crying? He wasn't in any way indifferent to Samanta's death, and he certainly hadn't reached some epiphany that it was "only a game." It wasn't only a game. What awareness did Samanta have of her imminent end? No avatar isn't sentient.

Every Skype session with his great-grandfather began with "I see you" and ended with "See you." Sam was bothered by the knowledge that one such conversation would be their last, and that there ought to, at some point, be some acknowledgment of some version of that fact. They had skyped early the previous morning, as Sam hastily packed for Model

UN—Isaac awoke before the sun rose, and went to bed before it set. They never talked for more than five minutes—despite having had it explained to him a hundred times that skyping doesn't cost anything ever, Isaac refused to believe that longer conversations didn't cost more—and this one had been particularly brief. Sam shared the vaguest description of the upcoming school trip, confirmed that he wasn't sick or hungry and that no, he wasn't "seeing anyone."

"And everything is ready for your bar mitzvah?"

"Pretty much."

But as he was about to click off—"Mom is waiting for me downstairs, so I should probably go"—Sam felt the expected discomfort, only this time with an urgency, or longing. He wasn't sure the longing was his.

"Go," Isaac said. "Go. We've already been on for too long."

"I just wanted you to know that I love you."

"Yeah, I know, sure. And I love you. OK, now go."

"And I'm sorry that you're moving."

"Go, Sameleh."

"I don't see why you can't just stay."

"Because I can't take care of myself anymore."

"I mean *here*."

"Sameleh."

"What? I don't get it."

"I couldn't go up and down the stairs."

"So we'd get one of those chairlift things."

"They're very expensive."

"I'll use my bar mitzvah money."

"I have lots of medicines I need to take."

"I have lots of vitamins I need to take. Mom is great with things like that."

"I don't want to make you upset, but soon I won't be able to take baths or go to the toilet on my own."

"Benjy can't take baths on his own, and we're constantly cleaning up Argus poop."

"I am not a child, and I am not a dog."

"I know, I'm just say—"

"I take care of my family, Sameleh."

"You take such good care, but—"

"My family doesn't take care of me."

"I understand, but—"

"And that is that."

"I'm gonna ask Dad—"

"No," Isaac said, with a sternness Sam had never heard.

"Why not? I'm sure he'll say yes."

There was a long pause. If it weren't for Isaac's blinking eyes, Sam would have wondered if the image had frozen. "I told you no," Isaac finally said, severely.

The connection weakened, the pixels enlarged.

What had Sam done? Something wrong, something unkind, but what?

Tentatively, in an effort to compensate for whatever hurt he'd accidentally inflicted in his effort to love, he said, "Also, I have a girlfriend."

"Jewish?" Isaac asked, his face only a handful of pixels.

"Yes," Sam lied.

"I see you," Isaac said, and clicked off.

The addition of the *I*, the only letter that takes up less space than a space, changed everything. The longing was his great-grandfather's.

Sam's second synagogue was as he'd left it. He had no avatar with which to explore, so he quickly and crudely made a blocky figure to drop in. The foundation had been poured and the walls were framed, but without the drywall he could have shot an arrow, or his gaze, all the way through it. He—Sam knew that his new avatar was a man—went to one of the walls, gripped the studs like prison bars, and pushed it over. Sam was at once controlling this and witnessing it. He went to another wall and pushed it over.

Sam wasn't destroying, and he wasn't Sam. He was carving a space out of a larger space. He didn't yet know who he was.

The exuberantly branching edifice was shrinking toward its center, like a failing empire that pulls its army back to the capital, like the blackening fingers of a stranded climber. No more social hall, no more basketball court or changing rooms, no more children's library, no more classrooms, no more offices for any administrator or cantor or rabbi, no more chapel, no more sanctuary.

What remained after all those walls came down?

Half a dozen rooms.

Sam hadn't intended this configuration, he'd merely created it. And he wasn't Sam.

A dining room, a living room, a kitchen. A hall. A bathroom, a guest bedroom, a TV room, a bedroom.

Something was missing. It was longing for something.

He went to the ruins of the first synagogue and took the largely intact window of Moses floating down the Nile, as well as a handful of rubble. He replaced one of the kitchen windows with the Moses window and put the rubble in the fridge, among the ginger ale.

But something was still missing. There was still a longing.

A basement. It needed a basement. The sentient synagogue, aware that even as it was being constructed it was being destroyed, longed for an underground. He had no money to buy a shovel, so he used his hands. He dug it like a grave. He dug until he wouldn't have been able to feel the arms that he couldn't feel. He dug until a family could have hidden behind the displaced earth.

And then he stood inside his work, like a cave painter inside his painting of a cave.

I see you.

Sam gave himself white hair, restored Firefox to the desktop, and googled: How is bubble wrap made?

THE EARTHQUAKE

When they got to the house, Julia was on the stoop, her arms holding her bent knees to her chest. The sun settled on her hair like yellow chalk dust, shaking free with the tiniest movement. Seeing her there, as she was then, in that moment, Jacob spontaneously shook free the resentment that had settled in his heart like gravel. She wasn't his wife, not right then, she was the woman he married—a person rather than a dynamic.

As he approached, Julia gave a weak smile, the smile of resignation. That morning, before leaving for the airport, he'd read a *National Geographic* sidebar about a broken weather satellite that could no longer do whatever it had been created to do, but would, because of the great expense and limited need to capture it, orbit the planet doing nothing until it ultimately fell to Earth. Her smile was remote like that.

"What are you doing here?" Jacob asked. "I thought you weren't going to be home until later."

"We decided to come back a couple of hours early."

"Where's Sam?" Max asked.

"Is that something you can decide? As the chaperone?"

"If Mark runs into a problem, I can be there in fifteen minutes."

Jacob hated hearing that fucking name. He felt his heart refilling with gravel and sinking.

"Sam's upstairs," Julia told Max.

"I suppose you can follow me," Max said to Barak, and the two went inside.

"I'm going to defecate," Irv said, shuffling past, "and then I'll rejoin the party. Hey, Julia."

Tamir emerged from the car and extended his arms.

"Julie!"

No one called her Julie. Not even Tamir called her Julie.

"Tamir!"

He embraced her in one of his hug dramas: holding her at arm's length, looking her up and down, then bringing her back into his body, then holding her at arm's length for another examination.

"Everyone else gets older," he said.

"I'm not getting any younger," she said, unwilling to return his flirtation, but unwilling to smother it, either.

"I didn't say you were."

They exchanged a smile.

Jacob wanted to hate Tamir for sexualizing everything, but he wasn't sure if the habit resulted from free choice or environmental conditioning—how much of Tamir's way was simply the Israeli way, cultural misinterpretation. And maybe desexualizing everything was Jacob's own way, even when he was sexualizing everything.

"We're so happy to have you for the extra time," Julia said.

Why was no one mentioning the earthquake, Jacob wondered. Was Julia afraid that they hadn't heard about it yet? Did she want to present the news in a thoughtful and controlled way, free of potential interruptions? Or had she not yet heard about it? More puzzling, why wasn't Tamir, he who mentioned everything, mentioning it?

"It's not an easy trip," Tamir said. "I would say you know, but you don't. Anyway, I thought we'd come a little early and make the most of it—let Barak get to know his American family."

"And Rivka?"

"She sends her regrets. She very much wanted to come."

"Everything's OK?"

Jacob was surprised by her forthrightness and reminded of his own restraint.

"Of course," Tamir said. "Just some old obligations she couldn't rearrange. Now: Jake mentioned you'd prepared some food?"

"Did he?"

"I didn't. I didn't even think you were going to be back until later in the afternoon."

"Don't lie to your wife," Tamir said, giving Jacob a wink that Jacob wasn't positive Julia saw, so he told her, "He winked at me."

"Let's put some food together," Julia said. "Head in. Max will show you where to put your things down, and we'll catch up around the kitchen table."

As Tamir entered the house, Julia took Jacob's hand. "Can we talk for a second?"

"I didn't say that."

"I know."

"They're driving me crazy."

"I need to tell you something."

"Something else?"

"Yes."

Years later, Jacob would remember this moment as a vast hinge.

"Something's happened," she said.

"I know."

"What?"

"Mark."

"No," Julia said, "not that. Not me."

And then, with a great flush of relief, Jacob said, "*Oh*, right. We already heard."

"What?"

"On the radio."

"The *radio*?"

"Yeah, it sounds horrible. And really scary."

"What does?"

"The earthquake."

"Oh," Julia said, at once clear and confused. "The earthquake. Yes." It was then that Jacob realized they were still holding hands.

"Wait, what were *you* talking about?"

"Jacob—"

"Mark."

"No, not that."

"I was thinking about it on the drive over. I was thinking about everything. After we got off the phone, I—"

"Stop. Please."

He felt the blood rush to his face like a tide, then recede as quickly.

He'd done something horrible, but he didn't know what. It wasn't the phone. There was nothing more to learn there. The money he'd taken out of ATMs over the years? For stupid, harmless things he was embarrassed to admit wanting? What? Had she somehow looked through his e-mails? Seen how he spoke about her to those who might understand or at least sympathize? Had he been stupid enough, or forced by his subconscious, to leave himself signed in on some device?

He put his hand on top of her hand on top of his hand: "I'm sorry."

"It's not your fault."

"I'm so sorry, Julia."

He was sorry, so sorry, but for what? There was so much to apologize for.

At his wedding, Jacob's mother told a story that he had no memory of, and didn't believe was true, and was hurt by, because even if it wasn't true, it could have been, and it exposed him.

"You were probably expecting my husband," Deborah began, eliciting a good laugh. "Perhaps you've noticed that he usually does the talking. *And talking*."

More laughter.

"But this one I wanted. The wedding of my son, whom I grew in my body, and fed from my body, and gave everything of myself so that one day he would be able to let go of my hand and take the hand of another. To his credit, my husband didn't argue or complain. He just gave me the silent treatment for three weeks." More laughter, especially from Irv. "They were the happiest three weeks of my life."

More laughter.

"Don't forget our honeymoon!" Irv called.

"Did we go on a honeymoon?" Deborah asked.

More laughter.

"You might have noticed that Jews don't exchange wedding vows. The covenant is said to be implicit in the ritual. Isn't that wonderfully Jewish? To stand before one's life partner, and before one's god, at what is probably the most significant moment of your life, and to assume it goes without saying? It's hard to think of *anything else* that a Jew would assume goes without saying."

More laughter.

"I'll never get over what a strange and easily explained people we are.

But perhaps some of you are like me, and cannot help but hear the familiar vows: 'for richer, for poorer, in sickness and in health.' They might not be our words, but they are in our collective subconscious.

"There was a year in Jacob's childhood—" She looked to Irv and said, "Maybe it was even more than a year? A year and a half?" Then she looked back to those gathered. "There was a period of time that felt like longer than it was"—laughter—"when Jacob would pretend he was disabled. It started with the announcement, one morning, that he was blind. 'But you're closing your eyes,' I told him."

More laughter.

" 'That's only because there's nothing to look at,' he said, 'so I'm resting them.' Jacob was a stubborn child. He could keep up a resistance for days, and weeks. Irv, can you imagine from where he might have gotten that?"

A laugh.

Irv called back, "Nature from me, nurture from you!"

Another laugh.

Deborah continued: "He stuck with the blindness for three or four days—a long time for a child, or anyone, to keep his eyes closed—but then came to dinner one night batting lashes and once again adept with silverware. 'I'm happy to see you've recovered,' I said. He shrugged his shoulders and pointed to his ears. 'What is it, love?' He went to the cabinet, got a pen and paper, and wrote, 'I'm sorry, I can't hear you. I'm deaf.' Irv said, 'You aren't deaf.' Jacob mouthed the words 'I am deaf.'

"Maybe a month later, he limped into the living room with a pillow under the back of his shirt. He didn't say anything, just limped to the shelf, took down a book, and limped back out. Irv called out, 'Ciao, Quasimodo,' and went back to his reading. He thought it was a phase among phases. I followed Jacob to his room, sat beside him on his bed, and asked, 'Did you break your back?' He nodded yes. 'That must be incredibly painful.' He nodded. I suggested we reset his spine by taping a broom to his back. He walked around like that for two days. He recovered.

"I was reading to him in bed a couple of weeks later—his head propped on the pillow that had been the hump on his back—and he pulled up the sleeve of his pajama top and said, 'Look what happened.' I didn't know what I was supposed to be seeing, only that I was supposed to be seeing it, so I said, 'That's looks horrible.' He nodded. 'I got a very bad burn,' he said. 'So I see,' I said, very gently touching it. 'Hold on, I have some ointment in the medicine cabinet.' I came back with moisturizer.

'For use on extreme burns,' I said, pretending to read the directions on the back. 'Apply liberally across burn. Rub into skin as if massaging. Full recovery expected by morning.' I rubbed his arm for half an hour, a massage that went through seasons of being pleasurable, and meditative, and intimate, and, apparently, sedating. When he came into our bed the next morning, he showed me his arm and said, 'It worked.' I said, 'A miracle.' 'No,' he said, 'just medicine.'"

More laughter.

"*Just medicine.* I still think about that all the time. No miracle, just medicine.

"The disabilities and injuries continued to come—a cracked rib, loss of feeling in his left leg, broken fingers—but with less and less frequency. Then, one morning, maybe a year after he'd gone blind, Jacob didn't come down for breakfast. He often overslept, especially after nights when he and his father stayed up to watch the Orioles. I tapped on his door. No answer. I opened it, and he was perfectly still on his bed, arms and legs straight, with a note balanced in the well of his sternum: 'I am feeling extremely sick, and think I might die tonight. If you are now looking at me, and I'm not moving, it is because I am dead.' If it were a game, he'd have won it. But it wasn't a game. I could rub cream into a burn, I could set a broken back, but there is nothing to be done for the dead. I had loved the intimacy of our secret understanding, but I no longer understood. I looked at him lying there, my stoic child, so still. I started crying. Just as I'm about to do now. I got on my knees beside Jacob's body, and I cried and cried and cried."

Irv went to the dance floor and put his arm around Deborah. He whispered something into her ear. She nodded, and whispered something back. He whispered something back.

She collected herself and said, "I cried a lot. I put my head on his chest and made little rivers in the channels between his ribs. You were so skinny, Jacob. No matter how much you ate, you were just bones. Just bones," she sighed.

"You let me go on for a long time, then coughed, and jerked your legs, and coughed again, and slowly came back to life. I was never more angry than when you put yourself in danger. When you didn't look both ways, when you ran with scissors—I wanted to hit you. I actually had to stop myself from hitting you. How could you be so *careless* with the thing I most loved?

"But I wasn't angry then. Only devastated. 'Don't ever do that again,' I told you. 'Don't you ever, *ever* do that again.' Still flat on your back, you turned your head to face me—do you remember this?—and you said, 'But I have to.'"

Deborah started crying again, and handed Irv the page from which she'd been reading.

"In sickness and in health," he said. "Jacob and Julia, my son and daughter, there is only ever sickness. Some people go blind, some go deaf. Some people break their backs, some get badly burned. But you were right, Jacob: you *would* have to do it again. Not as a game, or rehearsal, or tortuous effort to communicate something, but for real and forever."

Irv looked up from the page, turned to Deborah, and said, "Jesus, Deborah, this is depressing."

More laughter, but now from trembling throats. Deborah laughed, too, and took Irv's hand.

He kept reading: "In sickness and in sickness. That is what I wish for you. Don't seek or expect miracles. There are no miracles. Not anymore. And there are no cures for the hurt that hurts most. There is only the medicine of believing each other's pain, and being present for it."

After having made love for the first time as husband and wife, Jacob and Julia lay side by side. Side by side, they looked at the ceiling.

Jacob said, "My mom's speech was great."

"It was," Julia said.

Jacob took her hand and said, "But only the deafness part was true. None of the rest."

Sixteen years later, alone with the mother of his three children, on the stoop of their home and under only the infinite ceiling, Jacob knew that everything his mother had said was true. Even if he couldn't remember it, even if it hadn't happened. He chose illness, because he knew of no other way to be seen. Not even by those looking for him.

But then Julia pressed his hand. Not hard. Just enough pressure to communicate love. He felt love. Spousal, co-parental, romantic, friendly, forgiving, devoted, resigned, stubbornly hopeful—the kind didn't matter. He had spent so much of his life standing at thresholds, parsing love, withholding comfort, forcing happiness. She applied more pressure to her still-husband's hand, and held his eyes in the fingers of her eyes, and told him, "Your grandfather died."

"I'm sorry," he said, words that originated in his spine.

"Sorry?"

"Wait, *what*? I didn't hear you."

"Your grandfather. Isaac. He's dead."

"What?"

IV

FIFTEEN DAYS OF
FIVE THOUSAND YEARS

DAY 2

Asked to estimate how many are trapped in the rubble, the chief of Israel's recovery effort says, "One is ten thousand too many." The journalist follows up: "Are you suggesting ten thousand?"

DAY 3

Statement from the Israeli interior minister's office: "This is not a time for petty squabbling. If the Islamists want control, they can have control. If they want their holy sites preserved, they can have that. But they cannot have both."

To which the *waqf* responds: "The Zionists have a history of underestimating Arabs, and of keeping what it borrows."

To which the interior minister himself responds: "Israel never estimates, and Israel never borrows."

DAY 4

New York Times public editor: "Many readers have responded to the use of the word 'disproportionate' in yesterday's front-page projection of casualties in the Middle East."

In Lebanon, the leader of Hezbollah gives a TV address that contains the sentence "The earthquake was not a work of nature, and it was not an earthquake."

CBS Evening News anchor: "And finally, tonight, a glimmer of hope amid the rubble. Here is the story of young Adia, the three-year-old Palestinian girl who lost her parents and three sisters in Nablus. Wandering amid the ruins, without even a last name, she took the hand of the American photojournalist John Tirr, and refused to release it."

DAY 5

The Israeli ambassador's response: "Perhaps we should ask the thirty-six Japanese citizens we 'unilaterally, clumsily, and brutally' rescued, at the expense of our own blood, if they would prefer to be airlifted back onto the Temple Mount."

Military analyst on Fox News, on the subject of Turkey's uncoordinated use of Israeli airspace for supply transport: "Israel's nonreaction is either an unprecedented gesture of cooperation or a sign of the unprecedented weakness of the Israeli Air Force."

A twenty-two-year-old Arab Israeli citizen with four missing siblings explains: "The glass bottle is useless as a weapon, so it is deadly as a symbol." The rioting, no longer spontaneous, is known as the "tdamar," the resentment.

The Syrian president: "Taking effect immediately, the truce and strategic alliance will include the eleven largest rebel groups."

DAY 6

In Rome, the Pope announces: "The Vatican will fund and oversee the restoration of the Holy Sepulcher."
    Response from the synod of the Greek Orthodox Church: "The Vatican will do no such thing."
    Response from the catholicos of the Armenian Church: "The ruins shall not be altered."

The British Parliament passes a resolution "to condition the shipment of British aid to be delivered directly to the intended recipients, rather than through Israeli channels."

Junior (and Jewish) senator from California: "No doubt Israel is doing everything in her power to oversee the broadest, most effective recovery effort. Clearly, Israel cannot hold territories and renounce responsibility for the population."

The German chancellor: "As Israel's closest friend in Europe, we counsel her to use this tragedy as an opportunity to reach out to her Arab neighbors."

Secret communiqué from the king of Jordan to the prime minister of Israel: "Our need for aid has become so extreme and urgent, we are no longer in a position to question its source."

Response: "Is that a request, or a threat?"

Response: "It is a statement."

The American Israel Public Affairs Committee announces the creation of two lists of public officials: "Defenders of Israel" and "Betrayers of Israel." The first posting identifies 512 Defenders and 123 Betrayers.

Poster in Amman: STOP CHOLERA.

DAY 7

The Egyptian foreign minister's response: "With regard to the March of a Million, we cannot prevent free people from demonstrating their brotherhood with the suffering victims of the earthquake."

The Turkish ambassador to the UN claims: "Israel has halved the number of aid ships allowed to enter Israeli waters."

Al Jazeera claims: "Medical supplies intended for the West Bank are being held at Israeli-controlled border crossings."

The American secretary of state claims: "Israel is fully cooperating with all good-faith partners."

Syria claims: "We have moved ground forces to our southern border for the purpose of self-defense."

World Health Organization statement: "Epidemic cholera, which has now been confirmed in more than a dozen cities in the Palestinian Territories and Jordan, poses an even greater risk than either aftershocks or war."

In a phone call to the Israeli prime minister, the American president reaffirms his country's commitment to help secure Israel "with whatever is required, without limitations," but adds: "This horrible disaster must inspire a fundamental change in the Middle East axioms."

CNN anchor, forefinger to earpiece: "I'm sorry to interrupt. We're getting reports that just before seven p.m., local time, another dramatic earthquake struck the Middle East, magnitude 7.3."

DAY 8

From the head of Israeli civil engineering's report, delivered by secure videoconference to the homes of Knesset members: "Among the critical structures damaged beyond use: the Defense Ministry headquarters; the Geophysical Institute in Lod; Ben Gurion International Airport; Tel Nof and Hatzor Air Force Bases. All highways have at least partial obstructions. North–south access was blocked for ninety minutes. Railways are inoperative. Ports are minimally functioning. As for the Kotel, the portions that collapsed have not compromised the integrity of the Temple Mount, but further geological events will likely lead to catastrophic failure."

In the wake of the aftershock, Saudi Arabia and Jordan sign an agreement of "temporary unification." Asked why Saudi Arabia's unprecedentedly large supply line of aid also includes ground troops, the Saudi king replies: "To assist in the recovery." Asked why it includes two hundred combat aircraft, he replies: "It doesn't."

Israel refuses to recognize "Transarabia," thereby naming it.

Iran promises, "Jordan will know no greater ally than Iran," thereby refusing to recognize Transarabia.

The UN Human Rights Council passes a resolution condemning "the catastrophic crisis created by Israel's unilateral, unannounced, and complete withdrawal from the Occupied Territories." No member states abstain. No member states vote against the resolution.

Asked by what means Egypt is abrogating its treaties with Israel, the Egyptian Army chief responds: "All agreements and understandings were created within a set of conditions that no longer exist." Asked if Egypt would continue to recognize the State of Israel: "This is semantics."

Chanting outside a Georgetown University lecture hall, in which a visiting Israeli molecular biologist is presenting a paper on differentiating pluripotent embryonal carcinoma cells: "Shame on Israel! Shame on Israel!"

375 Defenders and 260 Betrayers.

"And finally, tonight, an update on a story that has captured the hearts of so many around the world—that of young Adia. It's with concern, but also hopes and prayers, that we report that the improvised orphanage in which Adia had been staying partially collapsed in yesterday's aftershock. It's believed that some of the building's occupants were able to escape, although, as with so many, Adia's whereabouts are unknown."

DAY 9

Under the cover of repairmen, a squad of Israeli extremists penetrates the Dome of the Rock and sets it on fire. The arsonists are quickly detained. The prime minister of Israel issues a statement calling the "attempted arson" a "terrorist plot."

Financial Times: "Hamas's declaration of allegiance to the Islamic State marks another step toward the unprecedented unification of the Muslim world."

From the Israeli minister of health's report to the prime minister: "Hospitals are operating at five-thousand percent capacity, and the influx of American supplies is neither fast enough nor large enough. A cholera epidemic is inevitable, as are dysentery and typhoid. As war approaches, it is necessary to make difficult decisions regarding priorities."

In a hastily arranged speech in Azadi Square in Tehran, before a crowd estimated at two hundred thousand, the Ayatollah intones: "O Jews, your time has come! You have burned down our Dome of the Rock, and now your fire will be met by fire! We will burn your cities and your towns, your schools and your hospitals, your every home! No Jew will be safe!"

DAY 10

In his daily address to the nation, the Israeli prime minister says, "Our reasons for this morning's action are simple: by expelling the *waqf* from the Temple Mount and deploying the IDF to control it, we can show the world that the damage to the Dome of the Rock is minimal and protect the site for as long as it is in danger."

Europe's three largest supermarket chains remove kosher food from their shelves amid fears over protesters. In response, a Tory MP tweets: "JEWS are not ISRAELIS! How DARE YOU! #JewsAreKosher."

American political commentator, responding to the joint declaration of war by Syria, Egypt, Lebanon, and Transarabia: "It was a necessary response to the IDF taking the Temple Mount, but there have been rocket attacks and air skirmishes for a week. This only makes it official."

The ultra-Orthodox population in Jerusalem spreads a rumor that "the Messiah is at the door."

The American president, addressing a joint session of Congress: "Israel must immediately relinquish control of the Temple Mount to an international peacekeeping force, refrain from any military reprisals, and resume its participation in rescue efforts in the Occupied Territories. If Israel fulfills its responsibilities, she will have America's unconditional and unlimited support."

AIPAC adds the president to its list of Betrayers.

DAY 11

Guardian editorial: "The issue isn't so much who raised the Israeli flag on the Temple Mount, but why hasn't it been taken down? Israel's inaction seems designed to inflame."

The caliph of the Islamic State declares temporary unity with the "infidel Syrian government and Hezbollah."

Turkish Air Force spokesman: "The computer virus that attacked our air control system, leading to this morning's multiple crashes, was an act of war."

The Israeli prime minister assures the American president that Israel neither created nor implemented the alleged virus.

The American president offers the Turkish prime minister unprecedented aid and advanced weaponry in exchange for a vow to stay out of the war.

Algeria, Bahrain, Comoros, Djibouti, Iraq, Iran, Kuwait, Libya, Mauritania, Morocco, Oman, Pakistan, Qatar, Somalia, Sudan, Tunisia, the United Arab Emirates, and Yemen declare war on Israel.

The United States ends "executive hold" on the pending sale of 60 Harpoon missiles, 185 M1A1 Abrams main battle tank "upgrade kits," 20 F-16 fighter jets, and 500 American-made Hellfire II missiles to Egypt. The State Department declines to comment.

President of Columbia University's Hillel chapter, commenting on the first anti-Israel demonstrations led by Jewish students: "The pursuit of justice, especially when it requires introspection and humility, is at the heart of our mission: to enrich the lives of Jewish students so that they may enrich the Jewish people and the world."

CNN: "We have confirmed reports that an American cargo plane, on its way to an airfield in the Negev, has crashed."

289 Defenders and 246 Betrayers.

DAY 12

Cover of the *New York Post*: the still-raised Israeli flag beneath the headline DOME OF THE MOCK!

Albania, Azerbaijan, Bangladesh, the Gambia, Guinea, Kosovo, Kyrgyzstan, the Maldives, Mali, Niger, Senegal, Sierra Leone, Tajikistan, Turkmenistan, and Uzbekistan declare war on Israel.

The Ayatollah publishes an open letter to "Iran's Arab brothers" that concludes: "Your reluctance to allow us into the theater of battle will be your own demise. Whatever our differences, this is our moment."

The American secretary of state offers the Israeli prime minister "as much aid as is needed" in exchange for control over the war and Israel's nuclear arsenal. After summarily rejecting the proposal, the prime minister asks, "Why isn't the president on the phone with me right now?"

Young mother in Tel Aviv: "The rockets are relentless, but the city's sewage has flooded the shelters, so we just wait outside for whatever will happen."

In Brussels, the president of the European Union delivers a speech in which he says, "The catastrophe in the Middle East reveals a failed experiment."

Israel declares war "against all of those seeking to destroy the Jewish state."

DAY 13

NPR: "The 'March of a Million' has never been a fitting name. When it was a coherent march, it numbered fewer than fifty thousand. Now it is numerous, uncoordinated campaigns—many origins, with the shared destination of Jerusalem—which some have numbered at two million."

A PEW poll finds that fifty-eight percent of American Jews believe the United States should enter the war.

Associated Press reports: "Several Bedouin tribes in the Negev claim that Israeli authorities are handing out potassium iodide to the Jewish population near the nuclear site in Dimona, but not to them."

Israel offers no response to this, or to Turkey's belligerent rhetoric, or to claims that Israel is targeting civilian utilities in the largest cities of Syria, Egypt, Lebanon, and Transarabia, or to the Transarabian Army's occupation of the tourist city of Eilat, or to the IDF's decision to categorically purge Arab Israelis from the Israeli Army, while simultaneously conscripting all Jewish men and women above the age of sixteen for "paramilitary support."

In major newspapers across America, full-page ads, signed by one hundred evangelical leaders, assert: "We are all Zionists."

United Nations statement: "With the number of earthquake refugees estimated to exceed twenty million; epidemic cholera, dysentery, and typhoid causing more fatalities than either the earthquake or the war; and an extreme shortage of food, potable water, and medical supplies, the Middle East is facing a humanitarian crisis of unprecedented proportions. We will either respond to this crisis immediately and with overwhelming resolve, or face decades of global instability, and the greatest loss of civilian life since the Second World War."

DAY 14

Transarabian spokesperson: "Bethlehem and Hebron have not been conquered, they have been reclaimed. This historic victory would not have been possible without our brave brothers from Morocco, Algeria, Libya, and Pakistan."

The American president to the Israeli prime minister: "It was Mossad. Our plane and Turkey's."

"What interest would Israel have in downing a plane of our last noncombatant in the region, much less our closest and most necessary ally?"

"That's a question for you to ask yourself."

"I give you my word: Israel was in no way involved with the downing of the American plane."

Turkey declares war, "in partnership with our Muslim brothers, against the Zionist Entity."

301 Defenders and 334 Betrayers.

Military assessment given to Israel's prime minister: "The IDF is nearing collapse in the north and east. The 5th, 7th, and 9th Divisions of the Syrian Army have full control of the Golan Hights, and are preparing an offensive to capture the Galilee. The Transarabian Army has penetrated the Negev."

Spokesperson for the Israeli settlers, resisting evacuation: "We will die in our homes."

DAY 15

Ministry of Defense memorandum to the prime minister of Israel:

> To follow is our response to your request for three viable strategies to win the war.

> Strategy 1: Attrition
> Israel has superior medical resources, the disease epidemics are killing at a faster rate than warfare, and a defensive position is less costly to maintain than an offensive one. We will pull back to our defensible borders, enhance our already robust military deployment, and allow the war to be won biologically. We will hasten the process by disrupting lines of medical supply, and more crucially, of water. There are options for taking more proactive steps in this regard, to be discussed in person.

> Strategy 2: Overwhelming Act
> A nuclear strike would be the most overwhelming display of force, but comes with too many risks, in terms of unmanageable consequences, including reprisals and the American response. Instead, we recommend two dramatic conventional attacks—one in the east, one in the west. The most effective target in the west is the Aswan Dam. Ninety-five percent of Egypt's population lives within twelve miles of the Nile, and the dam provides more than half of Egypt's power. With the destruction of the dam, Lake Nasser would run downstream, flooding virtually all of Egypt— massive civilian casualties, certainly in the millions. Egypt would cease to be a functioning society. In the east, we will bomb Transarabia's main oil wells, crippling the Arabs' ability to prosecute the war.

Strategy 3: Reverse Diaspora

While the war has exposed a widening gap between American and Israeli leadership, and between American and Israeli Jews, Israel will, with the proper public relations campaign, culminating with a speech delivered by the prime minister, persuade one hundred thousand American Jews to come to Israel to support the war effort.

It will be an enormously costly logistical effort, one that diverts men, equipment, and strategic focus from the planning and execution of military operations. The vast majority of the volunteers will have had no military training or experience, will not be in fighting condition, and will not speak Hebrew. But their presence will force America's hand militarily. The president of the United States could watch eight million Israeli Jews be slaughtered, but not one hundred thousand American Jews.

Pending your response, we will prepare a full and detailed course of action.

V

NOT TO HAVE A CHOICE IS ALSO A CHOICE

THE I-WORD

"Good afternoon. I want to extend to the people of the region affected by yesterday's earthquake the deep condolences and unwavering support of the American people. The full extent of the devastation is still unknown, but the images that we've seen of entire neighborhoods in ruins, of fathers and mothers searching the rubble for their children, are heartbreaking. Indeed, for a region that is no stranger to suffering, this tragedy seems especially cruel and incomprehensible. Our thoughts and prayers are with the people of the Middle East, and also with all of those around our country who do not yet know the fates of loved ones back home.

"I have directed my administration to respond with the full resources of the United States in the urgent task of rescuing those still trapped beneath the rubble, and to deliver the humanitarian relief that will be needed in the coming days and weeks. In that effort, our government, especially USAID and the Departments of State and Defense, is working closely with our partners in the region and around the world.

"There are several urgent priorities. First, we're working quickly to account for U.S. embassy personnel and their families in Tel Aviv, Amman, and Beirut, as well as the many American citizens who live and work in the region. Americans trying to locate family members are encouraged to contact the State Department at 299-306-2828."

"Say it," Tamir told the screen.

"Second," the president continued, ignoring Tamir, "we've mobilized resources to help rescue efforts. In disasters such as this, the first days are absolutely critical to saving lives and avoiding even greater tragedy, so

I have directed my teams to be as forward-leaning as possible in getting help on the ground and coordinating with our international partners as well."

"Say the word!"

"Third, given the many different resources that are needed, we are taking steps to ensure that assisting governments act in a unified way. I've designated the administrator of the U.S. Agency for International Development, Dr. Philip Shaw, to be our unified disaster coordinator.

"Now, this rescue and recovery effort will be complex and challenging. As we move resources into the Middle East, we will be working closely with partners on the ground, including local government agencies, as well as the many NGOs, the United Nations missions—which appear to have suffered their own losses—and our partners in the region and around the world. This must truly be an international effort."

"Say the word!"

For the first time in decades, perhaps ever, Jacob remembered the Texas Instruments Speak & Spell he'd had as a child. He brought it to the beach one summer; it melted onto a picnic table and wouldn't stop repeating *"Say it,"* not even when it was turned off—like a ghost: *"Say it, say it, say it . . ."*

"And, finally, let me just say that this is a time when we are reminded of the common humanity that we all share. Despite the fact that many are experiencing tough times here at home, I would encourage those Americans who want to support the urgent humanitarian efforts to go to WhiteHouse.gov, where you can learn how to contribute. This is not a time to withdraw behind borders, but to extend ourselves—our compassion and our resources—to the people of the Middle East. We must be prepared for difficult hours and days ahead as we learn about the scope of the tragedy. We will keep the victims and their families in our prayers. We will be aggressive and resolute in our response. And I pledge to the region that you will have a friend and partner in the United States of America, today and going forward. May God bless you, and those working on your behalf. Thank you very much."

"He just couldn't bring himself to say it."

"Neither can you, apparently."

Tamir gave Jacob that most annoying of all looks: the put-on assumption that Jacob must be joking—surely he was joking.

"What? *Military? Aid?*"

Tamir muted the television, which had moved on to images of fighter jets coring massive apples of smoke, and said: "Israel."

"Don't be silly."

"Don't *you.*"

"Of course he said it."

"Of course he didn't."

"He did. He said, *the people of Israel.*"

"Of *the region.*"

"Well, he definitely said Tel Aviv."

"But he definitely didn't say Jerusalem."

"He *did.* But if he didn't—and I'm sure he did—it's only for all of the perfectly reasonable reasons you know."

"Remind me of what I know."

Tamir's phone started ringing, and as with every call he'd received since the earthquake, it didn't have to ring twice. It might be news from Rivka or Noam. It might be a response to one of his dozen attempts to get home. E-mail had come back early that morning, so he knew they were safe. But there were innumerable unaccounted-for family and friends.

It was Barak calling from upstairs, asking if he could use the iPad.

"What's wrong with yours?"

"We want two."

Tamir hung up.

"It's a regional catastrophe," Jacob resumed, "not an Israeli one. It's geological, not political."

"Nothing is not political," Tamir said.

"This isn't political."

"Give it a few minutes."

"And if you were somewhat less insistent on hearing your name, it would be somewhat easier to say."

"*Ah . . .*"

"What?"

"It's our fault."

"That came out wrong."

"And can I ask you," Tamir went on, "who *you* is? When you say, 'If you were somewhat less insistent,' who is the *you?*"

"*You.*"

"Me, Tamir?"

"Yeah. Israelis."

"*Israelis.* OK. I just wanted to be sure you didn't mean Jews."

"Look, it was a statement, and he was being careful."

"But this isn't political."

"He didn't want to *make* it political."

"So what's the plan?" Julia asked, walking into the room.

"Dumbarton Oaks," Jacob said.

"Julia," Tamir said, turning to face her, "let me ask you. Do you feel a need to be careful when one of your friends is injured?"

"Theoretically?"

"No, in life."

"What kind of injury?"

"Something serious."

"I don't know that I've ever had a seriously injured friend."

"Some life."

"Theoretically? Yes, I'd be careful. If it were necessary."

"And you?" Tamir asked Jacob.

"Of course I would be careful."

"We're different in that way."

"You're reckless?"

"I'm loyal."

"Loyalty doesn't require recklessness," Julia said, as if she were taking Jacob's side, which she didn't feel like doing, especially without knowing what they were talking about.

"Yes, it does."

"And no one is helped by a loyalty that makes the situation worse," Jacob said, wanting Julia to feel that he had her back.

"Unless the situation is going to get worse anyway. Your father would agree with me."

"Which only proves the sanity of my argument."

Tamir laughed at that. And with his laugh, the rising temperature was halved, the pressure relieved.

"What's the best sushi in Washington?" Tamir asked.

"I don't know," Jacob said, "but I know it isn't as good as the worst sushi in Israel, which is better than the best sushi in Japan."

"I'll probably stick around here while you guys go out today," Julia said. "I've got some things to catch up on."

"What kind of things?" Tamir asked, as only an Israeli would.

"Bar mitzvah stuff."

"I thought it was canceled."

Julia looked at Jacob. "You told him it was canceled?"

"I did not."

"Don't lie to your wife," Tamir said.

"Why do you keep saying that?"

"He keeps saying it?" Julia asked.

"You can't see it," Jacob told Julia, "but he's nudging me right now. So you know."

Tamir gave Jacob another invisible nudge and said, "You told me that with Isaac's death, the earthquake, and what happened between the two of you—"

"I did not say anything," Jacob said.

"Don't lie to your wife, Jacob."

"What, about Mark?" Julia asked. "And did you tell him about your phone?"

"I hadn't told him about anything that you just told him about."

"And it's none of my business," Tamir said.

Addressing only Julia, Jacob said, "What I told him was that we were talking about how to *modify* the bar mitzvah, in light of, you know, everything."

"Modify what?" Sam asked.

How do children do that? Jacob wondered. Not only enter rooms silently, but at the worst possible moment.

"Your bar mitzvah," Max said. And where did *he* come from?

"Mom and I were talking about how to make sure the bar mitzvah feels good within the context of, you know."

"The earthquake?"

"What earthquake?" Benjy asked, without looking up from the maze he was drawing. Had he always been there?

"And Great-Grandpa," Jacob said.

"Dad and I—"

"You can just say *we*," Sam said.

"We don't think we can have a band," Jacob said, taking over the parental side of the conversation in an effort to demonstrate to Julia that he was also capable of delivering difficult news.

"Fine," Sam said. "They sucked shit anyway."

It's very hard to have a productive dialogue with a thirteen-year-old boy, as every gently broached subject becomes an Ultimate Conversation, requiring defense systems and counterattacks to attacks that were never launched. What begins as an innocent observation about his habit of leaving things in the pockets of dirty clothes ends with Sam blaming his parents for his twenty-eighth-percentile height, which makes him want to commit suicide on YouTube.

"They didn't suck," Jacob said.

Still focusing on his maze, Benjy said, "When Mom parked the car, it wasn't right, so I picked it up and put it in the right place."

"Thank you for that," Julia said to Benjy. And then, to Sam: "There's a nicer way to put it."

"Jesus," Sam said, "I'm not allowed to have an opinion anymore?"

"Now, hold on a minute," Jacob said. "*You* chose them. Mom didn't. I didn't. *You* did. You watched the videos of half a dozen bands, and it was *your* opinion that Electric Brigade should be the band for your bar mitzvah."

"They were the least pathetic of three totally pathetic options, and I chose them under duress. That's not the same as being a groupie."

"What duress?"

"The duress of being forced to have a bar mitzvah when you know I find all of this shit to be bullshit."

Jacob tried to spare Julia from having to be the one, yet again, to object to bad language: "*Shit to be bullshit*, Sam?"

"Is that poor usage?"

"Impoverished. And try to believe me when I tell you I would have been every bit as happy not to pay the utterly mediocre Electric Brigade five thousand dollars to play bad covers of bad songs."

"But the rite of passage is nonnegotiable," Sam confirmed.

"Yes," Jacob said, "that's correct."

"Because it was nonnegotiable for you, because it was nonnegotiable for—"

"Correct again. That's what Jewish people do."

"Not negotiate?"

"Have bar mitzvahs."

"Ah . . . I'd *completely* misunderstood the whole thing. And now that I realize we have bar mitzvahs because we have bar mitzvahs, what I *really* feel moved to do is marry a Jewish woman and have Jewish children."

"You need to slow down," Julia said.

"And I *definitely* don't want to be buried," Sam said, the Ultimate now within sight. "Especially if Jewish law requires it."

"So be cremated like me," Max said.

"Or don't die," Benjy suggested.

Like a conductor zipping up a piece of music, Julia gave a quick and stern *"Enough,"* and that was it. What was so scary about her? What about that five-foot-four woman, who never inflicted physical or emotional violence, or even saw a punishment all the way through, terrified her husband and children to the point of unconditional surrender?

Jacob broke down the breakdown: "The thing we want to be sensitive to is the appearance of enjoying life too much in the face of Great-Grandpa's death. Not to mention the earthquake. It would be in poor taste, and also just feel bad."

"The *appearance* of enjoying life?" Sam asked.

"I'm just saying that some sensitivity is required."

"Let me tell you the right way to think about it," Tamir began.

"Maybe later," Jacob said.

"So no band," Sam said. "Is that enough to make sure we don't appear to enjoy life?"

"In Israel we don't even have bar mitzvah parties," Tamir said.

"Mazel tov," Jacob told him. And then, to Sam: "I might also skip the sign-in board."

"Which I always wanted to skip," Sam said.

"Which I spent three weeks making for you," Julia said.

"You made it *over the course of three weeks,*" Jacob corrected.

"What?"

"You didn't spend three weeks making it."

"Why do you think that's an important clarification?"

He all of a sudden didn't, so he changed course: "I think we should also consider editing the centerpieces."

"Why?" Julia asked, beginning to understand that he was taking things from *her*, not Sam.

"I've never understood the desire of American Jews to speak words you don't understand," Tamir said. "Finding meaning in the absence of meaning—I don't get it."

"They're . . . *festive*," Jacob said.

"They're *elegant*."

"Wait a minute," Sam said, "what's left?"

"What's left?"

"Exactly," Tamir said.

"What's *left*," Jacob said, resting his hand on Sam's shoulder for the instant before Sam recoiled, "is you becoming a man."

"What's *left*," Julia said, "is being with your family."

"You are the luckiest people in the history of the world," Tamir said.

"We're trying," Jacob said to Sam, who lowered his eyes and said, "This sucks."

"It won't," Julia said. "We'll make it really special."

"I didn't say it *will* suck. I said it *sucks*. Presently."

"You'd rather be in a fridge like Great-Grandpa?" Jacob asked, as surprised as anyone by his words. How could he have thought them, much less vocalized them? Or these: "You'd rather be trapped under a building in Israel?"

"Those are my choices?" Sam asked.

"No, but they are your much-needed perspective. Look at that," Jacob said, pointing to the muted TV, which showed images of massive earth-moving machines, tires with ladders built into them, pulling apart rubble.

Sam took this in, nodded, averted his eyes to a place yet farther from where they would have met his parents'.

"No flowers," he said.

"No *flowers*?"

"Too beautiful."

"I'm not sure beauty is the problem," Julia said.

"The problem," Tamir said, "is that—"

"It's part of the problem," Sam said, talking over Tamir, "so lose 'em."

"Well, I don't know about *losing* them," Jacob said, "as they've already been paid for. But we can ask if it's still possible to shift the design toward something more in keeping with—"

"And let's ditch the monogrammed yarmulkes, too."

"Why?" Julia asked, hurt as only someone who had spent six hours choosing a font, palette, and material for monogrammed yarmulkes could be.

"They're decorative," Sam said.

"OK," Jacob said, "maybe they'd be a bit gauche, considering."

"*Gauche* they are not," Julia said.

"The problem—" Tamir began, again.

"And it probably goes without saying," Sam said, as he always did when he was about to say something that did not go without saying, "that we're not going to have party favors."

"I'm sorry, I have to draw a line," Julia said.

"I actually think he's right," Jacob said.

"You do?" Julia said. *"Actually?"*

"I do," Jacob said, not liking that mimicked *actually*, actually. "Party favors imply a party."

"The problem—"

"Of course they don't."

"*Party* favor, Julia."

"They imply a social convention, the lack of whose fulfillment would imply extreme rudeness. *Jacob.*"

"Social convention at the conclusion of a *party.*"

"So we punish his friends for plate tectonics and the death of Sam's great-grandfather?"

"Punishing thirteen-year-old children is encumbering them with garbage bags full of tourist tchotchkes from places Sam's distant and uncared-about relatives live and calling it a *favor.*"

"You imply an asshole," Julia said.

"Whoa," Barak said.

Where had he come from?

"Excuse me?" Jacob said, exactly as Julia would have.

"I'm not chanting Torah," Julia said. "We *know* what these words mean."

"What's gotten into you?"

"It was always there."

The television filled with tiny flashes, like fireflies trapped in a jar.

"The problem," Tamir said, standing up, "is that you don't have nearly enough problems."

"Can I state the obvious?" Sam asked.

"No," his parents said simultaneously—a rare unity.

There was a woman on TV, of unknown ethnicity or nationality, pulling at her hair as she wailed, pulling with enough force to yank her head left and right. There was no ticker across the bottom of the screen. There was no commentary. There was no cause offered for her suffering. There was only the suffering. Only the woman, her hair gathered in the fists she beat against her chest.

ABSORB OR ABSOLVE

When Isaac should have been well into his decomposition in the ground, he was still maintaining freshness in a human crisper in Bethesda. Only for Isaac could the end of misery be the extension of misery. His final wish—made known both in his will and in far too many conversations with Irv, Jacob, and whoever else might be entrusted with the task—was to be buried in Israel.

"But why?" Jacob had asked.

"Because that's where Jews go."

"On Christmas break. Not for eternity."

And when Sam, who was along for the visit, pointed out that he would get far fewer visitors over there, Isaac pointed out that "the dead are dead" and visits are the last things on their brain-dead minds.

"You don't want to be buried with Grandma and the rest of the family?" Jacob asked.

"We'll all meet when the moment is right."

"What the hell does *that* mean?" Jacob didn't ask, because there are times when meaning itself means very little. A dying wish is such a time. Isaac had arranged the plot two decades before—it was expensive even then, but he didn't mind being grave-poor—so all that was required in order to fulfill his last and most lasting wish was to get his body on a plane and work out the logistics on the other side.

But when the time came to drop Isaac's body in the mailbox, the logistics were impossible: all flights were grounded, and when the airspace reopened, the only bodies the country allowed in were of those prepared to die.

Once the ritually mandated window for a burial-in-one-day had passed, there was no great rush to figure out a solution. But that's not to say that the family was indifferent to Jewish ritual. Someone had to be with the body at all times between death and burial. The synagogue had a crew for this, but as the days passed, enthusiasm for babysitting the cadaver waned, and more and more responsibility fell to the Blochs. And that responsibility had to be negotiated with the responsibility of hospitably hosting the Israelis: Irv could take them to Georgetown while Jacob sat with Isaac's body, and then in the afternoon Jacob could take them to the Air and Space Museum to see *To Fly!* on the perspective-swallowing IMAX while Deborah had the exact opposite experience with Isaac's body. The patriarch with whom they begrudgingly skyped for seven minutes once a week was now someone they visited daily. By some uniquely Jewish magic, the transition from living to dead transformed the perpetually ignored into the never to be forgotten.

Jacob accepted the brunt of the responsibility, because he considered himself the most able to do so, and because he most strongly wanted to escape other responsibilities. He *sat shmira*—an expression he'd never heard before he became a choreographer of *shmira sitters*—at least once a day, usually for several hours at a time. For the first three days, the body was kept on a table, under a sheet, at the Jewish burial home. Then it was moved to a secondary space in the back, and finally, at the end of the week, to Bethesda, where unburied bodies go to die. Jacob never got any closer than ten feet, and dialed the podcasts to hearing-impairing volumes, and tried not to inhale through his nose. He brought books, went through e-mail (he had to stand on the other side of the door to get cell reception), even got some writing done: HOW TO PLAY DISTRACTION; HOW TO PLAY GHOSTS; HOW TO PLAY INCOMMUNICABLE, FELT MEMORIES.

Sunday, mid-morning, when Max's ritualized complaints of there being nothing to do became intolerably exasperating, Jacob suggested Max come along for some *shmira sitting,* thinking, *This will make you grateful for your boredom.* Calling his bluff, Max accepted.

They were greeted at the door by the previous *shmira sitter*—an ancient woman from the shul who evoked so much chilliness and vacancy she might have been mistaken for one of the dead if her overapplication of makeup had not given her away: only living Jews are embalmed. They exchanged nods, she handed Jacob the keys to the front door, reminded him that *absolutely nothing* other than toilet paper (and number two, of course) could be flushed down the toilet, and, with somewhat less pomp and circumstance than happens outside Buckingham Palace, the changing of the guard was complete.

"It smells horrible," Max observed, seating himself at the reception area's long oak table.

"I breathe through my mouth when I have to breathe."

"It smells like someone farted into a vodka bottle."

"How do you know what vodka smells like?"

"Grandpa made me smell it."

"Why?"

"To prove that it was expensive."

"Wouldn't the price do that?"

"Ask him."

"Chewing gum helps, too."

"Do you have any gum?"

"I don't think so."

They talked about Bryce Harper, and why, despite the genre being too exhausted to raise an original finger, superhero movies were still pretty great, and as often happened, Max asked his dad to recount Argus stories.

"We took him to a dog training class once. Did I ever tell you that?"

"You did. But tell me again."

"So it was right after we got him. The teacher began by demonstrating a belly rub that would relax a dog when it became agitated. We were sitting in a circle, maybe twenty people, everyone working away at his dog's belly, and then the room filled with a loud rumbling, like the Metro running beneath the building. It was coming from my lap. Argus was snoring."

"That's so cute."

"So cute."

"He's not very well behaved, though."

"We dropped out. Felt like a waste of time. But a couple of years later, Argus got into the habit of pulling on the leash when we walked. And he'd just stop abruptly and refuse to take another step. So we hired some guy that people in the park were using. I can't remember his name. He was from Saint Lucia, kind of fat, had a limp. He put a choke collar on

Argus and observed as we walked with him. Sure enough, Argus stopped short. 'Give him a pull,' the guy said. 'Show him who's the alpha dog.' That made Mom laugh. I gave a pull, because, you know, I'm the alpha dog. But Argus wouldn't budge. 'Harder,' the guy said, so I pulled harder, but Argus pulled back as hard. 'You got to show him,' the man said. I pulled again, this time quite hard, and Argus made a little choking noise, but still wouldn't budge. I looked at Mom. The guy said, 'You've got to teach him, otherwise it'll be like this forever.' And I remember thinking: *I can live with this forever.*

"I couldn't sleep that night. I felt so guilty about having pulled him so hard that last time, making him choke. And that expanded to guilt about all of the things I'd ever tried to teach him: to heel, offer his paw on command, even to come back. If I could do it all again, I wouldn't try to teach him anything."

An hour passed, and then another.

They played a game of Hangman, and then another thousand. Max's phrases were always inspired, but it was hard to say by what: NIGHT BEFORE NIGHTTIME; ASTHMA THROUGH BINOCULARS; BLOWING A KISS TO AN UNKINDNESS OF RAVENS.

"That's what you call a group of ravens," he said after Jacob had solved it with only a head, torso, and left arm.

"So I've heard."

"A lamentation of swans. A glittering of hummingbirds. A radiance of cardinals."

"How do you know all that?"

"I like knowing things."

"Me, too."

"A minyan of Jews."

"Excellent."

"An argument of Blochs."

"A universe of Max."

They played a word game called Ghost, in which they took turns adding letters to a growing fragment, trying not to be the one to complete a word, while having a word in mind that the fragment could spell.

"A."

"A-B."

"A-B-S."

"A-B-S-O."

"A-B-S-O-R."

"Shit."

"Absorb."

"Yeah. I was thinking *absolve.*"

They played Twenty Questions, Two Truths and a Lie, and Fortunately Unfortunately. Each wished there were a TV to lighten their load.

"Let's go look at him," Max said, as casually as if he'd been suggesting they dig into the dried mango they'd brought along.

"Great-Grandpa?"

"Yeah."

"Why?"

"Because he's there."

"But why?"

"Why not?"

"Why not isn't an answer."

"Neither is *why.*"

Why not? It wasn't prohibited. It wasn't disrespectful. It wasn't, or shouldn't be, disgusting.

"I took a philosophy class in college. I can't remember what it was called, and can't even remember the professor, but I do remember learning that some prohibitions aren't ethically grounded, but rather because certain things *are not to be done.* One could reach for all sorts of reasons that it isn't right to eat the bodies of humans who died of natural causes, but at the end of the day, it's just not something we do."

"I didn't say *eat* him."

"No, I know. I'm just making a point."

"Who would *want* to eat a human?"

"It would almost certainly smell and taste good. But we don't do it, because it's not to be done."

"Who decides?"

"Excellent question. Sometimes the *not to be done* is universal, sometimes it's particular to a culture, or even to a family."

"Like how we eat shrimp, but don't eat pork."

"We don't eat shrimp as a practice. We on occasion eat some shrimp. But yes, like that."

"Except this isn't like that."

"What isn't?"

"Looking at Great-Grandpa."

He was right; it wasn't.

Max went on: "We're here to be with him, right? So why wouldn't we *be with him*? What's the point of coming all the way here, and spending all this time, just to be in a different room? We might as well have sat at home with popcorn and a streaming video of his body."

Jacob was afraid. It was a very simple explanation, even if the explanation for that explanation was harder to come by. What was there to be afraid of? The proximity to death? Not exactly. The proximity to imperfection? The embodied proof of reality, in its grotesque honesty? The proximity to life.

Max said, "See you on the other side," and entered the room.

Jacob remembered the night, decades before, when he and Tamir had snuck into the National Zoo.

"You OK?" he called to Max.

"Freaky," Max said.

"I told you."

"That's not what you told me."

"How does he look?"

"Come see for yourself."

"I'm comfortable where I am."

"He looks like he does on Skype, but farther away."

"He looks OK?"

"I probably wouldn't put it like that."

How did he look? Would the body have looked different if he'd died differently?

Isaac had been the embodiment of Jacob's history; his people's psychological pantry, the shelves collapsed; his heritage of incomprehensible strength and incomprehensible weakness. But now he was only a body. The embodiment of Jacob's history was only a body.

They used to take baths together when Jacob slept over as a child, and the long hairs of Isaac's arms, chest, and legs would float on the surface like pond vegetation.

Jacob remembered watching his grandfather fall asleep under the barber's cape, how his head slumped forward, how the straight razor mowed a path from the back of his hairline to the limits of the barber's reach.

Jacob remembered being invited to pull at the loose skin of his grandfather's elbow until it stretched to a web large enough to hold a baseball.

He remembered the smell after his grandfather used the bathroom: it didn't disgust him, it terrified him. He was mortally afraid of it.

He remembered how his grandfather wore his belt just below the nipples, and his socks just above the knees; and how his fingernails were as thick as quarters, and his eyelids as thin as tinfoil; and how between claps he turned his palms skyward, as if repeatedly opening and shutting an invisible book, as if unable not to give the book a chance, and unable not to reject it, and unable not to give it another chance.

Once, he fell asleep in the middle of a game of Uno, his mouth half full of black bread. Jacob might have been Benjy's age. He carefully replaced his grandfather's mediocre hand with all Wild Draw Fours, but when he shook his grandfather awake and they resumed the game, Isaac showed no wonder at his cards, and on his next turn drew from the stack.

"You don't have anything?" Jacob asked.

Isaac shook his head and said, "Nothing."

He remembered watching his grandfather change into a bathing suit wherever happened to be convenient, with no regard for his own privacy or Jacob's mortification: beside the parked car, in the middle of a men's room, even on the beach. Did he not know? Did he not care? Once, at the public pool they sometimes went to on Sunday mornings, his grandfather undressed poolside. Jacob could feel the glances of strangers rubbing together inside him, building and tending to a fire of rage: at the strangers for their judgment, at his grandfather for his lack of dignity, at himself for his humiliation.

The lifeguard came over and said, "There's a changing room behind the vending machines."

"OK," his grandfather said, as if he'd been told there was a Home Depot just off the Beltway.

"You can't change here."

"Why not?"

Jacob spent decades thinking about that *Why not?* Why not, because the changing room was over there, and here was right here? Why not, because why are we even talking about this? Why not, because if you'd seen the things I've seen, you would also lose your ability to comprehend embarrassment? Why not, because a body is only a body?

A body is only a body. But before he was a body, he was an embodiment. And that, at least for Jacob, was why not: his grandfather's body couldn't be only a body.

For how long could this continue?

Irv argued that they should just buy a plot in Judean Gardens, as close to the rest of the family as possible, and get on with death already. Jacob insisted they wait until things cleared up in Israel and then fulfill Isaac's unambiguous wish for his eternal resting place.

"And what if that takes a couple of months?"

"Then we'll owe the funeral home that much more rent."

"And if things never clear up?"

"Then we'll remember how lucky we were to have this as the biggest of our problems."

WHAT DO THE CHILDREN KNOW?

Julia wanted to rehearse the conversation with the kids. Jacob could have argued that it was unnecessary right then, as they weren't going to have the actual conversation until after the bar mitzvah and burial dust had cleared. But he agreed, hoping that Julia's ears would hear what her mouth said. And more, he interpreted her desire to rehearse as a desire to role-play—an acknowledgment that she wasn't sure. Just as she interpreted his willingness to rehearse as a sign that he was, in fact, ready to move forward with the end.

"'We need to talk about something'?" Julia suggested.

Jacob considered that for a moment, and countered: "'We need to have a family conversation'?"

"Why is that better?"

"It reaffirms that we're a family."

"But we don't have family conversations. It'll tip them off that something's wrong."

"Something *is* wrong."

"The entire point we're trying to convey with this conversation is that nothing is *wrong*. Something is *different*."

"Not even Benjy will buy that."

"But I don't even have money—" Benjy said.

"Benjy?"

"—to buy something."

"What's going on, love?"

"What would you wish?"

"What's that, baby?"

"In school, Mr. Schneiderman asked us what we would wish, and he took our wishes to the Wailing Wall, because he was going to Israel for vacation. I think I made the wrong wish."

"What did you wish for?" Jacob asked.

"I can't tell you or it won't come true."

"What do you think you *should have* wished for?"

"I can't tell you, in case I change my wish."

"If sharing them means they can't come true, why are you asking us to tell you our wishes?"

"Oh yeah," he said, then turned and walked out of the living room.

They waited until they heard his footsteps vanishing up the staircase before continuing.

"And anyway," Julia said, in a quieter voice than before, "we want to make them feel safe, and then build to the change."

"'Can you guys come into the living room for a minute?' Like that?"

"Not the kitchen?"

"I think here."

"And then what," Julia said, "we tell them to sit down?"

"Yeah, that's going to be a tip-off, too."

"We could just wait until we're all in the car at some point."

"That could work."

"But then we can't face them."

"Except in the rearview mirror."

"An unfortunate symbol."

That made Jacob laugh. She was trying to be funny. There was a kindness in her effort. If this were real, Julia would never make a joke.

"During dinner?" Julia suggested.

"That would first require explaining why we're eating dinner together."

"We eat dinner together all the time."

"We briefly assemble at the table occasionally."

"What's for dinner?" Max asked, tumbling into the room exactly like Kramer, despite never having seen *Seinfeld*.

Julia gave Jacob a look he'd seen a million times in a million contexts: *What do the children know?* What did Sam know when, two years ago, he walked into the room while they were having sex—missionary and under a sheet and without filthy talk, thank goodness. When Max picked up the phone while Jacob was angrily interrogating Julia's gynecologist about the benignness of a benign lump—what did he hear? When Benjy walked into their kitchen blow-up and said, "Epitome"—what did he know?

"We were just talking about dinner," Jacob said.

"Yeah, I know."

"You heard?"

"I thought you were calling us for dinner."

"It's only four thirty."

"I thought—"

"You're hungry?"

"What's for dinner?"

"What's that have to do with your hunger?" Jacob asked.

"Just wondering."

"Lasagna and some veggie or another," Julia said.

"Plain lasagna?"

"Spinach."

"I'm not hungry."

"Well, you have an hour to work up an appetite for spinach lasagna."

"I think Argus needs a walk."

"I just gave him a walk," Jacob said.

"Did he poo?"

"I can't remember."

"You would remember if he'd pooed," Max said. "He needs to poo. He's doing that thing where he licks at the beginning of a poo that needs to come out."

"Why are you telling us this, instead of just walking him?"

"Because I'm working on my speech for Great-Grandpa's funeral, and I need to concentrate."

"You're giving a speech?" Jacob asked.

"You aren't?"

Julia was touched by Max's charmingly narcissistic initiative. Jacob was ashamed by his own narcissistic thoughtlessness.

"I'll say a few words. Or actually, Grandpa will probably speak on our behalf."

"Grandpa doesn't speak on my behalf," Max said.

"Work on your speech," Julia said. "Dad will walk Argus."

"I *did* walk Argus."

"Until he poos."

Max went to the kitchen and came out with a box of unhealthy organic cereal, which he took back to his room.

Julia called up: "Cereal should be in your mouth or in the box. Nowhere else."

Max called down: "I can't swallow it?"

"Maybe it's a mistake to talk to all of them at once," Jacob said, careful with his volume. "Maybe we should talk to Sam first."

"I suppose I could see the—"

"Jesus."

"What?"

Jacob gestured at the TV that was now always on. There were images from a soccer stadium in Jerusalem, a stadium in which Jacob and Tamir had seen a game more than two decades before. There were a dozen bulldozers. It wasn't clear what they were doing, or why Israel would allow such images to be broadcast, and that not-knowing was terrifying. Could they be preparing a military site? Digging a mass grave?

The news that reached America was scattershot, unreliable, and alarmist. The Blochs did what they did best: balanced overreaction with repression. If in their hearts they believed they were safe, they overworried, talked and talked, whipped themselves, and one another, into foams of anguish. From the comfort of the living room, they followed the unfolding news like a sporting event, and at times caught themselves rooting for drama. There were even small, shameful disappointments when estimates of destruction were revised downward, or when what appeared to be an act of aggression turned out to be only an accident. It was a game whose unreal danger was to be talked up and savored, so long as the outcome was fixed. But if there was an inkling of any real danger, if the shit started to thicken—as it was soon to do—they dug until the blades of their shovels threw sparks: *It'll be fine, it's nothing.*

Tamir was largely absent. He spent part of every day trying to find a way home, but never with any success. If he talked with Rivka or Noam, he did so privately and didn't share anything. And to Jacob's amazement, he still wanted to sightsee, schlepping an unenthusiastic Barak from monument to monument, museum to museum, Cheesecake Factory to Ruth's Chris Steakhouse. It was so easy for Jacob to see in Tamir what he couldn't see in himself: a refusal to acknowledge reality. He sightsaw so he wouldn't have to look.

The scene at the stadium was replaced with the face of Adia, the young Palestinian girl whose entire family had been killed in the earthquake and who was found wandering the streets by an American photojournalist. The story touched the world, and kept touching it. Maybe it was as simple as her beautiful face. Maybe it was how they held hands. It was a feel-good piece amid the tragedy, but it was a tragedy, Jacob thought, or at least inauspicious, that the good feeling was between a Palestinian and an American. At some point, Max started sleeping with a newspaper photo of Adia under his pillow. When her orphanage collapsed and she went missing, Max went missing, too. Everyone knew where he was—it was only his voice, gaze, and teeth that were hidden—but no one knew how to find him.

"Hello?" Julia asked, shaking her hand in front of Jacob's face.

"What?"

"You've been watching while we've been talking?"

"Out of the corner of my eye."

"I realize the Middle East is collapsing, and that the entire world will get sucked into the vortex, but this is actually more important right now."

She got up and turned off the TV. Jacob thought he heard it sigh in relief.

"Go walk Argus, then let's finish this."

"He'll go to the door and whine when he really needs it."

"Why make him really need it?"

"When it's time, I mean."

"You think we should talk to Sam first? Before the others?"

"Or Sam and Max. Just in case one of them starts crying. Benjy is going to follow their lead, so we should give them a chance to digest and gather themselves."

"Or just let them all cry together," Julia said.

"Maybe just Sam first. He's probably going to have the strongest reaction—whatever that reaction will be—but he's also the most able to process it."

Julia touched one of the art books on the coffee table.

"What if I cry?" she asked.

The question embodied Jacob, made him want to touch her—grasp her shoulder, press his palm to her cheek, feel the ridges and valleys of their fingerprints align—but he didn't know if that was acceptable anymore. Her stillness throughout the conversation didn't feel standoffish, but it did create a space around her. What if she cried? Of course she would cry. They would all cry. They'd wail. It would be horrible. The kids' lives would be ruined. Tens of thousands of people would die. Israel would be destroyed. He wanted all of that, not because he craved horror, but because imagining the worst kept him safe from it—focusing on dooms-day allowed for the day to day.

On a drive to visit Isaac many years before, Sam had asked from the backseat, "God is everywhere, right?"

Jacob and Julia exchanged yet another where-the-hell-did-*that*-come-from look.

Jacob handled it: "That's what people who believe in God tend to think, yes."

"And God has always been everywhere?"

"I suppose so."

"So here's what I can't figure out," he said, watching the early moon follow them as they drove. "If God was everywhere, where did He put the world when He made it?"

Jacob and Julia exchanged another look, this one of awe.

Julia turned to face Sam, who was still looking out the window, his pupils constantly returning, like a typewriter carriage, and said, "You are an amazing person."

"OK," Sam said, "but where did He put it?"

That night, Jacob did a bit of research and learned that Sam's question had inspired volumes of thought over thousands of years, and that the most prevalent response was the kabbalistic notion of tzimtzum. Basically, God *was* everywhere, and as Sam surmised, when He wanted to create the world, there was nowhere to put it. So He made Himself smaller. Some refered to it as an act of contraction, others a concealment. Creation demanded self-erasure, and to Jacob, it was the most extreme humility, the purest generosity.

Sitting with her now, rehearsing the horrible conversation, Jacob wondered if maybe, all those years, he had misunderstood the spaces surrounding Julia: her quiet, her steps back. Maybe they weren't buffers of defense, but of the most extreme humility, the purest generosity. What if she wasn't withdrawing, but beckoning? Or both at the same time? Withdrawing and beckoning? And more to the point: making a world for their children, even for Jacob.

"You won't cry," he told her, trying to enter the space.

"Would it be bad to?"

"I don't know. I suppose, all things being equal, it would be best not to impose that on them. *Impose* isn't the right word. I mean . . . You know what I mean."

"I do."

He was surprised, and further embodied, by her *I do.* "We'll go over this a few dozen times and it'll feel different."

"It will never not destroy me."

"And the adrenaline in the moment will help hold the tears back."

"You're probably right."

You're probably right. It had been a long time—it had *felt* like a long time, Dr. Silvers would correct—since she'd deferred to his emotional judgment in any way. Since she hadn't reflexively bucked against it. There was a kindness in those words—*you're probably right*—that disarmed him. He didn't need to be right, but he needed that kindness. What if, all those times she reflexively bucked against, or simply dismissed, his perspective, she'd given him a *you're probably right*? He would have found it very easy to concede inside that kindness.

"And if you cry," Jacob said, "you cry."

"I just want to make it easy on them."

"No chance of that."

"As easy as it can be."

"Whatever happens, we'll find our way."

We'll find our way. What an odd assurance, Julia thought, when the point of the conversation they were rehearsing was precisely that they couldn't find their way. Not together. And yet the assurance took the form of togetherness: *we.*

"Maybe I'll get a glass of water," she said. "Do you want one?"

"I'll go to the door and whine when I really need it."

"You think the kids are losing?" she asked as she walked to the kitchen. Jacob wondered if the water was just an excuse to face away when asking that question.

"I'm just going to turn on the TV for one second. On mute. I just need to see what's happening."

"What about what's happening here?"

"I'm here. You asked if I think the kids are losing. Yes, I think that's the only way to describe it."

A map of the Middle East, swooping arrows indicating the movements of various armies. There had been skirmishes, mostly with Syria and Hezbollah in the north. The Turks were taking an increasingly hostile tone, and the newly formed Transarabia was amassing planes and troops in what had been Jordan. But it was containable, controllable, plausibly deniable.

Jacob said, "Rest assured, I'll be crying."

"What?"

"I'll have some water."

"I didn't hear what you said."

"I said, even if you don't see me crying, I'll be crying."

That was something—that *felt* like something—he needed to say. He'd always known—always *felt*—that Julia believed she had a stronger emotional engagement with the children, that being a mother, or a woman, or simply herself, created a bond that a father, man, or Jacob was incapable of. She'd subtly suggest it all the time—it *felt* like she was subtly suggesting it—and would every now and then outright say it, although it was always couched in talk of all the things that were special to his relationship with them, like having fun.

Her perception of their parental identities generally broke that way: depth and fun. Julia breast-fed them. Jacob made them crack up with over-the-top versions of airplane-into-the-mouth feeding. Julia had a visceral, uncontrollable need to check in on them while they slept. Jacob woke them up if the game went into extra innings. Julia taught them words like *nostalgia*, *angst*, and *pensive*. Jacob liked to say, "There's no bad language, only bad usage," as a way of justifying the supposedly good usage of words like *douche* and *shitty*, which Julia hated as much as the kids loved.

There was another way of looking at that dichotomy of depth and fun, one that Jacob had spent innumerable hours considering with Dr. Silvers: heaviness and lightness. Julia brought weight to everything, opening up a space for every intimated emotion, urging a fleshed-out conversation about each passing remark, perpetually suggesting the value of sadness. Jacob felt that most problems weren't problems, and those that were could be resolved with distraction, food, physical activity, or the passage of time. Julia always wanted to give the kids a life of gravity: culture, trips abroad, black-and-white movies. Jacob saw no problem with—saw the great good in—bubblier, dumber activities: water parks, baseball games, terrible superhero movies that brought great pleasure. She understood childhood as the period of soul formation. He understood it as life's only opportunity to feel safe and happy. Each saw the myriad shortcomings and absolute necessity of the other.

"Do you remember," Julia asked, "however many years ago, when my friend Rachel came to our seder?"

"Rachel?"

"From architecture school? Remember, she came with her twins?"

"And no husband."

"Right. He'd had a heart attack at the gym."

"Cautionary tale."

"You remember?"

"Sure, that year's sympathy invite."

"I guess she went to yeshiva as a girl, or had some kind of rigorous Jewish education. I hadn't realized that, and ended up feeling so embarrassed."

"By what?"

"What illiterate Jews we are."

"But she had a great time, didn't she?"

"She did."

"So save your embarrassment."

"It was years ago."

"Embarrassment is the Parmalat of emotions."

That got a great laugh—it *felt* great to Jacob—from Julia. An irrepressible laugh in the midst of so much tactical strategizing.

"What made you remember her now?"

Silence can be as irrepressible as laughter. And it can accumulate, like weightless snowflakes. It can collapse a ceiling.

"I'm not sure," Julia said.

Jacob tried to pitch the conversation's roof: "Maybe you were remembering how it felt to be judged."

"Maybe. I don't think she was judging. But I felt judged."

"And you're afraid of feeling judged?" Jacob asked.

A few nights before, Julia had awoken as if from a nightmare, although she had no memory of any dream. She went down to the kitchen, found the Georgetown Day student directory in the "crap drawer," and confirmed that Benjy would be the only child in his class with two addresses.

"I'm afraid of our family being judged," she said.

"Do you judge yourself?"

"Don't you?"

"I'm going to be the sympathy invite this year, aren't I?"

Julia smiled, grateful for the deflection.

"Why should this year be different from all other years?"

Their first shared laugh in weeks.

Jacob wasn't used to this warmth, and it confused him. This was not what he was expecting when rehearsing for this rehearsal of a conversation. He'd anticipated something subtly passive-aggressive. He assumed he'd have to sample a buffet of shit, never having the guts—never finding justification in the cost-benefit analysis of self-defense—to draw upon the small arsenal of retorts he'd prepared.

Dr. Silvers had urged him simply to be present, to sit with his pain (rather than send it back), and to resist the desire for certain outcomes. But Jacob felt the situation would call for some very un-Eastern responsiveness. He would have to avoid saying things that could be used against him at any future point, as everything would be entered into the permanent record. He would have to appear to yield (with gentle affirmations, and declared reversals to positions he already secretly held), without giving an inch. He would have to have the cunning of someone too cunning to read a book about the cunning of samurai.

But as the conversation took shape, Jacob felt no need for control. There was nothing to win; there was only losing to protect against.

"'There are many different kinds of families,'" Julia said. "Doesn't that seem like a good way to go?"

"It does."

"'Some families have two dads. Some have two moms.'"

"'Some families live in two houses'?"

"At which point Max will infer we're buying a vacation house, and get excited."

"A vacation house?"

"A house on the ocean. 'Some families live in two houses: one in the city, one by the ocean.'"

A *vacation house*, Julia thought, willfully confusing herself as completely as Max would. She and Jacob had talked about it—not a house on the ocean, they could never afford that, but something cozy and elsewhere. It was the big news she was going to mention to Mark that day, before he reminded her how newsless her life was. A vacation house would be nice. Maybe even nice enough to make things work for a while, or to simulate a functioning family until the next temporary solution could be found. *The appearance of happiness.* If they could sustain the appearance—not to others, but how life appeared to themselves—it might be a close-enough approximation of the experience of actual happiness to make things work.

They could travel more. The planning of a trip, the trip, the decompression: that would buy them some time.

They could go to couples therapy, but Jacob had implied a bizarre loyalty to Dr. Silvers, which would have made seeing someone else a transgression (a greater transgression, apparently, than requesting a shot of fecal cum from a woman who was not his wife); and when Julia faced the prospect of opening everything up, the time and expense of twice-a-week visits that would end in either painful silence or endless talking, she couldn't rouse herself to the necessary hopefulness.

They could have done exactly what she'd spent her professional life facilitating and her personal life condemning: a renovation. There was so much that could be improved in their house: revamp the kitchen (new hardware, at minimum, but why not new countertops, new appliances, ideally a reconfiguration for better flow and lines of sight); new master bath; new closets; open up the back of the house to the garden; punch in a couple of skylights above the top-floor showers; finish the basement.

"'One house where Mom will live, and one house where Dad will live.'"

"OK," Jacob said, "let me be Sam for a minute."

"OK."

"You're going to move at the same time?"

"We're going to try to, yes."

"And I'm going to have to carry my stuff back and forth every day?"

"We're going to live within walking distance of each other," Julia said, "and it won't be every day."

"Is that really something you can promise? I'm being me now."

"I think it's an OK promise for the situation."

"And how will we divide time?"

"I don't know," Julia said, "but not every day."

"And who's going to live here? I'm being Sam again."

"Hopefully a nice family."

"We're a nice family."

"Yes, we are."

"Did one of you have an affair?"

"Jacob."

"What?"

"He's not going to ask that."

"First of all, of course he might. Second, it's one of those things that, however unlikely, we absolutely need to have a prepared answer for."

"OK," Julia said, "so I'll be Sam."

"OK."

"Did one of you have an affair?"

"Who am I?" Jacob asked. "Me? Or you?"

"You."

"No. That's not what's going on here."

"But I saw your phone."

"Wait, *did he?*"

"I don't think so."

"You don't think so? Or he didn't?"

"I don't believe that he did."

"So why are you saying it?"

"Because the kids know things that we don't think they know. And when he helped me to unlock it—"

"He helped you unlock it?"

"I didn't know whose it was."

"And he saw—?"

"No."

"Did you tell him—"

"Of course not."

Jacob got back into the character of himself.

"What you saw was an exchange with one of the other writers on my show. We were sending lines back and forth for a scene in which, well, two people say some pretty inappropriate things to each other."

"Convincing," Julia said, herself.

"And you, Mom?" Jacob asked. "Did you have an affair?"

"No."

"Not with Mark Adelson?"

"No."

"You didn't kiss him at Model UN?"

"Is this really productive, Jacob?"

"Here, I'll be you."

"You'll be me?"

"Yes, Sam, I did kiss Mark at Model UN. It wasn't premeditated—"

"Not a word I would ever use."

"It wasn't planned. It wasn't even enjoyable. It simply happened. I am sorry that it happened. I have asked your father to accept my apology, and he has. Your father is a very good man—"

"We get the picture."

"Really, though," Jacob said, "how *are* we going to explain our reasoning?"

"Reasoning?"

They never used the word *divorce*. Jacob could bring himself to say it, because it wasn't going to happen. But he didn't want it aboveground. Julia couldn't say it, because she wasn't so sure. She didn't know where to put it.

If Julia were to be fully honest, she couldn't easily say her reasons for doing what they couldn't say. She was unhappy, although unconvinced that her unhappiness wouldn't be someone else's happiness. She felt unfulfilled desire—profound amounts of it—but presumably so did every other married and unmarried person. She wanted more, but didn't know if there was more to be found. Not knowing used to feel inspiring. It felt like faith. Now it felt agnostic. Like not knowing.

"What if they want to know if we're going to get remarried?" Julia asked.

"I don't know. *Are* you?"

"Definitely not," she said. "No chance."

"You're awfully sure."

"There is nothing I'm more sure of."

"You used to be so unsure of everything, in the best way."

"I suppose I used to have less evidence."

"The only thing you have evidence of is that our specific way of doing things didn't work for the specific person you are."

"I'm ready for the next chapter."

"Spinsterhood?"

"Maybe."

"What about Mark?"

"What about him?"

"He's nice. Handsome. Why not give that a try?"

"How can you be so ready to give me away?"

"No. No, it's just you seem to have a connection with him, and—"

"You don't need to worry about me, Jacob. I'll be fine."

"I'm not worried about you."

That didn't sound right.

He tried again: "I'm not any more worried about you than you are about me."

Also not right.

"Mark is a mensch," Billie said at the edge of the room. Do they spontaneously generate from the upholstery, like maggots from rotting meat?

"Billie?"

"Hello," she said, extending her hand to Jacob. "We haven't actually met, although I've heard a lot about you."

Precisely what? Jacob wanted to ask, but instead took her hand and said, "And I've heard a lot about you." A lie. "All good things, by the way." The truth.

"I was upstairs helping Sam with his bar mitzvah apology, and it occurred to us that we don't know what, exactly, qualifies as an apology. Does an apology require an explicit disavowal?"

Jacob shot Julia a look of *check out the vocabulary on this one.*

"Could he simply describe what happened and explain? Are the words *I'm sorry* strictly necessary?"

"Why isn't Sam asking?"

"He's walking Argus. And he asked me to."

"I'll come up in a bit and help out," Jacob said.

"I'm not sure that's necessary or, really, *wanted.* We just kind of need to know what's meant by apology."

"I think an explicit disavowal is required," Julia said, "but no need for the words *I'm sorry.*"

"That was my instinct," Billie said. "OK. Well, thanks."

She turned to leave the room, and Julia called her back: "Billie."

"Yes?"

"Did you hear any of the conversation we were having? Or just that Mark is nice?"

"I don't know."

"You don't know if you heard anything? Or you don't know if you feel comfortable answering?"

"The latter."

"It's just that—"

"I understand."

"We haven't yet spoken with the boys—"

"I really understand."

"And there's a lot of context," Jacob chimed in.

"My parents are divorced. I get it."

"We're just finding our way," Jacob said, "just figuring things out."

"Your parents are divorced?" Julia asked.

"Yes."

"When?"

"Two years ago."

"I'm sorry."

"I don't blame myself for their divorce, and neither should you."

"You're funny," Julia said.

"Thank you."

"The divorce obviously didn't get in the way of you becoming an amazing person."

"Well, we'll never know what I could have been otherwise."

"You're really funny."

"I really thank you."

"We know this puts you in an awkward position," Jacob added.

"It's fine," Billie said, and turned to leave once again.

"Billie?" Julia said.

"Yes?"

"Would you describe your parents' divorce as a loss?"

"For whom?"

"I want to change my wish," Benjy said.

"Benjy?"

"I ought to go," Billie said, turning to leave.

"You don't have to go," Julia said. "Stay."

"I wished for you to believe Sam."

"Believe him about what?" Jacob said, gathering Benjy onto his knee.

"I ought to," Billie said, and headed up.

"I don't know," Benjy said. "I just heard him talking to Max, and he said he wished you believed him. So I made his wish my wish."

"It's not that we don't *believe* him," Jacob said, re-finding his anger at Julia for being unable to take Sam's side.

"So what is it?"

"Do you want to know what Sam and Max were talking about?" Julia asked.

Benjy nodded.

"Sam got in trouble in Hebrew school because they found a piece of paper on his desk with some bad words on it. He says he didn't do it. His teacher is sure that he did."

"So why don't you believe him?"

"We don't not believe him," Jacob said.

"We always want to believe him," Julia said. "We always want to take the side of our children. But we don't think Sam is telling the truth this time. That doesn't make him a bad person. And it doesn't make us love him any less. This is how we love him. We're trying to help him. People make mistakes all the time. I make mistakes all the time. Dad does. And we all count on each other's forgiveness. But that requires an apology. Good people don't make fewer mistakes, they're just better at apologizing."

Benjy thought about that.

He craned his neck to face Jacob, and asked, "So why do *you* believe him?"

"Mom and I believe the same thing."

"You also think he lied?"

"No, I also think people make mistakes and deserve forgiveness."

"But do you think he lied?"

"I don't know, Benjy. And neither does Mom. Only Sam knows."

"But do you *think* he lied?"

Jacob put his palms on Benjy's thighs and waited for the angel to call out. But no angel. And no ram. Jacob said, "We think he isn't telling the truth."

"Could you call Mr. Schneiderman and ask him to change my note?"

"Sure," Jacob said, "we can do that."

"But how would you tell him my new wish without saying it?"

"Why don't you just write it and give it to him?"

"He's already there."

"Where?"

"The Wailing Wall."

"In Israel?"

"I guess."

"Oh, then don't worry. I'm sure his trip was canceled and you'll have a chance to change your wish."

"Why?"

"Because of the earthquake."

"What earthquake?"

"There was an earthquake in Israel last week."

"A big one?"

"You haven't heard us talking about it?"

"You talk about lots of things that you don't talk about to me. Is the Wall going to be OK?"

"Of course," Julia said.

"If anything's going to be OK," Jacob added, "it's the Wall. It's been OK for more than two thousand years."

"Yeah, but there used to be three other walls."

"There's a great story about that," Jacob said, hoping he would be able to remember what he'd just promised to deliver. The story had lain dormant since he was told it in Hebrew school. He couldn't remember the telling, and he hadn't thought about it since, yet there it was, a part of him—a part to be handed down. "When the Roman army conquered Jerusalem, the order was given to destroy the Temple."

"It was the Second Temple," Benjy said, "because the first was destroyed."

"That's right. Good for you for knowing that. Anyway, three of the walls went down, but the fourth one resisted."

"Resisted?"

"Struggled. Fought back."

"A wall can't fight back."

"Wouldn't be destroyed."

"OK."

"It stood firm against hammers, and pickaxes, and clubs. The Romans had elephants push against the wall, they tried to set fire to it, they even invented the wrecking ball."

"Cool."

"But nothing, it seemed, would bring the fourth wall down. The soldier in charge of the Temple's destruction reported back to his commanding officer that they had destroyed three of the Temple's walls. But instead of admitting that they couldn't knock down the fourth one, he suggested they leave it up."

"Why?"

"As proof of their greatness."

"I don't get it."

"When people would see the wall, they would be able to conjure the immensity of the Temple, the foe they defeated."

"What?"

Julia clarified: "They would see how huge the actual Temple must have been."

"Right," Benjy said, taking it in.

Jacob turned to Julia. "Isn't there some organization rebuilding destroyed synagogues in Europe from their foundations? It's like that."

"Or the 9/11 Memorial."

"There's a word for it. I heard it once . . . A *shul*. Right, *shul*."

"Like synagogue?"

"Wonderful coincidence, but no. It's Tibetan."

"Where would you have learned a Tibetan word?"

"No idea," Jacob said. "But I learned it."

"So? Are you going to make us pull down the Tibetan *Webster's*?"

"I could be getting this wrong, but I think it's a physical impression left behind. Like a footprint. Or the channel where water flowed. Or in Connecticut—the matted grass where Argus had slept."

"A snow angel," Benjy said.

"That's a *great* one," Julia said, reaching for his face.

"Only, we don't believe in angels."

Jacob touched Benjy's knee. "What I *said* was that while there are angels in the Torah, Judaism doesn't really encourage—"

"You're my angel," Julia told Benjy.

"And you're actually my tooth fairy," he said.

Jacob's wish would have been to have learned his life lessons before it was too late to apply them. But like the wall into which he'd have tucked it, the wish conjured an immensity.

After Benjy had left the room, and the rehearsal had wrapped up, and Max was fed a second dinner that wasn't spinach lasagna, and the door separating Sam and Billie from the rest of the world was judged sufficiently cracked, Jacob decided to go run some unnecessary errands at the hardware store: buy a shorter hose that would tuck away less awkwardly, replenish the AAA battery supply, maybe fondle some power tools. On his way, he called his father.

"I give in," he said.

"Are you on Bluetooth?"

"Yes."

"Well, get off it, so I can hear you."

"It's illegal to hold the phone while driving."

"And it gives you cancer, too. Cost of doing business."

Jacob brought the phone to his face and repeated, "I give in."

"That's great to hear. With reference to what?"

"Let's bury Grandpa here."

"Really?" Irv asked, sounding surprised, and pleased, and heartbroken. "What brought that on?"

The reason—whether he was persuaded by his father's pragmatism, or was tired of reorganizing his life to spend time with a dead body, or was too preoccupied with the burial of his family to keep up the fight—simply didn't matter all that much. It took them eight days, but the decision was made: they would bury Isaac in Judean Gardens, a very ordinary, pretty-enough cemetery about thirty minutes outside the city. He would get visitors, and spend eternity among his family, and while it might not be the nonexistent and tarrying Messiah's first or thousandth stop, He'd get there.

THE GENUINE VERSION

Eyesick, the threadbare beginnings of an avatar, was in the middle of a digital lemon grove—the clearly marked and barbed-wire-ringed private property of a lemonade corporation that used kinda funny videos, featuring kinda trustworthy actors, to persuade concerned-but-not-motivated consumers to believe that what they were drinking had something to do with authenticity. Sam hated such corporations nearly half as much as he hated himself for being just another spoon-fed idiot-cog who grinned and whatever the past tense of "bear it" is while hating, and announcing his hatred of, corporations. He would never trespass in life itself. He was too ethical, and too much of a coward. (Sometimes it was hard to differentiate.) But that was one of the many, many great things about Other Life—perhaps the explanation for his addiction to it: it was an opportunity to be a little less ethical, and a little less of a coward.

Eyesick was trespassing, yes, but he wasn't there to start a fire, chop down trees, *do* graffiti (or whatever is the proper way of saying that), or even to trespass, really. He'd gone there to be alone. Among the seemingly infinite columns of trunks, beneath the duvet of lemons, he could be by himself. It's not like he felt a great *need* to be alone. *Need* was a word that Sam's mom might use.

"Do you need to get any homework done before we go to dinner?"

"*Finished*," he would say, taking great pleasure in throwing the correction back at her.

"Do you need to get any homework finished before we go to dinner?"

"Need?"

"Yes. Need."

He took no pleasure in the great pleasure he seemed to take in being a smart-ass with her. But he *needed* to do it. He needed to push back against his instinct to cling to her; he needed to alienate what he needed to draw close, but more than anything, he needed not to be the object of her needs. It was bodily. It wasn't her continued need to kiss him that repulsed him, but her overt efforts to manage that need. He was disgusted—revolted, nauseated—by her stolen touches: fixing his hair for a moment longer than necessary, holding his hand while cutting his fingernails (something he knew how to do himself, but needed her to do, but only in exactly the right and limited way). And her stolen glances: when he was coming out of a pool, or worse, taking off a shirt for an impromptu load of laundry. What she stole was stolen from him, and it inspired not only disgust, and not only auger, but resistance. You can have what you want, but you cannot take it.

Eyesick was seeking aloneness in a lemon grove because Sam was sitting shiva for Isaac, avoiding conversations with relatives whose central processing units were programmed to shame him. Why else would a second cousin he hadn't seen in years feel a need to mention acne? To mention voice-dropping? To wink while asking about girlfriends?

Eyesick was seeking aloneness. Not to be by himself, but to be away from others. It's different.

> Sam?
> . . .
> Sam, is that you?
> Who are you talking to?
> YOU.
> Me?
> You. Sam.
> Who are you?
> I KNEW it was you.
> Who knew?
> You don't recognize me?

Recognize? The avatar addressing Eyesick was a lion with a plush rainbow mane; a brown suede vest with opalescent buttons, largely concealed beneath a white tuxedo with tails down to the end of his tail (which was itself adorned with a cubic zirconia heart); bleached teeth largely concealed by lipsticked lips (insofar as a lion has lips); a snout that was just a *bit* too moist; ruby pupils (not ruby-colored, but gemstones); and mother-of-pearl claws with peace signs and Stars of David etched into them. If it was good, it was very good. But was it good?

There was no recognition. Only the surprise of having been discovered in a moment of reflection, and the shame of having been named and known.

It would be possible, in theory, for someone with sufficient tech savvy and insufficient joie de vivre to trace Eyesick back to Sam. But it would require an effort that he couldn't imagine anyone he knew—anyone who *knew him*—making. Except *maybe* Billie.

Putting aside his parents' virtuosically lame and quarter-hearted attempts to "check in" on his computer usage, it never ceased to amaze Sam what he could get away with.

Proof: he shoplifted from the corner grocery that still had his family name above the door, the store his great-grandfather had opened with more dead brothers than words of English. Sam shoplifted enough junk food—enough bags of Cheetos (punctured with the sharpened end of a bent paper clip to release the air and allow for compression), enough Mentos boners in his pockets—from the earnest Korean immigrants, who kept lemon slices by the register to keep their fingers moist enough to grip cash, to open his own corner store, but this one with a different name, preferably with no name, preferably: STORE. Why did he do all that stealing? Not to eat what he took. He never did, never once. He always, always returned the goods—the returning requiring far more illicit prowess than the stealing. He did it to prove that he could, and to prove that he was horrible, and to prove that no one cared.

Proof: the volume (in terabytes) of porn he consumed, and the volume (in quarts) of semen he disseminated. *Under their noses* might be an unfortunate turn of phrase, but how could so-called parents be so completely oblivious to the mass grave being dug and filled with sperm in their own backyard?

The shiva reminded him of many things—the mortality of his grandparents and parents, his own mortality and Argus's, how undeniably comforting it can be to perform rituals you don't understand—but nothing more than the first time he jerked off, also at a shiva. It was his great-aunt Doris's funeral reception. Though they referred to her as Great-Aunt Doris, her relationship was more distant, involving at least some *once-removed*s. (And it had been suggested, by his grandfather, after a few glasses of very expensive vodka, that she wasn't a blood relative at all.) Whatever the case, she'd never married, and had no children, and flaunted her loneliness to sidle up closer to the trunk of the family tree.

The familiar gathering of unfamiliar family noshed away, and like Moses receiving the call to a needy bush, Sam galloped to his bathroom. Somehow he understood it was the moment, even if he didn't understand the method. He used hair gel that day, because it was nearby and viscous. The more he slid his fist up and down his shaft, the stronger was his suspicion that something of genuine significance was happening— not just pleasurable, but mystical. It felt better and better, he squeezed harder, and then it felt even better, and then, with one small thrust for man, mankind leaped giantly across the canyon separating crappy, pathetic, inauthentic life from the unself-conscious, unangry, unawkward realm he wanted to spend the rest of his days and nights on earth inhabiting. Out of his penis gushed a substance he would have to admit he loved more than he loved any person in his life, more than any idea, loved so much that it became his enemy. Sometimes, in less proud moments, he would even talk to his sperm as his semen congealed in his belly button. Sometimes he would look it in the hundred million eyes and say simply: "Enemies."

The first time was a revelation. The first several thousand times. He jerked off again that afternoon, and again and again that night. He jerked off with the determination of someone within sight of Everest's summit, having lost all his friends and Sherpas, having run out of supplemental oxygen, but preferring death to failure. He used hair gel every time, never questioning the potential dermatological effects of repeatedly applying to his penis a substance intended to sculpt hair. By the third day, his pubes were pipe cleaners and his shaft was leprous.

So he started jerking off with aloe. But the green was cognitively dissonant, made him feel like he was fucking an alien, but in a bad way. So he switched to moisturizer.

He was a mad-scientist masturbator, always searching for ways to make his hand more like a vagina. It would have helped to have had a bona fide experience with a bona fide vagina, but his inability not to hear "boner fide" made the chances of that as nugatory as did his use of the word *nugatory*. Anyway, the Internet was nothing if not a gynecological resource, and anyway, there were things one knew without having had a way to know, like how babies won't crawl off a cliff—a fact he was ninety-five percent sure of. When, five infinitely and cosmically unjustly long years later, he had his first sexual experience with a corporeal female—not Billie, tragically, but someone merely nice and smart and pretty—he was surprised by just how accurate his imaginings had been. He'd known all along, he'd known everything. Perhaps if he'd known that he'd known, those years would have been slightly easier to endure.

He used his dry fist, his fist lubricated with: honey, or shampoo, or Vaseline, or shaving cream, or rice pudding, or toothpaste (only once), or the remnants of the tube of A&D that his parents couldn't bring themselves to throw away, despite being able to throw away everything that actually mattered. He made an artificial vagina out of a toilet paper roll, covering one end with Saran wrap (held down with rubber bands), filling the tube with maple syrup, then covering the other end with Saran wrap (and more rubber bands) and giving it a slit. He fucked pillows, blankets, swimming pool vacuums, stuffed animals. He jerked off to the Victoria's Secret catalog, and the *Sports Illustrated* Swimsuit Issue, and the back-page ads in the *City Paper*, and JCPenney bra advertisements in *Parade* magazine, and basically anything that could, with the far reaches of his all-powerful and highly motivated imagination, be construed to be an asshole, vagina, nipple, or mouth (in that order). Of course, he had un-limited access to more free porn than could be watched over the course of the lifetimes of every citizen of China, but even an anus-crazed twelve-year-old appreciates the correlation between the mental work required and the magnitude of the nut, hence his ultimate fantasy of intercepting some Arab virgin on her way to get fucked by an actual martyr, tucking his head under her burka, and, in that deep-space, sensory-deprived black-ness, licking orbits around Heranus. Would anyone ever believe that this had nothing to do with religion, or ethnicity, or even taboo?

He tied rubber bands around his wrist—rubber bands being to mastur-bation what flour is to baking—to make his fingers go numb so he would no longer recognize them as his own. It worked terrifically well, and he almost lost his hand. He angled mirrors in such a way as to see his ass-hole without the rest of his body, and was able to convince himself that it was the asshole of a woman who wanted him in her asshole. He mas-turbated with his dominant and his recessive hand—his intact and his mangled hand—and rubbed Indian burns into his shaft with both hands at once. For several months he favored what he called—called to no one, of course—the "Roger Ebert grip": a half twist of the wrist, so that the thumb was pointing down. (For reasons he didn't understand, and felt no need to understand, this also gave the impression of his hand being someone else's hand.) He closed his eyes and held his breath until he started to black out. He fucked the soles of his feet like some kind of horndog maharishi. If he were actually trying to detach his penis from his body, he couldn't have squeezed or pulled it any harder, and it's a miracle he never actually hurt himself, although even when he was pleasuring himself, he felt that, in some deep and irreparable way, he was hurting himself, that it had to be so, and that that was another elemental bit of knowledge with which he was born.

He masturbated in Amtrak bathrooms, plane bathrooms, the bathrooms of his school and Hebrew school, bookstore bathrooms, Gap and Zara and H&M bathrooms, restaurant bathrooms, the bathrooms of every house he'd been in since gaining the ability to come into a toilet. If it flushed, he fucked it.

How many times did he try to suck his own dick? (Like Tantalus, as he reached, so did the fruit pull away.) He tried to fuck his own asshole, but that required pushing his boner in the direction it most didn't want to go, like a drawbridge being forced to touch the water. He was able to rub his scrotum around his asshole, but that only made him melancholy.

He once stumbled upon a sufficiently compelling argument, in an analingus community, for sticking his finger into his butt while jerking off. Once he'd trained his sphincter to stop reflexively impersonating a Chinese finger trap, it felt pretty good, if pretty strange. It felt like being a bowl whose rim was being wiped clean of cookie batter by the finger of someone—namely: *him*—who couldn't wait. He was, indeed, able to find his prostate, and as promised, he saw through walls when he came. But there was nothing to see except the next crappy room. It was the removal of his finger that ruined everything. First of all, immediately after coming, everything that seemed not only good but logical, necessary, and inevitable before coming instantly seems inexplicable, deranged, and repugnant. It's possible to play down, or even deny, almost anything you just said or did, but a finger in one's butthole cannot be played down or denied. It can only be left there or removed. And it cannot be left there.

Sam never felt comfortable in his body—not in clothing that never fit, not when performing his ridiculous impression of a nonspastic walker—except when masturbating. When masturbating, he both owned and existed in his body. He was effortless, a natural, himself.

> It's ME.
> That doesn't help. And stop abusing caps.
> it's me.
> Billie?
> Billie?
> Max?
> No.
> Great-Grandpa?
> NOAM.
> Stop shouting.
> noam. your cousin.
> My Israeli cousin Noam?
> No, your Swedish cousin Noam.
> Funny.
> And Israeli.
> Your dad and little brother are here.
> I know. My dad sent me an e-mail from the cemetery.
> That's weird. He said he couldn't contact you guys.
> He probably meant by phone. We e-mail all the time.
> We're sitting shiva at my grandfather's house.
> Yes, I know that, too. He e-mailed me a picture of the salmon.
> Why?
> Because it was there. And because the world lacks reality for him until he photographs it with his phone.
> You speak English better than me.
> "Better than I do."
> Right.
> Anyway, I wanted to tell you whatever is the genuine version of "I am sorry for your loss."
> I don't believe in genuine versions.
> I wish you less sadness. How about that?
> How did you find me?

> The same way you would have found me if you were looking. Not hard.

> I didn't know you were in Other Life.

> I used to spend most of every day here. But I've never been in this grove before.

> I've never been in this grove before, either.

> Do you like it when people unnecessarily repeat bits of speech? Like you just did? You could have said, "Me, neither," but you took what I said and made it your own. I said, "I've never been in this grove before," and you said, "I've never been in this grove before, either."

> I do like it when people unnecessarily repeat bits of speech.

> If I used emoticons, I would have used one here.

> I'm glad you don't.

> There isn't time for Other Life in the army.

> Too much real life?

> I don't believe in real life.

> ;)

> I really let myself go. Look at my nails.

> Look at you? Look at me! I still have placenta on my face.

> ???

> My dad committed avataricide.

> Why?

> He accidentally sniffed a Bouquet of Fatality.

> Why?

> Because he wears his sphincter like a necklace, and it choked blood flow to his brain. Anyway, I'm in the process of rebuilding myself, and I'm not exactly satisfied with my progress.

> You look . . . old.

> Yeah. I kinda became my great-grandfather.

> Why?

> Same reason I will in real life, I guess? I mean, this life.

> Do you need some resilience fruit?

> A few hundred thousand wouldn't hurt.

> I can give you mine.

> I was kidding.

> I wasn't.

> Why would you do that?

> Because you need them and I don't. Do you want 250,000?

> 250,000!

> Stop shouting.

> That must have taken you a year.

> Or three.

> I can't accept that.

> Sure you can. A bar mitzvah present.

> I don't even know if I'm having one.

> A bar mitzvah isn't something you have. It's something you become.

> I don't even know if I'm becoming one.

> Do babies know they're born?

> They cry.

> So cry.

> Where are you?

> At home for another couple of hours.

> I thought you were somewhere dangerous.

> You've met my mother.

> Your dad said you were in the West Bank.

> I was. But I came back the day before the earthquake.

> Shit, I can't believe we've talked for this long and I haven't yet asked how you're doing. I suck. I'm sorry.

> It's OK. Remember, I found you.

> I suck.

> I'm safe. We're all safe.

> What would have happened if you'd still been in the West Bank?

> I really don't know.

> Guess.

> Why?

> Because I'm curious.

> Well, if we'd been stuck there during the earthquake, I suppose we would have had to create a temporary base of some kind and wait to be rescued.

> What kind of base?

> Whatever kind we could put together. Maybe occupy a building.

> Surrounded by people who want to kill you?

> What else is new?
> They would have lobbed shit at you?
> Shit?
> Grenades or whatever.
> There is no "grenades or whatever." Weapons are precise.
> Right.
> Maybe. Maybe not. Maybe they would have been preoccupied
with their own problems.
> It wouldn't have been good.
> There is no scenario in which it would have been good.
> What scenario would have been worst?

Like his dad, Sam was drawn to worst-case scenarios. It was obvious
why they thrilled him, but hard to explain the comfort they offered. Perhaps they mapped a distance from his own safe life. Or perhaps coming
to terms with the most horrible outcomes allowed for a kind of mental
preparation and resignation. Maybe they were just more sharp objects—
like the videos he hated and needed—to allow his insides out.

When he was in sixth grade, his Hebrew school class was made to
watch a documentary about the concentration camps. It was never clear
to him if this was because his teacher was lazy (an acceptable way to get
rid of a couple of hours), or unable or unwilling to teach the material, or
felt the impossibility of teaching it in any way other than simply showing
it. Even at the time, Sam felt that he was too young to be seeing such a
thing.

They sat at chipboard desks for righties, and the teacher—whose name
they will all be able to remember for the rest of their lives—muttered a
few unmemorable words of context and inspiration and disclaimer, and
pressed Play. They watched lines of naked women, many pressing children
to their chests. They were crying—the mothers and the children—but
why were they only crying? Why were they so orderly? So good? Why
didn't the mothers run? Why didn't they try to save their children's lives?
Why didn't they protect their children? Better to get shot running away
than simply walk to one's death. A minuscule chance is infinitely greater
than no chance.

The still-children watched from their desks; they saw men digging
their own mass graves and then kneeling in them, their fingers interlaced

behind their heads. Why did they dig their own graves? If you're going to be killed anyway, why help with the killing? For the few extra moments of life? That might make sense. But how did they maintain that composure? Because they thought it might buy them a few extra moments of life? Maybe. A minuscule chance is infinitely greater than no chance, but a moment of life is an eternity. Be a good Jewish boy and dig a good Jewish grave and kneel like a mensch and, as Sam's nursery school teacher, Judy Shore, used to say, "You get what you get, and you don't get upset."

They saw grainy montages of humans who had become science experiments—dead twins, Sam could not not remember, still clutching each other on a table. Did they cling like that in life? He could not not wonder.

They saw images from the liberated camps: piles of hundreds or thousands of skeletal bodies, knees and elbows bending the wrong way, arms and legs at wrong angles, eyes so deeply sunken they could not be seen. Hills of bodies. Bulldozers testing a child's belief that a dead body doesn't feel anything.

What was he left with? The knowledge that Germans were—*are*—evil, evil, evil, not only capable of ripping children from their mothers and then ripping their small bodies apart, but *eager* to; that had non-Germans not intervened, the Germans would have murdered every single Jewish man, woman, and child on the planet; and that of course his grandfather was absolutely right, even if he sounded insane, when he said a Jewish person should never buy a German product of any kind or size, never put money into a German pocket, never visit Germany, never not cringe at the sound of that vile language of savages, never have any more interaction than what simply could not be avoided with any German of any age. Inscribe that on the doorpost of your house and on your gate.

Or he was left with the knowledge that everything that has happened once can happen again, is likely to happen again, *must* happen again, *will*.

Or the knowledge that his life was, if not the result of, then at least inextricably bound to, the profound suffering, and that there was some kind of existential equation, whatever it was and whatever its implications, between *his* life and *their* deaths.

Or no knowledge, but a feeling. What feeling? What was that feeling?

Sam didn't mention to his parents what he'd seen. Didn't seek explanation, or comfort. And he was given plenty of guidance—almost all of it unintentional and extremely subtle—never to ask about it, never even to acknowledge it. So it was never mentioned, always never talked about, the perpetual topic of nonconversation. Everywhere you looked, there it wasn't.

His dad was obsessed with displays of optimism, and the imagined accumulation of property, and joke-making; his mom, with physical contact before saying goodbye, and fish oil, and outer garments, and "the right thing to do"; Max, with extreme empathy and self-imposed alienation; Benjy, with metaphysics and basic safety. And he, Sam, was always longing. What was that feeling? It had something to do with loneliness (his own and others'), something with suffering (his own and others'), something with shame (his own and others'), something with fear (his own and others'). But also something with stubborn belief, and stubborn dignity, and stubborn joy. And yet it wasn't really any of those things, or the sum of them. It was the feeling of being Jewish. But what was that feeling?

THERE ARE THINGS
THAT ARE HARD TO SAY TODAY

Israel continued to describe the situation as manageable, but it also continued to close off its airspace, which left tens of thousands of Israelis stranded on vacation and prevented Jews who wanted to help from coming. Tamir tried hitching a ride on a Red Cross cargo plane, tried getting special clearance through the military attaché at the embassy, looked into chaperoning a shipment of construction equipment. But there was no way home. He might have been the only person grateful to be at the funeral—it gave him a few hours to rest in peace.

Sam wore his ill-fitting bar mitzvah suit to the cemetery. Wearing it was the only thing he hated more than the process of getting it: the torture chamber of mirrors, his mother's unhelpful help, the functionally pedophiliac survivor tailor who not once, not twice, but three times groped at Sam's crotch with his Parkinsonian fingers and said, "Plenty of room."

Tamir and Barak wore slacks with short-sleeve button-up shirts—their uniform for every occasion, whether it was going to synagogue, the grocery store, a Maccabi Tel Aviv basketball game, or the funeral of the family patriarch. They viewed any kind of formality—in dress, in speech, in affect—as some kind of gross infringement on a God-given right to at all times be oneself. Jacob found it obnoxious, and enviable.

Jacob wore a black suit with a box of Altoids in the pocket: artifacts of a time when he cared enough about how his breath smelled to attempt to echo it off his palm for sniffs.

Julia wore a vintage A.P.C. dress she'd found on Etsy for the equivalent of nothing. It wasn't exactly funeral attire, but she never had occasion to wear it, and she wanted to wear it, and since the neutering of the bar mitzvah, a funeral was as glamorous an occasion as she was going to get.

"You look beautiful, Julia," she said to Jacob, hating herself for saying it.

"Very beautiful," Jacob said, hating her for saying it, but also surprised that his assessment of her beauty continued to matter to her.

"The impact is lessened by it having been prompted."

"It's a funeral, Julia. And thank you."

"For what?"

"For saying I look handsome."

Irv wore the same suit he'd been wearing since the Six-Day War.

Isaac wore the shroud in which he had been married, the shroud he'd worn once a year on the Day of Atonement, the chest of which he'd beaten with his fist: *For the sin which we have committed before You with an utterance on the lips . . . For the sin which we have committed before You openly or secretly . . . For the sin which we have committed before You by a confused heart . . .* The shroud had no pockets, as the dead are required to be buried without any encumbrances.

A small—in number and physical stature—army from Adas Israel had passed through the grief like a breeze: they brought stools, covered the mirrors, took care of the platters, and sent Jacob an un-itemized bill that he was unable to question without requiring Jewish seppuku. There would be a small service, followed by burial at Judean Gardens, followed by a small kiddush at Irv and Deborah's, followed by eternity.

All the local cousins were at the funeral, and a few older, zanier Jews came in from New York, Philly, and Chicago. Jacob had met these people throughout his life, but only at rites of passage—bar mitzvahs, weddings, funerals. He didn't know their names, but their faces evoked a kind of Pavlovian existentialism: if you're here, if I see you, something significant must be happening.

Rabbi Auerbach, who'd known Isaac for several decades, had a stroke a month earlier and so left the officiating to his replacement: a young, disheveled, smart, or maybe dumb recent product of wherever rabbis are made. He wore unlaced sneakers, which felt, to Jacob, like a shabby tribute to someone who had probably *eaten* sneakers in the skyless forests of Poland. Then again, it might have been some kind of religious display of reverence, like sitting on stools or covering mirrors.

He approached Jacob and Irv before the service began.

"I'm sorry for your loss," he said, cupping his hands in front of him, as if they contained empathy, or wisdom, or emptiness.

"Yeah," Irv said.

"There are a few ritualistic—"

"Save your words. We're not a religious family."

"It probably depends on what is meant by *religious*," the rabbi said.

"It probably doesn't," Jacob corrected him, either in his dad's defense or in the absence of God's.

"And our stance is a choice," Irv said. "Not laziness, not assimilation, not inertia."

"I respect that," the rabbi said.

"We're as good as any Jews."

"I'm sure you're better than most."

Irv went right back at the rabbi: "What you do or don't respect isn't of great importance to me."

"I respect that, too," the rabbi said. "You're a man of strongly held beliefs."

Irv turned to Jacob: "This guy really can't take an insult."

"Come on," Jacob said. "It's time."

The rabbi walked the two of them through a few of the small rituals that, while entirely voluntary, they would be expected to perform in order to ensure Isaac's proper passage into whatever Jews believe in. After his initial reluctance, Irv seemed not only willing, but wanting, to cross his chets and dot his zayins—as if stating his resistance was resistance enough. He didn't believe in God. He couldn't, even if opening himself to that foolishness might have opened him to badly needed comfort. There had been a few moments—not of belief, but religiosity—every one of them involving Jacob. When Deborah went into labor, Irv prayed to no one that she and the baby would be safe. When Jacob was born, he prayed to no one that his son long outlive him, and acquire more knowledge and self-knowledge than him, and experience greater happiness. At Jacob's bar mitzvah, Irv stood at the ark and said a prayer of gratitude to no one that trembled, then broke, then exploded into something so beautifully unrestrained and full-throated that he was left with no voice to deliver his speech at the party. When he and Deborah didn't read the books they were staring at in the waiting room of George Washington Hospital, and Jacob almost pushed the doors off the hinges, his face covered in tears, his scrubs covered in blood, and did his best to form the words "You have a grandson," Irv closed his eyes, but not to darkness, and said a prayer to no one without any content, only force. The sum of those no ones was the King of the Universe. He'd spent enough of his life wrestling foolishness. Now, at the cemetery, all the wrestling felt foolish.

The rabbi said a small prayer, offering no translation or approximate sense of the meaning, and took a razor blade to Irv's lapel.

"I need this suit for my grandson's bar mitzvah."

Because he didn't hear Irv, or because he did, the young rabbi made a tiny incision, and directed Irv to open it—to create the actual rip—with his forefingers. It was ridiculous, this gesture. It was witchcraft, a relic from the time of stoning women for having their periods the wrong way, and it was an unconscionable thing to do to a Brooks Brothers suit. But Irv wanted to bury his father according to Jewish law and tradition.

He inserted his fingers into the incision, as if into his own chest, and pulled. And as the fabric tore, Irv's tears were released. Jacob hadn't seen his father cry in years. He couldn't remember the last time he'd seen his father cry. It suddenly seemed possible that he'd never seen him cry.

Irv looked at his son and whispered, "I don't have parents anymore."

The rabbi said that now was the moment, before the casket was taken from the hearse, for Irv to forgive his father, and to ask for forgiveness.

"It's OK," Irv said, dismissing the offer.

"I know," the rabbi said.

"We've said everything that needed to be said."

"Do it anyway," the rabbi suggested.

"I think it's foolish to speak to a dead person."

"Do it anyway. I wouldn't want you to regret missing this last chance."

"He's dead. It doesn't matter to him."

"You're living," the rabbi said.

Irv shook his head, and continued to shake it, but the object of the dismissiveness shifted: from the ritual to his inability to participate.

He turned to Jacob and said, "I'm sorry."

"You realize I'm not the dead one."

"Yeah. But both of us will be at some point. And here we are."

"Sorry for what?"

"An apology is only an apology if it's complete. I'm sorry for everything that I need to apologize for. No context."

"I thought we'd be monsters without context."

"We're monsters either way."

"Yeah, well, I'm a schmuck, too."

"I didn't say I was a schmuck."

"OK, so I'm the schmuck."

Irv put his hand on Jacob's cheek and almost smiled.

"Let's get this party started," he said to the rabbi, and approached the back of the hearse.

He tentatively put his hands on the casket and lowered his covered head. Jacob heard some of the words—he wanted to hear everything—but he couldn't make out the meaning.

The whispering went on—past "Forgive me," past "I forgive you." What was he saying? Why did the Blochs find it so hard to talk to one another while alive? Why couldn't Jacob lie in a casket long enough to hear his family's unspeakable feelings, but then return to the world of the living with what he'd learned? All the words were for those who couldn't respond to them.

It was way too humid, and one extemporaneous speech would have been way too many. The men sweated through their underwear, through their white shirts and black suits, sweated all the way into the folds of the handkerchiefs in their breast pockets. They were losing their body weight in sweat, as if trying to become salt, like Lot's wife, or become nothing, like the man they were there to bury.

While most of the cousins felt obliged to say a few words, none had felt obliged to prepare a few words, so everyone was made to endure, in that humidity, more than an hour of rambling generalities. Isaac was courageous. He was resilient. He loved. And the embarrassing inversion of what the goyim say about their guy: he survived for us.

Max told the story of the time his great-grandfather took him aside and, apropos of no birthday, Hanukkah, glowing report card, recital, or rite of passage, said, "What do you want? Anything. Tell me. I want you to have the thing that you want." Max told him he wanted a drone. The next time Max visited, Isaac again took him aside, and presented him with a board game called Reversi—either a knockoff of Othello, or what Othello knocked off. Max pointed out to the mourners that if one were to try to think of the word that sounded least like *drone*, it might be *Reversi*. Then he nodded, or bowed, and returned to his mother's side. No moral, consolation, or meaning.

Irv, who'd been working on his speech since long before Isaac's death, chose silence.

Tamir stood at a distance. It was hard to tell if he was trying to repress emotion or generate some. More than once, he used his phone. His casualness knew no limits, there was nothing he couldn't shrug off: death, natural catastrophe. It was something else about him that angered Jacob and that Jacob almost certainly envied. Why couldn't Tamir be more like Jacob? That was the question. And why couldn't Jacob be more like Tamir? That was the other question. If they could meet halfway, they'd form a reasonable Jew.

Finally, the rabbi stepped forward. He cleared his throat, pushed his glasses up his nose, and took a small spiral-bound pad from his pocket. He flipped through a few pages, then put it back, having either committed the contents to memory or realized he'd accidentally brought the wrong pad.

"What can we say about Isaac Bloch?"

He left enough pause to generate some rhetorical uncertainty. Was he actually asking a question? Admitting that he didn't know Isaac well enough to know what to say?

What can we say about Isaac Bloch?

Quickly, the wet cement of annoyance that Jacob felt at the hearse dried into something to break fists against. He hated this man. Hated his lazy righteousness, his bullshit affectations, his obsessive beard-stroking and Central Casting hand gestures, his too-tight collar and untied shoelaces and off-center yarmulke. This feeling sometimes subsumed Jacob, this unnuanced, swift, and eternal loathing. It happened with waiters, with David Letterman, with the rabbi who accused Sam. More than once he had come home from lunch with an old friend, someone with whom he had been through dozens of seasons of life, and casually said to Julia, "I think we reached the end." In the beginning, she didn't know what he meant—*the end of what? why the end?*—but after years of living beside such a binary, unforgiving person, someone so agnostic about his own worth he was compelled to a religious certainty about others', she came to know him, if not understand him.

"What can we say about someone about whom there is too much to say?"

The rabbi put his hands in his jacket pockets, closed his eyes, and nodded.

"Words don't fail us, time does. There isn't time—not from now until time's end—to recount the tragedy, and heroism, and *tragedy* of Isaac Bloch's life. We could stand here speaking about him until our own funerals, and it wouldn't be enough. I visited Isaac the morning of his death."

Wait, *what*? Was this possible? Wasn't he just the schmuck rabbi, here because half of the actually good rabbi's mouth had stopped functioning? If they'd stopped at Isaac's on the way back from the airport, would they have crossed this man's path?

"He called, and he asked me to come over. I heard no urgency in his voice. I heard no desperation. But I heard need. So I went. It was my first time in his home. We'd only met once or twice at shul, and always in passing. He had me sit at his kitchen table. He poured me a glass of ginger ale, served me a plate of sliced pumpernickel, some cantaloupe. Many of you have had that meal at that table."

A gentle chuckle of recognition.

"He spoke slowly, and with effort. He told me about Sam's bar mitz-vah, and Jacob's show, and Max's early long division, and Benjy's bike-riding, and Julia's projects, and Irv's mishegas—that was *his* word."

A chuckle. He was winning.

"And then he said, 'Rabbi, I feel no despair anymore. For seventy years I had only nightmares, but I have no nightmares anymore. I feel only gratitude for my life, for every moment I lived. Not only the good moments. I feel gratitude for every moment of my life. I have seen so many miracles.'"

This was either the most audacious heaping and steaming mountain of Jewshit ever shoveled by a rabbi or anyone, or a revelatory glimpse into Isaac Bloch's consciousness. Only the rabbi knew for sure—what was accurately recounted, what was embellished, what was fabricated out of whole tallis. Had anyone ever heard Isaac use the word *despair*? Or *grat-itude*? He'd have said, "It was horrible, but it could have been worse." But would he have said *that*? Thankful for *what*? And what were all these miracles he'd witnessed?

"Then he asked me if I spoke Yiddish. I told him no. He said, 'What kind of rabbi doesn't speak Yiddish?'"

A proper laugh.

"I told him my grandparents spoke Yiddish to my parents, but my parents would never let me hear it. They wanted me to learn English. To *forget* Yiddish. He told me he'd done the same, that he was the last Yiddish-speaker in his family, that the language would be in the casket, too. And then he put his hand on my hand and said, 'Let me teach you a Yiddish expression.' He looked me in the eye and said, '*Kein briere iz oich a breire.*' I asked him what it meant. He took back his hand and said, 'Look it up.'"

Another laugh.

"I *did* look it up. On my phone, in his bathroom."

Another laugh.

"*Kein briere iz oich a breire.* It means 'Not to have a choice is also a choice.'"

No, those words couldn't have been his. They were too faux-enlightened, too content with circumstance. Isaac Bloch was many things, and resigned was not one of them.

If having no choice were a choice, Isaac would have run out of choices once a day after 1938. But the family needed him, especially before the family existed. They needed him to turn his back on his grandparents, his parents, and five of his brothers. They needed him to hide in that hole with Shlomo, to walk with rigid legs toward Russia, eat other people's garbage at night, hide, steal, forage. They needed him to forge documents to board the boat, and tell the right lies to the U.S. immigration officer, and work eighteen-hour days to keep the grocery profitable.

"Then," the young rabbi said, "he asked me to pick up toilet paper for him at the Safeway, because they were having a sale."

Everyone chuckled.

"I told him he didn't need to buy toilet paper anymore. It would be taken care of by the Jewish Home. He gave me a knowing smile and said, 'But that price . . .'"

A louder, freer laugh.

"'That's it?' I asked. 'That's it,' he said. 'Was there something you wanted to hear? Something you wanted to say?' He said, 'There are two things that everybody needs. The first is to feel that he is adding to the world. Do you agree?' I told him I did. 'The second,' he said, 'is toilet paper.'"

The loudest laugh yet.

"I'm thinking about a Hasidic teaching that I learned as a rabbinical student. There are three ascending levels of mourning: with tears, with silence, and with song. How do we mourn Isaac Bloch? With tears, with silence, or with song? How do we mourn the end of his life? The end of the Jewish epoch that he participated in and exemplified? The end of Jews who speak in that music of broken instruments; who arrange their grammar counterclockwise and miss the point of every cliché; who say *mine* instead of *my, the German people* instead of *Nazis,* and who implore their perfectly healthy relatives to be healthy instead of feeling silent gratitude for health? The end of hundred-and-fifty-decibel kisses, of that drunken European script. Do we shed tears for their disappearance? Silently grieve? Or sing their praises?

"Isaac Bloch was not the last of his kind, but once gone, his kind will be gone forever. We *know* them—we have lived among them, they have shaped us as Jews and Americans, as sons and daughters, grandsons and granddaughters—but our time of knowing them is nearly complete. And then they will be gone forever. And we will only remember them. Until we don't.

"We *know* them. We know them with tears for their suffering, with silence for all that cannot be said, and with song for their unprecedented resilience. There will be no more old Jews who interpret a spot of good news as the guarantee of imminent apocalypse, who treat buffets like grocery stores before blizzards, who touch a finger to the bottom lip before turning a page of their people's Maxwell House epic."

Jacob's hatred was softening—not evaporating, not even melting, but losing its shape.

The rabbi paused, brought his hands together, and sighed. "As we stand at Isaac Bloch's grave, there is a war going on. There are two wars. One is on the brink of breaking out. The other has been happening for seventy years. The imminent war will determine the survival of Israel. The old war will determine the survival of the Jewish soul.

"Survival has been the central theme and imperative of Jewish existence since the beginning, and not because we chose it to be that way. We have always had enemies, always been hunted. It's not true that everyone hates Jews, but in every country we've ever lived, in every decade of every century, we have encountered hatred.

"So we've slept with one eye open, kept packed suitcases in the closet and one-way train tickets in the breast pockets of our shirts, against our hearts. We've made efforts not to offend or be too noisy. To achieve, yes, but not to draw undue attention to ourselves in the process. We've organized our lives around the will to perpetuate our lives—with our stories, habits, values, dreams, and anxieties. Who could blame us? We are a traumatized people. And nothing else has trauma's power to deform the mind and heart.

"If you were to ask one hundred Jews what was the Jewish book of the century, you would get one answer: *The Diary of Anne Frank.* If you were to ask what was the Jewish work of art of the century, you would get the same answer. This despite it having been created neither as a book nor as a work of art, and not in the century in which the question was asked. But its appeal—symbolically, and on its own terms—is overpowering."

Jacob looked around to see if anyone else was as surprised by the direction this was taking. No one seemed fazed. Even Irv, whose head only ever rotated on the axis of disagreement, was nodding.

"But is it good for us? Has it been good to align ourselves with poignancy over rigor, with hiding over seeking, victimization over will? No one could blame Anne Frank for dying, but we could blame ourselves for telling her story as our own. Our stories are so fundamental to us that it's easy to forget that we choose them. We *choose* to rip certain pages from our history books, and coil others into our mezuzot. We *choose* to make life the ultimate Jewish value, rather than differentiate the values of kinds of life, or, more radically, admit that there are things even more important than being alive.

"So much of Judaism today—regarding Larry David as anything beyond very funny, the existence and persistence of the Jewish American Princess, the embrace of klutziness, the fear of wrath, the shifting emphasis from argument to confession—is the direct consequence of our choice to have Anne Frank's diary replace the Bible as our bible. Because the Jewish Bible, whose purpose is to delineate and transmit Jewish values, makes it abundantly clear that life itself is not the loftiest ambition. *Righteousness* is.

"Abraham argues with God to spare Sodom because of the *righteousness* of its citizens. Not because life is inherently deserving of saving, but because *righteousness* should be spared.

"God destroys the earth with a flood, sparing only Noah, who was *'righteous in his own time.'*

"Then there is the concept of the Lamed Vovniks—the thirty-six righteous men of every generation, because of whose merit the entire world is spared destruction. Humankind is saved not because it is worth saving, but because the righteousness of a few justifies the existence of the rest.

"A trope from my Jewish upbringing, and perhaps from yours, was this line from the Talmud: 'And whoever saves a life, it is considered as if he saved an entire world.' This is a beautiful idea, and one worth living by. But we shouldn't ascribe more meaning to it than it contains.

"How much greater the Jewish people might be today if instead of *not dying*, our ambition was *living righteously*. If instead of 'It was done to me,' our mantra was 'I did it.'"

He paused. He held a long blink and bit at his lower lip.

"There are things that are hard to say today."

He almost smiled, as Irv had almost smiled when touching Jacob's face.

"Judaism has a special relationship with words. Giving a word to a thing is to give it life. 'Let there be light,' God said, and there was light. No magic. No raised hands and thunder. The articulation made it possible. It is perhaps the most powerful of all Jewish ideas: expression is generative.

"It's the same with marriage. You say, 'I do,' and you do. What is it, really, to be married?"

Jacob felt a burning across his scalp. Julia needed to move her fingers.

"To be married is to say you are married. To say it not only in front of your spouse, but in front of your community, and, if you are a believer, in front of God.

"And so it is with prayer, with *true* prayer, which is never a request, and never praise, but the expression of something of extreme significance that would otherwise have no way to be expressed. As Abraham Joshua Heschel wrote, 'Prayer may not save us. But prayer may make us worthy of being saved.' We are made worthy, made righteous, by expression."

He bit again at his lower lip and shook his head.

"There are things that are hard to say today.

"It is often the case that everyone says what no one knows. Today, no one says what everyone knows.

"As I think about the wars in front of us—the war to save our lives, and the war to save our souls—I think about our greatest leader, Moses. You might remember that his mother, Jochebed, hides him in a reed basket, which she releases into the current of the Nile, as a last hope of sparing his life. The basket is discovered by Pharaoh's daughter. 'Look!' she says. 'A crying Hebrew baby!' But how did she know that he was a Hebrew?"

The rabbi paused, and held the agitated silence in place, as if forcefully saving the life of a bird that only wanted to fly away.

Max spoke up: "Probably because Hebrews were trying to keep their kids from getting killed, and only someone in that situation would ever put her baby in a basket and send it down the river."

"Perhaps," the rabbi said, showing no condescending pleasure in Max's confidence, only admiration for his thought. "Perhaps."

And again he forced silence.

Sam spoke up: "So, I say this fully seriously: maybe she saw that he was circumcised? Right? She says, 'Look.'"

"That could be," the rabbi said, nodding.

And he dug a silence.

"I don't know anything," Benjy said, "but maybe he was crying in Jewish?"

"How would one cry in Jewish?" the rabbi asked.

"I don't know anything," Benjy said again.

"Nobody knows anything," the rabbi said. "So let's try to learn together. How would one cry in Jewish?"

"I guess babies don't really speak."

"Do tears?"

"I don't know."

"It's strange," Julia said.

"What is?"

"Wouldn't she have *heard* him crying? That's how it works. You hear them crying, and you go to them."

"Yes, yes."

"She said, 'Look! A crying Hebrew baby.' *Look*. She *saw* that he was crying, but didn't *hear*."

"So tell me what that implies," he said—no patronizing, no self-righteousness.

"She knew he was a Hebrew because only Jews cry silently."

For an instant, for a stitch, Jacob was overwhelmed by the terror that he had managed to lose the most intelligent person on earth.

"Was she right?" the rabbi asked.

"Yes," Julia said. "He was a Hebrew."

"But was she right that Jews cry silently?"

"Not in my experience," Julia said, with a chuckle that drew a depressurizing chuckle from the others.

Without moving, the rabbi stepped into the grave of silence. He looked at Julia, almost unbearably directly, as if they were the only two living people left, as if the only thing that distinguished those buried from those standing was ninety degrees.

He looked into her and said, "But in your experience, do Jews cry silently?"

She nodded.

"And now I'd like to ask *you* a question, Benjy."

"OK."

"Let's say we have two choices, as Jews: to cry silently, as your mother has said, or to cry in Jewish, as you said. What would it sound like to cry in Jewish?"

"I don't know."

"Nobody knows, so you can't be wrong."

"I don't even have a guess."

"Maybe like laughing?" Max suggested.

"Like laughing?"

"I don't know. That's what we do."

For an instant, for a stitch, Jacob was overwhelmed by the terror that he had managed to ruin the three most beautiful human beings on earth.

He remembered when Sam was young, how every time he got a scrape, cut, or burn, after every blood test, every fall from every tree branch that was forever after deemed "too high," Jacob would urgently pick him up, as if the ground were suddenly on fire, and say, "You're fine. It's OK. It's nothing. You're fine." And Sam would always believe him. And Jacob would be thrilled by how well it worked, and ashamed by how well it worked. Sometimes, if a greater lie was needed, if there was visible blood, Jacob would even say, "It's funny." And his son would believe him, because sons have no choice. But sons do feel pain. And the absence of the expression of pain is not the absence of pain. It is a different pain. When Sam's hand was crushed, he said, "It's funny. It's funny, right?" That was his inheritance.

The columns of Jacob's legs couldn't bear the weight of his heavy heart. He felt himself buckling, in weakness or genuflection.

He put his arm on Julia's shoulder. She didn't turn to him, she showed no acknowledgment of his touch, but she kept him standing.

"So," the rabbi said, reassuming his authority, "what can we say about Isaac Bloch, and how should we mourn him? There are only two kinds of Jews of his generation: those who perished and those who survived. We swore our allegiance to the victims, were good on our promise never to forget them. But we turned our backs on those who endured, and forgot them. All our love was for the dead.

"But now the two kinds of Jews have equal mortal standing. Isaac might not be with his brothers in an afterlife, but he is with his brothers in death. So what can we now say about him, and how should we mourn him? It was not because they lacked strength that his brothers died, but it was because of his strength that Isaac lived and died. *Kein briere iz oich a breire*. Not to have a choice is also a choice. How will we tell the story of he who never had no choice? At stake is our notion of righteousness, of a life worth saving.

"What was Moses crying about? Was he crying for himself? Out of hunger or fear? Was he crying for his people? Their bondage, their suffering? Or were they tears of gratitude? Perhaps Pharaoh's daughter didn't hear him crying because he *wasn't* crying until she opened the wicker basket.

"How should we mourn Isaac Bloch? With tears—what kind of tears? With silence—what silence? Or with what kind of song? Our answer will not save him, but it might save us."

With all three, of course. Jacob could see the rabbi's moves from five thousand years away. With all three, because of the tragedy, because of our reverence, because of our gratitude. Because of everything that was necessary to bring us to this moment, because of the lies that lie ahead, because of the moments of joy so extreme they have no relation to happiness. With tears, with silence, with song, because he survived so we could sin, because our religion is as gorgeous, and opaque, and brittle, as the stained glass of Kol Nidre, because Ecclesiastes was wrong: there isn't time for every purpose.

What do you want? Anything. Tell me. I want you to have the thing that you want.

Jacob cried.

He wailed.

THE NAMES WERE MAGNIFICENT

Jacob carried the casket with his cousins. It was so much lighter than he'd imagined it would be. How could someone with such a heavy life weigh so little? And the job was surprisingly awkward: they nearly fell over a few times, and Irv was only a half teeter from tumbling into the grave with his father.

"This is the worst cemetery *ever*," Max said to no one in particular, but loud enough for everyone to hear.

Finally, they were able to position the simple pine coffin on the broad strips of fabric that eased it into the grave.

And there it was: the fact of it. Irv bore the responsibility—the privilege of the mitzvah—of shoveling the first dirt onto his father's coffin. He took a heaping mound, turned his body to the hole, and tipped the shovel, letting it fall. It was louder than it should have been, and more violent, as if every particle of soil hit the wood at once, and as if it had been dropped from a far greater height. Jacob winced. Julia and the boys winced. Everyone winced. Some were thinking of the body in the coffin. Some were thinking of Irv.

HOW TO PLAY EARLY MEMORIES

My earliest memories are hidden around my grandfather's final house like afikomens: dish-soap bubble baths; knee-football games in the basement with the grandchildren of survivors—they always ended in injury; the seemingly moving eyes of Golda Meir's portrait;

instant-coffee crystals; pearls of grease on the surface of every liquid; games of Uno at his kitchen table, just us two humans, just yesterday's bagel, last week's Jewish Week, and juice from concentrate from whenever in history was the last significant sale. I always beat him. Sometimes we'd play one hundred games a night, sometimes both nights of the weekend, sometimes three weekends a month. He always lost.

What I think of as my earliest memory couldn't possibly be my earliest memory—it's too far into my life. I am confusing foundational with earliest, in the same way that, as Julia used to point out, the first floor of a house is usually the second, and sometimes the third.

This is my earliest memory: I was raking the leaves in front of the house when I saw something against the side door. Ants were beginning to envelop a dead squirrel. For how long had it been there? Had it eaten poison? What poison? Had a neighborhood dog killed it and then, full of a dog's remorse, delivered his shame? Or perhaps his pride? Or had the squirrel died trying to get in?

I ran inside and told my mother. Her glasses were steamed over; she was stirring a pot she couldn't see. Without looking up she said, "Go tell Dad to take care of it."

Through the open door—on the safe side of the threshold—I watched my father cover his hand with the clear plastic bag that the morning's Post had come in, pick up the squirrel, and then pull his hand out, turning the bag inside out with the squirrel in it. While my father washed his hands in the bathroom sink, I stood at his side and asked him question after question. I was always being taught lessons, and so came to assume that everything conveyed some necessary piece of information, some moral.

Was it cold? When do you think it died? How do you think it died? Didn't it bother you?

"Bother me?" my father asked.

"Gross you out."

"Of course."

"But you just went out there and did it like it was nothing."

He nodded.

I followed his wedding ring through the soap.

"Did you think it was disgusting?"

"I did."

"It was so gross."

"Yes."

"I couldn't have done it."

He laughed a father's laugh and said, "One day you'll do it."

"What if I can't?"

"When you're a dad, there's no one above you. If I don't do some-thing that has to be done, who is going to do it?"

"I still couldn't do it."

"The more you won't want to do it, the more of a dad you'll be."

The closet was filled with hundreds of plastic bags. He had cho-sen a clear one to teach me a lesson.

I obsessed over that squirrel for a few days, and then didn't think about it again for a quarter century, until Julia was pregnant with Sam, at which point I started having a recurrent dream of dead squir-rels lining the streets of our neighborhood. There were thousands of them: pushed against curbs, filling public garbage cans, prone in final poses while automatic sprinkler systems soaked through their fur. In the dream I was always returning home from somewhere, always walking up our street, it was always the end of the day. The window shades of the house were illuminated like TV screens. We didn't have a working fireplace, but smoke poured from the chimney. I had to walk on tiptoes to avoid stepping on squirrels, and sometimes it couldn't be avoided. I apologized—to whom? There were squirrels on the windowsills, and on stoops, and pouring from the gutters. I could see their silhouettes on the undersides of awnings. They hung half-way out of mail slots, in apparent attempts to find food or water, or simply to die inside—like that squirrel that had wanted to die inside my childhood home. I knew I was going to have to take care of all of them.

Jacob wanted to go to his father's side, as he had as a child, and ask him how he managed to shovel dirt into his father's grave.

Did you think it was disgusting?

I did, his father would have said.

I couldn't have done it.

His father would have laughed a father's laugh and said, *One day you'll do it.*

What if I can't?

Children bury their dead parents, because the dead need to be buried. Parents do not need to bring their children into the world, but children need to bring their parents out of it.

Irv handed the shovel to Jacob. Their eyes met. The father whispered into the son's ear: "Here we are and will be."

When Jacob imagined his children surviving him, he felt no version of immortality, as it's sometimes unimaginatively put, usually by people who are trying to encourage others to have children. He felt no contentment or peace or satisfaction of any kind. He felt only the overwhelming sadness of missing out. Death felt less fair with children, because there was more to miss. Whom would Benjy marry? (Despite himself, Jacob couldn't shake his Jewish certainty that of course he would want to marry, and *would* marry.) To what ethical and lucrative profession would Sam be drawn? What odd hobbies would Max indulge? Where would they travel? What would their children look like? (Of course they would want to have children, and *have* children.) How would they cope and celebrate? How would each die? (At least he would miss their deaths. Maybe that was the compensation for having to die himself.)

Before returning to the car, Jacob went for a walk. He read the gravestones like pages in an enormous book. The names were magnificent— because they were Jewish haiku, because they traveled in time machines while those they identified were left behind, because they were as embarrassing as pennies collected in paper rolls, because they were as beautiful as boats in bottles brought over on boats, because they were mnemonics: *Miriam Apfel, Shaindel Potash, Beryl Dressler* . . . He wanted to remember them, to use them later. He wanted to remember all of it, to use it all: the rabbi's shoelaces, the untied melodies of grief, the hardened footprints of a visitor in the rain.

Sidney Landesman, Ethel Keiser, Lebel Alterman, Deborah Fischbach, Lazer Berenbaum . . .

He would remember the names. He wouldn't lose them. He would use them. He would make something of the no longer anything.

Seymour Kaiser, Shoshanna Ostrov, Elsa Glaser, Sura Needleman, Hymie Rattner, Simcha Tisch, Dinah Perlman, Ruchel Neustadt, Izzie Reinhardt, Ruben Fischman, Hindel Schulz . . .

Like listening to a Jewish river. But you *can* step in it twice. You can—Jacob could; he believed he could—take all that was lost and re-find it, reanimate it, breathe new life into the collapsed lungs of those names, those accents, those idioms and mannerisms and ways of being. The young rabbi was right: no one would ever have such names again. But he was wrong.

Mayer Vogel, Frida Walzer, Yussel Offenbacher, Rachel Blumenstein, Velvel Kronberg, Leah Beckerman, Mendel Fogelman, Sarah Bronstein, Schmuel Gersh, Wolf Seligman, Abner Edelson, Judith Weisz, Bernard Rosenbluth, Eliezer Umansky, Ruth Abramowicz, Irving Perlman, Leonard Goldberger, Nathan Moskowitz, Pincus Ziskind, Solomon Altman . . .

Jacob had once read that there are more people alive now than have died in all of human history. But it didn't feel that way. It felt as if everyone were dead. And for all the individuality—for the extreme idiosyncrasy of the names of those extremely idiosyncratic Jews—there was only one fate.

And then he found himself where two walls met, at the corner of the vast cemetery, at the corner of the vast everything.

He turned to face the immensity, and only then did it occur to him, or only then was he forced to acknowledge what he'd forced himself not to: He was standing among suicides. He was in the ghetto for those unfit to be buried with the rest. This corner was where the shame was cordoned off. This was where the unspeakable shame was put beneath the ground. Milk on one set of plates, meat on the other: never the two should meet.

Miriam Apfel, Shaindel Potash, Beryl Dressler . . .

He had some vague awareness of the prohibition against taking one's own life, and the price—beyond death—for having done so. The punishment wasn't for the criminal, but the victims: those left behind and now forced to bury their dead in the other-earth. He remembered it like he remembered the prohibition against tattoos—something about desecrating the body—which would also land you in the other-earth. And—less spiritual, but every bit as religious—the prohibition against drinking Pepsi, because Pepsi chose to market to Arab countries and not Israel. And the prohibition against touching a shiksa in any of the ways one was dying to, because it was a shanda. And the prohibition against resisting when elders touched any part of your body they wanted, in any way they wanted, because they were dying, perpetually dying, and it was a mitzvah.

Standing in that unwalled ghetto, he thought about eruvs—a wonderfully Jewish loophole that Julia had shared, before he even knew the prohibition it was circumventing. She'd learned about them not in the context of a Jewish education, but in architecture school: an example of a "magical structure."

Jews can't "carry" on Shabbat: no keys, no money, no tissues or medicine, no strollers or canes, not even children who can't yet walk. The prohibition against carrying is technically against carrying from private to public domains. But what if large areas were made to be private? What if an entire neighborhood were a private domain? A city? An *eruv* is a string or wire that encloses an area, making it private, and thus permitting carrying. Jerusalem is enclosed by an eruv. Virtually all of Manhattan is enclosed by an eruv. There is an eruv in nearly every Jewish community in the world.

"In D.C.?"

"Of course."

"I've never seen it."

"You've never looked for it."

She took him to the intersection of Reno and Davenport, where the eruv turned a corner and was most easy to see. There it was, like dental floss. They followed it down Davenport to Linnean, and Brandywine, and Broad Branch. They walked beneath the string as it ran from street sign to lamppost to power pole to telephone pole.

As he stood among the suicides, his pockets were full: a paper clip that Sam had somehow bent into an airplane, a crumpled twenty, Max's yarmulke from the funeral (apparently acquired at the wedding of two people Jacob had never heard of), the dry-cleaning ticket for the pants he was wearing, a pebble Benjy had taken from a grave and asked Jacob to hold, more keys than there were locks in his life. The older he got, the more he carried, the stronger it should have made him.

Isaac was buried in a pocketless shroud, six hundred yards from his wife of two hundred thousand hours.

Seymour Kaiser: loving brother, loving son; head in the oven. *Shoshanna Ostrov*: loving wife; wrists slit in the bath. *Elsa Glaser*: loving mother and grandmother; hanging from the ceiling fan. *Sura Needleman*: loving wife, mother, and sister; walked into a river, pockets full of stones. *Hymie Rattner*: loving son; wrists slit over the bathroom sink. *Simcha Tisch*: loving father, loving brother; steak knife in the gut. *Dinah Perlman*:

loving grandmother, mother, and sister; leaped from the top of the stairs. *Ruchel Neustadt*: loving wife and mother; letter opener in the neck. *Izzie Reinhardt*: loving father, husband, and brother; jumped from Memorial Bridge. *Ruben Fischman*: loving husband; drove his car into a tree at one hundred miles per hour. *Hindel Schulz*: loving mother; serrated bread knife across the wrist. *Isaac Bloch*: loving brother, husband, father, grand-father, and great-grandfather; hanging by a belt in his kitchen.

Jacob wanted to pull the thread from his black suit, tie it around the tree in the corner, and walk the perimeter of the suicide ghetto, enclos-ing it as he unraveled. And then, when the public had been made private, he would carry away the shame. But to where?

Every landmass is surrounded by water. Was every coast an eruv?

Was the equator an eruv around the earth?

Did Pluto's orbit enclose the solar system?

And the wedding ring still on his finger?

REINCARNATION

> So what's new?
> You're the one in the middle of a crisis.
> That isn't new.
> Everything's the same here, except my great-grandfather is dead.
> Your family is OK?
> Yeah. I think my dad is pretty upset, but it's hard to tell, because he always seems a bit upset.
> Right.
> And it's not like it was his dad, anyway. Just his grandfather. Which is still sad, but less sad. Far less sad.
> Right.
> I really do like it when people repeat bits of language. Why is that?
> I don't know.
> Your dad and brother seem to be having a good time. They're worried about you, obviously. They talk about you constantly. But if they can't be there, it's good that they're here.
> Have they found anything?
> What do you mean?
> A house.
> For what?
> To buy.
> Why would they buy a house here?
> My father hasn't mentioned it?

> Mentioned what?

> Maybe to your dad?

> You guys are moving?

> He's been talking about it for a few years, but when it was time for me to join the army, he started looking. Just on websites, and maybe with the help of some brokers over there. I thought it was just talk, but when I was deployed to the West Bank, he started searching more seriously. I think he found a few places that seemed promising, and that's why he's over there now. To see them in person.

> I thought it was for my bar mitzvah.

> That's why he's staying more than a few days.

> I had no idea.

> He might be embarrassed.

> I didn't know he was capable of feeling embarrassment.

> Feeling it, yes. Showing it, no.

> Your mom wants to move?

> I don't know.

> Do you want to move?

> I doubt I'll live with my parents again. After the army, school. After school, life. I hope.

> But what do you think about it?

> I try not to.

> Do you find it embarrassing?

> No. That's not the right word.

> Do you think your dad cheats on your mom?

> That's a strange question.

> Is it?

> Yes.

> Yes, it's a strange question? Or yes, you think your dad cheats on your mom?

> Both.

> Jesus. Really?

> Someone who asks that question shouldn't be so surprised by the answer.

> What makes you think he cheats on her?

> What makes you ask the question?

> I don't know.

> So ask yourself.
> What makes me ask the question?

He was not asking for no reason. He was asking because he'd found his dad's second phone a day before his mom had. *Found* is probably not the right word, as coming upon it was the result of snooping through his dad's favorite hiding places—beneath a pile of socks in the dresser, in a box in the back of the "gift closet," atop the grandfather clock his grandfather had given them on the occasion of Benjy's birth. The loot was never anything more salacious than a porno—"Why," he wanted to ask but could never ask, "why would anyone with a desktop, laptop, tablet, or smartphone *pay* for pornography?"

He had found a stack of fifties, presumably for some indulgence his dad didn't want his mom to know about—something perfectly innocent like a power tool he was afraid his mom would point out he would never actually use. He had found a tiny bag of pot, which never, in the year and a half that he would check on it, diminished in size. He'd found a stash of Halloween candy—just sad. He'd found a stack of papers with a cover sheet labeled "Bible for *Ever-Dying People*"—

HOW TO PLAY DESIRE

Don't. You have everything you could ever need or want. You are healthy (for now) and it's great. Do you have any idea how much suffering and toil was necessary to make this moment possible? Possible for you? Reflect on how great it is, how lucky and fully satisfied you are.

—too boring to investigate further.

But then, while nosing around in the drawer of his dad's bedside table, Sam found a phone. His dad's phone was an iPhone. Everyone knew that, because everyone suffered his endless complaints about how amazing it was, and how dependent he was on it. ("This is literally ruining my life," he would say as he performed some utterly unnecessary function, like checking the weather three days out. "Chance of rain. Interesting.") This was a generic smartphone, the kind they give you for free with a criminally overpriced plan. Maybe a relic that his dad was too nostalgic to throw out? Maybe it was filled with photos of Sam and his brothers, and his dad wasn't smart enough to transfer them to his iPhone (despite feeling too smart to ask for help at a phone store, or even from his technologically proficient son), so he saved it, and over time the drawer would probably fill with phones filled with photos.

Nothing could have been easier than figuring out how to unlock it—his dad cycled through the same three lamely predictable variations of the family password for all his security needs.

Generic wallpaper: a sunset.

No games. No apps cooler than a calculator. Why even *have* a smartphone?

It was a mom phone. A private phone between them. It was hard to understand the need for it, but maybe the lack of need was the point. It was actually kind of sweet. Kind of lame, but kind of romantic, which was kind of gross. Unless it had some sort of straightforward justification, as it now-that-he-thought-about-it probably did, like being the phone they took on trips, with prepaid international minutes.

As he scrolled through the messages, it became clear that those explanations were wrong, extremely wrong, and that either his parents weren't who he thought they were, not even close, or there was more than one Julia in the world, because the Julia that was his mom would never—no, *never*—move her thumbs in such a way as to form the words *take the wetness from my pussy and use it to get my asshole ready for you.*

He took the phone to the bathroom, locked the door, and scrolled.

i want two of your fingers in each of my holes

What, like Spock? What the fuck was going on?

on your stomach, legs spread to the corners, your hands behind you, opening your ass as wide as it will go, your pussy dripping onto the sheets . . .

What the *fuck* was going on?

But before Sam could ask the question a third time, the front door opened, the phone dropped behind the toilet, his mom said, "I'm home," and he tried to beat the footsteps on the stairs to his room.

He'd never met Dr. Silvers, but he knew what Dr. Silvers would have said: he left the phone on purpose. Like everyone in the family who wasn't his dad, Sam loathed Dr. Silvers and was jealous of his dad for having such a confidant, and was jealous of Dr. Silvers for having his dad. What good, of any kind, could come, for anyone, from the discovery of the phone?

> Is your dad cheating on your mom, or something?

Suddenly, back in real unreal life, Eyesick stumbled away a few yards. He limped a bit, walked with a stutter. After making circles around nothing—like a planet around no sun, or a bride around no groom—he picked up the fossil of a bird from one of the earliest generations of Other Life, maybe three years before: the Twitter logo. Eyesick looked at the rock dumbly, then put it down, then picked it up again, then motioned as if to throw it, then tapped it against his head, as if testing his own ripeness.

> Are you seeing this glitch?
> No glitch. I started the transfer.
> Of what?
> Resilience fruit.
> I told you not to.
> You didn't. And if you had, I would have ignored you.

A flood of digital images, each blooming on the screen and then receding as soon as it could be processed: some were stored moments from Samanta's other life, conversations she'd had, experiences; others were more impressionistic. He saw screens that he'd looked at, mixed with screens Noam must have looked at: a contrail in a blue sky; crocheted rainbows on Etsy; the shovel of a bulldozer making contact with an old woman; cunnilingus, from behind, in a changing room; a thrashing lab monkey; conjoined twins (one laughing, one crying); satellite photos of the Sinai; unconscious football players; nail polish color wheels; Evander Holyfield's ear; a dog being euthanized.

> How many are you transferring?
> All of them.
> What?
> 1,738,341.
> HOLY FUCKING SHIT! You have that many banked?
> I'm giving you a total transfusion.

> What?
> Listen, I have to get myself ready to go.
> Where?
> Jerusalem. My unit was mobilized. But don't tell my father, OK?
> Why not?
> He'll worry.
> But he should worry.
> But his worrying won't help him, and it won't help me.
> I don't even need all of this. I only had 45,000 when my dad killed me.
> Make yourself great.
> My avatar.
> Your great-grandfather.
> This is too much.
> I should let it rot? Make resilience cider?
> You should use it.
> But I won't. And you will.

The images came more quickly, so quick they could enter only subliminally; they overlapped, blended, and from the corner a light, bleeding from a few pixels to stain the screen, and spreading, a light like the darkness a broken pipe leaves on the ceiling, a light flooding the perpetually refreshing images, and then more light than image, and then an almost entirely white screen, but brighter than white, vague images as if seen through an avalanche.

In perhaps the purest moment of empathy of Sam's life, he tried to imagine what Noam was seeing on his screen at that moment. Was a darkness like light spreading? Was he receiving warnings about low levels of vitality? Sam imagined Noam clicking IGNORE to those warnings, over and over, and ignoring the annoying alerts, and clicking CONFIRM when finally prompted to confirm his ultimate choice.

The lion walked to the old man, knelt beside him, laid his immense and proud paws on Eyesick's stooped shoulders, licked at whatever one calls a white five o'clock shadow (a five o'clock brightness?), licked him over and over, as if to will Eyesick back to life, when in fact he was willing himself back to what comes before life.

> Look at you, Bar Mitzvah.

He rested his massive head on Eyesick's sunken chest. Eyesick hid his fingers in the lion's streaming mane.

In the middle of his great-grandfather's funeral reception, Sam started to cry. He didn't cry often. He hadn't cried since Argus returned from his second hip replacement, two years before, his back half shaved to reveal Frankenstein stitches, his eyes lowered in his lowered head.

"It's just what getting better looks like," Jacob had said. "In a month, he'll be his old self."

"A *month*?"

"It'll pass quickly."

"Not for Argus, it won't."

"We'll spoil him."

"He can barely walk."

"And he shouldn't walk any more than is necessary. The vet said that's the most important thing for his recovery, to keep him off his leg as much as possible. All walks have to be on-leash. And no stairs. We have to keep him on the first floor."

"But how will he come up to bed?"

"He's going to have to sleep down here."

"But he'll go up."

"I don't think so. He knows how weak his leg is."

"He'll go up."

"I'll put some books on the stairs to block the way."

Sam set his alarm for 2:00 a.m., to go down and check on Argus. He snoozed once, and then again, but with the third buzz, his guilt was awakened. He plodded down the stairs, only half aware of being out of bed, nearly paralyzed himself with the help of the stacked *Grove Encyclopedia of Art*, and found his father on top of a sleeping bag, spooning Argus. That's when he cried. Not because he loved his dad—although in that moment he certainly did—but because, of the two animals on the floor, it was his dad he felt more sorry for.

> Look at you, Bar Mitzvah.

He was by the window. The cousins were on PlayStation, killing representations. The adults were upstairs, eating the disgusting, smelly, smoked, and gelatinous foods Jews suddenly need in times of reflection. No one noticed him, which was what he wanted, even if it wasn't what he needed.

He wasn't crying about anything in front of him—not the death of his great-grandfather or the death of Noam's avatar, not the collapse of his parents' marriage, or the collapse of his bar mitzvah, or the collapsed buildings in Israel. His tears were reaching back. It took Noam's moment of kindness to reveal the yawning absence of kindness. His dad had slept on the floor for thirty-eight days. (The extra week to play it safe.) Was it easier to extend such kindness to a dog because it didn't risk rejection? Or because the needs of animals are so animalistic, whereas the needs of humans are so human?

He might never become a man, but crying at that window—his great-grandfather completely alone in the earth twenty minutes away; an avatar returning to pixelated dust in some refrigerated data storage center somewhere near nothing; his parents just on the other side of the ceiling, but a ceiling without edges—Sam was reborn.

JUST THE WAILING

Judaism gets death right, Jacob thought. It instructs us what to do when we know least well what to do, and feel an overwhelming need to do *something*. You should sit like this. *We will*. You should dress like this. *We will*. You should say these words at these moments, even if you have to read from transliteration. *Na-ah-seh*.

Jacob had stopped crying more than an hour ago, but he still had what Benjy called "after-crying breath." Irv brought him a glass of peach schnapps, said, "I told the rabbi he was welcome to come, but I doubt he'll come," and went back to his windowsill citadel.

The dining table was covered with platters of food: everything and pumpernickel bagels, everything minibagels, everything flagels, bialys, cream cheese, scallion cream cheese, salmon spread, tofu spread, smoked and pickled fish, pitch-black brownies with white chocolate swirls like square universes, blondies, rugelach, out-of-season hamantaschen (strawberry, prune, and poppy seed), and "salads"—Jews apply the word *salad* to anything that can't be held in one's hand: cucumber salad, whitefish and tuna and baked salmon salad, lentil salad, pasta salad, quinoa salad. And there was purple soda, and black coffee, and Diet Coke, and black tea, and enough seltzer to float an aircraft carrier, and Kedem grape juice—a liquid more Jewish than Jewish blood. And there were pickles, a few kinds. Capers don't belong in any food, but the capers that every spoon had tried to avoid had found their way into foods in which they *really* didn't belong, like someone's half-empty half-decaf. And at the center of the table, impossibly dense kugels bent light and time around them. It was too much food by a factor of ten. But it had to be.

Relatives exchanged stories about Isaac while they piled their plates toward the ceiling of the floor above. They laughed about how funny he was (on purpose, and by accident), what an obstinate pain in the ass he could be (on purpose, and by accident). They reflected on what a hero he had been (on purpose, and by accident). There was a bit of crying, there were some awkward silences, there was gratitude for having had an occasion to gather as a family (some of the cousins hadn't seen each other since Leah's bat mitzvah, some not since Great-Aunt Doris's death), and everyone looked at his phone: to check on the war, the score of the game, the weather.

The kids, having already forgotten about any first-person sadness they might have felt over Isaac's death, were playing first-person video games in the basement. Max's pulse doubled as he spectated at an assassination attempt by someone he thought was a second cousin. Sam sat off to the side with his iPad, wandering in a virtual lemon grove. This was how it always went, this vertical segregation. And inevitably, the adults with enough sense to escape the adult world would migrate down. Which is what Jacob did.

There were at least a dozen cousins—many from Deborah's side, a few from Julia's. The younger ones unpacked all the board games, one at a time—not to play them, but to unpack them and commingle the small pieces. Every now and then one would spontaneously freak out. The older cousins were surrounding Barak as he performed virtuosic acts of extreme violence on a TV so large one had to sit against the opposite wall to see its edges.

Benjy was on his own, stuffing crumpled Monopoly money between the venetian blinds.

"You're being very generous with the window," Jacob said.

"It's not real money."

"No?"

"I know you're joking."

"You haven't seen Mom around, have you?"

"No."

"Hey?"

"What?"

"Have you been crying, buddy?"

"No."

"Are you sure? You look like you have."

"Holy shit!" a cousin shouted.

"Language!" Jacob shouted back.

"I haven't," Benjy said.

"Are you sad about Great-Grandpa?"

"Not really."

"So what's upsetting you?"

"Nothing."

"Dads know these things."

"Then why don't you know what's upsetting me?"

"Dads don't know everything."

"Only God does."

"Who told you that?"

"Mr. Schneiderman."

"Who's that?"

"My Hebrew school teacher."

"*Schneiderman*. Right."

"He said that God knows everything. But that didn't make sense to me."

"It doesn't make sense to me, either."

"But that's because you don't believe in God."

"I only ever said I was unsure. But if I *did* believe in God, it *still* wouldn't make sense to me."

"Right, because if God knows everything, why do we have to write notes to put in the Wall?"

"That's a good point."

"Mr. Schneiderman said that God knows everything but sometimes forgets. So the notes are to remind him of what's important."

"God forgets? Really?"

"That's what he said."

"What do you think about that?"

"It's weird."

"I think so, too."

"But that's because you don't believe in God."

"If I believed in God, he would be a remembering God."

"Mine would, too."

Despite being as agnostic about God's existence as he was about the question's meaning (could any two people really be referring to the same thing when speaking about God?), Jacob wanted Benjy to believe. Or Dr. Silvers did, anyway. For several months, Benjy's anxiety about death had been slowly and steadily ramping up, and now risked tipping from adorable to problematic. Dr. Silvers said, "He has the rest of his life to form answers to theological questions, but he'll never get back this time of developing his first relationship to the world. Just make him feel safe." That struck Jacob as right, even if the thought of evangelizing made him squirm. The next time Benjy raised his fear of death, just when Jacob's instinct urged him to agree that an eternity of nonexistence was certainly the most horrible of all things to imagine, Jacob remembered Dr. Silvers's command: *Just make him feel safe.*

"Well, you know about heaven, right?" Jacob said, causing a nonexistent angel to lose its wings.

"I know that you think it isn't real."

"Well, no one knows for sure. I certainly don't. But you know what heaven is?"

"Not really."

So Jacob gave his most comforting explanation, sparing neither extravagance nor intellectual integrity.

"And if I wanted to stay up late in heaven?" Benjy asked, now planking on the sofa.

"As late as you want," Jacob said, "every single night."

"And I could probably eat dessert before dinner."

"You wouldn't have to eat dinner at all."

"But then I wouldn't be healthy."

"Health won't matter."

Benjy turned his head to the side: "Birthdays."

"What about them?"

"What are they like?"

"Well, they're never-ending, of course."

"Wait, it's *always* your birthday?"

"Yes."

"You have a party and get presents every day?"

"All day every day."

"Wait, do you have to write thank-you notes?"

"You don't even have to *say* thank you."

"Wait, does that mean you're zero, or infinity?"

"What do you want to be?"

"Infinity."

"Then you're infinity."

"Wait, is it always everyone's birthday?"

"Only yours."

Benjy rose to his feet, raised his hands above his head, and said, "I want to die right now!"

Just don't make him feel too safe.

In Irv and Deborah's basement, facing a more nuanced theological question, Jacob again resisted his instinct for truth in favor of Benjy's emotional safety: "Maybe God does remember everything but sometimes chooses to forget?"

"Why would he do that?"

"So that *we* remember," Jacob said, pleased with his improvisation. "Like the wishes," he continued. "If God knew what we wanted, *we* wouldn't have to."

"And God wants us to know for ourselves."

"Could be."

"I used to think Great-Grandpa was God," Benjy said.

"You did?"

"Yeah, but he's dead, so obviously he wasn't God."

"That's one way to think about it."

"I know Mom isn't God."

"How is that?"

"Because she would never forget about me."

"You're right," Jacob said, "she wouldn't."

"No matter what."

"No matter what."

Another round of expletive mutterings from the cousins.

"Anyway," Benjy said, "that's what was making me cry."

"Mom?"

"My note for the Wailing Wall."

"Because you were thinking about how God is forgetful?"

"No," Benjy said, pointing at the TV, which wasn't displaying a video game, as Jacob had thought, but the effects of the most recent, and most severe, aftershock, "because the Wall crumbled."

"The *Wall?*"

They came spilling into the world: every wish tucked into every crevice, but also every wish tucked into every Jew's heart.

"No more proof of how great they were," Benjy said.

"What?"

"The thing you told me about the Romans."

How much do the children know, and how much do they remember?

"Jacob!" Irv called from upstairs.

"The Wailing Wall," Jacob said, as if by saying its name aloud, it would exist again.

Jacob could make his children feel safe. But could he keep them safe?

Benjy shook his head and said, "Now it's just the Wailing."

LOOK! A CRYING HEBREW BABY

Tamir's presence had not only made a full reckoning impossible, it required Julia to be a buoyant host. And the death of Jacob's grandfather required her to at least perform love and care, when all she felt was sadness and doubt. She was good enough to manage her blossoming resentment, good enough, even, to suppress her passive-aggression, but at a certain point, the requirements of being a good person inspire hatred for oneself and others.

Like any living person, she had fantasies. (Although her immense guilt about being human required a constant reminder—that she was "like any living person.") The houses she designed were fantasies, but there were others.

She imagined a week alone in Big Sur. Maybe at the Post Ranch Inn, maybe one of the ocean-facing rooms. Maybe a massage, maybe a facial, maybe a "treatment" that treats nothing. Maybe she'd walk through a redwood tunnel, the growth rings bending around her.

She imagined having a personal chef. Vegans live longer, and are healthier, and have better skin, and she could do that; it would be easy, if someone shopped, cooked, and cleaned for her.

She imagined Mark noticing small things about her that she'd never noticed about herself: lovably misused idioms, what her feet do when she flosses, her funny relationship to dessert menus.

She imagined going for walks without destinations, thinking about things of no logistical importance, like whether Edison bulbs are actually obnoxious.

She imagined a secret admirer anonymously subscribing her to a magazine.

She imagined the disappearance of crow's feet, like the disappearance of crow's footprints from a dusty road.

She imagined the disappearance of screens—from her life, from her children's lives. From the gym, from doctors' offices and the backs of cabs, hanging behind bars and in the corners of diners, the iWatches of people holding iPads on the Metro.

She imagined the deaths of her air-filled clients and their dreams of heavier and heavier kitchen appliances.

She fantasized about the death of the so-called teacher who chuckled at one of Max's answers four years ago, requiring a month of bedtime talks to reinstill his enjoyment of school.

Dr. Silvers would have to die at least a couple of times.

She imagined Jacob's sudden disappearance—from the house, from existence. She imagined him dropping dead at the gym. Which required imagining him *going* to the gym. Which required imagining him once again possessing a desire to be attractive in ways other than professional success.

Of course, she didn't actually want him to die, no part of her did, not even subconsciously, and when she fantasized about his death, it was always painless. Sometimes he would panic in awareness as he tried to reach through his chest to grab his stammering heart. Sometimes he would think of the children. The end of sometimes: he would be gone forever. And she would be alone, and finally unalone, and people would grieve for her.

She would cook all the meals (as she already did), do all the cleaning (as she already did), buy the graph paper for Benjy's solutionless mazes, the teriyaki-roasted seaweed snacks for Max, a cool-but-not-trying-too-hard messenger bag for Sam when the last one she bought for him fell apart. She would dress them in end-of-the-year Zara and Crewcuts sale clothing and get them off to school (as she already did). She would have to support herself (which she couldn't, with her present lifestyle, but wouldn't have to, given Jacob's life insurance policy). Her imagination was strong enough to hurt her. She was weak enough to keep the hurt to herself.

And then came the most hurtful thought, the thought that can never be touched with even the whorls of the fingers of one's brain: the deaths of her children. She'd had the most horrible thought many times since she became pregnant with Sam: imagined miscarriages; imagined SIDS; imagined tumbles down stairs, trying to shield his body from the treads as they fell; imagined cancer every time she saw a child with cancer. There was the knowledge that every school bus she ever put one of her children on was going to roll down the side of a hill and into a frozen lake, whose ice would re-form around its silhouette. Every time one of her children was put under general anesthesia, she said goodbye to him as if she were saying goodbye to him. She wasn't naturally anxious, much less apocalyptic, but Jacob was right when, after Sam's injury, he said it was too much love for happiness.

Sam's injury. It was the place she was unwilling to go, because there was no road back. And yet the trauma center of her brain was always pushing her there. And she was always never fully returning. She'd found peace with why it happened—there was no why—but not how. It was too painful, because whatever the sequence of events, it wasn't necessary or inevitable. Jacob never asked her if she had been the one to open the door. (It was far too heavy for Sam to have opened himself.) Julia never asked Jacob if he had closed it on Sam's fingers. (*Maybe* Sam could have gotten it moving, and inertia would have taken care of the rest?) It was five years ago, and the journey—the century-long morning in the ER, the twice-a-week visits to the plastic surgeon, the year of rehab—brought them closer than they'd ever been. But it also created a black hole of silence, from which everything had to keep a safe distance, into which so much was swallowed, a teaspoon of which weighed more than a million suns consuming a million photos of a million families on a million moons.

They could talk about how lucky they were (Sam very nearly lost his fingers), but never how unlucky. They could speak in generalities, but never recount the details: Dr. Fred repeatedly sticking needles into Sam's fingers to test for feeling, while Sam looked into his parents' eyes and begged, pleaded, for it to stop. When they came home, Jacob put his bloody shirt in a plastic bag and walked it to the garbage can on the corner of Connecticut. Julia put her bloody shirt in an old pillowcase and tucked it halfway into a stack of pants.

Too much love for happiness, but how much happiness was enough? Would she do it all again? She always believed that her ability to endure pain was greater than anyone else's—certainly than her children's or Jacob's. A burden would be easiest carried by her, and regardless, it would ultimately be carried by her anyway. Only men can unhave babies. But if she could do it all again?

She often thought of those retired Japanese engineers who volunteered to go into failing nuclear plants to fix them after the tsunami. They knew they'd be exposed to fatal amounts of radiation, but given that their life expectancies were shorter than the time it would take for the cancer to kill them, they saw no reason not to get the cancer. In the hardware gallery, Mark had said it wasn't too late in life for happiness. When, in Julia's life, would it be late enough for honesty?

It was amazing how little changed as everything changed. The conversation was continually expanding, but it was no longer clear what they were talking about. When Jacob showed her listings for places to which he might move, was it any more real than when he used to show her listings for places to which *they* might move? When they shared their visions for happy independent lives, was it any less make-believe than when they used to share their visions for living together happily? The rehearsal of how they would tell the kids took on a quality of theater, as if they were trying to get the scene right, rather than get life right. She had the sense that to Jacob it was a kind of game, that he enjoyed it. Or worse, that planning their separation was a new ritual that kept them together.

Domestic life stagnated. They talked about Jacob starting to sleep elsewhere, but Tamir was in the guest room, Barak was on the sofa, and leaving for a hotel after everyone was asleep and arriving before anyone woke up felt both cruel and profligate. They talked and talked about what kind of schedule was most likely to facilitate good stretches with the kids, and good transitions, and as little missing as possible—but they didn't take any steps either to repair what was broken or to leave it behind.

After the funeral . . .

After the bar mitzvah . . .

After the Israelis leave . . .

After the semester ends . . .

There was a nonchalance to their desperation, and maybe talking about it was enough for now. It could wait until it couldn't.

But funerals, like airplane turbulence and fortieth birthdays, force the issue of mortality. Had it been another day, she and Jacob would have found ways to continue living inside their purgatory. They would

have created errands to run, diversions, emotional escape hatches, fantasies. The funeral made a conversation almost a crime, but it also inspired
an unrelenting questioning in Julia. All that could be deferred on any
other day was now urgent. She remembered Max's obsession with time,
how little there was. "I'm wasting my life!"

She went to the bedroom, to the dozens of coats piled on the bed. They
looked like dead bodies, like Jewish dead. Those images had imprinted
Julia's childhood, too, and she now found certain resonances impossible to escape. Those images of naked women holding their children to
their chests. She hadn't seen them since she first saw them, but she
never stopped seeing them.

The rabbi had looked across the patiently waiting grave and into Julia.
He asked, "But in your experience, do Jews cry silently?" Did he see what
no one could hear?

She found her coat, put it on. The pockets were filled with receipts,
and a small arsenal of candies for bribing, and keys, and business cards, and
assorted foreign currency from trips she could remember planning and
packing for but not taking. In two fistfuls she transferred all this to the
garbage, like tashlich.

She went to the front door without stopping: past the white cab-
bage salad, black coffee, bluefish, and blondies; past the purple soda and
peach schnapps; past the chatter about investments, and Israel, and cancer.
She walked past the drone of the Mourner's Kaddish, past the covered
mirrors, past the photos of Isaac on the console: with the Israelis at their
last visit; at Julia's fortieth; on his sofa, looking off into the near distance.
When she reached the door, she noticed, for the first time, the sign-in
book resting open on an accent table. She flipped through it, looking to
see if her boys had written anything.

Sam: *I'm sorry.*
Max: *I'm sorry.*
Benjy: *I'm sorry.*

She was sorry, too, and she touched the mezuzah as she crossed the
threshold, but didn't kiss her fingers. She remembered when Jacob suggested they select their own text to scroll into the mezuzah of the front
door of their home. They chose a line from the Talmud: "Every blade of
grass has an angel watching over it, whispering, 'Grow! Grow!'" Would
the next family to live in the house even know?

THE LION'S DEN

Tamir and Jacob stayed up late that night. Julia was somewhere, but she wasn't there. Isaac wasn't there, wasn't anywhere. The kids were supposed to be asleep in their rooms, but Sam was in Other Life while snapchatting with Billie, and Max was looking up words that he didn't understand in *The Catcher in the Rye*—pissed, as Holden had taught him to be, that he had to use a paper dictionary. Barak was in the guest room, asleep and expanding. Downstairs, it was only the two cousins—old friends, middle-aged men, the fathers of still-young children.

Jacob got some beers from the gently humming fridge, muted the TV, and with a heavy, affected sigh took a seat across the table from Tamir.

"That was hard today."

"He lived a good, long life," Tamir said, and then took a good, long drink.

"I suppose so," Jacob said, "except for the *good* part."

"The great-grandchildren."

"Whom he referred to as his 'revenge against the German people.'"

"Revenge is sweet."

"He spent his days clipping coupons for things he would never buy, while telling anyone who would listen that no one listened to him." A drink. "I once took the kids to a zoo in Berlin—"

"You've been to Berlin?"

"We were shooting there, and it coincided with a school break."

"You've taken your children to Berlin and not to Israel?"

"As I was *saying*, we went to a zoo in the East, and it was pretty much the most depressing place I've ever been. There was a panther, in a habitat the size of a handicapped parking space, with flora about as convincing as a plastic Chinese food display. He was walking figure eights, over and over and over, the exact same path. When he turned, he would jerk his head back and squint. Every time. We were mesmerized. Sam, who was maybe seven, pressed his palms to the glass and asked, 'When is Great-Grandpa's birthday?' Julia and I looked at each other. What kind of seven-year-old asks such a question at such a moment?"

"The kind who worries that his great-grandfather is a depressed panther."

"Exactly. And he was right. The same routine, day after day after day: instant black coffee and cantaloupe; crawl through the *Jewish Week* with that enormous magnifying glass; check the house to make sure all the lights are still off; push a walker on tennis balls to shul to have the same Sad Libs conversations with the same macular degenerates, substituting different names into the news about prognoses and graduations; thaw a brick of chicken soup while flipping through the same photo albums; eat the soup with black bread while advancing through another paragraph of the *Jewish Week*; take a nap in front of one of the same five movies; walk across the street to confirm Mr. Kowalski's continued existence; skip dinner; check the house to make sure all the lights are still off; go to bed at seven and have eleven hours of the same nightmares. Is that happiness?"

"It's a version."

"Not one that anyone would choose."

"A lot of people would choose that."

Jacob thought of Isaac's brothers, of hungry refugees, of survivors who didn't even have family to ignore them—he was ashamed both of the inadequate life he tolerated for his great-grandfather and of judging it inadequate.

"I can't believe you took the kids to Berlin," Tamir said.

"It's an incredible city."

"But before Israel?"

Google knew how far Tel Aviv was from Washington, and a tape measure could determine the width of the table, but Jacob couldn't even approximate his emotional distance from Tamir. He wondered: Do we understand each other? Or are we near-strangers, just assuming and pretending?

"I regret that we didn't keep in better touch," Jacob said.

"You and Isaac?"

"No. *Us*."

"I suppose if we'd wanted to, we would have."

"I'm not so sure," Jacob said. "There are a lot of things I wanted to do, but didn't."

"Wanted at the time, or looking back?"

"Hard to say."

"Hard to *know*? Or hard to *say*?"

Jacob swallowed a mouthful of beer and used his palm to dry the ring left on the table, wishing, as he did, that he were the kind of person to let such things go. He thought about all that was happening behind the walls, above the ceiling, and under the floor—how little he understood the workings of his home. What was going on at the outlet when nothing was plugged in? Was there water in the pipes at that moment? There must have been, as it came out as soon as the faucet was opened. So did that mean the house was constantly filled with sitting water? Wouldn't that weigh an enormous amount? When he'd learned in school that his body was more than sixty percent water, he'd done as his father had taught, and doubted. Water simply wasn't heavy enough for that to be true. Then he'd done as his father had taught, and sought the truth from his father. Irv filled a trash bin with water and challenged Jacob to lift it. As Jacob struggled, Irv said: "You should feel blood."

Jacob brought the beer to his lips. There were images of the Wailing Wall on the TV. He leaned back and said, "Remember when we snuck out of my parents' house? Years and years ago?"

"No."

"When we went to the National Zoo?"

"The National Zoo?"

"Really?" Jacob asked. "A few nights before my bar mitzvah?"

"Of course I remember. You're not remembering that I mentioned it in the car on the way from the airport. And it was the night before your bar mitzvah. Not a few nights before."

"Right. I know. I knew. I don't know why I changed it like that."

"What would your Dr. Silvers say?"

"I'm impressed you remember his name."

"You've made it easy."

"What would Dr. Silvers say? Probably that I was protecting myself with the vagueness."

"How much do you pay this man?"

"I pay him a preposterous shitload. And insurance pays the other two-thirds."

"Protecting yourself from what?"

"From caring more?"

"Than I do?"

"I'm not making an argument for my enlightenment here."

And not only behind the walls, above the ceiling, and under the floor—the room itself was filled with activity of which Jacob had only the dimmest awareness: radio broadcasts, TV stations, cell phone conversations, Bluetooth, Wi-Fi, leakage from the microwave, radiation from the oven and lightbulbs, solar rays from the biggest oven and lightbulb of them all. All of it constantly passing through the room, some of it cultivating tumors or killing sperm, none of it noticed.

"We were so dumb," Tamir chuckled.

"We still are."

"But we were even dumber then."

"But we were also romantic."

"Romantic?"

"About life. Don't you remember what that was like? To believe that life itself could be the object of love?"

While Tamir went for another beer, Jacob texted Julia: *where are you? i called maggie and she said you weren't there.*

"No," Tamir said into the fridge. "I don't remember that."

Their socks had become sweat sponges at the zoo that morning thirty years before. Everything in D.C. in the summer was a purification ritual. They saw the famous pandas, Ling-Ling and Hsing-Hsing, the elephants and their memories, the porcupines and their shields of writing implements. The parents argued about which city's weather was less sufferable, D.C.'s or Haifa's. Each wanted to lose, because losing was how you won. Tamir, who was a highly significant six months older than Jacob, spent most of the time pointing out how little security there was, how easy it would be to sneak in, perhaps not realizing that the zoo was open, and they were there, and it was free.

After the zoo, they took Connecticut Avenue to Dupont Circle—Irv and Shlomo up front, Adina and Deborah in the back, Jacob and Tamir facing backward in the Volvo's rear—had sandwiches at an unmemorable café, then spent the afternoon at the National Air and Space Museum waiting in line for the twenty-seven glorious minutes of *To Fly!*

To make up for the crappy lunch, they went to Armand's that evening for "the best Chicago pizza in D.C.," then had sundaes at Swensen's, then watched a dull action movie at the Uptown, just to experience the awe of a screen so big it felt like the opposite of being buried, and maybe even the opposite of dying.

Five hours later, the only light coming from the security system's keypad, Tamir shook Jacob into wakefulness.

"What are you doing?" Jacob asked.

"Let's go," Tamir whispered.

"What?"

"Come on."

"I'm asleep."

"Sleeping people don't talk."

"It's called talking in one's sleep."

"We're going."

"Where?"

"The zoo."

"What zoo?"

"Come on, shithead."

"It's my bar mitzvah tomorrow."

"Today."

"Right. And I need to sleep."

"Sleep during your bar mitzvah."

"Why would we go to the zoo?"

"To sneak in."

"Why would we do that?"

"Don't be a pussy."

Maybe Jacob's common sense was still offline, or maybe he actually cared about being a pussy in Tamir's estimation, but he sat up, rubbed his eyes, and put on his clothes. A phrase formed in his mind—*this is so unlike me*—that he would find himself repeating throughout the night, until the moment he became his own opposite.

They walked down Newark in the darkness, took a right at the Cleveland Park branch of the public library. Silently, more like sleepwalkers than Mossad agents, they padded down Connecticut, over the Klingle Valley

Bridge (which Jacob was incapable of crossing without imagining jumping), past the Kennedy-Warren apartments. They were awake, but it was a dream. They came to the verdigris lion and the large concrete letters: zoo.

Tamir had been right: nothing could have been easier than hopping the waist-high concrete barrier. It was so easy as to feel like a trap. Jacob would have been happy enough to cross the border, make the transgression official, and turn right back around, newly acquired trespassing badge in trembling hand. But Tamir wasn't content with the story.

Like a tiny commando, Tamir crouched, searched his field of vision, then gave Jacob a quick beckoning gesture to follow. And Jacob followed. Tamir led him past the welcome kiosk, past the orientation map, farther and farther away from the street, until they lost sight of it, as sailors lose sight of the shore. Jacob didn't know where Tamir was leading him, but he knew that he was being led, and would follow. *This is so unlike me.*

The animals, as far as Jacob could tell, were asleep. The only sounds were the wind moving through the copious bamboo, and the ghostly buzzing vending machines. Earlier, the zoo had resembled an arcade on Labor Day. Now it felt like the middle of the ocean.

Animals were always mysteries to Jacob, but never more than when they slept. It felt possible to outline—if only a crude, gross approximation— the consciousness of a waking animal. But what does a rhinoceros dream about? Does a rhinoceros dream? A waking animal never startled into sleep—it happened slowly, peacefully. But a sleeping animal seemed always on the verge of startling into wakefulness, into violence.

They reached the lion enclosure and Tamir stopped. "I haven't stopped thinking about this since we were here this morning."

"About what?"

He put his hands on the rail and said, "I want to touch the ground."

"You *are* touching the ground."

"In there."

"*What?*"

"For a second."

"Fuck you."

"I'm serious."

"No you're not."

"Yes. I am."

"Then you're fucking crazy."

"Yes. But I'm also fucking serious."

Tamir had taken them, Jacob then realized, to the only part of the enclosure where the wall was short enough for some DSM-5 exemplar to be able to climb back out. He'd obviously found it earlier in the day, maybe even measured it with his eyes, maybe—certainly—played out the scene in his mind.

"Don't," Jacob said.

"Why not?"

"Because you know why not."

"I don't."

"Because you will be *eaten by a lion*, Tamir. Jesus fucking Christ."

"They're asleep," he said.

"They?"

"There's three of them."

"You counted?"

"Yes. And it also says so on the plaque."

"They're asleep because nobody is invading their territory."

"And they're not even out here. They're inside."

"How do *you* know?"

"Do you see them?"

"I'm not a fucking zoologist. Of all the things that are going on right now, I probably see about none of them."

"They're asleep inside."

"Let's go home. I'll tell everyone you jumped in. I'll tell them you killed a lion, or got a blowjob from a lion, or whatever will make you feel like a hero, but let's get the fuck out of here."

"Nothing I want here has to do with anyone else."

Tamir had already begun to hoist himself over.

"You're going to die," Jacob said.

"So are you," Tamir responded.

"What am I supposed to do if a lion wakes up and starts running for you?"

"What are *you* supposed to do?"

That made Jacob laugh. And his laughter made Tamir laugh. With his small joke, the tension eased. With his small joke, the stupidest of all ideas became reasonable, even almost sensible, maybe even genius. The alternative—sanity—became insane. Because they were young. Because one is young only once in a life lived only once. Because recklessness is the only fist to throw at nothingness. How much aliveness can one bear?

It happened so quickly, and took forever. Tamir jumped down, landing with a thud he obviously didn't anticipate, because his eyes met Jacob's with a flash of terror. And as if the ground were lava, he tried to get off it. He wasn't quite able to reach the rail on his first jump, but the second try looked easy. He pulled himself up, Jacob hoisted him over the glass, and together they fell onto the pavement, laughing.

What did Jacob feel, laughing with his cousin? He was laughing at life. Laughing at himself. Even a thirteen-year-old knows the thrill and terror of his own insignificance. *Especially* a thirteen-year-old.

"Now you," Tamir said as they picked themselves up and brushed themselves off.

"No fucking way."

This is so unlike me.

"Come on."

"I'd rather die."

"You can have it both ways. Come on, you have to."

"Because you did it?"

"Because you want to do it."

"I don't."

"Come on," he said. "You'll be so happy. For years you'll be happy."

"Happiness isn't that important to me."

And then, firmly: "*Now*, Jacob."

Jacob tried to laugh off Tamir's flash of aggressiveness.

"My parents would kill me if I died before my bar mitzvah."

"This will *be* your bar mitzvah."

"No way."

And then Tamir got up in Jacob's face. "I'm going to punch you if you don't do it."

"Give me a break."

"I am literally going to punch you."

"But I have glasses and acne."

That small joke diffused nothing, made nothing almost sensible. Tamir punched Jacob in the chest, hard enough to send him into the railing. It was the first time Jacob had ever been punched.

"What the fuck, Tamir?"

"What are you crying about?"

"I'm not crying."

"If you're not crying, then stop crying."

"I'm not."

Tamir rested a hand on each of Jacob's shoulders, and rested his forehead against Jacob's. Jacob had breast-fed for a year, been given baths in the kitchen sink, fallen asleep on his father's shoulder a thousand times—but this was an intimacy he had never experienced.

"You have to do it," Tamir said.

"I don't want to."

"You do, but you're afraid."

"I don't."

But he did. But he was afraid.

"Come," Tamir said, bringing Jacob to the wall. "It's easy. It will take only a second. You saw. You saw that it wasn't a big deal. And you'll remember it forever."

This is so unlike me.

"Dead people don't have memories."

"I won't let you die."

"No? What will you do?"

"I'll jump in with you."

"So we die together?"

"Yes."

"But that doesn't make me any less dead."

"It does. Now *go*."

"Did you hear something?"

"No, because there was nothing to hear."

"Seriously: I don't want to die."

Somehow it happened without happening, without any decision having been made, without a brain sending any signal to any muscle. At a certain point, Jacob was halfway over the glass, without ever having climbed it. His hands were shaking so violently he could only barely hold on.

This is so unlike me.

"Let go," Tamir said.

He held on.

This is so unlike me.

"Let go."

He shook his head and let go.

And then he was on the ground, inside the lion's den.

This is the opposite of me.

There, on the dirt, in the middle of the simulated savannah, in the middle of the nation's capital, he felt something so irrepressible and true that it would either save or ruin his life.

Three years later he would touch his tongue to the tongue of a girl for whom he so happily would have cut off his arms, if only she had let him. And the following year an air bag would tear his cornea and save his life. Two years after that he would gaze with amazement at a mouth around his penis. And later that year he would say *to* his father what for years he had been saying *about* him. He would smoke a bushel of pot, watch his knee bend the wrong way during a stupid touch-football game, be inexplicably moved to tears in a foreign city by a painting of a woman and her baby, touch a hibernating brown bear and an endangered pangolin, spend a week waiting for a test result, pray silently for his wife's life as she screamed as new life came out of her body—many moments when life felt big, precious. But they made up such an utterly small portion of his time on earth: Five minutes a year? What did it sum to? A day? At most? A day of feeling alive in four decades of life?

Inside the lion's den, he felt surrounded and embraced by his own existence. He felt, perhaps for the first time in his life, safe.

But then he heard it, and was brought back. He looked up, met Tamir's eyes, and could see that Tamir heard it, too. A stirring. Flattening foliage. What did they exchange in their glance? Fear? But it felt like laughter. Like the greatest of all jokes had passed between them.

Jacob turned and saw an animal. Not in his mind, but an actual animal in the actual world. An animal that didn't deliberate and expound. An uncircumcised animal. It was fifty feet away, but its hot breath was steaming Jacob's glasses.

Without saying a word, Tamir climbed back over the fence and extended his hand. Jacob leaped for it but couldn't reach. Their fingers touched, which made the distance feel infinite. Jacob jumped again, and again their fingertips brushed, and now the lion was running, halving the distance between them with each stride. Jacob had no time to gather himself or contemplate how he might get an extra inch or two, he simply tried again, and this time—because of the adrenaline, or because of God's sudden desire to prove His existence—he caught hold of Tamir's wrist.

And then Jacob and Tamir were once again sprawled on the pavement, and Tamir started laughing, and Jacob started laughing, and then, or at the same time, Jacob started crying.

Maybe he knew. Maybe he was somehow aware, a teenager laughing and crying on that pavement, that he would never again feel anything like it. Maybe he saw, from the peak of that mountaintop, the great flatness before him.

Tamir was crying, too.

Thirty years later, they were still on the brink of the enclosure, but despite all the inches they'd grown, it no longer felt possible to enter. The glass had grown, too. It had grown more than they'd grown.

"I've never felt alive since that night," Jacob said, bringing Tamir another beer.

"Life has been that boring?"

"No. A lot of life has happened. But I haven't felt it.

"There are versions of happiness," Tamir said.

Jacob paused before opening the bottle and said, "You know, I'm not sure I believe that."

"You don't want to believe it. You want to believe that your work should have the significance of a war, that a long marriage should offer the same kind of excitement as a first date."

"I know," Jacob said. "Don't expect too much. Learn to love the numbness."

"That's not what I said."

"I've spent my life clinging to the belief that all the things we spoke about as children had at least a grain of truth to them. That the promise of a felt life isn't a lie."

"Did you ever stop to ask yourself why you put such an emphasis on feeling?"

"What else would one put an emphasis on?"

"Peace."

"I've got plenty of peace," Jacob said. "Too much peace."

"There are versions of peace, too."

A wind passed over the house, and deep inside the range hood, the damper flapped.

"Julia thinks I don't believe in anything," Jacob said. "Maybe she's right. I don't know if this counts as belief or disbelief, but I'm sure that my grandfather isn't somewhere other than in the ground right now. What we've got is what we're going to get. Our jobs, our marriages . . ."

"You're disappointed?"

"I am. Or devastated. No, something between disappointed and devastated. Dispirited?"

The stubborn recessed light over the sink went dark with a snapping sound. Some connection wasn't quite secure.

"It was a hard day," Tamir said.

"Yes, but the day has been decades."

"Even though it only felt like a few seconds?"

"Whenever someone asks me how I'm doing, I find myself saying, 'I'm going through a passage.' Everything is a transition, turbulence on the way to the destination. But I've been saying it for so long I should probably accept that the rest of my life is going to be one long passage: an hourglass with no bulbs. Always the pinch."

"Jacob, you really don't have enough problems."

"I've got enough," Jacob said while texting Julia again, "believe me. But my problems are so small, so domestic. My kids stare at screens all day. My dog is incontinent. I have an insatiable appetite for porn, but can't count on an erection when there's an analog pussy in front of me. I'm balding—which I know you've noticed, and thank you for not drawing attention to it."

"You aren't balding."

"I'm smaller than life."

Tamir nodded his head and asked, "Who isn't smaller than life?"

"*You.*"

"What's so big about me? I can't wait to hear."

"You've fought in wars, and live in the shadow of future wars, and Christ, Noam is in the middle of who-knows-what right now. The stakes of your life reflect the size of life."

"And that's worth envying?" Tamir asked. "One less beer and I'd be offended by what you just said." He drank down half the bottle. "One more and I'd be furious."

"There's no reason to be offended. I'm just saying you've escaped the Great Flatness."

"You think I want anything more than a boring white house in a boring neighborhood where no one knows each other because everyone's watching TV?"

"Yes," Jacob said. "I think you'd go as crazy as my grandfather."

"He wasn't crazy. You're the one who's crazy."

"I didn't mean—"

The light snapped back on, saving Jacob from having to know what he meant.

"Listen to yourself, Jacob. You think it's all a game, because you're only a fan."

"What's that supposed to mean?"

"Worse than a fan. You don't even know who you're rooting for."

"Hey. Tamir. You're running with something I didn't say. What's going on?"

Tamir pointed at the television—Israeli troops holding back an agitated crowd of Palestinians trying to get into West Jerusalem—and said, "That's what's going on. Maybe you haven't noticed?"

"But that's exactly what I'm talking about."

"The drama. Right. You love the drama. It's who we are that embarrasses you."

"*What?* Who does?"

"Israel."

"Tamir, stop. I don't know what you're talking about, or why this conversation took this turn. Can't I just bemoan my life?"

"If I can just defend my own."

With the hope that a bit of empowerment might bring Max out of his funk, Jacob and Julia had started to let him take neighborhood adventures on his own: to the pizza parlor, library, bakery. One afternoon he came back with a pair of cardboard X-ray glasses from the drugstore. Jacob covertly watched him try them on, then read the packaging again, then try them on again, then read the packaging. He wore them around the first floor, becoming increasingly agitated. "These completely suck!" he said, throwing them to the floor. Jacob delicately explained that they were a gag, intended to make other people think you could see through things. "Why wouldn't they make that clear on the packaging?" Max asked, his anger upshifting to humiliation. "And why would it be any less funny if they actually *could* see through things?"

What was going on inside Tamir? Jacob couldn't understand how the warm banter about happiness had downshifted to a heated political argument with only one participant. Something had been touched, but what?

"I work a lot," Tamir said. "You know that. I've always worked a lot. Some men work to get away from their families. I work to provide for mine. You believe me when I say that, right?"

Jacob nodded, unable to bring himself to say, "Of course I do."

"I missed a lot of dinners when Noam was young. But I took him to school every morning. It was important to me. I got to know a lot of the other parents that way. For the most part, I liked them. But there was one father I couldn't stand—a real asshole, like me. And so naturally I hated his child as well. Eitan was his name. So maybe you know where this story is going?"

"I have no idea, actually."

"When Noam entered the army, who should be in his unit?"

"Eitan."

"Eitan. His father and I exchange e-mails when one of us has some small bit of news to share. We never spend time together, and never even talk on the phone. But we write back and forth quite a bit. I didn't grow to like him—the more I deal with him, the more I hate him. But I love him." He wrapped his hand around the empty bottle. "Can I ask you a question?"

"Sure."

"How much money do you give to Israel?"

"How much *money*?" Jacob asked, going to the fridge to get Tamir another beer, and because he needed to move. "That's a funny question."

"Yes. What do you give to Israel? I'm serious."

"What, to the UJA? Ben-Gurion University?"

"Sure, include it all. And include your trips to Israel, with your parents, with your own family."

"You know I haven't been there with Julia and the boys."

"That's right, you went to Berlin. Well, imagine you had gone to Israel. Imagine the hotels you would have stayed in, the cab rides, falafel, the Jerusalem-stone mezuzot you would have brought back."

"I don't know what you're getting at."

"Well, I know that I give more than sixty percent of my salary."

"You mean in taxes? You *live* there."

"Which is all the more reason you should have to bear the financial burden."

"I really can't follow this conversation, Tamir."

"And it's not only that you refuse to give your fair share, you *take*."

"Take *what*?"

"Our future. Did you know that more than *forty percent* of Israelis are considering emigrating? There was a survey."

"That's somehow my fault? Tamir, I understand that Israel isn't a college town, and it must be torture to be away from your family right now, but you're going after the wrong guy."

"Come on, Jacob."

"What?"

"You're complaining about how fucking dispirited you are, about how small your life is." Tamir leaned forward. "I'm scared."

Jacob was moved to speechlessness. It was as if he had entered the kitchen that night with cardboard X-ray glasses and thrown them to the ground in frustration, and instead of explaining that they were only intended to make others think you could see through things, Tamir made himself transparent.

"I'm scared," he said again. "And I'm sick of bonding with Eitan's dad."

"You have more than Eitan's dad."

"That's right: we have the Arabs."

"Us."

"Us? Your children are asleep on organic mattresses. My son is in the middle of *that*," he said, pointing at the television again. "I give more than half of everything I have, and you give one percent, tops. You want to be part of the epic, and you feel entitled to tell me how to run my house, and yet you give and do nothing. Give more or talk less. But no more referring to *us*."

Like Jacob, Tamir preferred not to keep his phone in his pocket and would rest it on tables or counters. Several times, despite it looking nothing like Jacob's phone, Jacob instinctively picked it up. The first time, the home screen was a photo of Noam as a child, lining up a corner kick. The next time, it was a different photo: Noam in his uniform, saluting. The next time: Noam in Rivka's arms.

"I understand that you're worried," Jacob said. "I'd be losing my mind. And if I were you, I'd probably resent me, too. It's been a long day."

"Remember how you were obsessed with our bomb shelter? When you first visited? Your father, too. I practically had to drag you out of there."

"That's not true."

"When we defeated half a dozen Arab armies in '48—"

"*We?* You weren't even born."

"That's right, I shouldn't have said *we*. It includes you, and you had nothing to do with it."

"I had as much to do with it as you did."

"Except that my grandfather risked his life, and therefore risked my life."

"He had no choice."

"America has always been a choice for us. Just as Israel has for you. Every year you end your seder with 'Next year in Jerusalem,' and every year you choose to celebrate your seder in America."

"That's because Jerusalem is an idea."

Tamir laughed and banged the table. "Not for the people who live there, it isn't. Not when you're putting a gas mask on your child. What did your father do in '73, when the Egyptians and Syrians were pushing us toward the sea?"

"He wrote op-eds, led marches, lobbied."

"You know I love your father, but I hope you can hear yourself, Jacob. Op-eds? My father commanded a tank unit."

"My father helped."

"He gave what he could give without sacrificing, or even risking, anything. Do you think he considered getting on a plane and coming to fight?"

"He didn't know how to fight."

"It's not very hard, you just try not to die. In '48 they gave rifles to skeletons as they got off their boats from Europe."

"And he had a wife at home."

"No kidding."

"And it wasn't his country."

"Bingo."

"America was his country."

"No, he was homelandless."

"America was his home."

"America was where he rented a room. And do you know what would have happened if we'd lost that war, as so many, and so many of *us*, feared would happen?"

"But you didn't lose."

"But if we had? If we *had* been pushed into the sea, or just slaughtered where we were?"

"What's your point?"

"Your father would have written op-eds."

"I'm not sure what you're getting at with this mental exercise. You're trying to demonstrate that you live in Israel and I don't?"

"No, that Israel is dispensable to you."

"Dispensable?"

"Yes. You love it, support it, sing about it, pray for it, even envy the Jews who live there. And you will survive without it."

"In the sense that I wouldn't stop breathing?"

"In that sense."

"Well, in *that* sense, America is dispensable to me, as well."

"That's absolutely right. People think the Palestinians are homeland-less, but they would die for their homeland. It's you who deserves pity."

"Because I won't die for a country?"

"You're right. I've said too little. You won't die for *anything*. I'm sorry if that hurts your feelings, but don't pretend it's unfair or untrue. Julia was right: you don't believe in anything."

It would have been the moment for one or both of them to storm off, but Jacob took his phone from the table and calmly said, "I'm gonna take a piss. And when I come back, we're going to pretend the last ten minutes didn't happen." Tamir showed nothing.

Jacob closed himself in the bathroom, but he didn't pee, and he didn't pretend the fight hadn't happened. He took his phone from his pocket. The home screen was a photo taken on Max's sixth birthday. He and Julia had given Max a suitcase filled with costumes. A clown costume. A fireman costume. An Indian. A bellboy. A sheriff. The first one he tried on, commemorated digitally, was the soldier costume. Jacob flushed nothing down the toilet, went into his phone's settings, and replaced the photo with one of the stock generic images: a treeless leaf.

He went back to the kitchen and took his seat across from Tamir. He'd decided to try the joke about the difference between a Subaru and an erection, but before he could get the first word out, Tamir said, "I don't know where Noam is."

"What do you mean?"

"He was home for a few days. We exchanged some e-mails, and talked. But he was deployed this afternoon. Rivka doesn't know to where. And I haven't heard anything. He tried calling, but I stupidly didn't have my phone on. What kind of father am I?"

"Oh, Tamir. I'm so sorry. I can't even imagine what you're feeling."

"You can."

"Noam will be OK."

"You can promise me that?"

Jacob scratched at no itch on his arm and said, "I wish I could."

"I believed a lot of what I said. But a lot of it I didn't believe. Or I'm not sure I believe."

"I also said some things I didn't believe. It happens."

"Why can't he send even a one-sentence e-mail? Two letters: O-K."

Jacob said, "I don't know where Julia is," trying to meet Tamir's realness with his own. "She's not on a work trip."

"No?"

"No. And I'm scared."

"Then we can talk."

"What have we been doing?"

"Making sounds."

"It's all my fault. Julia. The family. I acted as if my home were dispensable."

"Slow down. Tell me what—"

"She found a phone," Jacob said, as if that statement needed something to interrupt in order to be spoken. "A secret phone of mine."

"Shit. Why did you have a secret phone?"

"It was really stupid."

"You had an affair?"

"I don't even know what that word means."

"You would know if it were Julia having an affair." Which released the emergency brake of Jacob's mind: Was she having sex with Mark at that moment? Was he fucking her while they talked about her? Tamir asked, "Did you fuck her?"

Jacob paused, as if he needed to consider the question, as if he didn't even know what the word *fuck* meant.

"I did."

"More than once?"

"Yes."

"Not in the house."

"No," Jacob said, as if offended by the suggestion. "In hotels. Once in the office. It was just permission to acknowledge our unhappiness. Julia was probably even grateful that it happened."

"Everyone is so grateful for the permission that no one wants."

"Maybe."

"It's the same conversation we were just having. The same."

"I thought it was revealed to be bullshit?"

"Some, yes, but not this part: you can't say, 'This is who I am.' You can't say, 'I'm a married man. I have three great kids, a nice house, a good job. I don't have everything I want, I'm not as respected as I might wish, I'm not as rich or loved or fucked as I might wish, but this is who I am, and choose to be, and admit to being.' You can't say that. But neither can you admit to needing more, to wanting more. Forget about other people, you can't even admit your unhappiness to yourself."

"I'm unhappy. If that's what you need to hear me say, there it is. I want more."

"That's just making sounds."

"What *isn't* making sounds?"

"Going to Israel. To live."

"OK, now you're kidding."

"I'm saying what you already know."

"That if I moved to Israel my marriage would improve?"

"That if you were capable of standing up and saying, 'This is who I am,' you'd at least be living your own life. Even if who you are is ugly to others. Even if who you are is ugly to you."

"I'm not living my own life?"

"No."

"Whose life am I living?"

"Maybe your grandfather's idea of your life. Or your father's. Or your own idea. Maybe no life at all."

Jacob suspected he should take offense, and he had the instinct to strike back at Tamir, but he also felt humbled, and grateful.

"It was a long day," he said, "and I don't know that either of us is saying what he means anymore. I like having you here. It reminds me of when we were kids. Let's cut our losses."

Tamir took the last third of his beer down in one gulp. He placed the bottle back on the table, more gently than Jacob had seen him do anything, and said, "When do we stop cutting our losses?"

"You and I?"

"Sure."

"As opposed to what? Losing it all?"

"Or reclaiming what's ours."

"Yours and mine?"

"Sure."

He finished Jacob's unfinished beer and tossed the two empty bottles in the garbage.

"We recycle," Jacob said.

"I don't."

"You have enough towels upstairs?"

"What do you think I do with towels?"

"Just trying to be a good host."

"Always trying to be something."

"Yes. I'm always trying to be something. That says something good about me."

"OK."

"And you're always trying to be something, too. And so is Barak. And Julia and Sam and Max and Benjy. Everybody."

"What am I trying to be?"

Jacob paused for a beat, careful.

"You're trying to be bigger than you actually are."

Tamir's smile revealed the force of the blow.

"Ah."

"Everybody is trying to be something."

"Your grandfather isn't."

What was that? A stupid joke? Some kind of lazy stab at wisdom?

"He stopped trying," Jacob said, "and it killed him."

"You're wrong. He's the only one of us who actually succeeded."

"At *what*?"

"At becoming something."

"*Dead?*"

"Real."

Jacob almost said, *Now you've lost me.*

He almost said, *I'm heading up.*

He almost said, *I don't agree with anything you've said, but I understand you.*

The night could end, the conversation could close, what was shared could be processed, digested, and expelled, save for the nutrients.

But instead, Jacob asked, "You want another beer? Or is that just going to get us drunk and fat?"

"I'll have whatever you're having," Tamir said. "Including drunkenness and fatness."

"And baldness."

"No, you're taking care of that for both of us."

"You know," Jacob said, "I have a bag of pot upstairs. Somewhere. It's probably as old as Max, but pot never goes bad, does it?"

"Not any more than kids do," Tamir said.

"Shit."

"What's the worst that could happen? We don't get high?"

IN THE HINGE

It took Julia three hours to walk to Mark's apartment. Jacob texted and called and texted and called, but she didn't text or call ahead to see if Mark was there. Her finger was releasing the buzzer to his apartment as it was pressing it—the circuit completed for a startling instant, like a bird hitting a window.

"Hello?"

She stood motionless and silent. Could the microphone detect her breathing? Was Mark listening to her exhalations, four floors above?

"I can see you, Julia. There's a little camera just above the buzzers."

"It's Julia," Julia said, as if she could snip out those last couple of seconds and respond to "Hello?" like a normal human being.

"Yes, I'm looking at you."

"This is an unpleasant feeling."

"So get out of the frame and come on up."

The door opened itself.

And then the elevator doors opened for her, and then opened for her again.

"I wasn't expecting you," Mark said, ushering her in.

"I wasn't expecting me, either."

Reflexively, she scanned the apartment. Everything was new and new-looking: phony moldings, floors glossy enough for bowling, fat plastic dimmer slides.

"As you can see," Mark said, "it's a work in progress."

"What isn't?"

"A lot of furniture is arriving tomorrow. Tomorrow it will look completely different."

"Well, then I'm glad I got to see the *before*."

"And it's temporary. I needed a place, and this . . . was a place."

"Do you think I'm judging you?"

"No, but I think you're judging my apartment."

She looked at Mark, the efforts he made: he worked out, used hair product, bought clothes that someone—in a magazine or store—told him were cool. She looked around the apartment: how high were the ceilings, how tall the windows, how glossy the appliances.

"Where do you eat?"

"Out, usually. Always."

"Where do you open mail?"

"That sofa is where I do everything."

"You sleep on it?"

"Everything but sleep."

Everything but sleep: it was unbearably suggestive. Or so Julia felt. But everything felt unbearably suggestive to her right then, because she was unbearably exposed. Before the skin regrew and healed, some of the inside of Sam's hand was on the outside, and infection was a constant concern. Childishly, Julia didn't want to blame her child's hand for its vulnerability, and so saw him as having stayed the same and the world as having become more threatening. They went straight from the hospital to ice cream. "*Every* topping?" the server asked. As her hand pressed on the door—the first door she'd opened since the heavy one shut—Julia noticed the back of the OPEN sign. "Look," she said, finding, in the joke, another reason to hate herself, "the world is closed."

"No," Sam said. "*Close*. Like near."

Another reason to hate herself.

There were so many things she could have said to Mark. There was so much available small talk. It was at sleepaway camp that she learned how to make a bed with hospital corners. It was at the hospital that she learned how to press tightly folded words between massive seconds. But she didn't want things to be tidy or concealed right then. But she didn't want things to be as disheveled and exposed as they felt.

What did she want?

"What do I want?" she asked, quiet as a spacewalk.

She wanted some of her insides on the outside, but which insides and how much?

"What?" Mark asked.

"I don't know why I'm asking you."

"I didn't hear what you asked," he said, closing the distance between them, perhaps to hear better.

She'd tried everything: juice cleanses, poetry binges, knitting, writing letters by hand to people she'd let go of, moments of the unmediated honesty they'd promised each other in Pennsylvania sixteen years before. She'd tried meditating half a dozen times, but always felt lost when guided to "remember" her body. She knew what was meant, but was incapable, or unwilling.

She took a step toward Mark, closing the distance, perhaps so that all she couldn't say could be better heard.

But now, and without trying, she remembered her body. She remembered her breasts, which hadn't been seen by another man, not sexually, since she was young. She remembered their heaviness, that they were the slowly descending weights powering her biological clock. They had appeared too early, but grew too slowly, and were referred to by the only college boyfriend whose birthday she still remembered as "Platonic." They became so sensitive when she had her period that she held them as she walked around the house. Years after it was turned off for the last time, she still occasionally heard the asthmatic Medela breast pump struggling not to die. She had grown to know her breasts more intimately as there was more to fear, but she looked away when, each of the last three years, they were pressed between mammogram plates—each time the tech made the unsolicited promise that the machine delivered less radiation than she would be exposed to on a transatlantic flight. When Jacob took her to Paris for her forty-first birthday, she imagined the kids searching the sky for her plane, her breasts glowing like poisoned beacons for them.

What did she want?

She wanted everything on the outside.

She wanted something impossible, whose fulfillment would destroy her.

And then she understood Jacob. She had believed him when he said his words were only words, but she never understood him. Now she understood: he needed to stick his hand in the hinge. But he didn't want to close the door on himself.

"I need to go home," she said.

She needed something impossible, whose fulfillment would save her.

"That's what you came here to tell me?"

She nodded.

He stood straight, now taller than he had been. "I get it that you're on some sort of journey," he said. "Nobody gets that better than I do. And I'm really glad to have served as a rest stop where you could stretch your legs, get some gas, and pee."

"Please don't be mad," she said, almost like a girl.

Her skin was burning with fear—of his anger, of deserving it, of being, finally, justly punished for her badness. She could be forgiven for allowing her children to be hurt, but there is no punishment great enough for hurting one's children knowingly. She was going to destroy her family—on purpose, and not because there were no alternatives. She was going to choose not to have a choice.

"I hope I facilitated a lot of growth," Mark went on, now making no effort to contain his hurt. "I do. I hope you learned something with me that you can apply later with someone else. But if I can offer a little free advice?"

"I just need to go home," she said, terrified of what he would say next, that by some magical justice it would kill her children.

"You're not the problem, Julia. Your life is the problem."

Kindness was worse than what she'd been most afraid of.

He opened the door. "And I say this wishing only for peace for both of us: know that next time I see your face on the screen, I'm not even going to watch you wait."

"I need to go home," she said.

"Good luck with that," he said.

She left.

She took a cab to a hotel whose renovation she'd nearly been hired to oversee.

There was a cartoonishly large, unnaturally symmetrical floral arrangement centered under ten thousand chandelier crystals.

And a bellhop said something into a palmed microphone whose cord ran up his sleeve and down his side to a transmitter clipped to his belt—there had to be a better way to communicate.

And the desk clerk, who could *almost* have been Sam in fifteen years, but with a perfect left hand, asked, "How many keys will you be needing?"

She thought of saying, "All of them." She thought of saying, "None."

WHO'S IN
THE UNOCCUPIED ROOM?

By the time Jacob came back downstairs with the pot, Tamir had already turned an apple into a pipe, seemingly without tools.

"Impressive," Jacob said.

"I am an impressive person."

"Well, you can certainly turn a piece of fruit into drug paraphernalia."

"Still smells like pot," Tamir said, opening the innermost bag. "That's a good sign."

They cracked some windows and smoked in a silence broken only by Jacob's humiliating coughing. They sat back. They waited.

Somehow the station had changed to ESPN. Had the television achieved sentience and will? There was a documentary about the 1988 trade that sent Wayne Gretzky from the Edmonton Oilers to the L.A. Kings—the effects it had on Gretzky, Edmonton, L.A., the sport of hockey, planet Earth, and the universe. What at any other time would have compelled Jacob to either smash his TV or blind himself was suddenly the happiest reprieve. Had Tamir put it on?

They lost track of how much time passed—it could have been forty-five seconds or forty-five minutes. It mattered as little to them as it did to Isaac.

"I feel good," Jacob said, leaning as he'd been told to do at the Passover seders of his childhood, as befits a free man.

"I feel very good," Tamir said.

"Just basically, fundamentally . . . *good*."

"I know the feeling."

"But the thing is, my life isn't good."

"Yeah."

"Yeah, you know? Yeah, yours isn't, either?"

"Yeah."

"Childhood is good," Jacob said, "the rest is pushing things around. If you're lucky, you give a shit about the things. But it's different only by degrees."

"But those degrees matter."

"Do they?"

"If one thing matters, everything matters."

"That is a seriously good impersonation of wisdom."

"Lo mein matters. Stupid, dirty jokes matter. Firm mattresses and soft sheets matter. The Boss matters."

"The Boss?"

"Springsteen. A heated toilet seat matters. The small things: changing a lightbulb, losing to your child at basketball, driving nowhere. There's your Great Flatness. And I could go on."

"Better still, do you think you could go back to the beginning and do that, *exactly* that, again, and I'll record it?"

"Chinese food matters. Stupid, dirty jokes matter. Firm mattresses and soft sheets—"

"I'm high."

"I'm looking at the chandelier from above."

"Is it dusty?" Jacob asked.

"Another person would ask if it was beautiful."

"People shouldn't be allowed to get married until it's too late to have kids."

"Maybe you could get enough signatures to make that happen."

"And having a gratifying career is impossible."

"For anyone?"

"For good fathers. But it's so hard to deviate. All these fucking Jewish nails driven through my palms."

"Jewish nails?"

"Expectations. Prescriptions. Commandments. Wanting to please everyone. And the rest of them."

"Them?"

"Did you ever have to read that poem, or journal entry, or whatever, by the kid who died in Auschwitz? Or maybe Treblinka? Not really the important detail, I just . . . The one about 'Next time you throw a ball, throw it for me'?"

"No."

"Really?"

"I don't think so."

"Consider yourself lucky. Anyway, I might not be getting it exactly right, but the gist is: don't mourn for me, live for me. I'm about to get gassed, so do me a favor and have fun."

"Never heard it."

"I must have heard it a thousand times. It was the theme song of my Jewish education, and it ruined everything. Not because every time you throw a ball you're thinking of the corpse of a kid who should have been you, but because sometimes you just want to veg out in front of shitty TV, and instead you think, 'I should really go throw a ball.'"

Tamir laughed.

"It's funny, except that throwing a ball becomes an attitude toward academic achievement, becomes measuring the distance from perfection in units of failure, becomes going to a college that murdered kid would have killed to go to, becomes studying things you aren't interested in but are good and worthy and remunerative, becomes getting married Jewishly and having Jewish kids and living Jewishly in some demented effort to redeem the suffering that made your increasingly alienating life possible."

"You should smoke a bit more."

"The problem is," Jacob said, taking back the apple, "the fulfillment of the expectations feels amazing, but you only fulfill them once—'I got an A!' 'I'm getting married!' 'It's a boy!'—and then you're left to experience them. Nobody knows it at the time, and everybody knows it later, but nobody admits it, because it would pull a foundational log from the Jewish tower of Jenga. You trade emotional ambition for companionship, a life of inhabiting a nerve-filled body for companionship, exploration for companionship. There's a good in commitment, I know. Things have to grow over time, mature, become full. But there's a price, and just because we don't talk about it doesn't mean it's endurable. So many blessings, but did anyone ever stop to ask why one would want a blessing?"

"Blessings are just curses that other people envy."

"You should smoke more pot, Tamir. It turns you into fucking Yoda, or at least Deepak Chopra."

"Maybe it allows you to listen differently."

"You see! That's exactly what I mean."

"You're becoming funny," Tamir said, bringing the apple to his mouth.

"I was always funny."

"So maybe I'm the one listening differently."

Tamir took another hit.

"What was Julia's reaction? To the texts?"

"Not good. Obviously."

"You'll stay together?"

"Yeah. Of course. We have the kids. And we've had a life together."

"You're sure?"

"I mean, we've *talked* about separating."

"I hope you're right."

Jacob took another hit.

"Have I ever told you about my TV show?"

"Of course."

"No, I mean *my* TV show."

"I'm high, Jacob. Pretend I'm a six-year-old."

"I've been writing a show about us."

"You and me?"

"Well, no, not you. Or not yet."

"I'd be great in a TV show."

"My family."

"I'm in your family."

"My family *here*. Isaac. My parents. Julia and the kids."

"Who would want to watch that?"

"Everybody, probably. But that's not the point. The point is, it's probably really good, and probably the writing I was born to do, and for the last ten or so years I've been pretty singularly devoted to it."

"Ten years?"

"And I've never shared it with anyone."

"Why not?"

"Well, before Isaac died, it was because I was afraid of betraying him."

"With?"

"With the truth of who we are, and what we're like."

"How would that be a betrayal?"

"I was listening to the radio the other morning, a science podcast I like. They were interviewing a woman who'd lived in that massive geodesic dome for two years—nothing goes in, nothing goes out. That one. It was pretty interesting."

"Let's listen to it now."

"No, I'm just searching for a metaphor."

"It would make me so happy to listen to it right now."

"I can't even tell if you're serious or making fun of me."

"Please, Jacob."

"I still can't tell. But anyway, she talked about how living in that closed environment made her aware of the interconnectedness of life: this thing eats this thing, then poops, which feeds this thing, which blah blah blah. Then she went on to talk about something I already knew—not because I'm so fucking smart, but because it's just one of those things that most people know—that with every inhalation, you are likely breathing in molecules that were breathed out by Pol Pot, or Caesar, or even the dinosaurs. I could be wrong about that dinosaur bit. I've found myself really interested in dinosaurs recently. I don't know why. I spent about thirty years not thinking about them at all, and then suddenly I was interested again. I heard, in another podcast—"

"You listen to a lot of podcasts."

"I know. I really do. It's embarrassing, right?"

"You're asking me if you're embarrassed?"

"It's humiliating."

"I don't know why."

"What kind of person sneaks off to unoccupied rooms and presses an almost-muted phone to his ear so that he, and only he, will hear a putterer's exploration of something as irrelevant as echolocation. It's humiliating. And the humiliation is humiliating." With his beer bottle, Jacob drew a ring of condensation on the table. "Anyway, this other podcast did this whole thing about how all the dinosaurs—not just most of them, but all of them—were destroyed at once. They roamed the earth for some large number of millions of years, and then, in something like an hour, *gone*. Why do people always use the word *roam* when referring to dinosaurs?"

"I don't know."

"They do, though. Dinosaurs *roamed* the earth. It's weird."

"It is."

"*So* weird, right?"

"The more I think about it, the weirder it becomes."

"Jews roamed Europe for thousands of years . . ."

"And then, in something like a decade . . ."

"But I was saying something else. About the dome woman . . . dinosaurs . . . maybe Pol Pot?"

"Breathing."

"Right! With each inhalation we take in molecules yada yada. Anyway, my eyes started to roll, because it just sounded like trite cocktail science shit. But then she went further, to say that our exhalations are just as certainly going to be inhaled by our great-great-great-great-great-great-great-grandchildren."

"And future dinosaurs."

"And future Pol Pots."

They laughed.

"But it really upset me, for some reason. I didn't start crying or anything. I didn't have to pull over. But I did have to turn off the podcast. It suddenly became too much."

"Why do you think?"

"Why do I think at all?"

"No. Why do you think it upset you to imagine your great-great-great-great-great-great-great-grandchildren breathing your breath?"

Jacob released a breath that would be inhaled by the last of his line.

"Try," Tamir said.

"I guess"—another breath—"I guess I was raised to understand that I'm not worthy of all that came before me. But no one ever prepared me for the knowledge that I'm not worthy of all that will come after me, either."

Tamir lifted the apple from the table, held it so that the chandelier light passed straight through its cored center, and said, "I want to fuck this apple."

"What?"

"But my cock is too big," he said. And then, trying to push his hairy-knuckled forefinger into it: "I can't even finger-fuck it."

"Put the apple down, Tamir."

"It's the Apple of Truth," Tamir said, ignoring Jacob. "And I want to fuck it."

"Jesus."

"I'm serious."

"You want to fuck the Apple of Truth, but your cock is too big?"

"Yes. That is exactly the predicament."

"The present predicament? Or the predicament of life?"

"Both."

"You're high."

"So are you."

"The scientist who was talking about the dinosaurs—"

"What are you talking about?"

"That podcast. The scientist said something so beautiful I thought I would die."

"Don't die."

"He asked the listener to imagine a bullet being fired through water, and how it would leave a conical wake of emptiness behind it—a hole in the water—before the water had time to come back together. He said that an asteroid would create a similar wake—a rip in the atmosphere— and that a dinosaur looking at the asteroid would see a nighttime hole in a daytime sky. That's what he would see just before being destroyed."

"Maybe it's not that you wanted to die, but that you became like the dinosaur."

"Huh?"

"It saw something incredibly beautiful before it was destroyed. You heard about it, and thought it was incredibly beautiful, and so assumed you would be destroyed."

"They give MacArthurs to all the wrong people."

"I lied."

"About what?"

"Most things."

"OK?"

"Rivka and I have been talking about moving."

"Really?"

"Talking."

"Moving where?"

"You're going to make me say it?"

"I guess I am."

"Here."

"You're kidding me."

"Just talking. Just thinking about it. I get job offers every now and then, and a month ago I got a really good one, a great one, with a tech firm. Rivka and I were playing make-believe at the dinner table, imagining what it would be like if I took the job, and then the conversation stopped being make-believe."

"I thought you were happy there? And all that shit about renting a room in America?"

"Did you hear anything I said before?"

"When you were begging me to make aliyah?"

"So I can make hayila."

"Which is what?"

"*Aliyah* backward."

"You just did that in your head?"

"While you were talking."

"And what, there's some sort of Bloch-Blumenberg Constant that has to be maintained?"

"A Jew Constant. Ideally, American Jews and Israeli Jews would just switch places."

"Is this what we were talking about the whole time? Your guilt about leaving Israel?"

"No, we were talking about your guilt about leaving your marriage."

"I'm not leaving my marriage," Jacob said.

"And I'm not leaving Israel," Tamir said.

"All just talk?"

"Whenever I would turn down an offer of my father's—for another piece of halvah, an evening walk—he'd say, '*De zelbe prayz*.' Same price. It was the only time he used Yiddish. He hated Yiddish. But he'd say that. And not only in Yiddish, he'd imitate my grandfather's voice. It doesn't cost me anything to talk about leaving Israel. Same price as not talking about it. I can really hear my father imitating my grandfather: *de zelbe prayz*."

Tamir woke up his phone and showed Jacob pictures of Noam: from the hospital, first steps, first day of school, first soccer game, first date, first time in his army uniform. "I've been obsessed with these pictures," Tamir said. "Not with looking at them, but seeing that they're still there. Sometimes I check under the table. Sometimes I go to the bathroom to do it. Remember going to the supermarket with your kids when they were small? That feeling that the second they were out of your sight, they would disappear forever? It's like that."

All the dinosaurs were wiped out, but some mammals survived. Most of them were burrowers. Underground, they were protected from the heat that consumed every living thing aboveground. Tamir was burying himself in his phone, in the photos of his son.

"Are we good men?" Tamir asked.

"What a strange question."

"Is it?"

"I don't think there's any higher power judging us," Jacob said.

"But how should we judge ourselves?"

"With tears, with silence, with—?"

"Even my confession was a lie."

"I must have given you reasons to lie."

"I want to leave. Rivka doesn't."

"You want to leave Israel? Or you want to leave your marriage?"

"Israel."

"Did you have an affair?"

"No."

"Did she?"

"No."

"I'm always tired," Jacob said. "Always exhausted. I've never wondered about it before, but what if this whole time I haven't been tired at all? What if my tiredness is just a hiding place?"

"There are worse hiding places."

"And what if I decided that I would never be tired again? If I simply refused to be tired. My body could be tired, but not me."

"I don't know, Jacob."

"Or what if I can't get out of my hiding place on my own? If it's too familiar, too safe? And I need to be smoked out?"

"I think you're smoking yourself out right now."

"What if I need Julia to smoke me out?"

Jacob looked at the apple between them. He understood what Tamir meant, about wanting to fuck it. It wasn't a sexual longing, but an existential one—to enter one's truth.

"You know what I'd like to do right now?"

"What?" Tamir asked.

"Shave my head."

"Why?"

"So I can see how bald I really am. And so everyone can see."

"What if we made some popcorn instead?"

"It would be awful. But I'm ready for it. But it would be awful. But I'm ready for it."

"You keep saying the same thing over and over."

"I think I'm falling asleep."

"So sleep."

"But . . ."

"What?"

"I've also been lying."

"I know that."

"You do?"

"Yes. I just don't know which parts."

"I didn't have an affair."

"No?"

"Or I did, but I didn't fuck her."

"What *did* you do?"

"Just a bunch of texts. And not even that many."

"Why did you lie about it?"

"Because I didn't want to get caught."

"To *me*."

"Oh. I don't know."

"There was a reason."

"I'm high."

"But it's the only thing you lied about."

"When Julia found my phone and I told her the truth—that nothing actually happened—she believed me."

"That's good."

"But it wasn't that she trusted me. She said she knew I wasn't capable of it."

"And you wanted me to think you were capable of it."

"That's my interpretation of myself, yes."

"Even though you *aren't* capable of it."

"Affirmative."

"You asked before, what kind of person sneaks around to listen to science podcasts?"

"Yes."

"The kind of person who uses the same phone to sext a woman he won't touch."

"It was a different phone."

"It was the same hand."

"So now you've shaved my head," Jacob said, closing his eyes. "Tell me what I can't see."

"You're balder than I thought, and less bald than you think."

Jacob felt the reflexive jerking, the fall down the elevator shaft that marked the onset of sleep. He couldn't account for the passage of time, or movement between thoughts, or stretches without thought.

What would happen to the sound of time? If all that he and Julia had rehearsed were performed? If it weren't the *same price* to explore an idea? No more candlelit whispering into the boys' ears. No more dishwashing musings about that afternoon's birthday party. No more scrape of the rake as the leaves were pulled against the curb so they could be jumped into just one last time. What would he listen for to hear his life? Or would he be deaf to it?

The next thing he was aware of was a hand, a voice. "There's news," Tamir said, shaking Jacob by the forearm.

"What?"

"You were asleep."

"No. I wasn't. I was just thinking."

"There's something big on the news."

"Gimme a second."

Jacob blinked away the glazing, rolled his head from shoulder to shoulder, and walked to the sofa.

Two hours earlier, while Jacob and Tamir were getting stoned, some Israeli extremists entered the Dome of the Rock and set it on fire. The flames caused hardly any damage, the Israelis claimed, but the effort caused more than enough. The television, which had somehow switched from ESPN to CNN, showed images of rage: men—always men—punching the sky, shooting broken rivers of bullets at the sky, trying to kill the sky. Jacob had seen this before, but the images had always come from the vicinity of the quake, primarily Gaza and the West Bank. Now, however, CNN was bouncing from feed to feed, with a seemingly endless supply of fury: a circle of men burning an Israeli flag in Jakarta; men in Khartoum swinging sticks at an effigy of the Israeli prime minister; men in Karachi, and Dhaka, and Riyadh, and Lahore; men with bandanas over their mouths smashing a Jewish storefront in Paris; a man, whose accent was so thick it's unlikely he knew one hundred words of English, screaming, "Death to Jews!" into a camera in Tehran.

"This is bad," Jacob said, transfixed and intoxicated by the images.

"Bad?"

"Very bad."

"I need to go home."

"I know," Jacob said, too groggy to understand, or even to be sure that he wasn't still asleep. "We'll figure it out."

"*Now.* We need to go to the embassy."

"Yeah. OK."

Tamir shook his head and said, "*Now, now, now.*"

"I get it. Let me put some clothes on."

But neither moved from the sofa. The television filled with Jewish rage: black-hatted men screaming in Hebrew in London; dark men from one of the last remaining kibbutzim waving fingers at the camera, hysterically repeating words Jacob didn't understand; Jewish men clashing with Jewish soldiers guarding the Temple Mount.

Tamir said, "You need to come, too."

"Of course. Give me a minute."

"No," Tamir said, grabbing Jacob's shoulders with the force he used at the zoo three decades before. "You need to come home."

"I am home. What?"

"To Israel."

"What?"

"You need to come to Israel with me."

"*I do?*"

"Yes."

"Tamir, you want to *leave* Israel."

"Jacob."

"Now you want *me* to go?"

Tamir pointed at the TV. "Are you looking at this?"

"I've been looking at that for a week."

"No. No one has ever seen this before."

"What are you talking about?"

"This is how it ends," he said. "Like this." And for the first time since Tamir had arrived in D.C., for the first time ever, Jacob saw the family resemblance. He saw the panicked eyes of his boys—the terror he looked into before blood tests and after injuries that drew blood.

"How it *ends?*"

"How Israel is destroyed."

"Because Muslims are screaming in Jakarta and Riyadh? What are they going to do, walk to Jerusalem?"

"Yes. And ride horses, and drive shitty cars, and be bussed, and take boats. And it's not only them. Look at us."

"It will pass."

"It won't. This is how it will all end."

Neither the images on the screen nor Tamir's words scared Jacob as much as the terror he saw in his children's eyes in Tamir's eyes.

"If you really believe that, Tamir, you need to get your family out of Israel."

"I can't!" he said, and then Jacob saw, in Tamir's clenched teeth, Irv's fury—the deep inner sadness that knew no expression but directionless rage.

"Why?" Jacob asked. "What could possibly be more important than your family's safety?"

"I can't get them out, Jacob. There are no flights in or out. Don't you think I've tried? What do you think I do all day? Go to museums? Go shopping? I'm trying to keep my family safe. I can't get them out, so I have to go. And you have to go, too."

Jacob was now too awake for nonchalant bravery.

"Israel isn't my home, Tamir."

"That's only because it hasn't been destroyed yet."

"No, it's because it isn't my home."

"But it's *my* home," he said, and now Jacob saw Julia. He saw the pleading he hadn't been able to see when her home still could have been saved. He saw his own blindness.

"Tamir, you—"

But the words wouldn't form, because there was no thought for them to express. It didn't matter: Tamir had stopped listening. He was angled away and texting. Rivka? Noam? Jacob didn't ask, because he felt it wasn't his place.

His place was the unoccupied room, typing: *you're begging me to fuck your tight pussy, but you don't deserve it yet.*

His place was the unoccupied room, the same hand pressing a different phone to his ear so that he, and only he, could hear: "Blind people can see. It's true. Making clicking sounds in their mouths, they can orient themselves by the echoes returning from nearby objects. Doing this, blind people are able to go on hikes in rocky terrain, navigate city streets, even ride bikes. But is that seeing? Brain scans of people echolocating show activity in the same visual centers as in the brains of people with sight; they are simply seeing through their ears, instead of their eyes."

His place was the unoccupied room, reading: *my husband is away this weekend with the kids, come fuck me for real.*

His place was the unoccupied room, hearing: "'So why aren't more blind people on bikes? According to David Spellman, the preeminent teacher of echolocation, it's because few are given the necessary freedom to learn how.'

"'It's the rare parent, maybe one in a hundred, probably fewer, who is able to watch her blind child approach an intersection and not grab his arm. It's with love that they're holding him back from danger, but they're also holding him back from sight. When I teach children to ride bikes, there are inevitably crashes, just as there are with sighted children. But parents of blind children almost always take it as proof that too much is being asked of their child, and they step in to protect him. The more the parents want their children to see, the less possible they make it, because that love gets in the way.'

"'How were you able to overcome that and learn?'

"'My father left before I was born, and my mother had three jobs. The absence of love allowed me to see.'"

DE ZELBE PRAYZ

Tamir went upstairs, and Jacob sat there, trying to replay the last few moments, and the last two hours, and the last two weeks, and the last thirteen, and sixteen, and forty-two years. What had happened?

Tamir had said Jacob wouldn't die for anything. Even if that were true, why would it matter? What's so inherently good about such ultimate devotion? What's so wrong with making good-enough money, eating good-enough food, living in a nice-enough house, striving to be as ethical and ambitious as circumstances allow? He had tried, he had come up short every single time, but against what measure? He had given his family a good-enough life. It felt as if an only life should be better than good enough, but how many efforts for more have ended with having nothing?

Years before, in the time when he and Julia would still share their work with each other, Julia came to the basement with a mug of tea in each hand and asked how it was going.

Jacob leaned back in his Aeron and said, "Well, it's nowhere near as good as it could be, but I suppose it's as good as I can make it right now."

"Then it's as good as it could be."

"No," Jacob said, "it could be a lot better."

"How? If someone else wrote it? If you wrote it at a different time in your life? We'd be talking about something else."

"If I were a better writer."

"But you're not," she said, putting a mug on his desk, "you're only perfect."

For all that he couldn't give Julia, he had given her a lot. He wasn't a great artist, but he worked hard (enough), and was devoted (enough) to his writing. It is not a weakness to acknowledge complexity. It is not a retreat to take a step back. He wasn't wrong to be envious of those wailing men on prayer mats in the Dome of the Rock, but maybe he was wrong to see reflected in their devotion his own existential pallor. Agnosticism is no less devout than fundamentalism, and maybe he'd destroyed what he loved, blind to the perfection of good-enough.

He called Julia's cell. She didn't answer. It was two in the morning, but there was no time of day, those days, when she would answer his call.

Hi, you've reached Julia . . .

But she would see that he had reached for her.

At the beep he said, "It's me. I don't know if you've been watching the news, but some extremists set fire to the Dome of the Rock, or tried to. Jewish extremists. I suppose they succeeded, technically. It was a very small fire. But, you know, it's a huge deal. Anyway, you can watch. Or read about it. I don't even know where you are. Where are you? So—"

The voice mail cut him off. He called again.

Hi, you've reached Julia . . .

"I got cut off. I don't know how much got through, but I was saying that the Middle East just blew up, and Tamir is totally hysterical, and he wants me to take him to the embassy tonight, like now, at two in the morning, to try to somehow get him on a plane. And the thing is, he says I need to go with him. And at first I just thought he meant—"

The voice mail cut him off. He called again.

Hi, you've reached Julia . . .

"And . . . it's me. Jacob. Obviously. Anyway, I was just saying that Tamir is freaking out, and I'm taking him to the embassy—I'll wake up Sam and let him know that we're going out, and that he has to—"

The voice mail cut him off. The allowed increments seemed to be shrinking. He called again.

"Jacob?"

"Julia?"

"What time is it?"

"I thought your phone was off."

"Why are you calling?"

"Well, I basically said it in the messages, but—"

"What time is it?"

"It's like two or so."

"*Why*, Jacob."

"Where are you?"

"Jacob, why are you calling me at two in the morning?"

"Because it's important."

"Are the kids OK?"

"Yes, everyone's fine. But Israel—"

"Nothing happened—?"

"No. Not to the kids. They're sleeping. It's Israel."

"Tell me in the morning, OK?"

"Julia, I wouldn't call if it weren't—"

"If the boys are OK, whatever it is can wait."

"It can't."

"Believe me, it can. Good night, Jacob."

"Some extremists tried to set fire to the Dome of the Rock."

"Tomorrow."

"There's going to be a war."

"Tomorrow."

"A war against us."

"We have a ton of batteries in the fridge."

"What?"

"I don't know. I'm half asleep."

"I think I'm going to go."

"Thank you."

"To Israel. With Tamir."

He heard her shift, and muffled static.

"You're not going to Israel."

"I'm really thinking about it."

"You'd never let such a dumb sentence slip into one of your scripts."

"What's that supposed to mean?"

"It means let's talk in the morning."

"I'm going to Israel," he said, and this time, removing the *I think*, expressed something entirely different—a certainty that when spoken aloud revealed to Jacob his lack of certainty. The first time he'd wanted to hear her say, "Don't go." But instead she didn't believe him.

"And why would you do that?"

"To help."

"What, write for the army paper?"

"Whatever they ask me to do. Fill sandbags, make sandwiches, fight."
She laughed herself into a fuller wakefulness: *"Fight?"*

"If that's what's necessary."

"And how would that work?"

"They need men."

She chuckled. Jacob thought he heard her chuckle.

"I'm not seeking your respect or approval," he said. "I'm telling you because we're going to need to figure out what the next couple of weeks will look like. I assume you'll come home and—"

"I respect and approve of your desire to be a hero, especially right now—"

"What you're doing sucks."

"No," she said, her voice now aggressively clear, "what *you're* doing sucks. Waking me up in the middle of the night with this idiotic Kabuki enactment of . . . I don't even *know* what. Resolution? Bravery? Selflessness? You assume I'll come home? That's nice. And then what? I'll single-handedly take care of the kids for however long your paintball adventure lasts? That shouldn't be any problem: preparing three meals a day for them—make that *nine* meals, as no two will ever eat the same thing—and chauffeuring to cello lessons, and speech therapy, and soccer, and soccer, and Hebrew school, and various health professionals? Yeah. I want to be a hero, too. I think being a hero would be awesome. But first, before we get measured for capes, let's see if we can maintain what we already have."

"Julia—"

"I'm not finished. You woke me up with this absurd shit, so now I'm entitled to hold the conch. If we were actually to entertain this utterly ridiculous notion of you in combat for a moment, then we would have to acknowledge that any army that would include you among its fighting ranks is desperate, and desperate armies tend not to be in the business of treating every life as if it were all of humankind, and without having any military expertise, I'm guessing you're not going to be called upon for specialized operations, like bomb defusing or surgical assassinations, but something more like 'Stand in front of this bullet so your meat will at least slow it before it enters the person we actually value.' And then you'll be dead. And your kids will be fatherless. And your father will become a yet more public asshole. And—"

"And you?"

"What?"

"What will you become?"

"In sickness and in sickness," Jacob's mother had said at his wedding. "That is what I wish for you. Don't seek or expect miracles. There are no miracles. Not anymore. And there are no cures for the hurt that hurts most. There is only the medicine of believing each other's pain, and being present for it."

Jacob had regained the hearing he'd pretended to lose as a child, and acquired a kind of pet interest in deafness that stayed with him into adulthood. He never shared it with Julia or anyone, as it felt distasteful, wrong. No one, not even Dr. Silvers, knew that he was able to sign, or that he would attend annual conventions for the D.C. chapter of the National Association of the Deaf. He didn't pretend he was deaf when he went. He pretended he was a teacher at an elementary school for deaf children. He explained his interest by saying he was the child of a deaf father.

"What will you become, Julia?"

"I have no idea what it is you're trying to get me to say. That contemplating having to raise three kids on my own makes me selfish?"

"No."

"Are you implying it's what I secretly want?"

"Is it? That hadn't even occurred to me, but it obviously occurred to you."

"Are you serious?"

"What will you become?"

"I have no idea what water it is you're trying to lead me to, but I'm fucking tired, and tired of this conversation, so if you have something to say—"

"Why won't you just tell me you want me to stay?"

"What?"

"I don't understand why you can't bring yourself to say that you don't want me to go."

"It's what I've been saying for the last five minutes."

"No, you've been saying it's unfair to the kids. That it's unfair to you."

"*Unfair* is your word."

"Not once have you said that you—you Julia—don't want me to go because you don't want me to go."

She opened a silence as the rabbi had opened the rip in Irv's jacket at the funeral.

"A widow," Jacob said. "That's what you'll become. You're constantly projecting your needs and fears onto the kids, or me, or whoever is within reach. Why can't you just admit that you—*you*—don't want to be a widow?"

He heard, he thought he heard, the springs of a mattress return to their state of rest. What bed was she rising from? How much of her body was uncovered, in what degree of darkness?

"Because I wouldn't be a widow," she said.

"Yes, you would."

"No, Jacob, I wouldn't. A widow is someone whose spouse has died."

"And?"

"And you're not my spouse."

In the 1970s there was no infrastructure to care for deaf children in Nicaragua—no schools, no educational or informational resources, there wasn't even a codified sign language. When the first Nicaraguan school for the deaf was opened, the teachers taught the lip-reading of Spanish. But on the playground the children communicated using the signs they had developed in their homes, organically generating a shared vocabulary and grammar. As generations of students moved through the school, the improvised language grew and matured. It is the only documented instance of a language being created entirely from scratch by its speakers. No adult helped, nothing was recorded on paper, there were no models. Only the children's will to be understood.

Jacob and Julia had tried. They had created signs, and they would spell words in front of the still-young kids, and there were codes. But the language they had created, and were even then creating, made the world smaller rather than clearer.

I'm not your spouse.

Because of those texts? Destroy everything because of the arrangement of a few hundred letters? What did he think was going to happen? And what did he think he was doing? Julia was right: it wasn't a moment of weakness. He pushed the exchange into sexuality, he bought the second phone, he was forming the words whenever he wasn't typing them, stealing off to read hers as soon as they came through. He'd more than once put Benjy in front of a movie so he could jerk off to a new message. *Why?*

Because it was perfect. He was a father to the boys, a son to his father, a husband to his wife, a friend to his friends, but to whom was he himself?

The digital veil offered a self-disappearing that made self-expression, finally, possible. When he was no one, he was free to be himself. It's not that he was bursting with stifled sexuality, though he was. It was the freedom that mattered. Which is why, when she texted, *my husband is away this weekend with the kids, come fuck me for real*, she got no response. And why *you can't STILL be jerking off!* got no response. And why *what happened to you?* were the last words to pass between their phones.

"I don't know how I could be any more sorry for what I did," he said.

"You could start by telling me you're sorry."

"I've apologized many times."

"No, many times you've told me that you've apologized. But you've never once apologized to me."

"I did that night in the kitchen."

"You didn't."

"In bed."

"No."

"On the phone in the car, when you were at Model UN."

"You told me you'd apologized, but you didn't apologize. I pay attention, Jacob. I remember. Exactly once, since I found the phone, did you say, 'I'm sorry.' When I told you your grandfather died. And you weren't saying it to me. Or to anyone."

"Well, it doesn't matter if that's the case—"

"It *is* the case, and it *does* matter."

"It doesn't matter if that's the case, because if you don't remember an apology, I obviously didn't apologize fully enough. So hear me now: I'm so sorry, Julia. I'm ashamed, and I'm sorry."

"It's not the texts."

The night Julia found the phone, she told Jacob, "You seem happy, but you aren't." And more: "You find unhappiness so threatening that you would rather go down with the ship than acknowledge a leak." What if she *wouldn't* go down with the ship? Because if it wasn't the texts, then it was everything. What if, when Jacob closed himself in the unoccupied room, he closed Julia in the unoccupied house? What if the thing he needed to apologize for was everything?

"Tell me," he said, "just tell me, why are you going to destroy this family?"

"Don't you dare say that."

"But it's true. You're destroying our family."

"I'm not. I'm ending our marriage."

He couldn't believe what she had just dared to say.

"Ending our marriage will destroy our family."

"No. It won't."

"Why? Why are you ending our marriage?"

"Who have I been having all of those conversations with for the last three weeks?"

"We were *talking.*"

She let that reverberate for a moment, then said, "*That's* why."

"Because we were talking?"

"Because you're always talking, and your words never mean anything. You hid your greatest secret behind a wall, remember that?"

"No."

"Our wedding. I walked seven circles around you, and I surrounded you with love, for years I did, and the wall toppled. I toppled it. But you know what I discovered? Your greatest secret is that you're wall all the way to the centermost stone. There is *nothing there.*"

And now he had no choice: "I'm going to Israel, Julia."

And either because of the addition of her name, or a shift in his tone, or more likely because the conversation had reached the point of breakage, the sentence took on a new meaning—one that Julia believed.

"I can't believe this," she said.

"I have to."

"For whom?"

"Our kids. And their kids."

"Our kids don't have kids."

"But they will."

"So that's the trade: lose a father, gain a kid?"

"You said it yourself, Julia: they're going to put me behind a computer."

"I didn't say that."

"You said they wouldn't be dumb enough to give me a gun."

"No, I didn't say that, either."

Jacob could hear the click of a lamp. A hotel? Mark's apartment? How could he ask her where she was in a way that didn't convey judgment or jealousy or imply that he was going to Israel to punish her for having gone to Mark's?

More than a thousand "constructed languages" have been invented—by linguists, novelists, hobbyists—each with the dream of correcting the imprecision, inefficiency, and irregularity of natural language. Some constructed languages are based on the musical scale and sung. Some are color-based and silent. The most admired constructed languages were designed to reveal what communication *could* be, and none of them is in use.

"If you're going to do this," Julia said, "if you're really going to do this, I need two things from you."

"What do you mean?"

"If you're going to go to Israel—"

"I am."

"—you need to do two things for me."

"OK."

"Sam needs to have a bar mitzvah. You can't leave without helping to see that through."

"OK. Let's do it tomorrow."

"As in, today?"

"Wednesday. And we'll do it here."

"Does he even know his whole haftorah yet?"

"He knows enough. We can invite whatever family can make it, whatever friends Sam wants. The Israelis are here. I can get ninety percent of what we need at Whole Foods. We'll skip the accoutrements, obviously."

"My parents wouldn't be able to be there."

"I'm sorry about that. We could skype with them?"

"And we need a Torah. That's not an accoutrement."

"Right. Shit. If Rabbi Singer won't participate—"

"He won't."

"My dad can call in a favor from that shul in Georgetown. He knows a bunch of people there."

"You'll take care of it?"

"Yes."

"OK. I can get the . . . And if I . . ." She trailed off into her interior plans, into that never-resting maternal lobe of her brain, the place that scheduled playdates two weeks out, and was vigilant about the food allergies of the kids' friends, and always knew everyone's shoe size, and needed no automated reminder to make appointments for biannual dental checkups, and kept track of the outflow of thank-you notes for birthday presents.

"What's the second thing?" Jacob asked.

"Sorry, what?"

"You said you needed me to do two things."

"You need to put down Argus."

"Put him down?"

"Yes."

"Why?"

"Because it's time, and because he's yours."

When Jacob was a boy, he used to stop spinning globes with his finger and imagine what life would be like if he lived in the Netherlands, or Argentina, or China, or Sudan.

When Jacob was a boy, he imagined that his finger brought the actual Earth to momentary rest. No one really noticed it, just as no one really noticed Earth's rotation, but the sun stayed where it was in the sky, the ocean went flat, and photos fell from fridges.

When Julia said those words—*Because it's time, and because he's yours*—her finger held his life in place.

Because it's time, and because he's yours.

The space where those clauses met was his home.

But could he live there?

At the last convention he attended, Jacob met two deaf parents and their eight-year-old deaf son. They'd recently moved to the States from England, the father explained, because the boy had been in a car accident and lost his left hand.

"I'm sorry," Jacob signed, making a ring around his heart with his fist.

The mother touched four fingers to her bottom lip, then straightened her arm, arcing the fingers down—like blowing a kiss without the kiss.

Jacob asked, "Are there better doctors here?"

The mother signed, "British Sign Language uses both hands for finger spelling. American uses only one. He would have managed in England, but we want to give him every best chance."

The mother and boy went off to the crafts tent while Jacob and the father hung back. They spoke for an hour, in silence, displacing the air between them with the stories of their lives.

Jacob had read of deaf couples who wanted deaf children. One couple even genetically selected for a deaf child. He found himself thinking about that quite often, the moral implications. Once they had shared enough for it not to feel like prying, Jacob asked the man how he felt when he learned that his son was deaf, like him.

"People would ask me if I was hoping for a boy or a girl," the father signed. "I told them I just wanted a healthy baby. But I had a very secret preference. Maybe you know that they don't perform the hearing test until you're about to leave the hospital?"

"I didn't know that."

"It works by sending a sound into the ear—if it echoes back, the baby can hear. So they leave as much time as they can for the ear to drain of amniotic fluid."

"If the sound doesn't echo back, the child is deaf?"

"That's right."

"Where does the sound go?"

"Into the deafness."

"So there was a period of not knowing?"

"A day. For a day, he was neither deaf nor hearing. When the nurse told us that he was deaf, I cried and cried."

Jacob once again circled his heart with his fist.

"No," the father signed. "A hearing baby would have been a blessing. A deaf baby was a special blessing."

"It was your preference?"

"My very secret preference."

"But what about giving him every best chance?"

"Can I ask if you're Jewish?" the man signed.

The question was so unlikely, Jacob wasn't sure he understood it correctly, but he nodded.

"We're Jewish as well." Jacob felt that old, embarrassing, singularly comforting recognition. "Where are your people from?"

"Everywhere. But mostly Drohobycz."

"We're *landsmen*," the father signed. He actually signed, "We're from the same place," but Jacob understood that his hands were speaking Yiddish.

"It's harder to be Jewish," the father signed. "It doesn't give you every best chance."

"It's different," Jacob signed.

The man signed, "I once read a line in a poem: 'You may find a dead bird; you won't see a flock of them anywhere.'" The sign for *flock* is two hands moving like a wave away from the torso.

Jacob returned home from the convention in time for Shabbat dinner. They lit the candles and blessed them. They blessed the wine and drank it. They uncovered the challah, blessed it, tore it, passed it, and ate it. The blessings disappeared into the universe's deafness, but when Jacob and Julia whispered into their children's tiny ears, the prayers echoed back. After the meal, Jacob and Julia and Sam and Max and Benjy closed their eyes and moved through their home.

VI

THE DESTRUCTION OF ISRAEL

COME HOME

In the end, they didn't need to rush the bar mitzvah—it took Tamir and Jacob eight days to find a way to Israel—but apparently there wasn't enough time to put Argus down. Jacob spoke with a few compassionate vets, but also watched a few horrible YouTube videos. Even when euthanasia was clearly a "good" thing—a genuinely suffering animal being given a genuinely peaceful end—it was horrible. He couldn't do it. He wasn't ready. Argus wasn't ready. They weren't ready.

The embassy continued to be unhelpful, and commercial flights to Israel continued to be halted. So they looked into getting press certification, volunteering for Doctors Without Borders, flying to another country and reaching Israel by boat—all nonstarters.

What changed their situation, and changed everything, was an internationally televised speech by Israel's prime minister—a speech that he must have known, when writing it, would either be memorized by future Jewish schoolchildren or be etched into memorial walls.

Looking directly into the camera, and directly into the Jewish souls of all Jews watching, he conveyed the unprecedented threat to Israel's existence, and asked that Jews between the ages of sixteen and fifty-five "come home."

Airspace would be opened to incoming flights, and commercial jumbo jets, emptied of seats to hold more bodies, would be flown continuously from airfields near New York, Los Angeles, Miami, Chicago,

Paris, London, Buenos Aires, Moscow, and other major Jewish population centers.

The planes weren't fueled until just before takeoff, as no one knew, even approximately, how heavy they would be.

TODAY I AM NOT A MAN

"We need to have a family conversation," Sam said. It was the night before his makeshift bar mitzvah. In twelve hours, catered food would begin to arrive. And not long after, the handful of cousins and friends who could make it on such short notice. Then manhood.

Max and Benjy sat on Sam's bed, their feet growing toward the floor, and Sam gave his ninety-two pounds to his beloved swivel chair—beloved because the range of motion made him feel capable, and beloved because it had been his dad's. His desktop flickered with footage of an army moving across the Sinai.

With parental gentleness, Sam recounted an age-appropriate version of what had happened with their father's phone, and what he knew—from the snippets Max had overheard in the car, what Billie had witnessed and inferred at Model UN, and his own piecing together—of their mother's relationship with Mark. ("I don't get what's the big deal," Benjy said. "People kiss people all the time and it's nice?") Sam shared what Billie had overheard of their parents' separation-conversation rehearsal (mortared with the results of Max's snooping), as well as what Barak had been told of their fathers' decision to go to Israel. Everyone knew that Jacob was lying when he said Julia had spent the night at a site visit, but they also sensed that he didn't know where she'd actually been, so no one mentioned it.

Sam often had fantasies of killing his brothers, but he also had fantasies of saving them. He'd felt the opposing pulls for as long as they'd been his brothers—with the same arms that cradled baby Benjy, he wanted to crush his rib cage—and the intensity of those coexisting impulses defined his brotherly love.

But not now. Now he only wanted to cradle them. Now he felt no possessiveness, no diminishment at their gain, no scorching, referentless annoyance.

When Sam reached the climax—"Everything is about to change"— Max started to cry. Reflexively, Sam wanted to say, "It's funny, it's funny," but a yet stronger reflex prevailed, and he said, "I know, I know." When Max started to cry, Benjy started to cry—like a reservoir that floods into an overflow reservoir, overflowing it. "It sucks," Sam said. "But it's all going to be OK. We just can't let it happen."

Through his tears, Benjy said, "I don't get it. Kissing is nice."

"What are we going to do?" Max asked.

"They keep putting everything off until after my bar mitzvah. They're going to tell us about their divorce after my bar mitzvah. Dad is going to move out after my bar mitzvah. And now he's going to go to Israel after my bar mitzvah. So I'm not going to have a bar mitzvah."

"That's a good plan," Benjy said. "You're smart."

"But they'll just force you to," Max said.

"What are they gonna do? Pinch my nose until I expel my haftorah?"

"Ground you."

"Who cares?"

"Take away your screen time."

"Who cares?"

"You do."

"I won't."

"You could run away?" Benjy suggested.

"Run away?" his brothers asked at the same time, and Max couldn't resist calling, "Jinx!"

"Sam, Sam, Sam," Benjy said, relieving his brother of his imposed silence.

"I can't run away," Sam said.

"Just until the war ends," Max said.

"I wouldn't leave you guys."

"And I would miss you," Benjy said.

When Jacob and Julia had shared the news that Sam and Max were going to get a little brother, Jacob made the mistake of suggesting the boys name him—a sweet idea that if carried out one hundred million times would never once produce an acceptable result. Max quickly settled on Ed the Hyena, after Scar's loyal henchman in *The Lion King*, assuming, presumably, that that's what his new brother would be: his loyal henchman. Sam wanted to name him Foamy, because it was the third word his finger landed on when he was riffling through the dictionary—he'd promised to commit to the first word, whatever it was, but it was *extortion*, and the second was *ambivalent*. The problem wasn't that the brothers disagreed, but that both were such terrific names—Ed the Hyena and Foamy. Great names that any human would be privileged to have and that would all but guarantee a cool life. They flipped a coin, and then did best out of three, then seven, and Julia, being Julia, gently folded the winning name into an origami bird that she released from an open window, but made the boys T-shirts with iron-on letters that read "Foamy's Brother," and, of course, a "Foamy" onesie. There was a photograph of the three of them in their Foamy-wear, asleep in the backseat of the Volvo that was christened Ed the Hyena as an easy-to-give concession to Max.

Sam patted his knees, beckoning Benjy over, and said, "I'd miss you, too, Foamy."

"Who's Foamy?" Benjy asked, climbing onto his brother.

"You almost were."

Max found all of this too emotional to acknowledge or name. "If you run away, I'm coming, too."

"No one is running away," Sam said.

"Me, too," Benjy said.

"We need to stay," Sam said.

"Why?" they asked.

"Jinx!"

"Benjy, Benjy, Benjy."

Sam could have said, *Because you need to be taken care of, and I can't do that myself.* Or, *Because it's only my bar mitzvah, so only I need to run from it.* Or, *Because life isn't a Wes Anderson movie.* But instead he said, "Because then our house would be completely empty."

"It should be," Max said. "It deserves to be."

"And Argus."

"He'll come with us."

"He can't walk to the corner. How would he run away?"

Max was becoming desperate: "So we'll put him to sleep, and then we'll run away."

"You would kill Argus to stop a bar mitzvah?"

"I would kill Argus to stop life."

"Yeah, his life."

"Our life."

"I have a question," Benjy said.

"What?" his brothers asked in unison.

"Jinx!"

"Jesus, Max."

"Fine. Sam, Sam, Sam."

"What's your question?"

"Max said you could run away until the war stops."

"No one is running away."

"What if the war never stops?"

O JEWS, YOUR TIME HAS COME!

Julia came home in time to put the boys to bed. It wasn't nearly as painful as either she or Jacob had imagined, but only because she had imagined a night of silence and Jacob had imagined a night of screaming. They hugged, exchanged gentle smiles, and got to work.

"My dad procured a Torah."

"And a rabbi?"

"It was a two-for-one."

"Please, not a cantor."

"Thank God, no."

"And you found everything at Whole Foods?"

"I got a caterer."

"The day before?"

"Not the best caterer. Some unsubstantiated accusations of salmonella."

"Rumors, I'm sure. We should have about what, fifteen people? Twenty?"

"We'll have food for one hundred."

"All those snow globes . . . ," Julia said, genuinely wistfully.

They were gridded on three linen-closet shelves, fifteen across and eight deep. They would stay there, untouched, for years—so much trapped water, like all the trapped air in the saved bubble wrap, like the words trapped in thought bubbles. There must have been tiny cracks in their domes, as the water slowly evaporated—maybe a quarter-inch a year?— and by the time Benjy was ready to have, or not have, a bar mitzvah, the snow was resting on dry city streets, still pure.

"The boys have no idea, by the way. I just told them you were visiting a site last night and they didn't ask anything else."

"We'll never know what they know."

"And neither will they."

"It was only a night," she said, loading dishes into the washer. "But I've never *chosen* to be away from them. It was always because I had to be. I feel awful."

Rather than try to diminish her feeling, Jacob tried to share it: "It's hard." But there was that other angel, its tiny feet nailed to Jacob's shoulder: "You were at Mark's?"

"When?"

"Is that where you went?"

There were many ways to answer that question. She chose: "Yes."

He brought the extra plates up from the basement. She took a shower, to release her shoulders and steam Sam's suit. He walked Argus to Rosedale, where they listened to other dogs play fetch in the dark. She ran a load of kids' underwear and socks and dish towels. And then they were back in the kitchen, putting away the clean, still-warm dishes.

Without intending to, Julia picked up where she'd left off earlier: "When they were tiny, I wouldn't take my eyes off them for two seconds. But there's going to come a time when we won't speak for days on end."

"There won't."

"There will. Every parent thinks it will never happen to them, but it happens to everyone."

"We won't let it happen."

"And at the same time we'll force it to happen."

Then they were upstairs. She searched her toiletries until she couldn't remember what she was searching for. He switched the placement of his sweaters and T-shirts—a little early this year. The windows were black, but she lowered the shades for the morning. He stood on an ottoman to reach a bulb. And then they were at the side-by-side sinks, brushing.

"There's an interesting house for sale," Jacob said, "in Rock Creek Park."

"On Davenport?"

"What?"

She spat, and said, "The house on Davenport?"

"Yeah."

"I saw it."

"You went to it?"

"The listing."

"Kind of interesting, no?"

"This house is better," she said.

"This is the best house."

"It's a very good house."

He spat, then alternated between rinsing the brush and brushing his tongue. "I should sleep on the sofa," he said.

"Or I can."

"No, I'll go. I should get used to sleeping in uncomfortable places, toughen myself up a bit." His joke applied pressure to something serious.

"The shabby-chic sofa isn't such a deprivation." Her joke pushed back.

"Maybe it would be a good thing if I set an alarm for quite early, and came back up to the bedroom so the boys could find us there together in the morning?"

"They're going to have to know at some point. And they probably already know."

"After the bar mitzvah. Let's give them this last bit. Even if everyone is in on the make-believe."

"Are we really not going to say any more about your going to Israel?"

"What else is there to say?"

"That it's insane."

"That's already been said."

"That it's unfair to me, and to the kids."

"That's already been said."

What hadn't been said, and what he wanted to hear, and what might even have made him choose differently, was "That I don't want you to go." But instead she'd given: "You're not my spouse."

The sofa was perfectly comfortable—more comfortable than the seven-thousand-dollar organic kelp and pony hair mattress Julia had insisted on buying—but Jacob couldn't sleep. He couldn't even make it to tossing and turning. He wasn't sure what he felt—it could have been guilt, it could have been humiliation, or just sadness—and as always, when he couldn't place a feeling, it became anger.

He went to the basement and turned on the TV. CNN, MSNBC, Fox News, ABC: it was all coverage of the Middle East, all interchangeable. Why could he never admit that he was just looking for his show, which wasn't even his show? It wasn't ego, it was self-flagellation. Which was ego.

There it was, syndicated on TBS. Sometimes Jacob convinced himself it was better with the swearing and brief flashes of nudity removed, that they were there only because the freedom to do such things had to be justified by exercising it. Jacob wondered what the executive producers were making for the airing, and switched the station.

He flipped past some sort of cooking reality show, some sort of X Games something or other, past one of the despicable *Despicable Me* iterations. Everything was another version of something that was never good to begin with. He made a full journey around the planet of television, ending at his point of departure: CNN.

Wolf Blitzer had once again relieved the horrible tension of his purgatorial beard—neither a beard nor not a beard—with yet another new pair of glasses. He was a man on TV standing in front of a TV, using this TV-in-a-TV to explain the geopolitics of the Middle East. Jacob zoned out. Normally, he would have taken this moment of mental meandering to contemplate masturbating, or whether whatever Pirate Booty rubble could be found at the bottom of the bag would justify the trip upstairs. But instead, inspired by the next day's bar mitzvah, he thought about his own, almost thirty years before. His portion was Ki Tissa, which, his bad luck, happened to be the longest portion in Exodus, and among the longest in the Torah. He remembered that much. *Ki Tissa* means "when you take," the first distinctive words in the portion, referring to the first census of the Jews. He had some vague memory of the melodies, but they could just as well have been generic Jewish-sounding musical phrases, the kind people fall back on when faking a prayer they are embarrassed not to know.

There was a lot of drama in the portion: the first census, Moses ascending Mount Sinai, the golden calf, Moses destroying the tablets, Moses ascending Mount Sinai a second time and returning with what would be the Ten Commandments. But what he remembered most clearly wasn't even in the parsha itself, but a related text, a passage of the Talmud, given to him by his rabbi, which addressed the question of what was done with the broken tablets. Even as an uninterested thirteen-year-old, it struck Jacob as a beautiful question. According to the Talmud, God instructed Moses to put both the intact tablets and the broken tablets in the ark. The Jews carried them—the broken and the whole—for their forty years of wandering, and placed them both in the Temple in Jerusalem.

"Why?" asked the rabbi, whose face Jacob couldn't visualize, and whose voice he couldn't conjure, and who was certainly no longer living. "Why didn't they just bury them, as would befit a sacred text? Or leave them behind, as would befit a blasphemy?"

By the time Jacob's focus shifted back to CNN, Wolf was addressing a hologram of the Ayatollah, speculating about the contents of his forthcoming speech—the first public comments out of Iran since the fire at the Dome of the Rock. There was apparently great anticipation in the Muslim and Jewish worlds for what he would say, as it would establish the most extreme response to the situation, draw the outer edge.

Jacob ran upstairs, grabbed the Pirate Booty—and a pack of roasted seaweed, and the last two Newman's Own Oreo imitations, and a bottle of Hefeweizen—and hustled back down in time to catch the beginning. Wolf hadn't mentioned that the speech would be delivered outside, in Azadi Square, in front of two hundred thousand people. He'd managed to commit the unpardonable sin of TV journalism: to undersell, to reduce expectations, to make *actually* necessary television seem optional.

A slightly chubby man approached the microphone: pitch-black turban, snow-white beard, black robe like a black balloon filled with shouting. There was an undeniable wisdom in his eyes, even a gentleness. There was absolutely nothing to distinguish his face from that of a Jew.

COME HOME

"It is now nine p.m. in Israel. Two p.m. in New York. It is seven p.m. in London, eleven a.m. in Los Angeles, eight p.m. in Paris, three p.m. in Buenos Aires, nine p.m. in Moscow, four a.m. in Melbourne.

"This speech is being broadcast around the world, on every major news outlet. It is being simultaneously translated into dozens of languages, and will be viewed by people of every religion and race and culture in the world. But I am speaking only to Jews.

"Since the devastating earthquake two weeks ago, Israel has endured calamity after calamity, some brought upon us by the indifferent hand of Mother Nature, some by the fists of our enemies. With ingenuity, strength, and resolve, we have done what Jews have always done: we have survived. How many more-powerful peoples have vanished from the face of the earth while the Jewish people have survived? Where are the Vikings? Where are the Mayans? The Hittites? The Mesopotamians? And where are our historical enemies, who have always outnumbered us? Where are the pharaohs, who destroyed our firstborn but could not destroy us? Where are the Babylonians, who destroyed our Holy Temple but could not destroy us? Where is the Roman Empire, which destroyed our Second Temple but could not destroy us? Where are the Nazis, who could not destroy us?

"They are gone.

"And here we are.

"Spread across the globe, we have different dreams in different languages, but we are joined in a richer, prouder history than can be claimed by any other people to have graced the earth. We have survived, and survived, and survived, and have come to assume that we always will. But brothers and sisters, descendants of Abraham, Isaac, and Jacob, Sarah, Rebecca, Rachel, and Leah, I come to you tonight to tell you that survival is the story of the Jewish people only because the Jewish people have not been destroyed. If we survive ten thousand calamities, and then, in the end, we are destroyed, the story of the Jews will be the story of destruction. Brothers and sisters, heirs of kings and queens, prophets and holy men—children, all of us, of the Jewish mother who released the wicker basket into the river of history—we are cast into the current, and this moment will determine our story.

"As King Solomon knew, 'A righteous man falls down seven times and gets up.' We have fallen down seven times, and seven times we have gotten up. We have been struck by an earthquake of unprecedented proportions. We have endured the collapse of our homes, the loss of basic utilities, aftershocks, disease, missile attacks, and now we are assailed on every side by enemies funded and armed by superpowers, while support for us has wavered, while our friends have averted their eyes. Our righteousness has not diminished, but we cannot fall down again. We were defeated two thousand years ago, and we were doomed to two thousand years of exile. As the prime minister of the State of Israel, I am here to tell you tonight that if we fall down again, the book of Lamentations will not only be given a new chapter, it will be given an end. The story of the Jewish people—*our* story—will be told alongside the stories of the Vikings and Mayans.

"Exodus recounts a battle between Israel and Amalek: man against man, army against army, people against people, with commanders observing from vantage points far behind their own lines. While he watches the battle, Moses notices that when his arms are raised, Israel makes advances, and when they are lowered, Israel takes losses. So he keeps his arms raised in front of him. But, as we are again and again reminded, Moses is only human. And no human can keep his arms raised forever.

"Fortunately, Moses's brother, Aaron, and brother-in-law, Hur, are nearby. He summons them, and they hold up his arms for the duration of the battle. Israel is victorious.

"As I speak to you, the Israeli Air Force, in collaboration with the other branches of the Israel Defense Forces, is commencing Operation Arms of Moses. Beginning in eight hours, El Al planes will be departing from major Jewish population centers around the world to bring Jewish men and women between the ages of sixteen and fifty-five to military stations in Israel. Those flights will be met by fighter jets, to ensure safe travel. Upon arriving in Israel, our brave brothers and sisters will be assessed and directed to how they can best support the effort of survival. Detailed information about the operation can be found at www .operationarmsofmoses.com.

"We have been preparing for this. We brought home our Ethiopian brothers and sisters from the desert. We brought home Russian Jews, and Iraqi Jews, and French Jews. We brought home those who survived the horrors of the Holocaust. But this will be an unprecedented undertaking—unprecedented in Israel's history, and unprecedented in world history. But this is an unprecedented crisis. The only way to prevent our total destruction is with the totality of our strength.

"By the end of the first twenty-four hours of flights, we will have brought fifty thousand Jews to Israel.

"By the end of the third day, three hundred thousand.

"On the seventh day, the Diaspora will be home: one million Jews, fighting shoulder to shoulder with their Jewish brothers and sisters. And with these Aarons and Hurs, our arms will not only be raised in victory, we will be able to dictate the peace."

TODAY I AM NOT A MAN

They unrolled the Torah on the kitchen island, and Sam chanted with a grace that had never before touched a member of the Bloch family—the grace of being fully present as oneself. Irv lacked such grace, was self-conscious about crying, and held in his tears. Julia lacked such grace, was too concerned with etiquette to respond to her most primitive instinct to go to her son and stand beside him. Jacob lacked such grace, and cared enough to wonder what others were thinking.

The Torah was closed and dressed and replaced in the cabinet that had been emptied of shelves and art supplies. The men who surrounded Sam took their seats, leaving him alone to chant his haftorah, which he did slowly, resolutely, with the care of an ophthalmologist performing surgery on his own eyes. The rituals were complete. All that remained was his speech.

Sam stood there, at the kitchen-island bimah. He imagined a cone of dusty light projecting from his forehead, creating everything in front of him: the yarmulke on Benjy's head (*Wedding of Jacob and Julia, August 23, 2000*), the tallis that wrapped around his grandfather like an unfinished ghost costume, the unoccupied folding chair on which his great-grandfather sat.

He walked around the island, then awkwardly between chairs, and put his arm on Max's shoulder. With a physical closeness that neither could have borne in any other moment, Sam took Max's face into his hands and whispered something into his ear. It wasn't a plan. It wasn't a secret. It wasn't information. Max softened like a yahrzeit candle.

Sam made his way back to the other side of the island.

"Hello, gathered. So. Right. Well. What can I say?

"You know how sometimes, when someone wins an award, they pretend that they were so sure they *weren't* going to win it, they didn't bother to prepare a speech? I don't believe that that has ever once, in human history, been true. Or at least not if it's for an Oscar, or something big like that, and the awards are televised. I guess people think that saying they didn't prepare a speech will make them sound modest, or even worse, down-to-earth, but they actually sound like totally disingenuous narcissists.

"I guess a bar mitzvah speech is like a plane in a storm: once you're in it, there's no way out but through. Great-Grandpa taught me that expression, even though he hadn't been in a plane for like thirty years. He loved expressions. I think they made him feel American.

"This isn't really a speech. To be honest, I didn't think I'd be here, so I didn't prepare anything, other than my original bar mitzvah speech, which wouldn't make any sense now, given that everything has completely changed. But I did work on it a lot, so if anyone wants it, I suppose I could e-mail it to them later. Anyway, I brought up that thing about actors who say they didn't prepare a speech, because maybe demonstrating my awareness of the untrustworthiness of saying you are unprepared might give you a reason to believe me. The real question is why I care if you believe me.

"Anyway, Grandpa Irv used to do this thing where he'd give Max and me five bucks if we made a speech that convinced him of something. Anytime, anything. So we were constantly making little speeches: why people shouldn't have dogs as pets, why escalators encourage obesity and should be illegal, why robots will defeat humans in our lifetime, why Bryce Harper should be traded, why it's OK to swat flies. There was nothing we wouldn't argue, because even though we didn't need the money, we wanted it. We liked how it accumulated. Or we wanted to win. Or to be loved. I don't know. I'm mentioning it because I guess it made us pretty good at speaking off the cuff, which is what I am now about to do. Thanks, Grandpa?

"I never wanted to have a bar mitzvah in the first place. My objection wasn't moral or intellectual, I just thought it would be a colossal waste of time. Maybe that's moral? I don't know. I assume I would have continued to object even if my parents had genuinely listened to me, or proposed other ways of thinking about a bar mitzvah. We'll never know, because I was simply told that it's what we do, because it's what we do. In the same way that not eating cheeseburgers is what we don't do, because it's what we don't do. Even though we do sometimes eat real-crab California rolls, even though it's what we don't do. And we often don't observe Shabbat, even though it's what we do. I don't have any problem with hypocrisy when it's self-serving, but applying the logic of *what we do* to having a bar mitzvah didn't serve me.

"So I made efforts to sabotage it. I tried not to learn my haftorah, but Mom would put on the recording whenever we were in the car, and it's actually unbelievably catchy—everyone in the family can recite it, and Argus starts beating his tail with the first verse.

"I was incredibly obnoxious to my tutor, but he was happy enough eating my crap if it meant cashing my parents' checks.

"As some of you might know, I was accused of writing some inappropriate words in Hebrew school. As terrible as it felt not to be believed, I was happy to get in trouble if it would get me out of this. Which it clearly didn't.

"I've never thought about it until right now, but it occurs to me that I don't know if I've ever actually tried to stop anything from happening in my life. I mean, obviously I've tried to get out of the way of inside pitches, and I make a lot of efforts not to use urinals without vertical privacy shields, but an *event*. I never tried to stop a birthday or, I don't know, Hanukkah. Maybe my inexperience made me think it would be easier. But for all of my efforts, Jewish manhood only got nearer.

"Then the earthquake happened, and that changed everything, and my great-grandfather died, and that also changed everything, and Israel got attacked by everyone, and a whole lot of other things happened that this is not the right time or place to get into, and suddenly everything was different. And as everything kept changing, my reasons for not wanting to have a bar mitzvah changed and became stronger. It wasn't just that it was a colossal waste of time—that time was already wasted, if you think about it. And it wasn't even that I knew that lots of bad things were going to happen after my bar mitzvah, so the effort to stop my bar mitzvah from happening was actually an effort to stop all kinds of bad things from happening.

"You can't stop things from happening. You can only choose not to be there, like Great-Grandpa Isaac did, or give yourself completely over, like my dad, who made his big decision to go to Israel to fight. Or maybe it's Dad who is choosing not to be there, which is *here*, and Great-Grandpa who gave himself over completely.

"We read *Hamlet* in school this year, and everybody knows the whole 'To be or not to be' business, and we talked about it for like three consecutive classes—the choice between life and death, action and reflection, whatever and whatever. It was kind of going nowhere until my friend Billie said something incredibly smart. She said, 'Isn't there another option besides those two? Like, to mostly be or mostly not be, that is the question.' And that got me thinking that also maybe one doesn't have to exactly choose. 'To be or not to be. That is the question.' To be *and* not to be. That is the answer.

"My Israeli cousin Noam—that's his dad, Tamir, over there—told me that a bar mitzvah isn't something you have, but something you become. He was right, and he was wrong. A bar mitzvah is both something you have *and* something you become. I am obviously *having* a bar mitzvah today. I chanted my Torah portion and haftorah, and no one was holding a gun to my head. But I want to take this opportunity to make clear to everyone that I am not *becoming* one. I did not ask to be a man, and I do not want to be a man, and I refuse to be a man.

"Dad once told me a story about when he was a kid and there was a dead squirrel on the lawn. He watched Grandpa take care of it. After, he said to Grandpa, 'I couldn't have done that.' And Grandpa said, 'Sure you could.' And Dad said, 'I couldn't.' And Grandpa said, 'When you're a dad, there's no one after you.' And Dad said, 'I still couldn't do it.' And Grandpa said, 'The more you won't want to do it, the more of a dad you'll be.' I don't want to be like that, so I won't.

"Now let me explain why I wrote all those words."

O JEWS, YOUR TIME HAS COME!

"O Muslims, the hour is here! The war of God against the enemies of God will end in triumph! Victory in the Holy Land of Palestine is within the reach of the righteous. We will have our revenge for Lydda, we will have our revenge for Haifa and Acre and Deir Yassin, we will have our revenge for the generations of martyrs, we will have our revenge, praise Allah, for al-Quds! Oh, al-Quds, raped by the Jews, treated like a whore by the sons of pigs and apes, we will restore to you your crown and your glory!

"They burned Qubbat Al-Sakhra to the ground. But it is they who will be burned. I say to you today the words that filled the hearts of a thousand martyrs: '*Khaybar, Khaybar, ya Yahud, Jaish Muhammad Saouf Ya'ud!*' As the Prophet Muhammad, peace be upon Him, defeated the perfidious Jews at Khaybar, so too will the armies of Muhammad inflict the final humiliation on the Jews today!

"O Jews, your time has come! Your fire will be met by fire! We will burn your cities and your towns, your schools and your hospitals, your every home! No Jew will be safe! I remind you, O Muslims, of what the Prophet, peace be upon Him, teaches us: that on Judgment Day even the stones and the trees will speak, with or without words, and say, 'O servant of Allah, O Muslim, there is a Jew behind me, come and kill him!'"

COME HOME

"'Watch me,' Gideon told his men, greatly outnumbered, facing the Midianites not far from where I now stand. 'Follow my lead. When I get to the edge of the camp, do exactly as I do. When I and all who are with me blow our trumpets, then from all around the camp blow yours and shout, "For the Lord and for Gideon."' At the sight and sound of our unity, the enemy scattered and fled.

"The majority of the Jewish people have chosen not to live in Israel, and Jews do not share any one set of political or religious beliefs, and do not share a culture or language. But we are in the same river of history.

"To the Jews of the world, those who came before you—your grandparents, your great-grandparents—and those who will come after you—your grandchildren, your great-grandchildren—are calling out: 'Come home.'

"Come home not only because your home needs you, but because you need your home.

"Come home not only to fight for Israel's survival, but to fight for your own.

"Come home because a people without a home is not a people, just as a person without a home is not a person.

"Come home not because you agree with everything Israel does, not because you think Israel is perfect, or even any better than other countries. Come home not because Israel is what you want it to be, but because it is *yours*.

"Come home, because history will remember what each of us chooses in this moment.

"Come home and we will win this war and establish a lasting peace.

"Come home and we will rebuild this state to be stronger and closer to its promise than it was before the destruction.

"Come home and be another hand around the pen that writes the story of the Jewish people.

"Come home and hold the arms of Moses aloft. And then, when the guns have cooled, and the buildings have risen where they once stood, only prouder, and the streets are filled with the sounds of children playing, you will find your name not in the book of Lamentations, but the book of Life.

"And then, wherever you choose to go next, you will always be home."

TODAY I AM NOT A MAN

"A couple of weeks ago, everybody was obsessing over what kind of apology I would give during my bar mitzvah speech. How would I explain my behavior? Would I even fess up to it? When I was being blamed, I didn't feel like explaining myself, much less apologizing. But now that other things have taken everyone's attention, and no one really cares anymore, I'd like to explain myself and apologize.

"My friend Billie, whom I mentioned before, told me I was repressed. She's really beautiful, and intelligent, and good. I told her, 'Maybe I just have inner peace.' She said, 'Peace between what parties?' I thought that was such an interesting question.

"I told her, 'I'm really not repressed.' She said, 'That's exactly what a repressed person would say.' So I said, 'And I suppose you aren't repressed?' And she said, 'Everyone is somewhat repressed.' 'OK,' I said, 'then I'm no more repressed than an average person.'

"'Say the hardest thing,' she said.

"I was like, 'What?'

"And she said, 'I don't mean right this second. You couldn't even know what it is without thinking long and hard about it. But once you figure it out, I dare you to say it.'

"'And if I do?'

"'You won't.'

"'But if.'

"She said, 'I would invite you to choose the terms, but I know you're too repressed to tell me what you'd actually want.'

"Which was obviously true.

"'So maybe *that's* actually the hardest thing to say,' I said.

"She said, 'What? That you want to kiss me? Doesn't even make the top hundred.'

"I thought a lot about what she said. And I was thinking about it in Hebrew school that day when I wrote those words. I was just seeing how each of them felt, seeing how hard it was to write them, and say them to myself. That's why I did it. But that's not the point.

"The point is: I made a mistake. I thought that the *worst* thing to say was the *hardest* thing to say. But it's actually pretty easy to say horrible things: retard, cunt, whatever. In a way, it's even easier because we know exactly how bad the words are. There's nothing scary about them. Part of what makes something really hard to say is the not knowing.

"The reason I'm here today is because I realized that the hardest thing to say isn't a word, or a sentence, but an event. The hardest thing to say couldn't be something you say to yourself. It requires the hardest person, or people, to say it to."

O JEWS, YOUR TIME HAS COME!

"O Muslims, God demands of his servants the deaths of these Jews. I call on the soldiers of the Qur'an to wage our final battle against those beasts who kill the prophets. O Muslims, must I tell you the story of the Jewish woman who gave the Prophet, peace be upon Him, poisoned lamb, to kill Him? The Prophet, peace be upon Him, said to his companions, 'Do not eat this lamb. It is telling me it has poison in it.' But it was too late for the companion Bishr ibn al-Bara, who died from the poison. The Jewess tried to kill our Prophet, peace be upon Him, but praise God, she failed. This is the nature of the Jews, these twice-cursed people! They will try to kill you, but Allah will plant knowledge of their wicked deeds in your hearts, and save you. You must do as the Prophet, peace be upon Him, did with the Jew Kenana ibn al-Rabi, who hid the treasure of the Jews, the Banu Nadir. The Prophet, peace be upon Him, told Az-Zubair ibn Al-Awwam, 'Torture this Jew until you learn from him what he knows.' He held hot steel to his chest and he nearly died. And then the Prophet, peace be upon Him, delivered the Jew Kenana to Muhammad ibn Maslamah, and he cut off his head! Then he took the Jews of Kenana as slaves. Muhammad, peace be upon Him, took the most beautiful woman of the Jews for himself! This is the way, O Muslims! Let the Prophet be your teacher in your dealings with the Jews!

"O brother Palestinians! Remember! When the Muslims, the Arabs, the Palestinians, make war against the Jews, they do so to worship Allah. They enter the war as Muslims! The hadith does not say, 'O Sunni, O Shiite, O Palestinian, O Syrian, O Persian, come fight.' It says, 'O Muslim'!

For too long we have battled ourselves and lost. Now we will battle together and be victorious.

"We are fighting in the name of Islam, because Islam commands us to wage war unto death against anyone who plunders our land. Surrender is the way of Satan!"

COME HOME

But then, after his final word, the camera stayed on the prime minister. His gaze held. And the camera held. At first it seemed like an awkward broadcasting mistake, but it was no accident.

His gaze held.

And the camera held.

And then the prime minister did something so outrageously symbolic, so potentially kitschy, so many miles over the top, it risked breaking the legs of its intended recipients just as they approached the necessary leap of faith.

He removed a shofar from beneath the lectern. And without any explanation of its meaning—its biblical or historical significance, its intent to awaken sleeping Jews to repent and return, without even sharing that this particular shofar, this twice-curled ram's horn, was two thousand years old, that it was the shofar discovered at Masada, stashed in a water hole and preserved by the dry desert heat, that its inside contained biological remnants of a noble Jewish martyr—he brought it to his lips.

The camera held.

The prime minister inhaled, and gathered into the ram's horn the molecules of every Jew who had ever lived: the breath of warrior kings and fishmongers; tailors, matchmakers, and executive producers; kosher butchers, radical publishers, kibbutzniks, management consultants, orthopedic surgeons, tanners, and judges; the grateful laugh of someone with more than forty grandchildren gathered in his hospital room; the false moan of a prostitute who hid children under the bed on which she kissed

Nazis on the mouth; the sigh of an ancient philosopher at a moment of understanding; the cry of a new orphan alone in a forest; the final air bubble to rise from the Seine and burst as Paul Celan sank, his pockets full of stones; the word *clear* from the lips of the first Jewish astronaut, strapped into a chair facing infinity. And the breath of those who never lived, but whose existence Jewish existence depended on: the patriarchs, matriarchs, and prophets; Abel's last plea; Sarah's laughter at the prospect of the miracle; Abraham offering his God and his son what could not be offered to both: "Here I am."

The prime minister aimed the shofar forty-five degrees, sixty degrees, and in New York, and in Los Angeles, and in Miami, Chicago, and Paris, in London, Buenos Aires, Moscow, and Melbourne, television screens trembled, they shook.

TODAY I AM NOT A MAN

"The hardest thing to say is the hardest thing to hear: forced to choose between my parents, I would be able to.

"And I've talked about it with Max and Benjy, and if forced to choose, each of them could choose as well. Two of us would have chosen one, and one of us the other, but we agreed that if forced to choose, we would all choose the same one, so that we could stay together.

"When I did Model UN a couple of weeks ago, the country we were representing, Micronesia, suddenly came into possession of a nuclear weapon. We didn't ask for a nuclear weapon, and didn't want a nuclear weapon, and nuclear weapons are, in pretty much every way, horrible. But there's a reason people have them, and it's to never have to use them.

"That's it. I'm finished."

He didn't bow, they didn't clap. No one moved or spoke.

As always, Sam didn't know what to do with his body. But the organism that was the roomful of family and friends seemed to depend on his movement. If he started to cry, someone would comfort him. If he ran out, someone would follow. If he'd just go talk to Max, everyone would schmooze. But if he continued to stand there, fists balled, they would continue to stand there.

Jacob thought maybe he could clap his hands, smile, and say something lame, like "Dig in!"

Julia thought maybe she could go to Sam, put her arm around him, and touch her head to his head.

Even Benjy, who, by virtue of never giving it any thought, always knew what to do, was motionless.

Irv longed to assume the authority of the family's new patriarch, but he didn't know how. Was there a five-dollar bill in his pocket?

From the middle of the room, Billie said, "Yet."

Everyone turned to her.

"What?" Sam asked.

There was no sound to overcome, but she screamed: "Yet!"

O JEWS, YOUR TIME HAS COME!

The cheering would continue long after the Ayatollah lowered his final raised arm of solidarity. Long after he made his way behind the temporary stage, surrounded by a dozen plainclothes bodyguards. The cheering—the applauding, the chanting, the hollering, the singing—would continue after he was greeted by a line of his closest advisers, each kissing him, blessing him. After he was put into a car with two-inch-thick windows and no door handles and driven away. The cheering continued, and intensified, but without a gravitational center, the crowd moved outward in every direction.

Wolf Blitzer and his panel started discussing the speech—without the time to digest the translation, they just pulled quote after quote until they'd reassembled it out of order—but the camera stayed on the crowd. The mass of people couldn't be contained by Azadi Square, which pumped them through the connecting streets like blood, and it couldn't be contained by the camera's frame.

Jacob imagined every street in Tehran packed with people throwing fists in the air, beating their chests. He imagined every park and gathering space overflowing like Azadi Square. The camera closed on a woman slapping the back of one hand into the palm of the other, over and over; a boy screaming from his father's shoulders, four arms in the air. There were people on balconies, on rooftops, on the branches of trees. People atop cars and corrugated metal awnings too hot to be touched with bare skin.

The Ayatollah's words had dripped into more than a billion open ears, and there had been two hundred thousand pairs of fixed eyes in the square, and 0.2 percent of the world was Jewish, but watching the replays of the speech—the Ayatollah's gesticulating fists, the crowd's undulations—Jacob thought only of his family.

Before they were allowed to take Sam home from the hospital when he was born, Jacob had to sit through a fifteen-minute course covering the Ten Commandments of Caring for a Newborn—the absolute rudiments of new parenting: YOU SHALL NOT SHAKE YOUR BABY; YOU SHALL CARE FOR THE UMBILICAL STUMP WITH A COTTON SWAB SOAKED IN WARM WATER AND SOAP, AT LEAST ONCE A DAY; YOU SHALL BE AWARE OF THE FONTANEL; YOU SHALL FEED YOUR BABY ONLY BREAST MILK OR FORMULA, BETWEEN ONE AND THREE OUNCES, EVERY TWO TO THREE HOURS, AND YOU SHALL NOT BE OBLIGATED TO BURP YOUR BABY IF HE FALLS ASLEEP AFTER A FEEDING; and so on. All things that anyone who had gone to a parenting class, or had ever spent time in the presence of a baby, or had simply been born Jewish, would already know. But the Tenth Commandment rattled Jacob. YOU SHALL REMEM-BER: IT WILL NOT LAST.

COME HOME

After the guests went home, after Uber came for the Torah, after Tamir took all the kids to the Nats game (where, thanks to Max's thoughtful ingenuity, Sam's bar mitzvah was announced on the scoreboard during the seventh-inning stretch), after a bit of unnecessary e-mailing, after a walk to the corner with Argus, Jacob and Julia were left to clean up. Before they had kids, if asked to conjure images of parenthood they would have said things like "Reading in bed," and "Giving a bath," and "Running while holding the seat of a bicycle." Parenthood contains such moments of warmth and intimacy, but isn't them. It's cleaning up. The great bulk of family life involves no exchange of love, and no meaning, only fulfill-ment. Not the fulfillment of feeling fulfilled, but of fulfilling that which now falls to you.

Julia couldn't bring herself to accept paper plates in the end, so there were a few loads of dishes to do. Jacob filled the machine to the brim and then hand-washed the rest, he and Julia taking turns with the soaping-up and the drying-off.

"You were right not to believe him," Jacob said.

"Apparently. But you were right that we should have believed him."

"Did we mishandle it?"

"I don't know," Julia said. "Is that even the question? Everything with kids is some kind of mishandling. So we try to learn, and mishandle it less badly in the future. But in the meantime, they've changed, so the lesson doesn't apply."

"It's a lose-lose."

They both laughed.

"A love-love."

The sponge was already well on its way to mush, the only clean dish towel was damp, and the dish soap had to be diluted with water for there to be enough, but they made it work.

"Listen," Jacob said. "Not fatalistically, but responsibly, I arranged a whole bunch of things with the accountant and lawyer, and—"

"Thank you," Julia said.

"Anyway, it's all pretty clearly spelled out in a document that I put on your bedside table—in a sealed envelope, in case one of the kids came upon it."

"You're not going to die."

"Of course not."

"You're not even going to go."

"I am."

She turned on the disposal, and Jacob had the thought that if he were a Foley artist tasked with creating the sound of Satan screaming out from hell, he might just hold a mic to what he was now hearing.

"Another thing," he said.

"What?"

"I'll wait till it's done."

She switched it off.

"Remember I mentioned that I've been working on a show for a long time?"

"Your secret masterpiece."

"I never described it like that."

"About us."

"Very loosely."

"Yes, I know what you're referring to."

"There's a copy of it in the bottom-right drawer of my desk."

"The whole thing?"

"Yes. And on top is the bible."

"The Bible?"

"For the show. It's a kind of guide for how to read it. For future actors, a future director."

"Shouldn't the work speak for itself?"

"Nothing speaks for itself."

"Sam sure does."

"If the show were Sam, it wouldn't need a bible."

"And if you were Sam, you wouldn't need a show."

"Correct."

"OK. So your show and its bible are in the bottom-right drawer of your desk. And in the event that you actually go to Israel and, what, perish in battle? I'm supposed to send it to your agent?"

"No. Please, Julia."

"Burn it?"

"I'm not *Kafka*."

"What?"

"I was hoping you'd read it."

"If you die."

"And only if."

"I don't know if I'm touched by how open you're being, or hurt by how closed off you are."

"You heard Sam: 'To be and not to be.'"

Julia wiped the suds from the counter and hung the dish towel over the faucet. "Now what?"

"Well," Jacob said, taking his phone from his pocket to check the time. "It's three o'clock, which is too early to go to sleep."

"Are you tired?"

"No," he said. "I'm just used to being tired."

"I don't know what that means, but OK."

"Aqua seafoam shame."

"Huh?"

"Don't assume it has to mean anything." Jacob put his palm on the counter and said, "It's you, of course. What Sam said."

"What he said about what?"

"You know. About whom he'd pick."

"Yes," she said with a kind smile, "of course it's me. The real question is, who was the dissenter?"

"That might very well have been a little weapon of psychological warfare."

"You're probably right."

They laughed again.

"Why haven't you asked me not to go to Israel?"

"Because after sixteen years, it goes without saying."

"Look! A crying Hebrew baby."

"Look! A pharaoh's deaf daughter."

Jacob slid his hands into his pockets and said, "I know sign language."

Julia laughed. "What?"

"I'm completely serious."

"No, you aren't."

"I've known it for as long as you've known me."

"You're full of shit."

"I'm not."

"Sign, *I'm full of shit.*"

Jacob pointed to himself, then moved his open right hand over the top of his left fist, then he held out his right hand with the thumb sticking up, grabbed the thumb in the fist of his left hand, and pulled his left hand up and off the thumb.

"How am I supposed to know if that's real?"

"It is."

"Sign, *Life is long.*"

Jacob made his hands into the shape that kids use for guns, aimed his forefingers at his belly, then traced them up his torso toward his neck. Then he extended his left arm, pointed at the fist with his right forefinger, and moved the finger along his arm up to his shoulder.

"Wait, are you crying?" Jacob asked.

"No."

"Are you about to?"

"No," she said. "Are you?"

"I'm always about to."

"Sign, *Look! A crying Hebrew baby.*"

Jacob held his right hand by his face, about eye level, raised his index and middle fingers, and pushed his arm forward—two eyes moving forward in space. Then he ran the forefinger of each hand down his cheeks, one at a time and alternating, as if painting tears onto himself. Then, with his right hand, he stroked an imaginary beard. Then he created a cradle of his arms, palms up and overlapped at belly level, and rocked it back and forth.

"That beard-stroking? That's the sign for *Hebrew*?"

"For *Hebrew*, for *Jew.* Yes."

"That manages to be at once anti-Semitic and misogynistic."

"I'm sure you know that most Nazis were deaf."

"Yes, I did know that."

"And French people, and English, and Spaniards, and Italians, and Scandinavians. Pretty much everyone who isn't us."

"Which is why your father is always shouting."

"That's right," Jacob laughed. "And by the way, the sign for *stingy* is the same as the sign for *Jew*, just with a clenched fist at the end."

"Jesus."

Jacob held his straightened arms out to his sides and tilted his head toward his right shoulder. Julia laughed and squeezed the sponge until her knuckles went white.

"I really don't know what to say, Jacob. I can't believe that you've kept an entire language secret."

"I wasn't keeping it secret. I just didn't tell anyone."

"Why?"

"When I write my memoir, I'm going to call it 'The Big Book of Whys.'"

"People hearing that title might think it's *w-i-s-e*."

"Let them think."

"And I thought you were calling it 'The Bible.'"

Julia turned off the radio, which had been broadcasting at no volume for who knows how long. "Different countries have different sign languages, right?"

"Yes."

"So what's the Jewish sign for *Jew*?"

"I have no idea," Jacob said. He picked up his phone and googled "Hebrew Sign Language for Jew." He turned his phone toward Julia and said, "It's the same."

"That's sad."

"It is, isn't it?"

"On a few levels."

"What would you make it?" Jacob asked.

"A Star of David would require some serious double-jointedness."

"Maybe a palm on the top of the head?"

"Not bad," Julia said, "but it doesn't account for women. Or the great majority of Jewish men, like you, who don't wear yarmulkes. Maybe palms open like a book?"

"Very nice," Jacob said, "but are illiterate Jews not Jews? Are babies?"

"I wasn't thinking that it was reading a book, but the book itself. The Torah, maybe. Or the Book of Life. How do you sign *life*?"

"Remember from *Life is long*?" he said, once again making his hands into guns, and then moving the forefingers up his torso.

"So like this," Julia said, putting her hands in front of her, unpeeling them like a book, and then moving those upturned palms up her torso, as if pushing a book through her lungs.

"I'll run it up the flagpole next time the Elders of Zion convene."

"What's the sign for *gentile*?"

"*Gentile?* Who fucking cares?"

Julia laughed, and Jacob laughed.

"I can't believe you knew a language all alone."

Eliezer Ben-Yehuda single-handedly revived Hebrew. Unlike most Zionists, he wasn't passionate about the creation of the State of Israel so that his people would have a home. He wanted his language to have a home. He knew that without a state—without a place for Jews to haggle, and curse, and create secular laws, and make love—the language wouldn't survive. And without a language, there wouldn't ultimately be a people.

Ben-Yehuda's son, Itamar, was the first native speaker of Hebrew in more than a thousand years. He was raised forbidden to hear or speak any other language. (His father once berated Itamar's mother for singing a Russian lullaby.) His parents wouldn't allow him to play with other children—none of them spoke Hebrew—but as a concession to his loneliness they gave him a dog with the name Maher, meaning "fast" in Hebrew. It was a kind of child abuse. And yet it is possible that he is even more responsible than his father for the first time a modern Jew ever told a dirty joke in Hebrew, ever told another Jew to fuck off in Hebrew, ever typed Hebrew into a court stenography machine, ever shouted unmeant words in Hebrew, ever, in Hebrew, moaned in pleasure.

Jacob put the last dried mugs back on the shelf upside down.

"What are you doing?" Julia asked.

"I'm doing it your way."

"And you're not hysterically concerned about their ability to dry without proper circulation?"

"No, but neither am I suddenly convinced they're going to fill with dust. I'm just tired of disagreeing."

God instructed Moses to put both the intact tablets and the broken tablets in the ark. The Jews carried them—the broken and the whole—for their forty years of wandering, and placed them both in the Temple in Jerusalem.

Why? Why didn't they just bury them, as would befit a sacred text? Or leave them behind, as would befit a blasphemy?

Because they were ours.

VII

THE BIBLE

HOW TO PLAY SADNESS

It doesn't exist, so hide it like a tumor.

HOW TO PLAY FEAR

For a laugh.

HOW TO PLAY CRYING

At my grandfather's funeral, the rabbi told the story of Moses being discovered by Pharaoh's daughter. "Look!" she said after opening the basket.
"A crying Hebrew baby." He asked the kids to try to explain what Pharaoh's
daughter said. Benjy suggested that Moses was "crying in Jewish."

The rabbi asked, "What would it sound like to cry in Jewish?"

Max took a step forward, toward the unfilled grave, and said, "Maybe
like laughing?"

I took a step back.

HOW TO PLAY LATE LAUGHTER

Use humor as aggressively as chemo. Laugh until your hair falls out.
There is nothing that can't be played for a laugh. When Julia says, "It's just
the two of us. Just you and me on the phone," laugh and say, "And God.
And the NSA."

HOW TO PLAY THE DEATH OF HAIR

No one has any idea how much hair he has—both because our hair can't be fully seen with our eyes (not even with multiple mirrors, believe me) and because our eyes are our own.

Sometimes, when they were still young enough not to question the question—and could be trusted not to mention it to others—I would ask the boys how bald I was. I'd bow to them, adjust my hair to reveal where I thought it was thinning, and ask them to describe me to me.

"Looks normal," they'd usually say.

"What about here?"

"Pretty much the same as everyone else."

"But it doesn't seem like there's less right here?"

"Not really."

"Not really? Or no?"

"No?"

"I'm asking for your help here. Could you give it a real look and then give me a real answer?"

What there was of my hair was a prop, the product of pharmaceutical intervention—the tiny hands of Aaron and Hur clutching my roots from inside my skull. I blamed my balding on genetics, and I blamed it on stress. In that way, it was no different from anything else.

The Propecia worked by suppressing testosterone. One of the well-documented and widely experienced side effects is decreased libido. That's a fact, not an opinion or defense. I wish I could have shared it with Julia. But I couldn't, because I couldn't let her know about the Propecia, because I couldn't admit that I cared how I looked. Better to let her think she couldn't make me hard.

I was taking a bath with Benjy a few months after the kids had started spending time at my house. We were talking about *The Odyssey*, a children's version of which we had recently finished, and how painful it must have been for Odysseus to keep his identity secret after finally making it home, but why it was necessary.

"It's not enough just to get home," he said. "You have to be able to stay there."

I said, "You're so right, Benjy." I always used his name when I was proud of him.

"You actually are kind of bald," he said.

"What?"

"You're kind of bald."

"I am?"

"Kind of, yeah."

"Have you been trying to protect my feelings all this time?"

"I don't know."

"Where am I bald?"

"I don't know."

"Touch the parts that are bald."

I bowed to him, but felt no touch.

"Benjy?" I asked, facing the water.

"You're not bald."

I lifted my head. "Then why'd you say it?"

"Because I wanted to make you feel good."

HOW TO PLAY TRUE BALDNESS

We used to go to Great Wall Szechuan House every Christmas, the five of us. We held the kids up to the aquarium until our arms trembled, and ordered every hot appetizer that didn't involve pork. The last such Christmas, my fortune was "You are not a ghost." When we read them aloud, as was the ritual, I looked at "You are not a ghost" and said, "There is always a way."

A dozen years later, I lost all my hair in the course of a month. Benjy showed up unexpectedly that Christmas Eve with enough Chinese food for a family of five.

"You got one of everything?" I asked, laughing out my love of the wonderfully ridiculous abundance.

"One of everything treyf," he said.

"Are you worried that I'm lonely?"

"Are you worried that I'm worried?"

We ate on the sofa, plates on our laps, the coffee table covered with steaming white boxes. Before refilling, Benjy put his empty plate on the crowded table, took my head between his hands, and angled it down. If it had been any less unexpected, I would have found a way out. But once it was happening, I gave myself over: rested my hands on my knees, closed my eyes.

"You don't have enough hands, right?"

"I don't need any."

"Ah, Benjy."

"I'm serious," he said. "Full head of hair."

"The doctor warned me, however many years ago, that this would happen: as soon as you stop taking the pill, you lose it all at once. I didn't believe him. Or I thought I'd be the exception."

"How does it feel?"

"Being able to slice bread with an erection?"

"I'm *eating*, Dad."

"Being able to do push-ups with my hands behind my back?"

"Sorry I expressed interest," he said, unable to pin the corners of his mouth.

"You know, I needed an egg once."

"Did you?" he asked, playing along.

"Yeah. I was doing some baking—"

"You often bake."

"All the time. I'm surprised I'm not baking as I tell this joke. Anyway, I was doing some baking, and found that I was one egg short. Isn't that the worst?"

"There is literally nothing worse."

"Right?" We were both starting to simmer in anticipation. "So rather than schlep to the store through the snow to buy eleven eggs I didn't want, I thought I'd see if I could borrow one."

"And that, right there, is why the 1998 National Jewish Book Award hangs in your office."

"*Yiddishe kop*," I said, tapping my forehead.

"I wish you were my real dad," Benjy said, his eyes moistening with suppressed laughter.

"So I opened the window—" I wasn't sure I'd make it to the punch line that was still forming as I approached it. "So I opened the window, wrote, directed, and starred in a five-second fantasy for which there aren't enough Xs, and my tumescent glans rang the doorbell of the neighbor across the street."

Almost convulsing with restraint, Benjy asked, "Did she have an egg?"

"*He.*"

"He!"

"And no, he didn't."

"What an asshole."

"And I accidentally blinded him."

"Injury to the insult."

"No, wait. Wait. Do it again. Ask me if she had an egg."

"I have a question."

"Let me try to answer it."

"Did she have an egg?"

"Your mom? She did."

"Wonder of wonders!"

"And I accidentally fertilized it."

The laughter we'd been containing never came. We sighed, smiled, sat back, and nodded for no reason. Benjy said, "It must be a relief."

"What must?"

"Finally looking like yourself."

I looked at "You will travel to many places" and said, "I am not a ghost."

Benjy was five when we started *Tales from the Odyssey.* I'd read it to Sam and Max, and both times, the further we got in, the slower we read, until we were making it through only a page a night. Benjy and I got all the way through the Cyclops that first bedtime. I had a rare instance of recognizing what was happening as it happened—he was my final child, and this was my final reading of the passage. It would not last. "'Why?'" I read. "'Why do you break the stillness of the night with your cries?'" I gave space to each pause, opening the sentences as far as they would go. "'Who harms you?' 'NO ONE!' Polyphemus shouted, writhing on the floor of his cave. 'No One tried to kill me! No One blinded me!'"

HOW TO PLAY NO ONE

I told Julia I didn't want her to go with us to the airport. I would tuck in the children, like any other night, no overly dramatic goodbyes, let them know I'd FaceTime as often as possible and be back in a week or two with a suitcase of tchotchkes. And then I'd leave while they slept.

"You can do it however you want," she said. "But can I ask you—or can you ask yourself—what it is you're waiting for?"

"What do you mean?"

"Everything is no big deal. You've raised your voice once in your entire life, to tell me I was your enemy."

"I didn't mean that."

"I know. But you don't mean the silence, either. If this isn't a big deal—saying goodbye to your children before going to war—what is? What is the big deal you're waiting for?"

My father drove us to MacArthur Airport in Islip, Long Island. I sat in the passenger seat, and Barak moved in and out of sleep against Tamir's chest in the back. Five hours. On the radio, there was coverage of the first day of Operation Arms of Moses. Reporters were stationed at the designated airfields around the world, but as it was still early, most of the reporting was just speculation about how many would heed the call. It was the opposite of the ride we'd made only a few weeks earlier, from Washington National to the house.

What conversations there were in the car were segregated front and back; I could hear little of what passed between Tamir and Barak, and my father, who lacked an indoor voice, found his whisper.

"Gabe Perelman will be there," he said. "I spoke to Hersch last night. We're going to see a lot of people we know."

"Probably."

"Glenn Mechling. Larry Moverman."

"Mom's OK, right? She was worryingly nonchalant this morning."

"She's a mother. But she'll be fine."

"And you?"

"What can I say? The price of speaking unpopular truths. I turned the ringer off on the home phone. And D.C.'s finest put a car on the corner. I told them not to. They insisted, told me it wasn't my choice. It'll pass."

"Not that. I mean with me going."

"You read what I wrote. Every part of me wishes you didn't have to go, but I know you do."

"I can't believe this is happening."

"That's because you haven't been listening to me for the past twenty years."

"Longer than that."

Eyes on the road, he rested his right hand on my thigh and said, "I can't believe it, either."

We stopped curbside. The airport was closed, save for flights to Israel. There were about two dozen cars unloading men, and no one waving a stumpy lightsaber and saying, "Keep it moving, keep it moving," but there were two men in army green with machine guns pressed to their chests.

We took our duffels from the trunk and stood by the car.

"Barak's not going to get out?" I asked.

"He's asleep," Tamir said. "We said goodbye in the car. It's better this way."

My father put his hand on Tamir's shoulder and told him, "You're brave."

Tamir said, "This doesn't count as bravery."

"I loved your father."

"He loved you."

My father nodded. He put his other hand on Tamir's other shoulder and said, "Since he's no longer here—" and that was all that was needed. As if the knowledge of what to do at that moment had been coiled into him at birth, Tamir put down his duffel, let his arms rest at his sides, and bowed slightly. My father placed his hands atop Tamir's head and said, "*Y'varech'cha Adonai v'yishm'recha.* May God bless you and guard you. *Ya'ar Adonai panav ay'lecha viy'hunecha.* May God make His face shine upon you and be gracious unto you. *Yisa Adonai panav ay'lecha v'yasaym l'cha shalom.* May God turn His face unto you and grant you peace."

Tamir thanked my father and told me he'd go for a walk, then meet me inside.

Once it was just the two of us, my father laughed.

"What?"

He said, "You know what Lou Gehrig's final words were, right?"

"'I don't want to die'?"

"'Damn, Lou Gehrig's disease, I should have seen that coming.'"

"Funny."

"We should have seen this coming," he said.

"You did."

"No, I just said I did."

Barak rose from his sleep, calmly looked around, and then, perhaps assuming he was in a dream, closed his eyes and rested his forehead against the window.

"You'll go to the house every day, right?"

"Of course," my father said.

"And take the kids out. Give Julia a break every now and then."

"Of course, Jacob."

"Make sure Mom eats."

"You've traded places."

"A friend at the *Times* said it's nowhere near as bad as it sounds. Israel is intentionally making the situation appear worse than it is with the hopes of getting more American support. He said they're drawing it out to achieve the most propitious peace."

"The *Times* is an anti-Semitic pap smear."

"I'm just saying don't be scared."

As if the knowledge of what to do at that moment had been coiled into me at birth, I bowed. My father put his hands atop my head. I waited. As if the knowledge of what to do at that moment had been coiled into him at my birth, his palms began to close, taking my hair into the grip of his fingers, holding me in place. I waited for a blessing that would never come.

HOW TO PLAY SILENCE

First ask, "What kind of silence is this?" EMBARRASSED SILENCE is not ASHAMED SILENCE. WORDLESS SILENCE is not SPEECHLESS SILENCE, is not SILENCE OF SUBTLE WITHHOLDING. And so on. And on and on.

Then ask, "What kind of suicide or sacrifice is this?"

HOW TO PLAY RAISED VOICES

I've raised my voice to a human only twice in my entire life. The first time was when Julia confronted me with the texts and, pushed beyond my self-control, into my self, I shouted: "You are my enemy!" She didn't remember that she had given me that line. When she was in labor with Sam—her only natural childbirth—she traced a forty-hour spiral into deeper and more isolating pain, until, surrounded by the same four walls, we were in different rooms. The doula said something absurd (something that, at any other moment, Julia would have dismissed with a roll of her eyes), and I said something loving (something that, at any other moment, Julia would have teared up about and thanked me for), and Julia moaned like a nonfemale nonhuman, grabbed the bed rail like it was a roller-coaster safety bar, looked at me with eyes more satanic than in any red-pupilled photograph, and snarled, "You are my enemy!" I hadn't meant to quote her thirteen years later, and it didn't even occur to me that I'd done so until I wrote about it after. Like so much that happened during labor, Julia seemed to have no memory of it.

The second time I raised my voice at a human was also at Julia, many years later. I found it so much easier to give what wasn't asked for or owed. Maybe I learned that from Argus—the only way to get him to drop a fetched ball was to appear indifferent. Maybe Argus learned that from me. Once Julia and I were living separate lives, it was not only possible to push my inner life through our still-shared conduit, I longed to. Because she appeared indifferent to it—*appeared*, or *was*.

Julia and I hadn't spoken in a long time, but she was the person I wanted to talk to. I called, she answered, we shared, just like old times weren't. I said, "I guess I wanted proof." She said, "I'm the gentle soul you called, remember?" I said, "Remember how they say the world is uniquely open?" She asked, "What happened to you?" She wasn't accusing or challenging me. She said it with the indifference necessary for me to give everything.

I've raised my voice at a human only twice in my entire life. Both times at the same human. Put differently: I've known only one human in my life. Put differently: I've allowed only one human to know me.

In a sadness beyond anger, pain, and fear, I screamed at Julia: "Unfair! Unfair! Unfair!"

HOW TO PLAY THE DEATH OF LANGUAGE

In the synagogue of my youth—which I left when I went to college and rejoined when Julia became pregnant with Sam—there was a memorial wall with tiny bulbs lit next to the names of those who had died in the given week of the year. As a boy, I rearranged the plastic letters that formed the names into whatever words I could. My father used to tell me that there were no bad words, only bad usage. And then, when I became a father, I told my boys the same thing.

There were more than fourteen hundred congregants of fighting age. Of the sixty-two who went to fight in Israel, twenty-four died. Two ten-watt, candelabra-base, flame-tip bulbs for each name. Only 480 watts of light. Fewer than in my living room chandelier. No one touched those names. But one day they will be rearranged into words. Or so is the hope.

It feels like it's been centuries since I wandered that building. But I can remember the smells: the siddurim like withered flowers, the must of the basket of yarmulkes, the new-car smell of the ark. And I can remember the surfaces: where the broad strips of linen wallpaper met; the Braille-like plaques affixed to the armrests of every velvet chair, immortalizing the largesse of someone unlikely ever to sit there; the cold steel banister of the plush-carpeted stairs. I can remember the heat of those bulbs, and the roughness of the letters. As I sit at a desk filled with thousands of pages, continuing to comment on the commentary, I wonder how one should judge the usage of words made from the dead. And the living. From everyone living and dead.

HOW TO PLAY NO ONE

There were several hundred men in the waiting area. Several hundred Jewish men. We were circumcised men, men who shared Jewish genetic markers, men who hummed the same ancient melodies. How many times, as a child, was I told that it didn't matter whether or not I thought of myself as Jewish, the Germans thought of me as a Jew? In the holding area of that airport, perhaps for the first time in my life, I stopped wondering if I felt Jewish. Not because I had an answer, but because the question stopped mattering.

I saw a few people I knew: old friends, familiar faces from the synagogue, some public figures. I didn't see Gabe Perelman or Larry Moverman, but Glenn Mechling was there. We nodded at each other across the enormous room. There was little interacting. Some sat in silence, or talked on their cell phones—presumably to their families. There were outbursts of singing: "Yerushalayim Shel Zachav" . . . "Hatikva" . . . It was emotional, but what was the *it*? The camaraderie? The most extreme version of the recognition I felt with the deaf father at the convention? The shared devotion? The sudden awareness of history, how small and big it is, how impotent and omnipotent an individual is inside it? The fear?

I had written books and screenplays my entire adult life, but it was the first time I'd felt like a character inside one—that the scale of my tchotchke existence, the *drama* of living, finally befitted the privilege of being alive.

No, it was the second time. The first time was in the lion's den.

Tamir was right: my problems were small. I'd spent so much of my finite time on earth thinking small thoughts, feeling small feelings, walking under doors into unoccupied rooms. How many hours did I spend online, rewatching inane videos, scrutinizing listings for houses I would never buy, clicking over to check for hasty e-mails from people I didn't care about? How much of myself, how many words, feelings, and actions, had I forcefully contained? I'd angled myself away from myself, by a fraction of a degree, but after so many years, finding my way back to myself required a plane.

They were singing, and I knew the song, but not how to join them.

HOW TO PLAY THE ITCH OF HOPE

I always believed that all it would take to completely change my life would be a complete change of personhood.

HOW TO PLAY HOME

The completion of *Tales from the Odyssey* left Max bereft.

"Why?" he asked, spinning to face his pillow. "Why did it have to end?"

I rubbed his back, told him, "But you wouldn't want Odysseus wandering forever, would you?"

"Well, then why did he have to leave home at all?"

The next morning, I took him to the farmer's market with the hope of finding some consolation in baked goods. Every other Sunday, a mobile pet rescue stationed itself by the main entrance, and we'd often stop and admire the animals. Max was drawn that morning to a golden retriever named Stan. We'd never spoken about getting a dog, and I certainly hadn't intended to get a dog, and I don't even know if he wanted that particular dog, but I told him, "If you would like to take Stan home, we can."

Everyone but me bounded into the house. Julia was furious, but didn't show it until we were alone at the top of the stairs. She said, "*Again*, you've put me in the position of either having to go along with a bad idea or be the bad guy."

Downstairs, the boys were calling: "Stan! Here, Stan! Come on, now!"

I had asked the woman running the pet rescue how he got the name Stan—it struck me as an odd choice for a dog. She said the dogs were given retired names of Atlantic storms. With so many dogs moving through the facility, it made things easy simply to use a list.

"Sorry, a retired name of what?"

"You know how storms get names? There's something like a hundred that are cycled through. But if a storm is especially costly or deadly, they retire the name—to be sensitive. There will never be another Sandy."

Just as there will never be another Isaac.

We don't know the name of my grandfather's grandfather.

When my grandfather came to America, he changed his name from Blumenberg to Bloch.

My father was the first person in our family to have an "English name" and a "Hebrew name."

When I became a writer, I experimented with different versions of my name: various uses of initials, the insertion of my middle name, pseudonyms.

The farther we got from Europe, the more identities we had to choose between.

"No One tried to kill me! No One blinded me!"

It was Max's idea to rename Stan. I said it might confuse him. Max said, "But we need to make him ours."

HOW TO PLAY NO ONE

We were given some simple forms to fill out, and an announcement was made that we were to pass, single file, in front of a middle-aged man in a white lab coat. He gave each person a quick visual inspection and pointed toward one of about a dozen long lines, which began to roughly correspond to age. The resonance with the selections upon entering the concentration camps was so explicit and undeniable, it was hard to imagine it wasn't intentional.

When I reached the front of my line, a stocky woman, perhaps seventy, invited me to sit opposite her at a plastic folding table. She took my papers and started filling out a series of forms.

"Atah medaber ivrit?" she asked without looking up.

"Sorry?"

"Lo medaber ivrit," she said, checking a box.

"Sorry?"

"Jewish?"

"Of course."

"Recite the Sh'ma."

"Sh'ma Yisrael, Adonai—"

"Do you belong to a Jewish community?"

"Adas Israel."

"How often do you attend services?"

"Maybe twice a year, every other year?"

"What are the two occasions?"

"Rosh Hashanah and Yom Kippur."

"Any languages besides English?"

"A little Spanish."

"I'm sure that will be very useful. Health conditions?"

"No."

"No asthma? High blood pressure? Epilepsy?"

"No. I do have some eczema. At the back of my hairline."

"Have you tried coconut oil?" she asked, still not looking up.

"No."

"So try it. Military training or experience?"

"No."

"Have you ever fired a gun?"

"I've never *held* a gun."

She checked a number of boxes, apparently feeling no need to ask the next sequence of questions.

"Can you function without your glasses?"

"Function highly?"

She checked a box.

"Can you swim?"

"Without my glasses?"

"Do you know how to swim?"

"Of course."

"Have you ever been a competitive swimmer?"

"No."

"Do you have any experience with knot tying?"

"Doesn't everyone?"

She checked two boxes.

"Can you read a topographical map?"

"I suppose I know what I'm looking at, but I don't know if that qualifies as reading."

She checked a box.

"Do you have any experience with electrical engineering?"

"I once took a—"

"You cannot disarm a simple bomb."

"I mean, *how* simple?"

"You cannot disarm a simple bomb."

"I cannot."

"What's the longest you've ever gone without eating?"

"Yom Kippur, a while ago."

"What is your tolerance for pain?"

"I don't even know how one would answer that question."

"You answered the question," she said. "Have you ever been in shock?"

"Probably. In fact, yes. Often."

"Are you claustrophobic?"

"Hugely."

"What is the greatest load you can carry?"

"Physically?"

"Are you sensitive to extremes of heat or cold?"

"Is anyone not?"

"Allergic to medications?"

"I'm lactose intolerant, but I guess that's not really what you were asking."

"Morphine?"

"Morphine?"

"Do you know first aid?"

"I didn't answer about morphine."

"Are you allergic to morphine?"

"I have no idea."

She wrote something down, which I tried, without success, to decipher.

"I don't want not to get morphine if I need morphine."

"There are other forms of pain relief."

"Are they as good?"

"Do you know first aid?"

"Sort of."

"That will sort of be a comfort to someone sort of in need of first aid."

While perusing the paperwork I'd filled out in line, she said, "Emergency contact information . . ."

"It's there."

"Julia Bloch."

"Yes."

"She's who?"

"What?"

"You didn't fill in your relationship."

"Sure I did."

"So you used invisible ink on that one."

"She's my wife."

"Most wives prefer permanent marker."

"I must have—"

"You are an organ donor in America."

"I am."

"If you are killed in Israel, would you allow your organs to be used in Israel?"

"Yes," I said, allowing the *s* to skid for a hundred feet.

"Yes?"

"Yes, if I'm killed—"

"What is your blood type?"

"Blood type?"

"You have blood?"

"I do."

"What type? A? B? AB? O?"

"You're asking for *giving*, or *receiving*?"

Finally, for the first time since we started speaking, she looked me in the eye. "It's the same blood."

HOW TO PLAY SUICIDE GROWTH RINGS

For left-handedness, or twins, or red hair, to run in one's family—as all of those do in mine—there need to be multiple occurrences. For suicide to run in one's family, there needs to be only one.

I received my grandfather's death certificate from the Maryland Department of Records. I wanted to know that I knew what I already knew. The coroner's handwriting was as good as typeset, the opposite of a doctor's: *asphyxiation by hanging*. He killed himself at approximately ten in the morning. The certificate said that it was Mr. Kowalski, the next-door neighbor, who made the report. That my grandfather's name was Isaac Bloch. That he had been born in Poland. That he hanged himself with a belt wedged between his kitchen door and its frame.

But when I was imagining it in bed that night, I saw him outside, hanging by a rope from a tree. The grass in the shadow of his feet slowly died and powdered to a little patch of dirt in an otherwise wild, overgrown garden.

Later in the night, I imagined plants ascending to meet his feet, as if the earth were trying to atone for its gravity. I imagined palm fronds holding him up like hands, the rope slack.

Even later—I barely slept—I imagined walking with my grandfather through a redwood forest. His skin was blue and his fingernails were an inch long, but otherwise he looked like the man at whose kitchen table I used to eat black bread and cantaloupe, the man who, when told not to change into his bathing suit in public, asked, "Why not?" He stopped at a massive overturned tree and pointed at the rings.

"This, here, is my parents' wedding. It was an arranged marriage. It worked. And here," he said, pointing at a different ring, "is when Iser fell from a tree and broke his arm."

"Iser?"

"My brother. You were named for him."

"I thought I was named for someone named Yakov."

"No. We just told you that."

"How does Iser become Jacob?"

"Iser is short for Israel. After wrestling with Jacob through the night, the angel renamed him Israel."

"How old was he?"

"And here," he said, pointing at another ring, "is when I left home. With Benny. Everyone else stayed—my grandparents and parents, my other five brothers—and I wanted to stay, but Benny convinced me. He forced me. And here is when Benny and I got on different boats, one for America, one for Israel." He touched a ring, and let his long fingernail slide outward toward the bark as he spoke. "This, here, is when you were born. Here you were a boy. Here you got married. Here is Sam's birth, here is Max's, here is Benjy's. And here"—he touched his fingernail to the rim of the trunk, like a record needle—"is right now. And out here"—he pointed to a spot in the air, about an inch outside the trunk—"is when you'll die, and here"—he gestured at the area slightly nearer to the trunk—"is the rest of your life, and here"—he pointed to just outside the trunk—"is what happens next."

I understood, somehow, that the weight of his hanging body had pulled the tree over, making our history visible.

HOW TO PLAY SEVEN RINGS

I could never anticipate which religious rituals Julia would find beautiful and which misogynistic, morally repugnant, or simply foolish. So I was surprised when she wanted to walk the seven rings around me under the chuppah.

In our preparatory reading—her preparatory reading; I gave up fairly quickly—she learned that the rings echo the biblical story of Joshua leading the Israelites into Canaan. When they came to the walled city of Jericho, and the first battle they would have to fight on their way to the Promised Land, God instructed Joshua to march the Israelites around the walls seven times. As soon as they had completed the seventh ring, the walls came tumbling down, and the Israelites conquered the city.

"You hide your greatest secret behind a wall," she said, with a tone that suggested both irony and earnestness, "and I will surround you with love, and the wall will topple—"

"And you will have conquered me."

"We will have conquered ourselves."

"All I have to do is stand there?"

"Just stand there and topple."

"What's my greatest secret?"

"I don't know. We're only beginning."

It wasn't until we were ending that she knew.

HOW TO PLAY THE LAST WHOLLY HAPPY MOMENT

"Let's do something special," I suggested a month before Julia's fortieth birthday. "Something unlike us. A party. A blowout: band, ice cream truck, magician."

"A magician?"

"Or a flamenco dancer."

"No," she said. "That's the last thing I'd want."

"Even if it's last, it's still on the list."

She laughed and said, "It's sweet of you to think of that. But let's do something simple. A nice dinner at home."

"Come on. We'll make it fun."

"Fun for me would be a simple family dinner."

I tried a few times to persuade her, but she made clear, with increasing force, that she didn't want "a big deal."

"You're sure you're not protesting too much?"

"I'm not protesting at all. The thing I most want is to have a nice, quiet dinner with my family."

The boys and I made her breakfast in bed that morning: fresh waffle, kale-and-pear smoothie, huevos rancheros.

We whispered wishes to the elephant at the zoo (an old birthday ritual, origin unknown), collected leaves in Rock Creek Park for pressing into the Book of Years (another ritual), ate lunch at one of the outside tables of her favorite Greek restaurant in Dupont Circle. We went to the Phillips Collection, where Sam and Max feigned interest so earnestly and poorly, Julia was moved to tell them, "I know you love me. It's OK to be bored."

It was getting dark when we made it home, with half a dozen bags of groceries for dinner supplies. (I insisted that we not shop for any other meals, even though there were things we needed. "Today," I said, "will not be utilitarian.") I gave Sam the key, and the boys ran ahead into the house. Julia and I unloaded the bags on the island and started putting away the perishables. Our eyes met, and I saw that she was crying.

"What is it?" I asked.

"You're going to hate me if I tell you."

"I'm sure I won't."

"You'll be extremely annoyed."

"I'm pretty sure there's an annoyance moratorium on birthdays."

And then, really letting the tears come, she said, "I actually wanted a big deal."

I laughed.

"It's not funny."

"It *is* funny, Julia."

"It's not that I knew what I wanted and hid it from you. I wasn't trying to be disappointed."

"I know that."

"I meant what I said at the time. I really did. It wasn't until right now—not even when we entered the house, but right this second—that I realized I really wanted a big deal. I did. It's so stupid. What am I, eight?"

"You're forty."

"I am, aren't I? I'm a forty-year-old who doesn't know herself until it's too late. And to make matters worse, I'm dumping it on you, as if you could respond with anything other than guilt or hurt."

"Here," I said, handing her a box of orecchiette. "Put these away."

"That's as far as your sympathy can reach?"

"What happened to the annoyance moratorium?"

"That's a one-way street, and you know it."

"Put the pretentious pasta away."

"No," she said. "No. Today, I won't."

I laughed.

"It's not funny," she said, banging the counter.

"It's so funny," I said.

She grabbed the box, ripped off the top, and poured the pasta on the floor.

"I made a huge mess," she said, "and I don't even know why."

I told her, "Put the empty box away."

"The *box*?"

"Yes."

"Why?" she asked. "To create a depressing symbol?"

"No," I said, "because understanding oneself isn't a prerequisite for being understood."

She inhaled, understanding something she didn't yet understand, and opened the pantry door. Out spilled the boys, and the grandparents, and Mark and Jennifer, and David and Hannah, and Steve and Patty, and someone turned the music on, and it was Stevie Wonder, and someone released the balloons from the hall closet, and they jangled the chandelier, and Julia looked at me.

HOW TO PLAY EXISTENTIAL SHAME

The IKEA encounter with Maggie Silliman haunted me for years. She was the embodiment of my shame. I would often wake in the middle of the night and write letters to her. Each began the same way: "You were wrong. I am not a good man." If I could have been the embodiment of my shame, I might have been spared it. I might even have been good.

HOW TO PLAY UNBROKEN RINGS

For his first trick, the magician asked Julia to pull a card from an invisible deck.

"Look at it," he said, "but don't let me see it."

With a roll of her eyes, she obeyed.

"You know your card?"

She nodded and said, "Yeah. I know my card."

"Now please throw it across the room."

With an overdramatized windup, she hurled the invisible card. The gesture was beautiful to watch: the fakeness of it, the generosity of its spirit, how quick it was and how long it took, the movement of her ring through the air.

"Max. Your name is Max, right? Can you go fetch the card your mother just threw?"

"But it's invisible," he said, looking to his mother for help.

"Get it anyway," the magician said, and Julia nodded permission.

So Max happily waddled across the room.

"OK, got it!" he said.

"And could you please tell us what the card is."

Max looked to his mother and said, "But I can't see it."

"Tell us, anyway," the magician said.

"And I can't remember what the different kinds of cards are."

"Hearts, spades, clubs, and diamonds. Any number two through ten. Or joker, jack, queen, king, or ace."

"Right," Max said, and again looked to his mother, who again let him know it was OK. He examined the invisible card, held it right up to his squinting eyes. "It's a seven of diamonds."

The magician didn't have to ask Julia if that was her card, because she was crying. Nodding and crying.

We ate some cake, we cleared out the dining room and did some silly dancing, we used paper plates and disposable cutlery.

The magician stuck around for a while, doing close-up magic for whoever would pay attention.

"That was really great," I told him, patting him on the back, surprised and repelled by his skinniness. "Just perfect."

"I'm glad. Feel free to recommend me. It's how I get my jobs."

"I certainly will."

He did the classic linked-rings trick for me. I'd seen it countless times, but it was still a thrill.

"My dad was the magician at my fifth birthday," I told him. "He opened with that."

"So you know how it's done?"

"Broken rings."

He handed them to me. I must have spent five full minutes searching for what had to be there.

"What happens if the trick goes wrong?" I asked, not yet ready to return the rings.

"How would it go wrong?"

"Someone takes the wrong card, or lies to you, or the deck falls."

"I never perform a trick," he said. "I perform a process. There's no outcome I need."

I told that to Julia in bed that night: "There's no outcome he needs."

"Sounds Eastern."

"Definitely not Eastern European."

"No."

I turned off the bedside light.

"That first trick. Or *process*. Max really said your card?"

"I didn't actually pick one."

"No?"

"I wanted to, but I just couldn't bring myself to."

"So why did you cry?"

"Because Max still could."

HOW TO PLAY NO ONE

The night I came back from Islip, I went straight to the kids' rooms. It was three in the morning. Benjy was contorted into one of those almost inconceivably bizarre sleeping-child positions: his tush way up in the air, his legs rigid, the weight of his body driving his cheek into the pillow. He had sweated through his sheets and was snoring like a tiny human animal. I reached out my hand, but before I'd even touched him, his eyes sprang open: "I wasn't asleep."

"It's OK," I said, brushing his damp hair with my hand. "Close your eyes."

"I was awake."

"You were doing sleep-breathing."

"You're home."

"I am. I didn't go."

He smiled. His eyes closed too slowly for it to be voluntary, and he said, "Tell me."

"Tell you what?"

He opened his eyes, saw that I was still there, smiled once again, and said, "I don't know. Just tell me."

"I came home."

He closed his eyes and asked, "Did you win the war?"

"You're asleep."

He opened his eyes and said, "I'm only thinking about how you were in a war."

"I didn't go."

"Oh. That's good." He closed his eyes and said, "I know what it is."

"What what is?"

"The n-word."

"You do?"

"I googled it."

"Ah. OK."

He opened his eyes. And though he didn't smile this time, I could hear, in his full exhalation, that he was again relieved by my permanence.

"I'll never use it," he said. "Never."

"Good night, love."

"I'm not asleep."

"You're falling asleep."

His eyes closed. I kissed him. He smiled.

"Is it a *g* like *gun*?" he asked. "Or like *ginger*?"

"What's that?"

"The n-word. I don't know how you say it."

"But you're never going to say it."

"But I still want to know how."

"Why?"

"You aren't going to go away again, are you?"

"No," I said, because I didn't know what to say—to my child, or to myself.

HOW TO PLAY LOVE

Love is not a positive emotion. It is not a blessing, and it is not a curse. It is a blessing that is a curse, and it is also not that. LOVE OF ONE'S CHILDREN is not LOVE OF CHILDREN, is not LOVE OF ONE'S SPOUSE, is not LOVE OF ONE'S PARENTS, is not LOVE OF ONE'S EXTENDED FAMILY, is not LOVE OF THE IDEA OF FAMILY. LOVE OF JUDAISM is not LOVE OF JEWISHNESS, is not LOVE OF ISRAEL, is not LOVE OF GOD. LOVE OF WORK is not LOVE OF SELF. Not even LOVE OF SELF is LOVE OF SELF. The place where LOVE OF NATION, LOVE OF HOMELAND, and LOVE OF HOME meet is nowhere. LOVE OF DOGS is to LOVE OF ONE'S CHILD'S SLEEPING BODY as LOVE OF DOGS is to LOVE OF ONE'S DOG. LOVE OF THE PAST has as much in common with LOVE OF THE FUTURE as LOVE OF LOVE has with LOVE OF SADNESS—which is to say, everything. But then, LOVE OF SAYING EVERYTHING makes one untrustworthy.

Without love, you die. With love, you also die. Not all deaths are equal.

HOW TO PLAY ANGER

"You are my enemy!"

HOW TO PLAY FEAR OF DEATH

"Unfair! Unfair! Unfair!"

HOW TO PLAY THE INTERSECTION OF LOVE, ANGER,
AND FEAR OF DEATH

At my annual cleaning, the dentist spent an unusual amount of time looking in my mouth—not at my teeth, but deeper—his instruments of pain slowly tarnishing, untouched, on the tray. He asked if I'd been having a hard time swallowing.

"Why do you ask?"

"Just curious."

"I suppose a bit."

"For how long?"

"A couple of months?"

"Did you ever mention it to your doctor?"

He referred me to an oncologist at Johns Hopkins.

I was surprised by my instinct to call Julia. We hardly ever spoke anymore: she had long since remarried; the kids were masters of their own logistics, being adults; and as one gets older, there is less and less news to share, until the final piece, which is delivered by someone else. The dialogue in the show is virtually identical to what actually transpired, with one significant exception: in life, I didn't cry. I screamed: "Unfair! Unfair! Unfair!"

JACOB
It's me.

JULIA
I recognize your voice.

JACOB
It's been a long time.

JULIA
And your number comes up on my phone.

JACOB
As Jacob?

JULIA
As opposed to what?

JACOB
Listen—

JULIA
Is everything OK?

JACOB
I was at the dentist this morning—

JULIA
But I didn't make an appointment for you.

JACOB
I've become remarkably capable.

JULIA
Necessity is the ex-wife of capability.

JACOB
He saw a lump in my throat.

Julia starts crying. Each is surprised by her reaction to nothing (yet), and it goes on for longer than either would have imagined or thought bearable.

JULIA
You're dying?

JACOB
The *dentist*, Julia.

JULIA
You're telling me he saw a lump, and you're calling me.

JACOB
Both a lump and a phone call can be benign, you know.

JULIA
So now what?

JACOB
I have an appointment with an oncologist at Hopkins.

JULIA
Tell me everything.

JACOB
You know everything I know.

JULIA
Have you had any other symptoms? Stiffness in your neck? Difficulty swallowing?

JACOB
Did you go to med school since we last spoke?

JULIA
I'm googling while we talk.

JACOB
Yes, I've had stiffness in my neck. And yes, I've had difficulty swallowing. Now will you please give me your undivided attention?

JULIA
Is Lauren being supportive?

JACOB
You'd have to ask the man she's presently dating.

JULIA
I'm sorry to hear that.

JACOB
And you're the first person I've told.

JULIA
Do the boys know?

JACOB
I told you, you're the first—

JULIA
Right.

JACOB
I'm sorry to have laid this on you. I know I haven't been your responsibility for a long time.

JULIA
You were never my responsibility.
    (beat)
And you still *are* my responsibility.

JACOB
I won't tell the kids anything until there's something real to tell
them.

JULIA
Good. That's good.
   (beat)
How are you holding up?

JACOB
I'm fine. He's just a dentist.

JULIA
It's OK to be scared.

JACOB
If he were so smart, he'd be a dermatologist.

JULIA
Have you cried?

JACOB
On November 18, 1985, when Lawrence Taylor ended Joe Theis-
mann's career.

JULIA
Enough, Jacob.

JACOB
He's just a dentist.

JULIA
You know, I don't think I've ever seen you cry. Other than tears of
happiness when the boys were born. Is that possible?

JACOB
At my grandfather's funeral.

JULIA
That's true. You wailed.

JACOB
I wept.

JULIA
But remembering it as the exception proves—

JACOB
Nothing.

JULIA
All those repressed tears metastasized.

JACOB
Yes, that's exactly what the dentist thought the oncologist will think.

JULIA
Throat cancer.

JACOB
Who said anything about cancer?

JULIA
Throat malignancy.

JACOB
Thank you.

JULIA
Is it too soon to observe how poetic that is?

JACOB
Way too soon. I haven't even been diagnosed, much less gone through super-fun chemo and recovery only to learn that they didn't get it all.

JULIA
You'll finally have your baldness.

JACOB
I already do.

JULIA
Right.

JACOB
No, really. I went off Propecia. I look like Mr. Clean. Ask Benjy.

JULIA
You saw him recently?

JACOB
He came by on Christmas Eve with Chinese food.

JULIA
That's sweet. How did he look?

JACOB
Enormous. And old.

JULIA
I didn't even know you were on Propecia. But I guess I wouldn't know what pills you take anymore.

JACOB
I've actually been on it for a long time.

JULIA
How long?

JACOB
Around when Max was born?

JULIA
Our Max?

JACOB
I was embarrassed. I kept them with my cummerbund.

JULIA
That makes me so sad.

JACOB
Me, too.

JULIA
Why don't you just cry, Jacob?

JACOB
Sure thing.

JULIA
I'm serious.

JACOB
This isn't *Days of Our Lives*. This is *life*.

JULIA
You're afraid that letting anything out will leave you open to letting things in. I know you. But it's just the two of us. Just you and me on the phone.

JACOB
And God. And the NSA.

JULIA
Is this the person you want to be? Always just joking? Always concealing, distracting, hiding? Never fully yourself?

JACOB
You know, I was hunting for sympathy when I called.

JULIA
And you killed it without having to fire a shot. This is what real sympathy is.

JACOB
    (after a long beat)
No.

JULIA
No what?

JACOB
No, I'm not the person I want to be.

JULIA
Well, you're in good company.

JACOB
Before I called, I found myself asking—literally asking aloud, over and over—"Who's a gentle soul? Who's a gentle soul?"

JULIA
Why?

JACOB
I guess I wanted proof.

JULIA
Of the existence of gentleness?

JACOB
Gentleness for me.

JULIA
Jacob.

JACOB
I mean it. You have Daniel. The boys have their lives. I'm the kind

of person whose neighbors will have to notice the smell for anyone
to realize he's dead.

JULIA
Remember that poem? "Proof of Your existence? There is nothing
but"?

JACOB
God . . . I do. We bought that book at Shakespeare and Company.
Read it on the bank of the Seine with a baguette and cheese and
no knife. That was so happy. So long ago.

JULIA
Look around, Jacob. There is nothing but proof of how loved you
are. The boys idolize you. Your friends flock to you. I bet women—

JACOB
You? What about you?

JULIA
I'm the gentle soul you called, remember?

JACOB
I'm sorry.

JULIA
For what?

JACOB
We're in the Days of Awe right now.

JULIA
I know I know what that means, but I can't remember.

JACOB
The days between Rosh Hashanah and Yom Kippur. The world is
uniquely open. God's ears are, His eyes, His heart. People, too.

JULIA
You've become *some* Jew.

JACOB
I don't believe any of it, but I believe in it.
    (*beat*)
Anyway, it's during these ten days that we're supposed to ask our loved ones to forgive us for all of the wrongs we committed— "knowingly and unknowingly."
    (*beat*)
Julia—

JULIA
He's just a dentist.

JACOB
I am so sincerely sorry for any times that I knowingly or unknowingly wronged you.

JULIA
You didn't *wrong* me.

JACOB
I did.

JULIA
We made mistakes, both of us.

JACOB
The Hebrew word for *sin* translates to "missing the mark." I am sorry for the times that I sinned against you by small degrees, and I am sorry for the times that I sinned against you by running directly away from what I should have been running toward.

JULIA
There was another line in that book: "And everything that once was infinitely far and unsayable is now unsayable and right here in the room."

The silence is so complete, neither is sure if the connection has been lost.

JACOB
You opened the door, unknowingly. I closed it, unknowingly.

JULIA
What door?

JACOB
Sam's hand.

Julia starts to cry, quietly.

JULIA
I forgive you, Jacob. I do. For everything. All that we hid from each other, and all that we allowed between us. The pettiness. The holding in and holding on. The measuring. None of it matters anymore.

JACOB
None of it ever mattered.

JULIA
It did. But not as much as we thought it did.
    (*beat*)
And I hope that you will forgive me.

JACOB
I do.
    (*after a long beat*)
I'm sure you're right. It would be good if I could let my sadness out.

JULIA
Your anger.

JACOB
I'm not angry.

JULIA
But you are.

JACOB
I'm really not.

JULIA
What are you so angry about?

JACOB
Julia, I'm—

JULIA
What happened to you?

They are silent. But it's a different silence than the kind they'd known. Not the silence of just joking, concealing, distracting. Not the silence of walls, but the silence of creating a space to fill.

With each passing second—and the seconds are passing, two by two—more space is created. It takes the shape of the home they might have moved to had they decided to give it one more shot, to go deeply and unconditionally into the work of re-finding their happiness together. Jacob can feel the pull of the unoccupied space, the aching longing to be allowed into what is wide open to him.

He cries.

When was the last time he cried? When he put down Argus? When he awoke Max to tell him he hadn't gone to Israel, and Max said, "I knew you wouldn't go"? When he tried to encourage Benjy's budding interest in astronomy, and took him all the way to Marfa, where they got a tour of the observatory and held galaxies in their eyes like oceans in shells, and when that night they lay on their backs on the roof of the Airbnb cabin and Benjy asked, "Why are we whispering?" and Jacob said, "I hadn't even noticed that we were," and Benjy said, "When people look at stars, they tend to whisper. I wonder why"?

HOW TO PLAY LATE MEMORIES

My earliest memory is of my father handling a dead squirrel.

My last memory of the old house is leaving the key in the mailbox in an envelope with a stamp and no destination or return address.

My last memory of my mother is spoon-feeding her yogurt. I reflexively made the airplane sound, though I hadn't done that for fifteen years. I was too embarrassed to acknowledge it with an apology. She winked, I was sure.

My last memory of Argus is hearing his breathing deepen, and feeling his pulse slow, and then watching myself reflected in his eyes as they rolled back.

Despite the texts and e-mails that we have continued to send back and forth, my last memory of Tamir is from Islip. I told him, "Stay." He asked, "Then who would go?" And I said, "No one." And he asked, "Then what would save it?" And I said, "Nothing." "Just let it go?" he asked.

My last memory of my family before the earthquake is by the front door, my parents about to take Benjy for the night, Sam and Julia about to leave for Model UN. Benjy asked, "What if I don't miss you?" Of course he didn't know what was about to happen, but how could I remember it any way other than as prophetic?

My last memory of my father is dropping him and his girlfriend at Dulles for his bucket-list trip to the Warsaw Ghetto—his Cooperstown— and my saying, "Who'd have thought it? Taking a shiksa to the Reverse Diaspora Prom?" I always felt that he withheld his laughter from me, but that got a good one. He patted my cheek and said, "Life amazes." Of course he didn't know he wouldn't make it onto the plane, but how could I remember it any way other than as ironic?

My last memory of being married to Julia: the burnished handle of the snack drawer; the seam where the slabs of soapstone met; the Special Award for Bravery sticker on the underside of the island's overhang, given to Max for what no one knew was his last pulled tooth, a sticker Argus saw many times every day, and only Argus ever saw. Julia said: "It's way too late in the conversation for that."

HOW TO PLAY "WHAT IS YOUR NAME?"

Max asked to have a bar mitzvah. Even if it was the expression of something subterranean, even if it was some kind of hypersophisticated act of aggression, it still pleased Julia and me. The year of study went off without a hitch or complaint, the service was beautiful (Julia and I stood together at the ark, which felt good and right), the party was themeless and genuinely fun, and he banked enough savings bonds to buy something pretty great just as soon as they matured to their face value in twenty years, at which point twice as much would seem like half as much.

Max's portion was Vayishlach, in which Jacob—the last of the patriarchs—is assaulted by an unknown assailant in the middle of the night. Jacob wrestles him down and refuses to let go, demanding a blessing of him. The assailant—an angel, or God himself—asks, "What is your name?" As Jacob holds on to the man with all his strength, he answers, "Jacob." (*Jacob* means "heel-grabber"—he grabbed the heel of his older brother, Esau, as he was being born, wanting to be the first out.) Then the angel says, "Your name shall no longer be Jacob, but Israel—which means 'wrestles God.'"

From the bimah, with a poise far beyond his years or mine, Max said, "Jacob wrestled with God for the blessing. He wrestled with Esau for the blessing. He wrestled with Isaac for the blessing, with Laban for the blessing, and in each case he eventually prevailed. He wrestled because he recognized that the blessings were worth the struggle. He knew that you only get to keep what you refuse to let go of.

"*Israel*, the historical Jewish homeland, literally means 'wrestles God.' Not 'praises God,' or 'reveres God,' or 'loves God,' not even 'obeys God.' In fact, it is the *opposite* of 'obeys God.' Wrestling is not only our condition, it is our identity, our name."

That last sentence sounded a lot like Julia.

"But what *is* wrestling?"

That sounded like Dr. Silvers.

"There is Greco-Roman wrestling, WWF wrestling, arm wrestling, sumo wrestling, lucha libre wrestling, wrestling with ideas, wrestling with faith . . . They all have one thing in common: closeness."

And there I was, the intended recipient of his speech, sitting so close to my ex-wife that the fabric of our clothing touched, on a pew with children half of whose lives I was missing.

"You only get to keep what you refuse to let go of," Max said.

"A Jewish fist can do more than masturbate and hold a pen," my dad once said.

"To see your lifeline you have to let go," I pulled from a fortune cookie one Christmas.

Max kept getting smarter and smarter. Julia and I had always assumed that Sam was the brains of the bunch—that Max was the artist and Benjy would be perpetually adorable—but it was Max who took chess seriously (he placed third in the D.C.-area sixteen-and-unders), Max who elected to have a Mandarin tutor twice a week (while his brain was still "supple"), and Max who was accepted to Harvard after his junior year of high school. (Not until he chose to apply a year early did I realize that all that extra credit—those supplemental courses, that summer school—was a way to be away more, and get away sooner.)

"Closeness," he said, surveying the congregation. "It's easy to *be* close, but almost impossible to *stay* close. Think about friends. Think about hobbies. Even ideas. They're close to us—sometimes so close we think they are part of us—and then, at some point, they aren't close anymore. They go away. Only one thing can keep something close over time: holding it there. Grappling with it. Wrestling it to the ground, as Jacob did with the angel, and refusing to let go. What we don't wrestle we let go of. Love isn't the absence of struggle. Love *is* struggle."

That sounded like the person I wanted to be, but couldn't be. It sounded like Max.

HOW TO PLAY NO ONE

I heard the shutter before I saw the photographer. It was the first and only shot of my war.

"Hey," I said, stomping toward him. "What the hell are you doing?"

Why the hell was I so upset?

"I'm here for the *Times*," he said, showing me the press pass hanging from his neck.

"You're supposed to be here?"

"The consulate gave me authorization, if that's what you're asking."

"Well, I didn't give you authorization to take a picture of me."

"You want me to delete the photo?" he asked, neither assertive nor conciliatory.

"It's fine," I said, "but don't take any more."

"I don't want a problem. I'm happy to delete it."

"Keep it," I said. "But no more."

He walked off to take pictures of other groups. Some of them posed. Some were either unaware of his presence or unwilling to recognize it. My knee-jerk anger—if that's even what it was—surprised me. But harder to explain was my insistence that he keep the photo he'd taken but not take any more. What two ways was I trying to have it?

My mind wandered to all those years of school portraits: the licked palms wrestling cowlicks under the pretense of a loving stroke; letting the boys watch a cartoon while sliding them into handsome, uncomfortable clothes; clumsy efforts to subliminally communicate the value of a "natural" smile. The pictures always came out the same: a forced grin with unparted lips, eyes vacantly gazing into the haze—something from the Diane Arbus scrap pile. But I loved them. I loved the truth they conveyed: that kids aren't yet able to fake it. Or they aren't yet able to conceal their disingenuousness. They're wonderful smilers, the best; but they're the very worst fake smilers. The inability to fake a smile defines childhood. When Sam thanked me for his room in my new house, he became a man.

One year Benjy was genuinely disturbed by his school portrait, unwilling to believe that the child in the picture was either him or not him. Max took it upon himself to prod Benjy's distress, explaining to him that everyone has a living self and a dead self existing in parallel—"kind of like your own ghost"—and that the only time we ever get to see our dead selves is in school portraits. Soon enough, Benjy was crying. In an effort to calm him, I took out my bar mitzvah album. We'd already looked through several dozen photos when Benjy said, "But I thought Sam's bar mitzvah was in the future."

At my bar mitzvah party, relatives, friends of my parents, and complete strangers handed me envelopes with savings bonds. When my suit's jacket pockets started to strain, I'd give the envelopes to my mother, who put them in the purse under her chair. My father and I tabulated the "righteous plunder" at the kitchen table that night. I can't remember the figure, but I remember that it was evenly divisible by eighteen.

I remember the albumin archipelago on the salmon. I remember how the singer smudged *ve-nismecha* in "Hava Nagila," like a kid singing the alphabet, believing that *l-m-n-o* is one letter. I remember being lifted in the chair, high above the Jewish masses, the coronation of the One-Eyed

Man. Back on the parquet, my father told me to go spend a few minutes with my grandfather. I venerated him, as I was taught to, but it was never not a chore.

"Hi, Grandpa," I said, offering the top of my head for his kiss.

"I put some money into your college account," he said, patting the empty chair beside him.

"Thank you."

"Did Dad tell you how much?"

"No."

He looked to both sides, beckoned my ear to his lips, and whispered, "One thousand four hundred forty dollars."

"Wow," I said, reestablishing a comfortable distance. I had no idea if that many dollars justified that presentation, but I knew what was expected of me: "That's so incredibly generous. Thank you."

"But also this," he said, straining to get a grocery bag from the ground. He placed it on the table and removed something wrapped in a napkin. I assumed it was a roll—he often stashed rolls in napkins in bags—but then I felt its weight. "Go on," he said. Inside was a camera, a Leica.

"Thank you," I said, thinking the gift was a camera.

"Benny and I went back after the war, in 1946. We thought maybe our family had found a way to survive. At least someone. But there was no one. A neighbor, one of my father's friends, saw us and brought us to his house. He had kept some of our things, in case we ever came back. He told us that even though the war was over, it wasn't safe, and that we had to go. So we went. I only took a few things, and this was one of them."

"Thank you."

"I sewed money and photographs into the lining of the jacket I wore on the boat. I was so worried that someone would try to steal my things. I promised myself I wouldn't take it off, but it was so hot, too hot. I slept with it in my arms, and one morning when I woke up, my suitcase was still at my side, but the jacket was gone. That's why I don't blame the person who took it. If he'd been a thief, he would have taken the suitcase. He was just cold."

"But you said it was hot."

"It was hot for me." He rested his finger on the shutter release as if it were the trigger of a land mine. "I have only one picture from Europe. It's of me. It was marking my place in my diary in my suitcase. The pictures of my brothers and parents were sewn into that jacket. Gone. But this is the camera that took them."

"Where's your diary?"

"I let it go."

What would I have seen in those lost pictures? What would I have seen in the diary? Benjy didn't recognize himself in his school portrait, but what did I see when I looked at it? And what did I see when I looked at the sonogram of Sam? An idea? A human? *My* human? Myself? An idea of myself? I had to believe in him, and I did. I never stopped believing in him, only in myself.

In his bar mitzvah speech, Sam said, "We didn't ask for a nuclear weapon, and didn't want a nuclear weapon, and nuclear weapons are, in pretty much every way, horrible. But there's a reason people have them, and it's to never have to use them."

Billie shouted something I didn't understand, but I understood the flicker of happiness in Sam's eyes. The tension in the room redistributed itself across paper plates and plastic cups; Sam's speech divided and re-divided into small talk. I brought him some food and told him, "You're so much better than I was at your age. Or am now."

"It's not a competition," he said.

"No, it's progress. Come with me for a second."

"Where?"

"What do you mean, where? Mount Moriah, of course."

I led him upstairs, to my dresser, and took the Leica from the bottom drawer.

"This was your great-grandpa's. He brought it over from Europe. He gave it to me on my bar mitzvah and told me that he had no pictures of his brothers or parents, but that this camera had taken pictures of them. I know he wanted you to have it."

"He told you that?"

"No. But I know that—"

"So *you're* the one who wants me to have it."

Who was leading whom?

"I am," I said.

He held it in his hands, turned it around a few times. "Does it work?"

"Gosh, I don't know. I'm not sure that's the point."

He said, "Shouldn't it be?"

Sam had the Leica refurbished; he brought it into the world and it brought him out of Other Life.

He studied philosophy in college, but only in college.

He left the Leica on a train in Peru on his honeymoon with his first wife.

At thirty-eight, he became the youngest judge ever appointed to the Court of Appeals for the D.C. circuit.

The boys took me to Great Wall Szechuan House for my sixty-fifth birthday. Sam raised his bottle of Tsingtao and gave a beautiful toast, ending with "Dad, you're always looking." I didn't know whether he meant *searching* or *seeing*.

Tamir was sitting on the terminal's floor, his back against the wall, his eyes on the phone in his hands. I went and sat beside him.

"I'm having second thoughts," I said.

He smiled, nodded.

"Tamir?"

He nodded again.

"Can you stop texting for a second and listen?"

"I'm not texting," he said, and turned his phone to face me: a grid of thumbnails of family photos.

"I'm having second thoughts."

"Only second?"

"Could you talk this through with me?"

"What is there to talk through?"

"You're returning to your family," I said. "I would be leaving mine."

"Would be?"

"Don't do that. I'm asking for your help."

"I don't think you are. I think you're asking for forgiveness."

"For what? I haven't even done anything."

"Every thought after the first thought will lead you back to Newark Street."

"That's not necessarily true."

"Not necessarily?"

"I'm here. I said goodbye to my children."

"You don't owe me an apology," he said. "It's not your country."

"Maybe I've been wrong about that."

"Apparently you were right."

"And like you said, even if it isn't my home, it's yours."

"Who are you, Jacob?"

For three consecutive years, Max's eyes were closed in his school portrait. The first time, it was a small disappointment, but mostly funny.

The second year, it was harder to excuse as an accident. We talked about why such photos are nice to have, how much his grandparents and great-grandfather cherished them, how it was a waste of money to spoil them on purpose. The morning of picture day that third year, we asked Max to look us in the eye and promise to keep his eyes open. "I'll try," he said, his eyes blinking wildly, as if to flush out a fly. "Don't try," Julia said, "do it." When the photos came back, all three boys had closed their eyes. But I've never seen more genuine smiles.

"Maybe this is who I am," I said to Tamir.

"You say that as if you couldn't choose to be who you wanted to be."

"Maybe I choose this."

"Maybe?"

"I don't know what I should do, and I'm asking you to talk this through with me."

"So let's talk it through. Who are you?"

"What?"

"You said, 'Maybe this is who I am.' So who, maybe, are you?"

"Come on, Tamir."

"What? I'm asking you to explain what you meant. Who are you?"

"It's not the kind of thing that can be articulated like that."

"Try. Who are you?"

"OK, never mind. I'm sorry I came over here."

"Who are you, Jacob?"

"Who are *you*, Tamir?"

"I am someone who goes home, no matter how difficult."

"Well then, you took the words out of my mouth."

"Maybe. But not out of your heart. Wherever you go, you won't be going home."

When my mother first got sick, she mentioned that my father visited Isaac's grave once a month. When I asked him about it, he deflected, as if I'd confronted him about a gambling addiction.

"Penance for burying him in America," he said.

"What do you do there?"

"Just stand around like a jerk."

"Can I go with you next time?" I asked my father; I told Tamir, "Stay."

"Then who would go?" Tamir asked.

"No one."

"Then what would save it?"

"Nothing."

"Just let it go?"

"Yes."

I was right: my father cleaned the site of twigs, leaves, and weeds; he wiped down the gravestone with a wet rag he'd brought in a ziplock in his jacket pocket; and from another ziplock he removed photos.

"The boys," he said, turning them toward me for a moment and then laying them on the ground, facedown, above his father's eyes.

I'd wanted to make an eruv around the suicides and carry the shame away from them, but how would I bear my own shame? How, coming home from Islip, would I face Julia and the boys?

"It feels like we were burying him five minutes ago," I said to my father; I said to Tamir, "It feels like we were picking you up at the airport five minutes ago."

My father said, "It feels like everything was five minutes ago."

Tamir brought his lips to my ear and whispered, "You are innocent."

"What?" I whispered, as if I were looking at stars.

"You are innocent."

"Thank you."

He pulled back and said, "No, like, too trusting. Too childlike."

"What, *gullible*?"

"I don't know that word."

"What are you trying to say?"

"Of course Steven Spielberg wasn't in the men's room."

"You made up that whole thing?"

"I did."

"You knew who he was?"

"You think we don't have electricity in Israel?"

"You're very good," I said.

"I see you," my grandfather would say from the other side of the glass.

"You're very innocent," Tamir said.

"See you," my grandfather would say.

"And yet we've never been older," my father said, and then chanted the Mourner's Kaddish.

HOW TO PLAY THE LAST THING ONE SEES BEFORE COMMITTING SUICIDE

Six closed eyes, three genuine smiles.

HOW TO PLAY THE LAST THING ONE SEES BEFORE BEING REINCARNATED

The EMERGENCY exit from MacArthur Airport's terminal; the EMERGENCY entrance to the world.

HOW TO PLAY SUICIDE

Unbuckle your belt. Slide it back out the five loops of your pants. Wrap it around your throat and tighten, buckle on the back of your neck. Place the other end of the belt over the door. Close the door, so that the belt is held firmly in place between the top of the door and the doorframe. Look at the refrigerator. Allow full body weight to fall. Eight closed eyes.

HOW TO PLAY REINCARNATION

A few months after moving out, on yet another day without a letter in the mailbox on my bedroom door, I was emptying the kids' hampers and found a poop in a pair of Max's underwear. He was eleven. I got several such dispatches in the coming weeks. Sometimes I was able to turn the underwear inside out over the toilet, scrub at any stain that was left, and throw them into the wash. Usually they weren't salvageable.

I didn't mention it to Dr. Silvers, for the same reason I didn't mention my persistent throat pain to my actual doctor: I suspected it was a symptom of something that I didn't want revealed. I didn't mention it to Julia, because I didn't want to hear that Max never did it at her house. And I didn't mention it to Max, because that was something I could spare him. Spare us.

As a child, I used to leave bowel movements on the lilac carpet of my grandfather's bathroom, a few inches from the toilet seat. It was on purpose. Why did I do such a thing? Why did Max?

I desperately wanted a dog, as a boy, but was told they were dirty. As a boy, I was told to wash my hands before going to the bathroom, because the world was dirty. But I was also told to wash my hands after.

My grandfather mentioned the poops on his floor only once. He smiled, covered the side of my head with his enormous hand, and said, "It's OK. It's great." Why would he say such a thing?

Max never mentioned the poops in his hamper, although he came upon me hanging a pair of his hand-washed underwear on the drying rack and said, "Argus died the day we started coming to this house. Do you think this ever would have felt like home to him?"

HOW TO PLAY MATTERS OF DEATH AND REBIRTH

Never speak about them.

HOW TO PLAY BELIEF

At Julia's second sonogram, we saw Sam's arms and legs. (Although he wasn't "Sam" yet, but "the peanut.") So began the exodus from idea to thing. What you think about all the time, but can't—without aids—see, hear, smell, taste, or touch has to be believed in. Only a few weeks later, when Julia was able to feel the peanut's presence and movements, it no longer *only* needed to be believed in, because it could also be *known*. As the months progressed—it turned, kicked, hiccupped—we knew more and more and had to believe less. And then Sam came, and belief fell away—it wasn't necessary anymore.

But it didn't fall away completely. There was some residue. And the inexplicable, unreasonable, illogical emotions and behavior of parents can be explained, or partially explained, by having had to believe for the better part of a year. Parents don't have the luxury of being reasonable, not any more than a religious person does. What can make religious people and parents so utterly insufferable is also what makes religion and parenthood so utterly beautiful: the all-or-nothing wager. The faith.

I watched Sam being born through the viewfinder of a video camera. When the doctor handed him to me, I put the camera on the bed and forgot about it until the nurse came to take him for measuring, or warming, or whatever utterly necessary thing they do with newborns that justifies the teaching of that most important life lesson: everyone, even your parents, will let you go.

But we had twenty minutes with him, so we have a twenty-minute video of the view of the dark window, with the soundtrack of new life—

Sam's new life, ours. I told Sam how beautiful he was. I told Julia how beautiful Sam was. I told her how beautiful she was. All of it was understatement, all of it imprecise—I used that same inadequate word to try to convey three entirely different, essential meanings: *beautiful, beautiful, beautiful*.

You can hear crying—everyone's.

You can hear laughter—Julia's and mine.

You can hear Julia calling me "Dad" for the first time. You can hear me whispering blessings to Sam, prayers: *be healthy, be happy, know peace*. I said it over and over—*be healthy, be happy, know peace*. It wasn't the kind of thing I would say, and I hadn't intended to say it; the words were drawn from some well far deeper than my life, and the hands raising the bucket weren't my own. The last thing you can hear on the video, as the nurse taps on the door, is me saying to Julia, "Before we know it, he'll be burying us."

"Jacob . . ."

"OK, so we'll be at his wedding."

"Jacob!"

"His bar mitzvah?"

"Can't we ease into it?"

"Into what?"

"The giving away."

I was wrong about almost everything. But I was right about the speed of the losing. Some of the moments were interminably long—the first cruel night of sleep training; cruelly (it felt) peeling him off a leg on the first day of school; pinning him down while the doctor who wasn't stitching his hand back together told me, "This is not a time to be his friend"—but the years passed so quickly I had to search videos and photo albums for proof of our shared life. It happened. It must have. We did all that living. And yet it required evidence, or belief.

I told Julia, the night after Sam's injury, that it was too much love for happiness. I loved my boy beyond my capacity to love, but I didn't love the love. Because it was overwhelming. Because it was necessarily cruel. Because it couldn't fit into my body, and so deformed itself into a kind of agonizing hypervigilance that complicated what should have been the most uncomplicated of things—nurturing and play. Because it was too much love for happiness. I was right about that, too.

Carrying Sam into the house for the first time, I implored myself to remember every feeling and detail. One day I would need to recall what the garden looked like when my first child first saw it. I would need to know the sound of the car seat's latch disengaging. My life would depend on my ability to revisit my life—there would come a day when I would trade a year of what remained to hold my babies for an hour. I was right about that, too, without even knowing that Julia and I would one day divorce.

I *did* remember. I remembered all of it: the drop of dried blood on the gauze around the circumcision wound; the smell of the back of his neck; how to collapse an umbrella stroller with one hand; holding his ankles above his head with one hand while wiping the insides of his thighs; the viscosity of A&D ointment; the eeriness of frozen breast milk; the static of a baby monitor set to the wrong channel; the economy of diaper bags; the transparency of new eyelids; how Sam's hands lurched upward, like those of his falling-monkey ancestors, whenever he was placed on his back; the torturing irregularity of his breathing; my own inability to forgive myself for the moments I looked away and something utterly inconsequential happened, but happened. It happened. All of it. And yet it made a believer out of me.

HOW TO PLAY TOO MUCH LOVE

Whisper into an ear, listen for an echo.

HOW TO PLAY PRAYER

Whisper into an ear, don't listen for an echo.

HOW TO PLAY NO ONE

The night I came home from Islip was the last night I spent in bed with Julia. She shifted when I got under the covers. She mumbled, "That was a short war."

I said, "I just kissed the kids."

She asked, "Did we win?"

I said, "As it turns out, there is no *we*."

She asked, "Did I win?"

"Win?"

She turned onto her side and said, "Survive."

HOW TO PLAY "HERE I AM"

A clause near the end of our legal divorce agreement stated that should either of us have more children, the children we had together would be treated "no less favorably" financially, either in life or in our wills. Despite all the longer thorns, and there were many, this one dug into Julia. But rather than acknowledge what at the time I assumed was the source of her distress—that because of our ages, having more children was realistic only for me—she attached herself to the issue that wasn't even there.

"I would never, in a million years, remarry," she told the mediator.

"This doesn't concern remarriage, but rather having children."

"If I were to have more children, which I will not, it would be in the context of a marriage, which is not going to happen."

"Life is long," he said.

"And the universe is even bigger, but we don't seem to be getting a lot of visits from intelligent life."

"That's only because we're not in the Jewish Home yet," I said, trying at once to calm her and to create a bit of innocent camaraderie with the mediator, who shot me a confused look.

"And it's not long," Julia said. "If life were long, I wouldn't be halfway through it."

"We aren't halfway through it," I said.

"*You* aren't, because you're a man."

"Women live longer than men."

"Only technically."

As ever, the mediator wouldn't take the bait. He cleared his throat, as if swinging a machete to clear a path through our overgrown history, and said, "This clause, which I should say is entirely standard for agreements like yours, won't affect you in the event that you don't have any more children. It merely protects you and your children if Jacob does."

"I don't want it in there," she said.

"Can we move on to something genuinely contentious?" I suggested.

"No," she said. "I don't want it in there."

"Even if that means forfeiting your legal protection?" the mediator asked.

"I trust Jacob not to treat other children more favorably than ours."

"Life is long," I said, winking at the mediator without moving an eyelid.

"Is that some kind of joke?" she asked.

"Obviously."

The mediator cleared his throat again and drew a line through the clause.

Julia wouldn't let it go, not even after we'd removed what wasn't there to begin with. In the middle of a discussion of something entirely unrelated—how to handle Thanksgiving, Halloween, and birthdays; whether it was necessary to legally forbid the presence of a Christmas tree in either's home—she might say, "Divorce gets an unfair rap; it was marriage that did this." Such out-of-context statements became part of the routine—at once impossible to anticipate and unsurprising. The mediator showed an almost autistic patience for her Tourettic eruptions, until one afternoon, when splitting the hairs of medical decision-making in the event that one parent couldn't be reached, she said, "I will literally die before I remarry," and, without clearing his throat or missing a beat, he asked, "Do you want me to put in some language legally codifying that?"

She started dating Daniel about three years after the divorce. To my knowledge, which was greatly limited by the kindness of kids who were trying to protect me, she didn't date very much before him. She seemed to relish the quiet and aloneness, just as she'd always said, and I'd never believed, she would. Her architecture practice flowered: two of her houses were built (one in Bethesda, one on the shore), and she got a commission to convert a grand Dupont Circle mansion into a museum showcasing the contemporary art collection of a local supermarket oligarch. Benjy—who was no less kind than his brothers, but far less psychologically sophisticated—would increasingly mention Daniel, usually in the context of his ability to edit movies on his laptop. That humble skill, which could be learned in an afternoon by someone willing to devote an afternoon to learning it, dramatically changed Benjy's life. All the "babyish" movies he had been making on the waterproof digital camera I got him two Hanukkahs before were suddenly brought to life as fully realized "adult films." (I never suggested that the camera should stay at my house, and we never corrected his terminology.) Once, when I was dropping the boys back at Julia's after a particularly fun weekend of adventures I'd spent the previous two weeks planning, Benjy grabbed at my leg and said, "You have to go?" I told him I did, but that he was going to have a great time and we'd see each other again in just a couple of days. He turned to Julia and asked, "Is Daniel here?" "He's at a meeting," she said, "but he'll be back any minute." "Aw, *another* meeting? I wanna make an adult film." When my car rounded the corner, I saw a man, about my age, in clothing I might wear, sitting on a bench, no reading material, no purpose but to wait.

I knew he went on the safari with them.

I knew he took Max to Wizards games.

At some point he moved in. I don't know when; it was never presented to me as news.

"What does Daniel do?" I asked the boys one night over Indian. We ate out a lot in those days, because it was hard for me to find the necessary time to grocery shop and cook, but more because I was obsessed with proving to them that we could still have "fun." And eating out is fun. Until someone asks, "Where are we having dinner tonight?" At which point it begins to feel depressing.

"He's a scientist," Sam said.

"But not a Nobel Prize winner or anything," Max said. "Just a scientist."

"What kind of scientist?"

"Dunno," Sam and Max said at the same time, but no one said "Jinx."

"He's an astrophysicist," Benjy said. And then: "Are you sad?"

"That he's an astrophysicist?"

"Yeah."

Julia asked a few times if I would go out for a drink with him, get to know him. She said it would mean a lot to her, and to Daniel, and that it could only be good for the boys. I told her, "Of course." I told her, "That sounds great." And I believed myself as I said it. But it never happened.

As we were saying goodbye after one of Max's teacher conferences, she told me that she and Daniel were going to get married.

"Does this mean you're dead?"

"Excuse me?"

"You would sooner die than remarry."

She laughed. "No, not dead. Reincarnated."

"As yourself?"

"As myself plus time."

"Myself plus time is my father."

She laughed again. Was her laugh spontaneous or generous? "The nice thing about reincarnation is that life becomes a process rather than an event."

"Wait, you're serious?"

"Just stuff from yoga."

"Well, it flies in the face of stuff from science."

"As I was saying. Life becomes a process rather than an event. Like that thing the magician told you, about tricks and outcomes. You don't need to achieve enlightenment, only move yourself closer to it. Only become a bit more accepting."

"Most things shouldn't be accepted."

"Accepting of the world—"

"Yes, I live in the world."

"Of yourself."

"That's more complicated."

"One life is too much pressure."

"So is the Marianas Trench, but such is reality. And by the way, what was all that shit about Max being too conscientious?"

"Staying in at recess to go over his homework?"

"He's diligent."

"He wants to control what is possible to control."

"Stuff from yoga?"

"I actually got myself a Dr. Silvers."

Why did that trigger my jealousy? Because my feelings about her marriage were too extreme to be felt directly?

"Well," I said, "I believe in a lot of things. But at the very top of the list of things I don't believe in is reincarnation."

"You're constantly coming back, Jacob. Just always as yourself."

I didn't ask if the kids knew before me, and if so, for how long. She didn't tell me when it was going to happen, or if I was going to be invited.

I asked, "Does this mean I'm going to be treated less favorably?" She laughed. I hugged her, told her how happy I was for her, and went home and ordered a video game system, as we'd always agreed we wouldn't.

The wedding was three months later, and I was invited, and the kids did know before me, but only by a day. I told them not to mention the video game system to her, and that was the actual missing of the mark.

I can't help but compare it to our wedding. There were fewer people, but many of the same people. What did they think when they saw me?

Those who had the guts to approach either pretended there was nothing remotely awkward going on, that we were simply making small talk at the wedding of a mutual friend, or they put their hands on my shoulder.

Julia and I were always good at catching eyes, even after the divorce. We just had a way of finding each other. It was a joke between us. "How will I find you in the theater?" "By being you." But it didn't happen once all afternoon. She was preoccupied, but she must also have been keeping track of where I was. I thought about slipping out at various points, but that was not to be done.

The boys gave a charming speech together.

I asked for red.

Daniel spoke thoughtfully, and lovingly. He thanked me for being there, for welcoming him. I nodded, I smiled. He moved on.

I asked for red.

I remembered my mother's speech at my wedding: "In sickness and in sickness. That is what I wish for you. Don't seek or expect miracles. There are no miracles. Not anymore. And there are no cures for the hurt that hurts most. There is only the medicine of believing each other's pain, and being present for it." Who will believe my pain? Who will be present for it?

I watched the horah from my table, watched the boys lift their mother in the chair. She was laughing so hard, and I was sure that with her up at that vantage we would catch eyes, but we didn't.

A salad was placed in front of me.

Julia and Daniel went from table to table to make sure they said hello to every guest, and for pictures. I saw it approaching, like the wave at a Nats game, and there was nothing to do but participate.

I stood at the margin. The photographer said, "Say *mocha*," which I did not. He took it three times to be sure. Julia whispered to Daniel, gave him a kiss. He walked off, and she took the seat beside me.

"I'm glad you came."

"Of course."

"Not of course. It was a choice you made, and I know it's not uncomplicated."

"I'm glad you wanted me here."

"Are you OK?" she asked.

"Very much so."

"OK."

I looked around the room: the doomed flowers, sweating water glasses, lipstick in purses left on chairs, guitars becoming detuned against speakers, knives that had attended thousands of unions.

"You want to hear something sad?" I said. "I always thought I was the happy one. The happier one, I should say. I never thought of myself as happy."

"You want to hear something even sadder? I thought I was the unhappy one."

"I guess we were both wrong."

"No," she said, "we were both right. But only in the context of our marriage."

I put my hands on my knees, as if to further ground myself.

"Were you there when my dad said that thing? 'Without context, we'd all be monsters'?"

"I don't think so. Or I don't remember it."

"Our context made monsters of us."

"No, not monsters," she said. "We were good, and we raised three amazing kids."

"And now you're happy, and I'm still me."

"Life is long," she said, trusting me to remember.

"The universe is bigger," I said, proving myself.

Sea bass was placed in front of me.

I picked up my fork, so as to touch something, and said, "Can I ask you a question?"

"Sure."

"What do you tell people when they ask why we got divorced?"

"It's been a long time since anyone has."

"What did you used to tell them?"

"That we realized we were just really good friends, good co-parents."

"Aren't those reasons not to get divorced?"

She smiled and said, "I had a hard time explaining it."

"Me, too. I always sounded like I was hiding something. Or guilty about something. Or just fickle."

"It's not really anyone else's business."

"What do you tell yourself?"

"It's been a long time since I asked myself."

"What did you used to tell yourself?"

She picked up my spoon and said, "We got divorced because that's what we did. It's not a tautology."

While the waiters were bringing dinner to the final tables, the first tables were being brought dessert.

"And the boys?" I asked. "How did you explain it to them?"

"They never really asked me. Sometimes they'd trace the outline, but they'd never enter. With you?"

"Never once. Isn't that odd?"

"No," she said, a bride in her dress. "It's not."

I looked at my boys being silly children on the dance floor and said, "Why did we put them in the position of having to ask?"

"Our love for them got in the way of being good parents."

I ran my finger around the rim of my glass, but no music came.

"I'd be a much better father if I could do it again."

"You can," she said.

"I'm not going to have any more kids."

"I know."

"And I don't have a time machine."

"I know."

"And I don't believe in reincarnation."

"I know."

"Think we could have made it?" I asked. "If we'd tried harder? Gone back into things?"

"Made what?"

"Life."

"We made three lives," she said.

"Could we have made one?"

"Is that the question?"

"Why not?"

"*Making it*. Not failing. There are more ambitious things to do with life."

"Are there?"

"I hope so."

On the drive to the party, I'd listened to a podcast about asteroids, and how unprepared we are for the possibility of one heading toward us. The physicist being interviewed explained why none of the possible contingencies would work: nuking it would just turn a cosmic cannonball into cosmic buckshot (and the debris would likely re-form in a few hours due to gravity); robotic landers could deflect the asteroid with mounted thrusters, if such things existed, which they don't and won't; similarly implausible would be sending up an enormous spacecraft as a "gravity tractor," using its own mass to pull the asteroid away from Earth. "So what *would* we do?" the host asked. "Probably nuke it," the physicist said. "But you said it would only break it into lots of asteroids that would hit us." "That's right." "So it wouldn't work." "Almost certainly not," the physicist said, "but it would be our best hope."

Our best hope.

The expression didn't awaken anything in me at the time. It took Julia's *hope* attaching itself to the other terminal of my mind to jump-start my sadness.

"Remember when I smashed the lightbulb? At our wedding?"

"Are you really asking me that?"

"Did you like that moment?"

"That's a funny question," she said. "But yes, I did."

"Me, too."

"I don't even know what it's supposed to symbolize."

"I'm glad you asked."

"I knew you would be."

"So, some people think it's to remind us of all the destruction that was necessary to bring us to the moment of our greatest happiness. Some people think it's a kind of prayer: let us be happy until the shards of this lightbulb reassemble. Some people think it's a symbol of fragility. But the interpretation I've never heard is the most straightforward one: this is what we're like. We are broken individuals, committing to what will be a broken union in a broken world."

"It's less inspiring your way."

It's not, I thought. *It's more inspiring.*

I said, "There is nothing more whole than a broken heart."

"Silvers?"

"In fact, the Kotzker Rebbe."

"Listen to you."

"I've been studying with the rabbi who did my grandfather's funeral."

"Curiosity converted the cat."

"Meowzel tov."

How I loved her laugh.

I looked at Julia, and in that moment I knew we never could have made it. But I also knew that she had been my best hope.

"Isn't it strange?" I said. "We had sixteen years together. They felt like everything when we were in them, but as time passes they will account for less and less of our lives. All of that everything was just a . . . what? A chapter?"

"That's not how I think about it."

She tucked her hair behind her ear, as I'd seen her do tens of thousands of times.

I asked, "Why are you crying?"

"Why am I crying? Why aren't *you* crying? This is *life*. I'm crying because this is my life."

Just as the sound of the scooper going into Argus's dog food used to bring him running from wherever in the house he was, the boys seemed almost telepathically drawn to their mother's tears.

"Why's everyone crying?" Sam asked. "Did someone win a gold medal?"

"Are you sad?" Benjy asked me.

"You don't have to worry about me," I told him.

"It's OK," Julia said. "Let it be OK."

There was nothing more painful than being the center of attention at my wife's wedding, save for continuing to think of her as my wife.

"Overjoyed?" Max asked, handing Benjy the maraschino cherry from his Shirley Temple.

"No."

"Flabbergasted? Cattywampussed? Diaphanous?"

I laughed.

"So, what?" Sam asked.

What? What was the feeling? My feeling?

"Remember when we talked about absolute value? For physics, maybe?"

"Math."

"And do you remember what it is?"

"Distance from zero."

"I have no idea what you're talking about," Benjy said.

Julia pulled him onto her lap and said, "Neither do I."

I said, "Sometimes feelings are like that—not positive, not negative, just a lot."

No one had any idea what I was talking about. I didn't know what I was talking about. I wished I could get Dr. Silvers on the phone, put him on speaker, and ask him to explain me to myself and my family.

After the divorce, I had a series of brief relationships. I was lucky to have met those women. They were smart, strong, fun, and giving. My explanations of what went wrong always came down to an inability to live fully honestly with them. Dr. Silvers pushed me to explore what I meant by "full honesty," but he never challenged my reasoning, never suggested that I was self-sabotaging or creating definitions that were impossible to meet. He respected me while feeling sorry for me. Or that's what I wanted him to feel.

"It would be very difficult to live like that," he told me. "Fully honestly."

"I know."

"You would not only open yourself to a great deal of hurt, you would have to inflict a great deal of hurt."

"I know."

"And I don't believe that it would make you happier."

"I don't, either."

He swiveled his chair and looked out the window, as he often did when thinking, as if wisdom could be found only in the distance. He swiveled back and said, "But if you were able to live like that . . ." And then he stopped. He removed his glasses. In my twenty years of knowing him, it was the only time he'd ever removed his glasses. He held the bridge of his nose between his thumb and forefinger. "If you were able to live like that, our work here would be finished."

I was never able to live like that, but our work finished a year later, when he had a fatal heart attack while jogging. I got a call from one of the therapists who had an office in the same suite. She invited me to come and talk about it, but I didn't want to talk to her. I wanted to talk to him. I felt betrayed. *He* should have delivered the news of his death.

And *I* should have delivered the news of my sadness to the kids. But just as his death precluded Dr. Silvers from sharing his death with me, my sadness kept my sadness from them.

The band members had assumed their positions, and forgoing any musical foreplay, went straight into "Dancing on the Ceiling." The sea bass that was once in front of me no longer was; it must have been taken away. The glass of wine that was once in front of me no longer was; I must have drunk it.

The boys ran to the dance floor.

"I'll slip out," I told Julia.

"Islip," she said.

"What?"

"Islip out." And then: "I'm sorry. I didn't—"

When we visited Masada, my father filled his pockets with rocks, and without knowing what he was doing, knowing only my need for his approval, I filled mine. Shlomo told us to put them back. It was the first time I'd ever heard him say no to one of us. He said that if everyone took a rock, Masada would be dispersed across mantels and bookshelves and coffee tables, and there would be no Masada. Even as a boy, I knew that was ridiculous—if anything is permanent, mountains are.

Islip out.

I walked to my car beneath a sky clotted with near-Earth objects.

Somewhere in the wedding guest book are my children's signatures. They developed their handwriting on their own. But I gave them their names.

I parked out front with two wheels on the curb. I might not even have closed the front door behind me.

Here I am, writing in my half-buried office while my family is dancing.

How many synagogues did Sam end up building? Did any survive? Even a wall?

My synagogue is made of words. All the spaces allow it to shift when the ground moves. At the threshold of the sanctuary is the mezuzah, a doorframe nailed to the doorframe: the growth rings of my family. Inside the ark are the broken and the whole: Sam's crushed hand, beside the hand that reached for his "I-know"; Argus lying in his own shit, beside the ever-panting tail-wagger who would pee as soon as Max entered the house; Tamir from after the war, beside Noam from before the war; my grandfather's never-unbending knees, beside my kiss on his great-grandson's nonexistent boo-boo; my father's reflection in a mirror draped with black cloth, beside my sons falling asleep in the rearview mirror, beside the person who will never stop writing these words, who spent his life breaking his fists against the door of his synagogue, begging to be allowed in, beside the boy who dreamed of people fleeing the enormous bomb shelter for the safety of the world, the boy who would have realized that the heavy, heavy door opens outward, that I was inside the Holiest of Holies all along.

VIII

HOME

In the long aftermath of the destruction of Israel, Jacob moved into his new house. It was a nice, if slightly less nice, version of his old house: slightly lower ceilings; slightly less old and less wide planked floors; a kitchen with hardware that if it was called *bespoke* was called that by Home Depot; a bathtub that probably leached BPA, and was probably from Home Depot, but held water; melamine closets with nearly level shelves that performed their function and were nice enough; a faint, not-pleasant attic smell filling the atticless house; Home Depot doorknobs; middle-aged, rotting sub-Marvin windows that served as visual thresholds rather than as barriers against the elements or sound; walls wavy with un-charming trapped moisture; ominous peeling at the corners; subtly sadis-tic wall colors; unflush light switch plates; a faux-porcelain Home Depot vanity with wood-grained melamine drawers, in a bathroom the color of discharge, whose toilet paper roll was out of reach of anyone who wasn't imported from Africa to dunk without jumping; ominous separation ev-erywhere: between the molding components, between the crown molding and the ceiling, the floor molding and the floor, separation of the sink from the wall, the mantel of the nonfunctioning fireplace from the wall, the unflush electrical plates from the wall, the doorframes from the wall, the more-plastic-than-plastic Home Depot rosettes from the jaun-diced ceiling, the floorboards from one another. It didn't really matter, but it didn't go unnoticed. He had to admit that he was more bourgeois than he'd have liked to admit, but he knew what was important. Those things were separating, too.

There was time, there was suddenly a life of it, and Jacob's needs were taking the shape of his needs, rather than his ability to fulfill them. He was declaring his independence, and all of it—from the interminable wait for the hot-water Messiah to the unflush plate through which not enough threads of the cable nipple were exposed—filled him with hope. Or a version of hope. Jacob might have forced her hand, but it was Julia who chose the separation. And while his return from Islip could be understood as the claiming of an identity, it could at least as easily be understood as the forfeiture of one. So maybe he didn't write his declaration of independence, but he was happy to sign it. It was a version of happiness.

Forty-two is *young*, he kept telling himself, like an idiot. He could hear his own idiocy loud and clear, and yet he couldn't stop announcing it. He would remind himself of advances in medical technology, of his own efforts to eat less unhealthily, of the gym to which he had a membership (albeit ceremonial), and of that fact Sam had once shared: with each passing year, life expectancy increases by a year. Everyone who didn't smoke would live to be one hundred. Practitioners of yoga would outlive Moses.

In time, his house would resemble his home—some rugs, better hardware, wall colors in keeping with the Geneva Convention, paintings and photos and lithos, calming lamplight, art books stacked on surfaces, throws not thrown but crisply folded and laid over sofas and chairs, maybe a wood-burning stove in the corner. And in time, everything that was possible would be actual. He'd get a girlfriend, or not. Buy an unexpected car, or probably not. Finally do something with the television show he'd been emptying his soul into for more than a decade. (The soul being the only thing that requires dispersal to accumulate.) Now that he no longer needed to protect his grandfather, he'd stop writing the bible and get back to the show itself. He'd take it to one of those producers who used to be interested in what he was doing, back when he was doing things that could be shared. A lot of time had passed, but they'd still remember him.

There had been more than one reason to keep the pages in a drawer—he wasn't only protecting others. But once there was nothing left to lose, even Julia would see that the show wasn't an escape from the challenges of family life, but a redemption of his family's destruction.

Israel wasn't *destroyed*—at least not in the literal sense. It remained a Jewish country, with a Jewish army, and borders only negligibly different from before the earthquake. Infinite debate corkscrewed the question of whether those new borders were *good for the Jews*. Although, tellingly, the expression most often used by American Jews was *good for the Israelis*. And *that*, the Israelis thought, was *bad for the Jews*.

Israel had been made weaker, but its enemies were made weaker still. Not much comfort can be taken, when sifting through your rubble with a bulldozer, in the knowledge that your enemy is sifting through his rubble by hand. But some comfort can be taken. As Isaac would have said, "It could be worse." No, he would have said, "It *is* worse."

Maybe he was right. Maybe it was worse to have survived, if continuing to *be* required destroying the reason to be. It's not as if American Jews stopped caring. They continued to vacation and bar mitzvah and *find themselves* in Israel. They winced as their small cuts were first touched by Dead Sea water, winced as their hearts were first touched by "Hatikvah," crammed folded wishes between the rubble of the Wailing Wall, recounted back-alley hummus spots, recounted the thrill of distant rocket strikes, winced as their eyes were first touched by the sun at Masada, recounted the perpetual thrill of seeing Jewish garbagemen, and Jewish firefighters, and Jewish homeless. But the feeling of having arrived, of finally finding a place of comfort, of being *home*, was disappearing.

For some, it was the inability to forgive Israel's actions during the war—even a massacre or two would have been easier to accept than the complete and explicit abdication of responsibility for non-Jews—the withdrawal of security forces and emergency personnel, the stockpiling of medical supplies that had urgent use elsewhere, the withholding of utilities, the rationing of food even amid a surplus, the blockade of aid shipments to Gaza and the West Bank. Irv—whose once-daily, occasionally inflammatory blog had become a rushing river of provocation—defended Israel at every step: "If it were a family in a time of emergency, and not a country, no one would judge parents for keeping food in the fridge and Band-Aids in the medicine cabinet. Things happen, especially when your death-loving neighbors hate you to death, and it is not unethical to care more about your own children."

"If the family lived only in its own house, you might almost be right," Jacob said. "And you might almost be right if every family were equally able to give preferential treatment to its own. But that's not the world we live in, and you know it."

"It's the world they created."

"When you look at that girl, Adia, your heart doesn't go out to her?"

"Of course it does. But like every heart, mine is of limited size, and if it came down to Adia or Benjy, I would pull the food from her hands to put into his. I'm not even arguing that that's right or good. I'm just saying it isn't bad, because it isn't a choice. '*Ought* implies *can*,' right? To be morally obliged to do something, you have to be able to do it. I love Noam, Yael, and Barak, but I cannot love them as much as I love Sam, Max, and Benjy. It's impossible. And I love my friends, but I can't love them as much as I love my family. And believe it or not, I am fully capable of loving Arabs, but not of loving them as much as I love Jews. These are not choices."

Irv genuinely and forcefully advocated for every Jewish American of fighting age going to Israel. Categorically. With the exception of the one he couldn't not love more than the others. He was a hypocrite, a father.

"And yet some people *can* choose otherwise," Jacob said.

"Like?"

"Well, the first example that comes to mind is the first Jew: Abraham."

"Senator, I served with Abraham. I knew Abraham. Abraham was a friend of mine. Senator, you're no Abraham."

"I'm not saying *I* could choose otherwise. Obviously I couldn't."

Was that obvious? Irv had collapsed the circle of concern to the youngest in his family, but was that the center? What about oneself? Julia had asked Jacob if it made him sad that they loved the kids more than each other. But did Jacob love his children more than he loved himself? He ought to, but could he?

For other American Jews, it wasn't Israel's actions that created an emotional distance, but how those actions were perceived—those whose good faith in Israel could always be counted on either switched sides or fell silent, and left American Jews feeling more alone than indignantly righteous.

For others, it was the discomfort of Israel being neither a scrappy underdog nor a bitty superpower capable of bombing its Stone Age neighbors back into the pre–Stone Age. David was good. Goliath was good. But you'd better be one or the other.

The prime minister had set the goal of bringing one million American Jews to Israel with Operation Arms of Moses. Twenty thousand went on the first day of flights—if not in the same ballpark as the hoped-for fifty thousand, at least playing the same sport. But instead of reaching three hundred thousand by the end of the third day, the numbers kept halving, like box office receipts. The *Times* estimated that fewer than thirty-five thousand American Jews ultimately went, and that three-quarters of those were forty-five or older. Israel survived without them—the army pulled back to its defensible borders and allowed disease to do the work of killing; the tragedy lasted five hundred televised hours. But neither Israelis nor American Jews could deny what was exposed.

Jacob still thought of Tel Aviv as vibrant and cultured, and Jerusalem as irresistibly spiritual. He still felt an almost sexual delight when he recalled the actual places where almost-make-believe things actually happened to almost-make-believe people. The women with guns still gave him an actual sexual delight. The ultra-Orthodox still disgusted him, and he still couldn't repress the misplaced gratitude he felt for them. But something had changed.

What was Israel to him? What were Israelis? They were his more aggressive, more obnoxious, more crazed, more hairy, more muscular brothers . . . *over there*. They were ridiculous, and they were *his*. They were more brave, more beautiful, more piggish and delusional, less self-conscious, more reckless, more themselves. *Over there*. That's where they were those things. And they were *his*.

After the near-destruction, they were still *over there*, but they were no longer *his*.

At each step, Jacob had made efforts to rationalize Israel's actions—to defend, or at least excuse, them. And at each step, he believed what he said. Was it right to regulate incoming aid shipments if it slowed down their delivery? It was necessary, in order to maintain order and security. Was it right to take the Temple Mount? It was necessary, in order to protect it. Was it right to withhold equal medical care from anyone with equal needs? It was necessary, in order to fully care for Israel's citizens, who, unlike its Arab neighbors, had nowhere else to turn. "*Ought* implies *can*." And yet the destination to which those defensible, or at least excusable, steps led was an Israel that sat on urgently needed aid, conquered the most contentious Muslim territory in the world, and forced the mothers of children who didn't need to die to pound on locked hospital doors. Even if there couldn't have been another way, there ought to have been.

Would anyone notice, the next morning, if the ocean widened by a foot overnight? If it widened by a mile? By half? The horizon conceals the distance, as does the distance itself. American Jews didn't think of themselves as having pulled back, and would never have described their relationship to Israel that way—not to others, not to themselves. But even as they claimed relief and joy that Israel had triumphed, even as they marched in parades and sent uncomfortably large checks to the rebuilding effort, the Israeli waves took longer to reach the American shore.

Unexpectedly, the distance between Irv and Jacob closed. For a year, they went to shul together and said Kaddish for Isaac, three times a day every day—or at least once, most days. And on the days they didn't go, they threw minyan to the wind and mourned in Irv's living room, facing the bookshelves, whatever their compass direction. They found a new language—not free of jokes, irony, and argument, but no longer dependent on them. Maybe it was a rediscovered language.

No one was less qualified than Irv to help Jacob move—he didn't know a fitted sheet from a slotted spoon—but no one helped him more. They made trips to IKEA together, to Pottery Barn, and Home Depot, and Gap Kids. They bought two brooms and talked about transitions, and beginnings, and impermanence, while brushing at what felt like infinite dust. Or they brushed in silence.

"It isn't good to be alone," Irv said, trying to figure out the vacuum cleaner.

"I'll try again," Jacob said. "I'm just not ready yet."

"I meant me."

"Did something happen with Mom?"

"No, your mother's the best of them all. I'm just thinking about the people I've pushed away."

Packing up his things had been emotionally easier than Jacob had imagined, but the logistics were surprisingly fraught. The problem wasn't the volume of things—despite having accumulated things for sixteen years, there was a surprising scarcity of things. The problem—at the end of the day, at the end of the end of their marriage—was addressing the question of what makes something yours and not someone else's. How did life reach the point where that question mattered? And what took life so long?

If he'd known that he was going to get divorced, he would have better set the table for the end—bought one of those old-fashioned "Library of Jacob Bloch" embossers and marked the title page of every book; perhaps stashed away money in small, unnoticeable increments; started moving things whose absence would never be noticed, but whose presence in his new home would make a real difference.

It was scary how quickly and completely his past could be rewritten, or overwritten. All those years felt worthwhile while they were happening, but only a few months on the other side of them and they were a gigantic waste of time. Of a life. It was an almost irrepressible urge of his brain to see the worst in that which had failed. To see it as something that had failed, rather than something that had succeeded until the end. Was he protecting himself from the loss by denying anything was lost? Or simply achieving some pathetic emotional nonvictory by not caring?

When a friend would express sympathy, why did Jacob insist on opposing it? Why did he have to turn his decade and a half of marriage into stupid puns and ironic observations? Why couldn't he express to a single person—to himself—that even if he understood that divorce was the right thing to do, even if he was hopeful about the future, even if there was happiness ahead, it was sad? Things can be for the best and the worst at the same time.

Three days after returning to Israel, Tamir e-mailed Jacob from an outpost in the Negev, where his tank unit was awaiting its next order: "Today I fired a gun, and my son fired a gun. I never doubted the rightness of my firing a weapon to defend my home, or of Noam doing so. But the fact of us both doing it on the same day cannot be right. Can you understand that?"

"You drive the tank?" Jacob asked.

"Did you read what I wrote?"

"I'm sorry. I don't know what to say."

"I reload the ammunition."

Five days later, as they turned to the bookshelves to say Kaddish, Irv said, "So listen," and Jacob knew something had happened. And more, he knew it was Noam. He hadn't seen it coming, but like someone watching the tracks from the back of a train, he saw that it couldn't have been any other way.

Noam had been injured. Critically, but not fatally. Rivka was with him. Tamir was on his way.

"How did you find out?" Jacob asked.

"Tamir called me last night."

"Did he ask you to tell me?"

"I think I'm a kind of father figure to him."

Jacob's first instinct was to suggest they go to Israel. He wouldn't get on the plane to fight beside his cousin, but he would go to sit at his cousin's son's bedside and offer the kind of strength that involves only heart muscle.

Tamir's first instinct was to cling to Rivka. If someone had told him, a month or year or decade earlier, that Noam would be wounded in a war, he would have predicted the end of his marriage. And yet when the unimaginable happened, it was just the opposite of what he'd imagined.

When the house shook with the middle-of-the-night knocking against the door, Tamir was at a forward operating base near Dimona; his commander woke him with the news. Later, he and Rivka would try to pinpoint the exact moment that each learned of what happened, as if something profound depended on who knew first, and what the amount of time was that one parent knew and the other still believed Noam to be OK. For those first five or thirty minutes, there would have existed a greater distance between them than the one that separated them before they met. Perhaps if Tamir had been home, the shared experience would have driven them apart, into competitive suffering, misplaced fury, blame. But the apartness drew them together.

How many times, in those first weeks, did he enter the room and stand by the door, unable to speak? How many times did she ask, "Do you need anything?"

And he would say, "No."

And she would say, "Are you sure?"

And he would say, "Yes," but think, *Ask again.*

And she would say, "I know," but think, *Come to me.*

And he would say, "Ask again."

And she would say, "Come to me."

And saying nothing, he would.

There they would be, side by side, her hand on his thigh, his head resting on her chest. If they had been teenagers, it would have looked like the beginning of love, but they'd been married for twenty years, and it was the exhumation of love.

After being informed of Noam's injury, Tamir was given a week's leave. He was with Rivka at the hospital three hours later, and when darkness fell, they were told they had to go home. Rivka instinctively went to sleep in the guest room. In the middle of the night, Tamir entered and stood by the door.

"Do you need anything?" she asked.

And he said, "No."

And she said, "Are you sure?"

And he said, "Yes."

And she said, "I know."

And he said, "Ask again."

And she said, "Come to me," and saying nothing, he went to her.

He needed the distance to traverse. So she gave it to him. Every night she would go to the guest room. Every night he would come to her.

When Tamir sat with his son's body, he thought of what Jacob had told him about sitting with Isaac's body, Max's desire to be close to it. Noam's face was misshapen, shades of a purple that appeared nowhere in nature, his cheeks and brow forced together by the swelling. Why isn't health as shocking as illness, as demanding of prayer? Tamir had been capable of going weeks without speaking to his son, but he wouldn't willingly leave his son's unconscious body.

Noam emerged from his coma the day before the cease-fire. It would take time to learn the extent of his injuries: the ways his body would never function as it once did, the psychological damage. He hadn't been buried alive or burned to death. But he had been broken.

When the cease-fire was signed, there was no celebrating in the streets. There were no fireworks, or passed bottles, or singing from windows. Rivka slept in the bedroom that night. The loving distance they'd found in crisis had closed with peace. Across the country and the world, Jews were already writing editorials blaming other Jews—for lack of preparedness, of wisdom, of ethics, of sufficient force, of help. The prime minister's coalition collapsed and elections were scheduled. Unable to sleep, Tamir took his phone from the bedside table and wrote a one-sentence text to Jacob: *We've won, but we've lost.*

It was nine in the evening in D.C. Jacob was in the Airbnb one-bedroom that he had been renting by the week, three blocks from his sleeping children. He went after putting the kids down and returned before they awoke. They knew he didn't spend the night at home, and he knew they knew it, but the charade felt necessary. Nothing would be harder for Jacob than this period between houses, which lasted half a year. Everything that was necessary was punishing: the pretending, the extreme early rising, the aloneness.

Jacob's thumb was constantly pushing his list of contacts, as if some new person might materialize with whom he could share the sadness he couldn't confess. He wanted to reach out to Tamir, but it was impossible: not after Islip, not after Noam's injury. So when the text from Tamir came through—*We've won, but we've lost*—Jacob was relieved and grateful, but careful about expanding his shame by revealing it.

Won what? Lost what?

Won the war. Lost peace.

But it sounds like everyone is accepting
the conditions of the armistice?

Peace with ourselves.

How is Noam?

He will be OK.

I'm so relieved to hear that.

When we were at your kitchen table,
stoned, you told me something
about a daytime hole in a nighttime sky.
What was that?

The dinosaur thing?

Yes, that.

So it was actually a nighttime hole in a daytime sky.

And how?

Imagine shooting a bullet through water.

That's all you had to say. Now I remember.

What made you think of it?

I can't sleep. So instead I think.

I haven't been sleeping too much, either.
For people who talk about being tired
as much as we do, we don't do a lot of sleeping.

We're not going to move.

I didn't think you were.

We were.
Rivka was coming around.
But not anymore.

What changed?

Everything. Nothing.

Right.

We are who we are.
Admitting that is what changed.

I'm working on that myself.

What if it had been night?

When?

When the asteroid came.

Then they would have
become extinct at night.

But what would they have seen?

A nighttime hole in a nighttime sky?

And what do you think that would look like?

Maybe like nothing?

Over the next few years, they would exchange brief texts and e-mails, all matter-of-fact updates, mostly about the kids, never with any tone or tangents. Tamir didn't come for Max's bar mitzvah, or Benjy's, or Julia's wedding (despite her kind invitation, and Jacob's appeal), or either Deborah's or Irv's funeral.

After the kids' first visit to his new house—the first and worst day of the rest of his life—Jacob closed the door, lay with Argus for half an hour, telling him what a good dog he was, the best dog, then sat with a cup of coffee that gave its heat to the room as he wrote a long, never-to-be-sent e-mail to Tamir, then stood up, keys in hand, finally ready to go to the veterinarian. The e-mail began: "We've lost, but we've lost."

Some of the losing was giving away. Some was having things taken. Jacob was often surprised by what he found himself clutching, and what he freely released—what he felt was his, what he felt he needed.

What about that copy of *Disgrace*? *He'd* bought it—he remembered finding it at the used bookstore in Great Barrington one summer; he even remembered the beautiful set of Tennessee Williams plays he didn't buy because Julia was there, and he didn't want to be forced to confront his desire to own books he had no intention of reading.

Julia had taken *Disgrace* from his bedside table, on the grounds of it having sat there untouched for more than a year. (*Untouched* was her word. *Unread* would have been his.) Did his having bought it entitle him to it? Did her having read—touched—it? Did her having touched and read it forfeit her claim to it, as it was now his to touch and read? Such thoughts felt disgraceful. The only way to be spared them was to give away everything, but only a more enlightened or stupid person would rub his palms together and think, *They're only things*.

What about the blue vase on the mantel? Her parents had given it to him as a gift. Not to *them*, but to *him*. It was a birthday present. Or Father's Day. He could remember, at least, that it was a gift placed in *his* hands, with an attached card addressed to *him*, that it had been carefully chosen for *him*, because they prided themselves on knowing him, which, to their credit, they did.

Was it somehow ungenerous to assume ownership of something paid for by her parents, which, while undeniably given to *him*, was clearly intended for their shared home? And beautiful as the vase was, did he want that psychic energy in his sanctuary and symbol of new beginnings? Would it really give his flowers the best chance of blooming?

Most things he could let go of:

He loved the Big Red Chair, curled into whose corduroy he'd done virtually all his reading in the last dozen years. Hadn't it absorbed something? Taken on qualities beyond chairness? Was the sweat stain on the back the only remnant of all that experience? What was trapped in the wide wales? *Let it go,* he thought.

The silverware. It had brought food to his mouth, to his children's mouths. The most fundamental of all human activities, that which we can't live without. He had washed them in the sink before positioning them in the dishwasher. He had unbent the spoons after Sam's clumsy psychokinesis; used knives to pry off the lids of paint cans and scrape hardened who-knows-what from the sink; guided forks down the back of his shirt to scratch an out-of-reach itch. *Let them go. Let it all go until it's all gone.*

The photo albums. He'd have liked some of those. But they shouldn't be separated any more than the volumes of the *Grove Encyclopedia of Art*. And there was no way around the fact that Julia had taken almost all the pictures: observe her absence among them. Was her absence her claim to ownership?

The growth chart, inscribed on the kitchen doorframe. On New Year's and Jewish New Year's, Jacob would make a production of calling everyone to be measured. They stood facing out, backs flat as surfboards, never on tiptoes but always willing tallness. Jacob pressed a black Sharpie flush with the tops of their heads and drew a two-inch line. Then the initials and date. The first measurement was SB 01/01/05. The last was BB 01/01/16. Between them, a couple dozen lines. What did it look like? A tiny ladder for tiny angels to ascend and descend? The frets on the instrument playing the sound of life passing?

He would have been happy enough to take nothing and simply start again at the beginning. *They're only things.* But that wouldn't be fair. More, it would be unfair. Very quickly, the fairness and unfairness took on

more importance than the things themselves. That feeling of aggrieve-
ment reached its peak when they started talking about amounts of money
that simply didn't matter. One spring afternoon, cherry blossoms stuck to
the window, Dr. Silvers told him, "Whatever the conditions of your life,
you're never going to be happy if you use the word *unfair* as often as you
do." So he tried to let it all go—the things, and the ideas he imbued them
with. He would begin again.

The first purchases for the new house were beds for the kids. Because
Benjy's room was on the small side, he needed a bed with storage drawers. Perhaps those were actually hard to find, or perhaps Jacob made the
task hard. He spent three full days researching online and visiting stores,
and ended up with something quite nice (from the offensively misnamed
Design Within Reach), made of solid oak, which cost more than three
thousand dollars. *Plus* tax, *plus* delivery.

The bed obviously needed a mattress—talk about obvious—and the
mattress obviously had to be organic—talk about unobvious—because
Julia would ask if it was, and then, not trusting his answer, would peel
back the sheets and have a look. Would it kill him simply to say, "I went
with something easy?" Yes, it would. But why? For fear of disappointing
her? For fear of her? Because she was right, and it mattered what chemicals children spend nearly half of their lives pressed up against? Another
thousand dollars.

The mattress needed sheets, obviously, but first it needed a mattress
cover, because even though Benjy was on the verge of the end of nighttime accidents, he was still on the wrong side of that verge—it occurred
to Jacob that the divorce might even inspire regression—and one such
accident could effectively ruin the thousand-dollar organic mattress. So
another hundred and fifty dollars. And then those sheets. The plural is
not only for the various kinds of sheet necessary to define a sheet set, but
for the second sheet set, because that's what people get. He often found
himself at the mercy of such logic: this has to be done in such and such
way because it has to, because it's what people do. People get two pieces
of silverware for every one they will ever use. People buy esoteric vin-
egars for salads that they might make once, if ever. And why is the func-
tionality of the fork so underrecognized? With a simple fork, one doesn't
need a whisk, a spatula, salad tongs (two forks for that), a "masher," or
pretty much any other highly specialized kitchen utensil whose real

function is to be bought. He found his share of peace by resolving that if he was going to buy things he didn't need, at least he was going to get crummy versions of them.

Imagine arriving in the afterlife and not knowing if you were in heaven or hell.

"Excuse me," you ask a passing angel, "where am I?"

"You're gonna wanna ask the angel at the information desk."

"And where would that be?"

But he's gone.

You look around. A strong case could be made for it being heaven. A strong case could be made for it being hell. That is what IKEA is like.

By the time he was finished preparing his new house for the boys, Jacob had made half a dozen trips to IKEA, and even then he couldn't discern if, on balance, he loved or loathed it.

He loathed the particleboard, the bookcases that needed books to keep them from floating away.

He loved imagining the scrutiny that had to be applied to every detail—the shortest functional length of a dowel that will be reproduced eighty million times—in order to sell things for prices that verged on magical.

He loathed the experience of passing someone whose cart's contents were not only identical to his, but identically stacked. And he loathed the carts: three mortal enemies and one palsy case for wheels, and turning radiuses like rainbows—not the shape, but actual rainbows.

He loved the unexpected object—beautifully designed, perfectly named, and actually made from materials denser than shaving cream. That black marble Ädelsten mortar and pestle. Was it a loss leader? An act of love?

He loathed the machine that punched that poor chair over and over, punched it all day every day and probably through the night, confirming both the resilience of the chair and the existence of evil.

Jacob sat himself on a sofa—green velvet-like upholstery holding in whatever is the opposite of kelp and pony hair—and closed his eyes. He'd been having a hard time falling asleep. For a long time. But this felt OK. Despite the river of strangers passing in front of him, and occasionally sitting beside him to test the comfort, this felt safe. He was in his own world in that world that was in its own world in the world. Everyone was looking for something, but there was an endless supply, so no one's gratification had to come at anyone else's expense—there was no need to fight, no need even to disagree. So what that it was utterly soulless? Maybe heaven wasn't populated by souls, but emptied of them? Maybe this was fairness?

He was awoken by what he at first thought was the punching of that depraved machine, as if his resiliency were being violently challenged again and again and again. But it was just the tapping of a friendly angel.

"We're closing in ten," she said.

"Oh, I'm really sorry," he said.

She asked, "For what?"

By the time of the earthquake, Jacob would walk downstairs every morning not wondering *if* Argus had pooped, but where and with what solidity. It was a horrible way to start a day, and Jacob knew it wasn't Argus's fault, but when time was of the essence and kids weren't cooperating robotically, poop in four places could force a meltdown.

"Jesus Christ, Argus!"

And then one of the kids would come to Argus's rescue: "He can't help it."

And then Jacob would feel miserable.

Argus made Rorschachs of persians and orientals, relocated the stuffing of upholstered furniture to closets and his stomach, and scratched wood floors like Grand Wizard Theodore. But he was theirs.

Everything would have been so much easier if Argus were suffering—not just uncomfortable, but in deep pain. Or if a vet could find cancer, or heart disease, even kidney failure.

When Jacob told Julia he was going to Israel to fight, she told him he had to put down Argus first. He didn't, and she didn't mention it again. But when he came home from not leaving, it was an open, if invisible, wound.

In the following months, Argus's condition worsened along with everything else. He started whining for no obvious reason, paced before sitting down, ate less and less until he hardly ate at all.

•

Julia and the boys would be there any minute. Jacob wandered through the house, noticing the imperfections, adding to the infinite mental punch list of things that should be taken care of: the cracked grout in the dripping shower; the sloppy bit of overpainting where the hallway wall met the floor; the torqued vent in the dining room ceiling; the fussy bedroom window.

The doorbell rang. Then rang again. Then rang again.

"Coming! Coming!"

He opened the door to smiles.

"Your doorbell sounds weird," Max said.

Your doorbell.

"It does sound a little weird. Weird good? Or weird bad?"

"Maybe weird good?" Max said, and that might have been his opinion, but it might have been kindness.

"Come in," Jacob said. "Come. I have some great snacks—Cheddar Bunnies; the truffle cheese you like, Benjy; those lime tortilla chips, Max. And the whole line of Italian sodas: aranciata, limonata, pompelmo, clementine."

"We're good," Sam said, smiling as if for a family photo.

"I've never even heard of pompelmo," Max said.

"Neither had I," Jacob said. "But we've got it."

"I love this place," Julia said, quite sincerely and convincingly, despite it being a scripted line. They'd rehearsed the visit, just as they'd rehearsed the divorce conversation, and how to share the new schedule of moving between houses, and so many other experiences too painful to have only once.

"So do you guys want a tour? Or do you want to just explore it yourselves?"

"Maybe explore?" Sam said.

"Go on. Your names are on the doors of your rooms, so you can't miss them."

He heard himself.

The boys went upstairs, slowly, deliberately. They didn't speak, but Jacob could hear them touching things.

Julia hung back, and waited until the kids were on the third floor before saying, "So far, so good."

"You think?"

"I do," she said. "But it'll take time."

Jacob wondered what Tamir would have to say about the house, should he ever see it. What would Isaac have said? He spared himself the move to the Jewish Home, unaware that he was also sparing himself Jacob's move—and sparing Jacob.

Jacob led Julia into what would become the living room—emptier now than if it had never been enclosed by walls. They sat on the only piece of furniture, the green sofa that Jacob had fallen asleep on a few weeks before. Not that exact sofa, but one of its two million identical siblings.

"Dusty," she said. And then: "Sorry."

"No, it is. Horribly."

"You have a vacuum?"

"I got the kind we have," Jacob said. "We *had*? *You* have? And I mop it, too. All the time, it feels like."

"There's dust in the air, from the work. It keeps settling."

"How does one get dust out of the air?"

"Just keep doing what you're doing," she said.

"And expect a different result? Isn't that the definition of insanity?"

"Do you have a Swiffer duster?"

"Excuse me?"

"I'll get you one. They're really useful."

"I can get it if you send me the link."

"At that point it's easier for me to just get it."

"Thanks."

"Do you feel OK about Argus?"

"No."

"You should."

"My feelings have never once cared about what they should be."

"You're good, Jacob."

"Compared to what?"

"Compared to other men."

"I feel like I'm bailing water with a colander."

"If life were easy, everyone would do it."

"Everyone does."

"Think about how many trillions of trillions of people are never born for every one who is."

"Or just think about my grandfather."

"I often do," she said. Her eyes raised, and scanned the room. "I don't know if it's annoying or helpful when I mention things—"

"Why so binary?"

"Right. Well. The walls are rather dark."

"I know. They are, right?"

"Disconsolate."

"I hired a colorist."

"You're kidding."

"I used that paint you like. Farrow whatever."

"Farrow and Ball."

"And they offered a colorist's services, I assumed as a courtesy because I was buying so much of their overpriced paint. And then I got a bill for twenty-five hundred dollars."

"No."

"Yes. Two thousand five hundred. And I feel like I'm living underneath a Union kepi."

"Excuse me?"

"Those Civil War hats. I've been listening to this history of—"

"You should have asked me."

"I can't afford you."

"Would have been pro bono."

"Didn't my father teach you there's no such thing as a free colorist?"

"There's paper everywhere," Benjy said, coming down the stairs. He seemed buoyant, unfazed.

"It's just protecting the floor while they finish the work," Jacob said.

"I'm going to trip a lot."

"It'll be long gone by the time you live here. The paper on the floor, the ladders, the dust. All of it will be gone."

Max and Sam came back down.

"Can I have a mini-fridge in my room?" Max asked.

"Definitely," Jacob said.

"For what?" Julia asked.

"Don't you think there's too much paper on the floors?" Benjy asked his brothers.

"For all those Italian sodas."

"I think Dad intended those as something special for your first time here."

"Dad?"

"They would definitely not be an everyday beverage."

"Sam, don't you think the paper on the floor is bad?"

"Fine, so I could keep the dead rats."

"Dead rats?"

"I gave the OK for a python," Jacob said, "and that's what they eat."

"Actually, they'd probably have to be frozen," Max said. "And I don't think those mini-fridges have little freezer sections in them."

"Why would you want a python?" Julia asked.

"Because I've wanted a python forever, because they're amazing, and Dad said now that we had the new house we could finally get one."

"Why doesn't anybody care that I'm going to trip all the time?" Benjy asked.

And then Sam, who had been quiet for an uncharacteristically long time, said, "My room seems nice. Thanks, Dad."

And that was the hardest thing for Jacob to hear. Julia saw that he needed help, and stepped in.

"So," she said, clapping her hands once, inadvertently raising more dust, "Dad and I were thinking it would be nice to give this house a name."

"Isn't it just Dad's House?"

"Right," Jacob said, composing himself with an imitation of optimism. "But we all want to think of it as one of our family's two houses."

"Yeah, the one that you live in. As opposed to the one that Mom lives in."

"I don't like this house," Benjy said, verbally cutting the lines of Jacob's emotional brakes.

"You will," Julia said.

"I don't like this house."

"I promise you will."

Jacob felt himself skidding out. It was unfair that he had to move, unfair that he was perceived as the one who left; that all this dust was his was unfair. But he also felt his dependency on Julia's efforts. He couldn't do this without her. He couldn't live without her without her.

"It's going to be great," she said, as if she could keep blowing her optimism into the punctured balloon of Benjy's happiness and it would keep its shape. "Dad said there's even room for a Ping-Pong table upstairs."

"Totally," Jacob said. "And I've been trolling eBay for an old Skee-Ball machine."

"You don't mean *trolling*," Max said. "You mean *trawling*."

"Although," Sam said, suddenly enlivened, "did you know that *trolling* actually comes from *trawling*. Not from, like, trolls?"

"I didn't," Max said, grateful for that little bit of knowledge. "I'd always assumed trolls."

"Right?"

The moment of normality suggested a normal life.

"What's Skee-Ball?" Benjy asked.

"It's kind of a combination of bowling and darts," Sam said.

"That's hard for me to imagine."

"Like at Chuck E. Cheese's."

"Ah, right."

A normal life? Was all this upheaval justified by that ambition?

"How about Arcade House?" Max suggested.

"Too much like Arcade Fire," Sam said.

"It's very dusty," Benjy said.

"The dust won't be here."

"How about Davenport House?"

"Why?"

"Because it's on Davenport Street."

"That sounds like an old-age home."

"I don't see what's wrong about calling it Dad's House," Sam said. "We can pretend it's something else, but that's what it is."

"Paper House," Benjy said, a bit to himself, a bit to no one.

"What?"

"Because there's so much paper everywhere."

"But the paper will be gone by the time you move in," Jacob said.

"And paper is what you write on, and you're a writer."

"He writes on a computer," Sam said.

"And paper rips and burns easily."

"Why would you want to name a house after something that rips and burns easily?"

"Give him a break, Max."

"What did I say?"

"Forget it," Jacob said. "We can just call it 2328, after the address."

"No," Julia said, "don't forget it. It's a nice idea, and we're five intelligent people. We can do it."

The five intelligent people thought. They applied their intelligence to what was ultimately not a question of intelligence, like applying a Phillips-head screwdriver to a crossword puzzle.

Some religions emphasize inner peace, some the avoidance of sin, some praise. Judaism emphasizes intelligence—textually, ritualistically, and culturally. Everything is learning, everything preparation, perpetually filling the mental toolbox until we are prepared for any situation (and it is too heavy to carry). Jews make up 0.2 percent of the world's population, but have been awarded 22 percent of all Nobel Prizes—24 percent if you don't include the Peace Prize. And with no Nobel for Being Exterminated, there was a decade when Jews wouldn't have had much of a chance, so the practical percentage is yet higher. Why? It's not because Jews are any smarter than anyone else; it's because Jews put their emphasis on the kinds of things Stockholm rewards. Jews have been training for Nobel Prizes for thousands of years. But if there were Nobel Prizes for Contentment, for Feeling Safe, or for the Ability to Let Go, that 22 percent—24 percent without Peace—would need a parachute.

"I still think we should call it Dad's House," Sam said.

"But it's not just my house. It's our house."

"We can't call it Our House," Sam said, "because the other house is our house, too."

"Clock House?"

"Why?"

"I don't know."

"Pompelmo House?"

"Anonymous House?"

"Dusty House?"

"To be continued," Julia said as she checked her phone for the time. "I've got to get these guys to haircuts."

"Right," Jacob said, knowing the inevitable, and wanting to defer it, if only for another few minutes. "Does anyone want a snack or drink first?"

"We're going to be late," Julia said. And then: "Everybody say 'bye to Argus."

"Later, Argus."

"Ciao, Argo."

"A *good* goodbye," she said.

"Why?"

"It's his first night in the new house," Jacob said.

"New House?" Sam suggested.

"Maybe," Jacob said. "Although it won't be new for long."

"We can change the name at that point," Sam said.

"Like the Old-New Synagogue in Prague," Julia said.

"Or move," Benjy said.

"No more moving," Jacob said.

"Gotta go," Julia said to the kids.

The kids said good goodbyes to Argus, and then Julia knelt down to be face-to-face with him. "Take care, hairy man."

She showed nothing, nothing that anyone but Jacob could see. But he could see. He couldn't describe the giveaway—her face revealed nothing, her body revealed nothing, and there was nothing in her voice—but she gave it all away. He could only ever manage repression. She was capable of composure. And he was in awe of it. She did it for the kids. She did it for Argus. But how did she do it?

"OK," Jacob said.

"OK," Julia said.

"I know what we should do," Benjy said.

"We should go," Julia said.

"No. We should walk around the house with our eyes closed. Like we used to do on Shabbat."

"How about next time you're here?" Jacob said.

Sam stepped forward, into the space of his adulthood: "Dad, we can do this for him."

And with that, Julia put down her bag. And Jacob took his hands from his pockets. No one watched anyone close their eyes, because that would have betrayed the spirit of the ritual. And no one peeked, because there was an instinct stronger than that instinct.

It was fun at first; it was funny. The nostalgia was sweet and untinged. The kids bumped into things on purpose, and made boy noises, and laughed a lot. But then, without anyone intending it, or noticing the shift, a silence bloomed. No one stopped talking, but there was no more talking. No one suppressed a laugh, but there was no more laughing. It went on for a long time—it felt like a different amount of time to each—the five of them like ghosts, or explorers, or newborns. No one knew if anyone's arms were extended for protection. No one knew if anyone crawled, or did leg sweeps for obstacles, or ran a finger against a wall that he kept to his right at all times. Julia's foot touched the leg of a folding chair. Sam found a light switch, pinched it between his thumb and forefinger, searched for the place between off and on. Max felt a thrill as his hands explored the stovetop. Julia opened her eyes; they were greeted by Jacob's open eyes.

"I figured it out," Benjy said, old enough to know that the world doesn't disappear when you aren't looking at it.

"What did you figure out?" Julia asked from across the room, not betraying him by looking at him.

"Wailing House."

Jacob didn't need anything when he made his final visit to IKEA. He'd just become so accustomed to IKEA satisfying his needs—hand towels for the top bathroom, a pot of lamb's ears, freestanding acrylic picture frames—that he came to believe IKEA knew his needs better than he did, in the same way that he scheduled physicals because the doctor knew better than Jacob if Jacob was sick.

He picked up a bright red step stool, a garlic press, three toilet brushes, a drying rack for laundry, a drying rack for dishes, half a dozen felt storage boxes that would be perfect for some still-unknown purpose, a level (despite never once, in the previous forty-two years, having had need of a level), a doormat, two letter trays, oven mitts, several glass jars with air-tight seals for the storage (and attractive display) of things like beans and lentils and split peas and popcorn and quinoa and rice, more hangers, LED light strings to connect the corners of Benjy's room, pedal bins for each bathroom, a crappy umbrella that wouldn't survive two storms but would survive one. He was among the textiles, spreading his fingers in a faux sheepskin, when he heard his name.

"Jacob?"

He turned to face a quite beautiful woman: warm brown eyes like old leather; a gold locket that drew his gaze to the top of her tight, unmottled cleavage; bracelets halfway down her hands as if she'd once been bigger. What was in that locket? He knew her, or had known her.

"Maggie," she said. "Silliman."

"Hi, Maggie."

She smiled a smile to bring a thousand ships to harbor.

"Dylan and Sam went to nursery school together. Leah and Melissa's class."

"Right. Of course."

"It's been a decade," she said kindly.

"No, I remember."

"I thought I saw you. Way back in living rooms. But I lost you in the shuffle. And I wasn't sure. But when I saw you here, I knew."

"Ah."

"I'm so relieved you're home."

"Oh, I don't live here," Jacob said, his reflexive flirtatiousness stimulating the thought that maybe she was the one whose husband had an aneurysm in the middle of the school year. "Just purchasing a few things for my actual home."

She didn't laugh. She was visibly moved. Was she the one for whom Julia brought over all those dinners?

"There was a list of everyone who went."

"Went?"

"To Israel. They hung it outside the sanctuary."

"I didn't know that," he said.

"I never used to pray. Never. But I started going. A lot of people did. Most mornings the sanctuary was full. Anyway, I looked at it every day."

He thought, *I can still tell the truth, but only now. After this, an awkward misunderstanding will be a lie that is worse than what it is concealing.*

"I had no idea," he said.

And there are smaller lies available (that I was turned back at the airport), and even half-truths (that there was a crisis at home that needed me even more than the crisis abroad).

"There were two lists, actually: one with the names of those who went to fight, and one with the names of those who died. Everyone on the second list was on the first list, obviously."

"Well, it's really nice to see you again," Jacob said, hating the truth, hating the lie, and knowing nothing between.

"They never took them down. Maybe they're supposed to be some kind of memorial? Or maybe even though the war is over, it somehow isn't?"

"Hard to say."

"What did you do?" she asked.

"What do you mean?"

"In Israel. Were you in logistics? Infantry? I don't know the terminology."

"I was in a tank unit."

Her eyes widened.

"Being in a tank must have been terrifying."

"Not as terrifying as being outside of one."

She didn't laugh. She brought her fingers to her mouth and said, "You didn't drive it, did you?"

"No. That requires a lot of training and experience. I reloaded the ammunition."

"Sounds grueling."

"I guess it was."

"And did you see battle? Is that the right way to put it? *See battle?*"

"I don't know how to put things, either. I was just a body. But yes, I saw battle. I imagine everyone did."

The sentence advanced, but his mind stayed back with *I was just a body.*

"Did you ever feel that you were in grave danger?"

"I don't know that I was feeling much of anything. It might sound clichéd, but there wasn't time to be afraid."

Without looking down, she took the locket between her thumb and forefinger. Her hand knew exactly where it would be.

"I'm sorry," she said. "I'm asking too much."

"No, that's not it," he said, seizing her offer of regret as an escape route. "I just have to get out of here in time to pick up Sam."

"Is he well?"

"He's doing great. Thank you for asking. And—?"

"Dylan."

"Of course."

"Dylan is having a hard time."

"Oh no. I'm sorry to hear that."

"Maybe," she began, but then shook the thought away.

"What?"

"I was just going to say, maybe if it's not too much to ask, you could come by sometime."

"I'm sure Sam would like that."

"No," she said, a vein in her neck suddenly visible, or suddenly noticed. "You. I meant you."

Jacob no longer understood. Could she be as brazen as she sounded? Or was she mistaking him for a parent who was a child psychologist, as he'd mistaken her for the wife of an aneurysm victim? He was attracted to her, he wanted her, but this couldn't go any further.

"Sure," he said. "I could come by."

"Maybe if you shared some of your experiences, it would make things less abstract for him. Less scary. I think part of what's so hard right now is not having any details."

"That makes sense."

Although it didn't.

"It wouldn't have to take a lot of your time. I'm not asking you to take him on or anything."

"It doesn't sound like it."

"You're a good man," she said.

"I'm not," he said.

And then, finally, she laughed. "Well, I suppose only you know for sure. But you seem good."

Once, Benjy called Jacob back into his room after tuck-in and asked, "Are there things that don't have names?"

"Sure," Jacob said, "lots of things."

"Like what?"

"Like this headboard."

"It's called headboard."

"Headboard is what it is. But it doesn't have its own name."

"True."

"Good night, love."

"Let's give them names."

"That was the first man's first job, you know."

"Huh?"

"Adam. From Adam and Eve. God told him to name the animals."

"We named Argus."

"That's right."

"But the first man was a monkey, right? So did he name himself?"

"Could be."

"I want to name everything."

"That would be a lot of work."

"So?"

"OK. But starting tomorrow."

"OK."

Jacob went to the threshold and waited, as he always did, and Benjy called him back, as he always did.

"Yes?"

"Are there names that don't have things?"

Names like the names on the gravestones in the suicide ghetto. Names like the names on the memorial wall, which Jacob had rearranged into words. Names like the names in his never-to-be-shared show. Jacob had written thousands and thousands of pages about his life, but it wasn't until that moment, her pulse visible in her neck, his choice finally visible, that he questioned if he was worthy of a word.

"OK," she said, and smiled, and nodded, and took a half step away. "Please say hello to Julia for me."

"I will," Jacob said.

He left the overflowing cartful of things where it was, followed the arrows back through LIVING ROOM, WORK SPACE, KITCHEN, DINING, and BEDROOM to the parking lot. He drove straight to the synagogue. Indeed, the lists were still there. But his name wasn't among those who had gone. He double- and triple-checked.

So what had just happened?

Had she misremembered?

Or maybe she had seen the Islip photograph in the newspaper and was remembering his image when she thought she was remembering his name?

Maybe she was giving Jacob the benefit of the doubt?

Maybe she knew everything and was destroying the life he'd saved?

With the hand that had cut three umbilical cords, he touched the names of the dead.

"Only you know for sure," she had said.

There were dozens of veterinarians far closer than Gaithersburg, Maryland, that he hadn't consulted—it felt essential to go to someone they hadn't seen, for both Argus's sake and Jacob's—but he needed to create some distance from home.

On the way there, he took Argus to a rest-stop McDonald's. He brought the food to a grassy hill beside the lot, and tried to feed Argus McNuggets, but Argus just turned away. Jacob kept stroking him under the chin, as he liked.

Life is precious, Jacob thought. *It is the most important of all thoughts, and the most obvious, and the most difficult to remember to have.* He thought: *How different my life would have been if I could have had that thought before I was forced to.*

They drove with the windows halfway down, Dan Carlin's "Hardcore History: Blueprint for Armageddon II" blaring. In the context of an argument Carlin was making about the significance of World War I, he spoke about a concept called the Great Filter—the moment at which a civilization becomes capable of destroying itself. Many mark 1945, and the use of nuclear weapons, as humanity's Great Filter. Carlin argued it was 1914, with the worldwide proliferation of mechanized warfare. He then digressed a bit, as was his genius, to Fermi's paradox. During a lunch break at Los Alamos, in 1950, a handful of the world's greatest physicists were joking about a recent spate of UFO sightings. Taking the matter ironically-seriously, they unfolded a paper napkin and tried to calculate the probability of intelligent life existing elsewhere. Assume there are 10^{24} stars in the observable universe—ten thousand stars for every grain of sand on Earth. Using the most conservative estimates, there are approximately one hundred billion billion Earth-like planets—one hundred for each grain of sand on Earth. If, after billions of years in existence, one percent of those developed life, and one percent of *those* developed intelligent life, there should be ten million billion intelligent civilizations in the universe—one hundred thousand just in our galaxy. Clearly we are not alone.

But then Enrico Fermi, the most celebrated and brilliant physicist at the table, spoke for the first time: "So where is everybody?" If they ought to be there, and they aren't there, why aren't they there? Clearly we are alone.

There are many responses to this paradox: that there's plenty of intelligent life in the universe, just no way of knowing about it because we're too far from one another for any messages to reach; that humans aren't listening properly; that other life is too alien to recognize, or to recognize us; that everyone is listening and no one adequately transmitting. Each of these struck Jacob as unbearably poetic: *we're too far for messages to reach; we aren't listening properly; no one is adequately transmitting.* Then Carlin returned to the notion of the Great Filter. At a certain point, every civilization will become capable of destroying itself (on purpose, or by accident), and face a kind of pass/fail test—whether it is possible to have the ability to commit suicide, and not commit suicide.

When did Isaac reach his Great Filter?

When did Israel?

When did Jacob and Julia's marriage?

When did Jacob?

He parked the car and walked Argus to the clinic door. No leash necessary anymore. Argus wasn't going anywhere. And yet Jacob wished he'd had a leash then, so it wouldn't feel like Argus was unknowingly walking himself to his own end. It would have been horrible to lead him there, but less horrible.

The place was called Hope Clinic. Somehow Jacob had forgotten that, or never bothered to know it. It reminded him of a Kafka quote: "Oh, there is hope, an infinite amount of hope, just not for us." Just not for you, Argus.

They went to the reception desk.

"This is a checkup?" the secretary asked.

"Yes," Jacob responded.

He just couldn't. He wasn't ready. He'd have another chance with the vet.

Jacob browsed a magazine without focusing his eyes. He remembered the first time one of his kids called him out for looking at his phone instead of at them.

"That's my boy," he said to Argus, scratching under his chin. Had he ever called him his *boy* before?

The tech came and led them to an examination room in the back. The vet took forever, and Jacob offered Argus treats from the glass jar on the counter. But Argus just turned away.

"You're good," Jacob told him, trying to be as calming as Max had been. "You're so good."

We live in the world, Jacob thought. That thought always seemed to insert itself, usually in opposition to the word *ideally*. Ideally, we would make sandwiches at homeless shelters every weekend, and learn instruments late in life, and stop thinking about the middle of life as late in life, and use some mental resource other than Google, and some physical resource other than Amazon, and permanently retire mac and cheese, and give at least a quarter of the time and attention to aging relatives that they deserve, and never put a child in front of a screen. But we live in the world, and in the world there's soccer practice, and speech therapy, and grocery shopping, and homework, and keeping the house respectably clean, and money, and moods, and fatigue, and also we're only human, and humans not only need but deserve things like time with a coffee and the paper, and seeing friends, and taking breathers, so as nice as that idea is, there's just no way we can make it happen. Ought to, but can't.

Over and over and over: *We live in the world.*

Finally, the vet came. He was an old man, maybe eighty. Old and old-fashioned: a pocket square in his white coat, a stethoscope around his neck. His handshake was arresting: so much softness to get through before the bone.

"What brings you here today?"

"They didn't explain?"

"Who?"

"I'd called."

"Why don't you tell me yourself."

Was this a ploy? Like when they make a young woman listen to a fetal heartbeat before she can get an abortion?

He wasn't ready.

"So, my dog has been suffering for a long time."

"Oh, OK," the vet said, clicking shut the pen with which he was about to start filling out a form. "And what's the name of your dog?"

"Argus."

"'This is the dog of a man who died far away,'" the vet bellowed.

"Impressive."

"I was a classics professor in another life."

"With a photographic memory?"

"There's actually no such thing. But I did love Homer." He slowly lowered himself onto a knee. "Hello, Argus." He held the sides of Argus's face and looked into his eyes. "It's not my favorite expression," he said, still looking at Argus. "*Putting down*. I prefer *letting go*."

"I prefer that, too," Jacob said, as grateful as he'd ever been.

"Are you in pain, Argus?"

"He whines a lot, sometimes through the night. And he has a hard time getting up and down."

"That doesn't sound good."

"It's been going on for quite a while, but it's gotten worse in the last half a year. He's barely eating. And he's incontinent."

"None of that is good news."

News. It was the first time since the earthquake he'd heard anything else referred to as news.

"Our vet, back in D.C., gave him a couple of months, but it's been almost half a year."

"You're a fighter," the vet said to Argus, "aren't you?"

Jacob didn't like that. He didn't like thinking of Argus fighting for the life that was about to be taken from him. And while he knew that age and illness were what Argus was fighting against, there they were: Argus and Jacob, and a vet to carry out Jacob's wishes at the expense of Argus's. It wasn't that simple. Jacob knew it wasn't. But he also knew there was a sense in which it was exactly that simple. There is no way to communicate to a dog that one is sorry that we live in the world but it is the only place that one can live. Or maybe there is no way not to communicate that.

The vet looked into Argus's eyes for another few moments, now in silence.

"What do you think?" Jacob asked.

"What do I think?"

"About this situation?"

"I think you know this dog better than anyone, and certainly better than some old vet who's spent a total of five minutes with him."

"Right," Jacob said.

"In my experience, and I've had a lot of it, people know when it's time."

"I can't imagine ever knowing. But I think that just says something about me, rather than Argus's condition."

"Might be."

"I *feel* that it's time. But I don't *know* that it's time."

"OK," the vet said, rising. "OK."

He took a syringe from a glass jar on the counter—a jar directly beside the treats—and a small vial from a cabinet.

"This is a very simple procedure, and I can assure you that Argus will neither anticipate it nor feel any pain whatsoever, other than the pinch of the needle, although I'm pretty good at concealing that. Within a second or two, he'll pass. I'll just warn you that the moment of death can be unpleasant. Usually it's just like falling asleep, and most owners describe their animals as appearing relieved. But each dog is different. It's not uncommon for a dog to empty its bowels, or for its eyes to roll into its head. Sometimes muscles seize. But it's all perfectly normal, and wouldn't suggest that Argus was feeling anything. For Argus it will be going to sleep."

"OK," Jacob said, but he thought, *I don't want this to happen. I'm not ready for this to happen. This cannot happen.* He'd had that feeling two other times: when holding down Sam as he got his hand stitched back together, and the moment before he and Julia told the kids they were separating. It was the feeling of not wanting to live in the world, even if it was the only place to live.

"It would be best if we can get Argus to lie down here on the floor. Perhaps you can get him to rest his head on your lap. Something comforting for him."

He filled the syringe while he spoke, always keeping it out of Argus's view. Argus went right to the floor, as if he knew what was expected of him, if not why. It was all happening so quickly, and Jacob couldn't suppress the panicked feeling that he wasn't ready. He gave Argus the sleep-inducing belly rub he'd learned in their one and only dog-training class, but Argus wouldn't sleep.

"Argus is old," Jacob said. There was no reason to say it, other than to slow things down.

"An old man," the vet said. "Must be why we get along so well. Try to keep him looking at you."

"One second," Jacob said as he stroked the length of Argus's side, his fingers slipping over and between his ribs. "I didn't know it was going to happen this quickly."

"Would you like another few minutes alone?"

"What happens to the body?"

"Unless you have other plans, we cremate it."

"What kind of plans might one have?"

"Burial."

"No."

"So then that's what we'll do."

"Immediately?"

"What's that?"

"You cremate him immediately?"

"Twice a week. There's a facility about twenty minutes from here."

Argus gave a small whine and Jacob told him, "You're good. You're good." And then he asked the vet, "Where are we in that cycle?"

"I'm not sure I know what you mean."

"I know it shouldn't matter, but I don't like the idea of Argus's body sitting around for four whole days."

Do people sit shmira for dogs? No one should be left alone.

"Today is Thursday," the vet said. "So it would be this afternoon."

"OK," Jacob said. "I'm relieved to know that."

"Would you like another few minutes? It's no problem at all."

"No, it's OK."

"You'll see me put some pressure on Argus's vein, so as to be sure the needle enters properly. You can hold him. Within a few seconds, Argus will take a deeper breath, then appear to sleep."

Jacob was disturbed by the vet's repeated use of Argus's name, his seeming unwillingness to refer to Argus as *him* or *he*. It felt cruel, the constant reminder of Argus's specific personhood, or of Jacob's identity as Argus's namer.

"Though completely unconscious, Argus might take a few more breaths. I've found that, for whatever reason, the older the dog, the longer the unconscious breathing goes on."

"That's interesting," Jacob said, and in an instant, as the *g* freed itself from the back of his hard palate, his discomfort with the vet's use of Argus's name morphed into anger at himself—the anger that was often deeply buried, and often projected, but was always there. *That's interesting.* What a stupid thing to say right then. What an unimportant, cheapening, disgusting remark. *That's interesting.* All day he'd been experiencing fear, and sadness, and guilt about not being able to give Argus a little longer, and pride at having given him this long, but now, at the arrival of the moment, he was only angry.

"You're ready to let him go?" the vet asked.

"Sorry. Not yet."

"Of course."

"You're good," Jacob said, pulling at the excess skin between Argus's shoulders, just as Argus liked.

Jacob must have given the vet a suggestive look, because he once again asked, "Are you ready?"

"You're not going to give him some sort of sedative or, I don't know, painkiller so he doesn't feel the shot?"

"Some vets do. I don't. It can just as often make them more anxious."

"Oh."

"Some people like to be left alone for a few minutes first."

Jacob gestured at the vial in the vet's hand and asked, "Why is that fluid so bright?"

"So it's never mistaken for something else."

"That makes sense."

He needed to let go, of the anger and everything else, but he needed help to do so, but he needed to do it alone.

"Could I stay with the body? Until the cremation?"

"I'm sure we could arrange that."

Jacob said, "Argus," naming him for the second time—once in the beginning, once at the end.

Argus's eyes rose to meet Jacob's. There was no acceptance to be found in them. No forgiveness. There was no knowledge that all that had happened was all that would happen. As it had to be, and as it should be. Their relationship was defined not by what they could share, but what they couldn't. Between any two beings there is a unique, uncrossable distance, an unenterable sanctuary. Sometimes it takes the shape of aloneness. Sometimes it takes the shape of love.

"OK," Jacob said to the vet, still looking into Argus's eyes.

"Don't forget how it ends," the vet said, readying the needle. "Argus dies fulfilled. His master has finally come home."

"But after so much suffering."

"He has peace."

Jacob didn't tell Argus, "It's OK."

He told him: "Look at me."

He told himself: *Life is precious, and I live in the world.*

He told the vet: "I'm ready."